A NOTE FROM THE AUTHOR:

Like all previous Darkover novels, this story is complete in itself and does not depend on knowledge of any other. More than any other Darkover book, however, this one was written by popular demand.

One result of writing novels as they occurred to me, instead of following strict chronological order, was that I began with an attempt to solve the final problems of the society; each novel thus suggested one laid in an earlier time, in an attempt to explain how the society had reached that point. Unfortunately, that meant that relatively mature novels, early in the chronology of Darkover, were followed by books written when I was much younger and relatively less skilled at story-telling; and of all these, the least satisfactory was *The Sword of Aldones*, perhaps because this book was, in essence, dreamed up at the age of fifteen.

In 1975 I made a landmark decision; that in writing *The Heritage of Hastur*, I would not be locked into the basically immature concepts set forth in *Sword*, even at the sacrifice of consistency in the series. After *Heritage* appeared in print, *Sword of Aldones* seemed even less satisfactory—for years, it seemed that everyone I met asked me when I was going to rewrite it. For years I replied "Never," or "I don't want to go back to it." But I finally decided that I had, in *Sword of Aldones*, developed a basically good idea, without the skill or maturity to handle it as well as it deserved; and that the characters deserved serious treatment by a matured writer. I decided not to rewrite, but to write an entirely new book based on events in the same time frame as *Sword*. The present book is the result.

Marion Zimmer Bradley

SHARRA'S EXILE

Marion Zimmer Bradley

This first hardcover edition published in Great Britain 1995 by
SEVERN HOUSE PUBLISHERS LTD of
9–15 High Street, Sutton, Surrey SM1 1DF.
This first hardcover edition published in the USA 1995 by
SEVERN HOUSE PUBLISHERS INC of
595 Madison Avenue, New York, NY 10022.

British Library Cataloguing in Publication Data
Bradley, Marion Zimmer
  Sharra's Exile. – New ed
  I. Title
  813.54 [F]

  ISBN 0-7278-4799-6

Typeset by Hewer Text Composition Services, Edinburgh.
Printed and bound in Great Britain by
Hartnolls Ltd, Bodmin, Cornwall.

Chapter Two of Book One appeared in a slightly
different form, as a short story entitled "Blood Will
Tell" in the volume *The Keeper's Price*, DAW 1980.

Prologue

The second year of exile

This was the home of my ancestors.

But I knew, now, that it would never be *my* home.

My eyes ached as I stared at the horizon where the sun
sank out of sight—a strange yellow sun, not red as a sun
should be, a glaring sun that hurt my eyes. But now, for a
moment just before twilight, it was suddenly red and huge
and sinking behind the lake in a sudden crimson glory that
made me ache with homesickness; and across the water a
streak of crimson.... I stood staring until the last gleams of
crimson faded; and over the lake, pale and silver, the solitary
moon of Terra showed the thinnest of elegant crescents.

Earlier in the day there had been rain, and the air was
heavy with alien smells. Not alien, really; they were known,
somehow, in the very depth of my genes. My ancestors had
climbed down from the trees of this world, had lived out the
long evolution which had patterned them into human, and
had later sent out the seedling ships, one of which—I had
heard the tale—had crash-landed on Darkover and settled
there, rooting into the new world so deeply that I, exiled from
my race's homeworld and returning, found homeworld alien
and longed for the world of my people's exile.

I did not know how long ago, or for how long my people
had dwelt on Darkover. Travel among the stars has strange
anomalies; the enormous interstellar distances play strange
tricks with time. There would never be any way for the folk
of the Terran Empire to say, three thousand years ago, or
fifteen thousand years ago, which particular colony ship
founded Darkover.... The elapsed time on Terra was something like three thousand years. Yet elapsed time on Darkover was somehow more like ten thousand, so that Darkover
had a history nearly as long as Earth's own history of civi-
lization and chaos. I knew how many years ago Terra, in the

7

days long before the Terran Empire had spread from star to star, had sent out the ship. I knew how many years had elapsed on Darkover. And there was no way for even the most accurate historian to reconcile them: I had long ago stopped trying.

Nor was I the only one with hopelessly torn loyalties, as deep as the very DNA in my cells. My mother had been earth born under this impossibly blue sky and this colorless moon; yet she had loved Darkover, had married my Darkovan father and borne him sons and, at last, been laid to rest in an unmarked grave in the Kilghard Hills on Darkover.

And I wish I were lying there beside her....

For a moment I was not sure that the thoughts were not my own. Then I shut them out, savagely. My father and I were too close...not the ordinary closeness of a Comyn telepath family (though that in itself would have been freakish enough to the Terrans around us) but entangled by common fears, common loss...shared experience and pain. Bastard, rejected by my father's caste because my mother had been half Terran, my father had gone to endless pains to have me accepted as a Comyn Heir. To this day I did not know whether it was for my sake or his own. My futile attempts at rebellion had entrapped us all in the abortive rebellion under the Aldarans, and Sharra....

Sharra. Flame burning in my mind...the image of a woman of flame, chained, restless, tresses of fire rising on a firestorm wind, hovering...rising, ravening...Marjorie caught in the fires, screaming, dying...

No! Merciful Avarra, no....

Black dark. Shut out everything. Close my eyes, bend my head, go away, not there at all, nowhere at all....

Pain. Agony flaming in my hand....

"Pretty bad, Lew?" Behind me I felt the calming presence of my father's mind. I nodded, clenching my teeth, slamming the painful stump of my left hand against the railing, letting the cold strangeness of the white moon-rim flood me.

"Damn it, I'm all right. Stop—" I fought for the right word and came up with "stop hovering."

"What am I supposed to do? I can't shut it out," he said quietly. "You were—what shall I say? Broadcasting. When you can keep your thoughts to yourself, I'll leave you alone with them. In the name of all the Gods, Lew, I was a technician in the Arilinn Tower for ten years!"

He didn't elaborate. He didn't have to. For three years, the happiest years of my life, perhaps, I too had been matrix mechanic in the Arilinn Tower, working with the complex matrix crystals which linked telepaths and minds in linkages to provide communication, technology to our metal-poor, machinery-poor world. I had learned, in Arilinn, what it was to be a telepath, Comyn of our caste, gifted or cursed with the linking of minds and the hypersensitivity to the other minds around me. You learned not to pry; you learned not to let your own thoughts entangle with others, not to be hurt too much by the pain, or the needs, of others, to remain exquisitely sensitive and at the same time to live without intruding or demanding.

I had learned this, too. But my own control had been burned out by the ninth-level matrix which I had tried, insanely, to handle with a circle of half-trained telepaths, we had hoped, vainly, to restore the old, high-level Darkovan technology, handed down as legend from the Ages of Chaos. And we had nearly done it, too, experimenting with the old Darkovan crafts, called sorcery and magic by the commoners. We knew that in truth they were a complex technology, which could have done anything—powered spaceships for Darkover to stand equal to the Empire, rather than remain poor relations, dependents of the Terran Empire, a cold, metal-poor planet.

We had nearly done it... but Sharra was too powerful for us, and the matrix which for years had been chained, peacefully bringing fire to the forges of the mountain smiths, had been freed, ravening and raging in the hills. A city had been destroyed. *And I, I had been destroyed too, burnt in those monstrous fires, and Marjorie, Marjorie was dead....*

And now within my matrix, now I could see nothing but flame and destruction and Sharra....

A telepath keys himself into the matrix stone he uses. At eleven I had been given such a matrix: if it had been taken from me, I would swiftly have died. I do not know what the matrix stones are. Some people say they are crystals which amplify the psychoelectrical emanations of the brain's activity in the "silent" areas where the Comyn powers reside. Others call them an alien life-form, symbiotic with the special powers of the Comyn. Whatever the truth, a Comyn telepath works through his own matrix; the larger matrixes, multilevel, are never keyed to the body and brain of the individual matrix worker, but relayed and transformed through his stone.

But Sharra had reached out for us all, and taken us into the fire...

"Enough!" My father spoke with the particular force of an Alton, forcing his mine on mine, wresting the image away. Grateful darkness descended behind my .eyes; then I could see the moon again, see something other than flames.

He said quietly, as I rested my eyes, covering them with my good hand, "You don't believe it now, but it *is* better, Lew. It comes when you let your guard down, yes. But there are long periods when you can break the domination of the Sharra matrix...."

"When I don't talk about it, you mean," I interrupted angrily.

"No," he said, "when it isn't there. I've been monitoring you. It's not nearly as bad as it was that first year. In the hospital, for instance...I couldn't get you out of it for more than a few hours at a time. Now there are days, even weeks...."

Yet I would never be free. When we went offworld, from Darkover, hoping to save the hand burned in Sharra's fires, I had taken the Sharra matrix, hidden in its elaborate sword; not because I wished to take it, but because after what had happened, I could no more be separated from it than parted from my own matrix. My own matrix hung around my neck; it had hung there since my twelfth year, and I could not remove it without pain and probably brain damage. Once it had been taken from me—a kind of deliberate torture—and I had come nearer to death than I like to think. Probably if it had been kept from me another day, I would have died, of heart failure or cerebral accident.

But the Sharra matrix...somehow it had overpowered my own. I need not wear it hanging round my neck, or be in physical contact with it, but I could not go beyond a certain critical distance, or the pain would begin, and the fire images surge in my brain, like static blurring out all else. My father was a competent technician, but he could do nothing; the technicians in the Arilinn Tower, where they had tried to save my hand, could do nothing. Finally they had taken me offworld, in a vain hope that Terran science could do more. It was illegal for the Warden of the Alton Domain, my father, Kennard Alton, to leave Darkover at the same time as his

Heir. He had done it anyway, and for that I knew that I should have been grateful to him. But all I felt was weariness, rage, resentment.

You should have let me die.

My father stepped out into the light of the dim moon and stars. I could only barely see his outline; tall, once heavy and imposing; now stooped with the bone disease which had crippled him for many years; but still powerful, dominating. I was never sure whether I saw my father's physical presence or the mental, commanding force which had overpowered my life since, at eleven, he had forced my mind open to the telepathic Alton Gift—the gift of forced rapport even with non-telepaths, which characterizes the Alton Domain. He had done it because there was no other way to prove to the Comyn Council that I was worthy to be the Alton Heir. But I had had to live with it—and with his domination—ever since.

My hand throbbed where I had slammed down what was left of the arm. Peculiar, that ache; I could feel it in my fourth and sixth fingers...as if I had burned off a nail. And yet there was nothing there, nothing but the empty scar...they had explained it to me; phantom pain, nerves remaining in the rest of the arm. Damned real for a phantom. At least the Terran medics, and even my father, now realized there was nothing more to be done for the hand, and they had done what they should have done at first, and taken it off. Nothing to be done, even with their (rightly) fabled medical science. My mind still flinched away from the memory of the twisted, terrifying thing which had crowned their latest, experimental technique at regeneration. Whatever it is in the cells of the body which bids a hand be a hand, with palm and fingers and nails, and not a claw or a feather or an eye, had been burned away by Sharra, and once, through the drugs, I had seen what my hand had become....

Force my mind away from that too...was there anything safe to think about? I stared into the quiet sky from which the last lingering trace of crimson had faded.

He said quietly "It's worse at twilight, I think. I wasn't even full-grown yet when I came first to Terra; I used to come here at sunset so that my cousins and foster-brothers wouldn't see. You get so tired—" His back was to me, and in any case it was too dark to see anything but the dark loom of his presence, but still, somewhere in my mind, I could see the wry deprecating half-smile, "of the same old moon. And my

Terran cousins thought it shameful for anyone my age to cry. So I made sure, after the first time, that they wouldn't see it."

There is a saying on Darkover; *only men laugh, only men dance, only men weep.*

But it had been different for my father, I thought in fierce envy. He had come here of his free will, and for a purpose; to build a bridge between our peoples, Terran and Darkovan. Larry Montray, his Terran friend, remaining on Darkover to be fostered in the Alton Domain: Kennard Alton coming here for a Terran education in the sciences of this world.

But I?

I had come here an exile, broken, maimed, my beloved Marjorie dead because I, like my father before me, had tried to build a bridge between Terran Empire and Darkover. And I had better reason: I was a son of both worlds, because Kennard, all Comyn, had married Montray's half-sister, Elaine. So I tried; but I had chosen the wrong instrument—the Sharra matrix—and failed, and lived on, with everything that made life real for me dead or abandoned on a world half a Galaxy away. Even the hope which had persuaded my father to bring me here—that my hand, burned in the fires of Sharra, might somehow be salvaged or regenerated—had proved worse than a mirage; even after all I had endured, that was gone too. And I was here on a hated world, alien and familiar at once.

My eyes were growing used to the darkness; I could see my father now, a man in late middle age, stooped and lame, his once-blazing hair all gray; his face was deeply lined with pain and conflict.

"Lew, do you want to go back? Would it be easier? I was here for a reason; I was an exchange student, on a formal mission. It was a matter of honor. But nothing binds you here. You can take ship and return to Darkover whenever you will. Shall we go home, Lew?" He did not glance at my hand; he didn't need to. *That* had failed, there was no reason to stay here hoping for a miracle.

(But I could still feel that dull pain like a torn-off nail around the thumb. And the sixth finger ached as if I had pinched it in a vise, or burnt it. Strange. Haunted by the ghost of a hand that wasn't there.)

"Lew, shall we go home?" I knew he wanted it; this alien land was killing him, too. But then he said the wrong thing.

"The Council wants me back. They know, now, I will father no other sons. And you are acknowledged Heir to Alton; when I went away, they said it was unlawful for the lord of Alton Domain and his Heir to leave the Domains at the same time. If you returned, the Council would be forced to acknowledge—"

"Damn the Council!" I said, so loudly that my father flinched. The same damned old political maneuvering. He had never stopped trying to get the Council to acknowledge me—it had made a nightmare of my childhood, forced him into the painful and dangerous step he had taken, forcing premature awakening of my *laran* gift. Later it had driven me to my Aldaran kinsfolk, and the ill-fated attempt to raise power through Sharra, and Marjorie.... I slammed the door shut in my mind, a closed place, black, blank. I would not think about that, *I would not*.... I wanted no part of their damned Council, nor of the Comyn, nor Darkover.... I turned my back and walked away toward the lake cabin, feeling him behind me, close, too close....

Get out of my mind! Get—out! Leave me alone! I slammed my mind shut like the cabin door, heard the door open and close, felt him there though I stood with closed eyes. I did not turn or look.

"Lew. No, damn it, don't shut me out again, listen to me! Do you think you are the only one in the world who has known what it is to lose a loved one?" His voice was rough but it was a roughness I knew; it meant that if his voice had been less rough he might have wept. It had taken me twenty-two years to know that my father could weep.

"You were two years old; and your sister died at birth. We both knew there should be no more. Elaine—" he had never before spoken her name in my hearing, though I knew it from his friends; always it had been the distant, formal *your mother*. "*Yllana*," he said again, saying the Darkovan version of the name this time. "She knew as well as I, how fragile is the rule of a man with only one son. And you were not a hardy child. Believe me, I did not demand it of her. It was her free choice. And for fifteen years I have borne *that* burden, and tried never to let Marius feel it...that I grudged him life at the cost of Yllana's...."

He had never said so much before. I could feel in his harsh voice what it had cost him to say it.

But it had been my mother's free choice, to risk her life in bearing my brother Marius. Marjorie had had no choice....

Fire. Ravening flames shooting into the sky, the great hovering wings of flame. Marjorie, burning, burning in the flames of Sharra.... Caer Donn, the world, Darkover, all in flames....

I slammed the barrier and the blackness down into my mind, heard myself shouting "No!" at the top of my voice, and once again brought up my maimed arm and slammed it down on anything, anything that would send pure physical pain crashing through my mind to the point where I could think of nothing else. *He should not make me look at this, that I had killed the only thing I had ever loved or would ever love....*

From very far away I heard him calling my name, felt the concerned touch of his thoughts...I slammed the barrier tighter, felt the dark close down. I stood there, not hearing, not seeing, until he went away.

BOOK ONE:

The Exile

Darkover: the third year of exile

CHAPTER ONE

Regis Hastur stood on a balcony of Comyn Castle, high over Thendara and the valley which lay ahead, looking over the city and the Terran Trade City beyond.

Behind him lay the castle, shadowed beneath the mountains. Before him lay the Terran Trade City, the spaceport beyond it—and the rising skyscrapers of the Terran Headquarters building. As he had thought many times before, he thought: *this has its own alien beauty.*

For many years he had had a dream. When he had come of age, he would leave Darkover behind him, take passage on one of those Terran starships, and go outward, among the stars, strange suns and worlds multiple beyond all telling. He would leave behind him all that he hated about his life; his own uneasy position, heir to an ancient household and a Regency which was more of an anachronism with every passing year; the continuing pressure to marry, young as he was, and provide heirs to the legacy of the Hasturs: the unknown potential of *laran,* the inbred psychic ability bred into bones and brain and genes. He would leave behind him the rulership of the contending Domains, each striving for something different in the ever-changing world that was modern Darkover. Regis was eighteen; legally of age three years ago, sworn to Hastur. Now he knew he would never have his dream.

He would not have been the first of the Comyn to leave Darkover and go into the Empire. Adventure, the lure of an alien society and a vast complex universe, had drawn more than one Darkovan, even of the highest nobility, into the Empire.

The Ridenow Domain, he thought. *They make no secret of their belief that Darkover should align with the Empire, become a part of this modern world. Lerrys Ridenow has traveled widely in the Empire, and no doubt at Council this season he will be singing their praises again. Kennard Alton was edu-*

17

cated on Terra, and he is there now, with his son Lew. And
then Regis wondered how Lew fared, somewhere in that alien
universe.

*If I were free of the burden of the Hastur heritage, I too
would go forth and never return.* And again the temptation
struck him, as he had planned it when he was a rebellious
child in his first year in the Cadets of the Guard—the necessary apprenticeship served by all Comyn sons. He and his
friend Danilo had plotted it together; they would ship outward
on one of the Terran ships, find a place for themselves
there...lose themselves in the immensities of a thousand
alien worlds. Regis smiled, reminiscently, knowing it had
been the dream of children. For better or worse, he was Heir
to Hastur, and the fate of Darkover was a part of his life, as
intimately as body or brain. Danilo was Heir to Ardais,
adopted by the childless Lord Dyan Ardais, being prepared
for that high office as Regis was prepared for his own. Last
year had been their third year in the cadets together; junior
officers, learning command and self-command. It had been
a peaceful time; but it was over. Regis had spent the winter
past in the city of Thendara, attending sessions of the *cortes,*
dealing with city magistrates, diplomatic envoys from the
other Domains and the Dry Towns beyond the Domains, the
representatives of the Terrans and the Empire; learning, in
short, to take his grandfather's place as representative of the
Domains.

Danilo had paid only one or two fleeting visits to the city
since that Festival Night when Council Season had ended;
he had had to return to Castle Ardais with Dyan and learn
the ordering of the Domain which, if Dyan died still childless,
would be his own. Then, Regis had heard, Danilo had been
called back to Syrtis by the grave illness of his own father.

Why is Danilo on my mind now, so suddenly? And then
he knew; he was not a powerful telepath, but the bond sworn
between himself and Danilo was a strong one, and he turned
abruptly away from the view of city and spaceport which lay
before him, thrusting the curtains closed behind him as he
went inside.

*It is a boy's idle dream, to stand there and dream of the
stars. My world lies here.* He went into the outer room of the
Hastur apartments just as one of the servants came in search
of him.

"*Dom* Danilo Syrtis, Heir and Warden of Ardais," he announced, and Danilo came into the room, a slender, handsome young man, dark-haired and dark-eyed. Regis moved to take him into a formal kinsman's embrace, but over his shoulder he saw the servant leave the room and the formal greeting somehow transformed itself into an enthusiastic mutual hug.

"Dani! I'm so glad to see you! You can't imagine how dull the city is in winter!"

Danilo chuckled, looking down at Regis affectionately. He was a little taller, now, than his friend. "I'd have chosen it. I swear to you that the climate of Ardais has much in common with that of Zandru's coldest hell. I don't think Lord Dyan was any colder than that in Nevarsin monastery!"

"Is Dyan still at Nevarsin?"

"No, he left it early last winter. We were at Ardais together all the winter; he taught me many things he said I should know as Regent of the Domain. Then we traveled south to Thendara together...Strange, I never thought I would take pleasure in his company, yet he has taken great pains to have me properly educated for the place I will have—"

"He would do that for the honor of his own house," said Regis dryly.

"Yet when my poor father died he was kindness itself."

"I am not surprised at that either," Regis said. "You have grown handsome, Dani, and Lord Dyan has always had an eye for beauty in a boy—"

Danilo laughed. They could laugh together about it, now, though three years ago it had been no laughing matter. "Oh, I am too old for Dyan now—he prefers lads who have not yet grown their beards, and you can see—" with a nervous finger he twisted the small, dark moustache on his upper lip.

"Why, I wonder, then, that you have not grown a full beard!"

"No," said Danilo, with a strange, quiet persistence. "I know Dyan better now. And I give you my word, never once has he offered me a word or a gesture unseemly between father and son. When my own father died, he showed him all honor; he said it was a pleasure to do honor to one who had deserved it; it made amends, perhaps, for the honor he had had to show to those of his kinsmen who deserved it not." The old Lord of Ardais had died three years ago, mad and senile after a long and disgraceful life of debauchery.

"Dyan said something like that to me once," Regis agreed.

"But enough of that—I am glad you are here, *bredu*. I suppose you are to sit in Council this year among the Ardais?"

"So Dyan says," Danilo agreed. "But Council will not begin till tomorrow, and tonight—well, I have not been in Thendara for years."

"I seldom go into the streets," said Regis, so quietly that it did not even sound bitter. "I cannot walk half a mile without a crowd following me..."

Danilo started to make a flippant answer; then withheld it, and the old sympathy began to weave between them again, a touch closer than words; the telepathic touch of *laran*, of sworn brotherhood and more.

Well, you are Heir to Hastur, Regis; it is part of the burden of being what you are. I would lighten it if I could, but no one alive can do that. And you would not have it otherwise.

You lighten it by understanding; and now that you are here I am not altogether alone...

No spoken words were necessary. After a time Danilo said lightly, "There is the tavern where the Guard officers go; they at least have grown used to Comyn and do not think we are all freaks or monsters, or that we walk without touching the ground like some heroes from old legends. We could have a drink there without anyone staring."

The Castle Guard of Thendara at least know that we are human, with all the human faults and failings, and sometimes more.... Regis was not entirely sure whether the thought was his own, or whether he picked it up from Danilo. They went down through the great labyrinth of the Comyn Castle, and out into the crowded streets of the first night of Féstival.

"Sometimes, at Festival, I come here masked," Regis said.

Danilo grinned. "What—and deprive every girl in the city of the joys of hopeless love?"

Regis made a nervous gesture—the gesture of a fencer who concedes a hit. Danilo knew he had struck too close to the nerve, but did not make it worse with an apology. Regis picked up the thought anyway; *The Regent is pressuring him to marry again, damned old tryant! At least my foster-father understands why I do not.* Then Danilo managed to shield his thoughts; they went into the tavern near the gates of the Guard Hall.

The front room was crowded with young cadets. A few of the boys saluted Regis and he had to speak a word or two to them, but they finally got through to the quieter back room,

where the older officers were drinking. The room was semi-
dark even at this hour, and some of the men nodded in a
friendly fashion to Regis and his companion, but immediately
turned back to their own affairs; not unfriendliness but a way
of giving the Hastur Heir the only privacy and anonymity
he ever could have these days. Unlike the boys in the outer
room, who enjoyed the knowledge that even the powerful
Hastur-lord was required by law and custom to return their
salutes and acknowledge their existence, these officers knew
a little of Regis's burden and were willing to let him alone
if he wished.

The tavernkeeper, who knew him too, brought his usual
wine without asking. "What would you like, Dani?"

Danilo shrugged. "Whatever he's brought."

Regis began to protest, then laughed and poured the wine;
the drinking was only an excuse, anyway. He raised his rough
mug, sipped and said, "Now tell me everything that's been
happening while you were away. I'm sorry about your father,
Dani; I liked him and hoped to bring him to court someday.
Did you spend all that time in the Hellers?"

Hours slipped away while they talked, the wine half forgotten between them. At last they heard the drum-roll of
"Early Quarters" beat out from the Guard Hall, and Regis
started, half rising, then laughed, remembering that he was
no longer obliged to answer to it. He sat down again.

"What a soldier you've become!" Danilo teased.

"I liked it," Regis said, after a moment. "I always knew
exactly what was expected of me, and who expected it, and
what to do about it. If there were war, it would have been a
different thing. But the worst trouble I ever had was in breaking up street riots, or escorting drunks to the lockup if they
were making a nuisance of themselves, or investigating when
a house was robbed, or making somebody tie up a troublesome
dog. Last year there was a riot in the marketplace—no, this
one is funny, Dani; a cattle-drover's wife had left him because,
she said, she had caught him in her *own* bed with her *own*
cousin! So she slipped into his stall, and stampeded the animals he'd brought to sell! There were upset stalls and broken
crockery all over the place...I happened to be officer of the
day, so I caught it! One of the cadets complained that he'd
left home so he *wouldn't* have to chase dairy animals all day
long! Well, we finally got them all rounded up again, and I
had to go and testify before the city magistrate. So the *cortes*

fined the woman twelve *reis* for all the damage the beasts
had caused, and it was the husband who had to pay the fine!
He protested that he had been the victim, and it was his wife
who let the animals loose, and the magistrate—she was a
Renunciate—said that it would teach him to conduct his love
affairs in decent privacy, in a way that didn't insult or hu-
miliate his wife!"

Danilo laughed, more at the reminiscent amusement in
Regis's face, than at the story. Out in the other room, he
heard the cadets jostling each other and bickering as they
paid their accounts and went back to barracks. "Did I see one
of your sister's sons among the cadets out there? They must
be great boys now."

"Not yet this year," said Regis. "Rafael is only twelve, and
young Gabriel only eleven...I suppose Rafael might have
been just old enough, but with his father the Commander of
the Guard, I suppose he felt it was early for that. Or my sister
did, which is the same thing."

Danilo looked startled. "Gabriel Lanart-Hastur is Commander of the Guards? How did that happen? Has Kennard
Alton not returned?"

"There's been no word from him; not even whether he is
dead or alive, my grandfather said."

"But the Command of Castle Guard is an Alton post,"
Danilo protested. "How comes it into Hastur hands?"

"Gabriel is one of the nearest kin to the Altons of Armida.
With Kennard and his Heir both offworld, what else could
they do?"

"But surely there are Altons nearer of kin than your
brother-in-law," protested Danilo. "Kennard's other son,
Marius—he must be fifteen or sixteen now."

"Even if he were acknowledged Heir to Alton," Regis said,
"he would hardly be old enough to command the Guard. And
Kennard's elder brother had a son, the one they found on
Terra...but he's chief technician at Arilinn Tower, and
knows no more of commanding soldiers than I know of embroidery stitches! Anyway, his Terran education's a handi-
cap—it doesn't hurt him out there at Arilinn, but they don't
want him in Thendara to remind them that there are Terrans
in the very heart of Comyn Council!" His voice sounded bitter.
"After all, they managed to get rid of Lew Alton, and the
Council refused again last year to give Marius any of the
rights—or duties—of a Comyn son. My grandfather told

me—" his smile only stretched his mouth a little— "that they had made that mistake with Lew, and they're not going to make it again, they said. Terran blood, bad blood, treachery."

"Lew deserves better of them than that," said Danilo quietly. "And if he does not, Kennard at least is guiltless of any treachery and should be consulted."

"Do you think I did not say that? I am old enough to sit in Council and listen to my elders, Dani, but do you think they listen to me when I speak? My grandfather said that he knew Lew and I had been *bredin* when I was a child—implying that would warp my judgment. If Kennard were *here* to be consulted, they might listen to him. Most people do. But they are not neglecting Marius, even though they have not allowed him status as Alton of Armida; they appointed Gabriel as his Guardian, and he has been sent to the Terran Headquarters for a proper Terran education. He's better educated than either you or I, Dani, and what he has learned there probably makes more sense in this day of Empire and star-travel than *this*—" He gestured around the tavern, at the Guardsmen wearing swords. Regis fully agreed with the Darkovan Compact, which forbade use of any weapon beyond arm's reach of the man using it, insisting that he who would kill must take his own chance with death. Still, swords were not weapons alone, but tokens of a way of life which seemed to make little sense in the presence of an interstellar Empire. Danilo followed his thoughts, but shook his head stubbornly.

"I don't agree with you, Regis. Marius deserves better of the Council than a Terran education. I don't think Kennard should have gone offworld, and certainly he should not have stayed this long. Hastur should recall him at once—unless your grandfather is greedy for another Domain to pass under the rule of the Hasturs. Already, it seems, he has taken over the Elhalyn Domain—or why is Derik not yet crowned, at eighteen?"

Regis made a wry face. "You do not know our Prince. He may be eighteen, but he is a child of ten—or might as well be. My grandsire wants nothing more than to be free of the burden of the Regency of Thendara—"

Danilo raised a skeptical eyebrow but said nothing. Regis repeated, "Derik is not yet ready to rule. The Council has deferred his crowning till he is twenty-five. There is precedent for that, and if Derik is simply slow to reach manhood and wisdom, well, that will give him time. If not—well, we will fly that falcon when his pinions are grown."

"And what if Derik, in Hastur's opinion, is never fit to rule?" Danilo asked. "There was a time when the Hasturs ruled all these Domains, and the rebellion against their tyranny split the Domains into a hundred little kingdoms!"

"And it was the Hasturs who united them all again, in the days of King Carolin," said Regis. "I have read history, too. In Aldones's name, Dani, do you think my grandsire is anxious to be King over all this country? Or do I look to you like a tyrant?"

Danilo said, "Certainly not. But in principle, each of the Domains should be strong—and independent. If Lord Hastur cannot crown Derik—and from what little I have seen of him, he looks not much like a King—he should look elsewhere for an Heir to Elhalyn. Forgive me, Regis, but I like it not, to see so much power in Hastur hands; first the Regency which controls the Heir to the Crown, and now the Altons under Hastur rule too. And the Alton Domain carries with it the command of Castle Guard. Where will Hastur turn next? Lady Callina of Valeron is unmarried; will he marry her, perhaps, to you, and bring the Aillard Domain as well under the Hasturs?"

"I am old enough to be consulted about my marriage," said Regis dryly. "And I assure you that if he has any such plan, he has not spoken of it to me. Do you think my grandfather is a spider at the center of such a web as that?"

"Regis, I am not trying to pick a quarrel with you." Danilo raised the wine pitcher; Regis shook his head, but Danilo poured it anyway, raised the rough mug to his lips and set it down untasted. "I know your grandsire is a good man, and as for you—well, you know well what I think, *bredhyu.*" He used the intimate inflection, and Regis smiled, but Danilo went on earnestly, "All this sets a dangerous precedent. After you, Hasturs may reign who are really not fit for such power. A day could come when all the Domains would be Hastur vassals."

"Zandru's hells, Dani!" said Regis impatiently. "Do you really think Darkover will remain independent of the Empire that long, or that the Comyn will rule over the Domains when that day comes? I think Marius Alton is the only one of us

who will be properly prepared for the direction in which Darkover will go."

"That day will come," Danilo told him quietly, "over the
dead bodies of the Ardais Domain."

"No doubt, on that day, there will be Hastur bodies lying
dead too, but it will come for all that. Listen, Dani," he said
urgently, "do you *really* understand the situation? A few generations ago, when the Terrans came here, it was because we
happened to be in the wrong place at the right time—a planet
located between the upper and lower spiral arms of the Galaxy, exactly where they needed to set up a spaceport as a
crossroads and transit point for Empire traffic. They'd have
preferred an uninhabited planet, and I'm sure they debated
making us into one. Then they discovered that we were a lost
Terran colony—"

"And Saint-Valentine-of-the-Snows lies buried in Nevarsin," Danilo said, exasperated. "I heard all that when we were
prisoners in Aldaran three years ago, Regis!"

"No, listen—the Terrans found us, speaking languages
long dead on Terra itself; but we were a primitive world,
which had lost its technology, or so they thought. They gave
us Closed World status, so that we would not be disturbed by
too-rapid social upheavals—they do that with all primitive
societies, so that they can evolve at their own rate. Then they
found out that we were not so primitive a planet after all,
and they found out about our *laran,* our matrix technology.
They found that the linked minds in the Tower circles could
mine metals, power aircraft, all those other things—well,
they wanted matrix technology, and they tried all sorts of
things to get some of it."

"Regis, I know all that, but—"

"Will you *listen?* You know as well as I; some Darkovans
wanted, and still want, the advantages of Terran technology,
a place in the Empire, status for Darkover as a colony with
political strength, representation in the Empire Senate—all
those things. Others, especially in the Comyn, felt that Empire citizenship would destroy our world and our people. That
we'd become just another colony like a dozen others, depen-
dent on Terran trade, offworld metals and luxuries, tour-
ists.... They've had their way so far. I can see that there will
have to be changes on Darkover. But I want them to come
at a rate we can assimilate."

"And I don't want them to come at all," Danilo said.

"Who would? But the Terrans are *here,* like it or not. And I will not be accused of trying to keep our people primitives, barbarians, so that my family and I can maintain our superstitious powers over them!"

He had spoken more forcefully than he realized, forgetting where they were. A languid voice said, "Bravo! The Heir to Hastur has come of age and learned that Terrans are a reality, not a crew of bogeymen to frighten little children!"

Regis started. He had forgotten they were not alone. He turned to see a tall thin man, fair-haired, with the stamp of the Comyn on his angular features; elegantly dressed in foppish Darkovan clothing, but with rich alien furs adorning his cloak. Regis bowed, his face set in rigid politeness.

"Cousin," he acknowledged. "I did not see you, Lerrys."

"Nor I you, *Dom* Regis," said Lerrys Ridenow, "but when you shout so loudly that the Terrans in their Headquarters could hear you across the city, why should I pretend I did not hear? I am glad to know that you understand the situation. I hope this means there will be another advocate for sanity in the Council this year, and that the Ridenow need not stand alone against that doddering conclave of maiden ladies of either sex!"

Regis said stiffly, "Please don't believe that I am altogether in agreement with you, *Dom* Lerrys. I do not like to think of the kind of social upheavals there would be, if we became just another Terran colony—"

"But we *are* another Terran colony," Lerrys said. "And the sooner we recognize it, the better. Social upheavals? Bah! Our people want the good things Terran citizenship will bring them, and they would accept the rest, once they were confronted with an accomplished fact. They simply haven't enough education to know what they want, and the Hasturs, and the worthy lords of the Comyn, have made sure they won't have it!" He half-rose. "Must we shout this from table to table? Will you not join us, cousin—and your friend as well?" He used the intimate inflection of the word, with its implications, and Regis, flicked raw, glanced at Danilo, half-wishing the other would refuse; but there was no reasonable cause for denial. Lerrys was Comyn and his kinsman. There was no reason for his distaste.

Only, perhaps, that we have more in common than I could wish. He flaunts abroad what I must, for the sake of my grandfather, keep discreetly within bounds. I envy him, perhaps,

*that he is a younger son of a minor Comyn house, that he is
not always in the public eye. Everything he does, does not
immediately become public property for gossip or censure.*

They took a seat at Lerrys's table and accepted a fresh
round of drinks, which neither of them wanted. After another
round or two, he thought, he would make some excuse, then
he and Danilo would go somewhere and dine; Early Quarters
had been some time ago. Soon there would be the sound of
Night Quarters from the Guard Hall and he could invent an
engagement somewhere. The places he chose to dine would
be too tame for Lerrys and his elegant hangers-on; most of
them, he could see, were Darkovan, but they wore elaborate
Terran clothing; not the functional uniform of the spaceports,
but brilliant and colorful things from the far corners of the
Empire.

Lerrys, pouring the wine he had ordered, went on, taking
up the conversation he had interrupted, "After all, we *are*
Terrans; we deserve all the privileges of our heritage. Everyone in the Domains could benefit from Terran medicine and
science—not to mention education! I happen to know you can
read and write, Regis, but you must admit you are a happy
exception. How many, even of the cadets, can do more than
scribble their names and spell their way through the arms
manual?"

"I think they have enough education for what they must
do in the world," said Regis. "Why should they burden themselves with idle nonsense, which is what most written matter
turns out to be? There are enough idle scholars in the world—
and in the Empire, for that matter."

"And if they are uneducated," Lerrys said with a sardonic
smile, "it is easier to keep them in superstitious bondage to
the Comyn, fabulous tales about the God-given rulership of
the Hasturs, kinfolk to the Gods...."

"Certainly I would agree with you that there is no excuse
for that kind of mental slavery," said Regis. "If you heard
what I was saying before, you would hear that I was pro-
testing against that sort of tyranny. But you cannot say that
we are Terrans and no more." He reached across the table;
took Lerrys's hand and laid his own palm-to-palm with it,
counting the six fingers; then touched the small leather bag
at his throat, where the matrix stone rested; a small warmth,
a pulse....

"The powers of the Comyn are real."

"Oh—*laran*," said Lerrys with a shrug. "Even some of the
Terrans who come among us have developed it; it, too, is part
of our Terran heritage, and we can teach them something of
this, too... Why should it be limited to the Comyn? In return
we will have their sciences; knowledge of weather control,
which would be like a blessing from the Gods in some of the
country across the Hellers; the Dry-town desert, perhaps,
reclaimed for agriculture, and some of the impassable mountains across the Wall Around the World, brought into contact
with the Domains; astronomy, star-travel—and in return,
laran and knowledge all through the Galaxy...."

"That could be dangerous, too dangerous to spread indis-
criminately through the Empire," said one of Lerrys's young
companions diffidently. "Were you there when Caer Donn
burned, Lerrys?"

"I was," Regis said, and looked sharply at the young
stranger. "I know you. Rakhal—Rafe—"

"Rakhal Darriell-Scott, *z'par servu*," said the young man.
"They call me Rafe Scott, in the Terran Zone. I saw then what
laran uncontrolled can do—and hope never to see it again!"

"No fear of that," Lerrys said. "The Sharra matrix was
destroyed. As far as we know, that was the only one of those
old matrixes from the Ages of Chaos left on our world. Besides, if there are such things, we should learn how to control
and use them, not hide like banshee-birds in the sunlight,
and pretend they do not exist. Believe me, the Terrans are
no more anxious than you to see *laran* out of control that
way."

"And, no matter what happens, there will always be those
who can use *laran* and those who cannot," said another youngster. There was something familiar about him, too; Regis
thought he was probably one of Rafe Scott's kinsmen. He was
not eager to remember that time at Castle Aldaran, and the
frightful time when Sharra had raged and ravened in the
hills across the river. He and Danilo, escaping from Aldaran,
had come near to dying in those hills....

"Still, we are all Terrans," said Lerrys, "and the Empire
is our heritage, as of right, not a privilege; we should not
have to ask for Empire citizenship or the benefits of Empire.
They gave us Closed World status, but it's high time to rectify
that mistake. Before we can do that, we must acknowledge
that the Terran Empire is our lawful government, not the
local bigwigs and aristocracy! I can understand that you,

Regis, would like to keep your place of power, but listen to me! In the face of an Empire which spans a thousand worlds, what does it matter what the peasants think of our nobles? As long as this is a Closed World, the local aristocrats can maintain their personal power and privilege. But once we acknowledge that we are a part of the Terran Empire—not that we wish to become part of the Empire, but that we are already so, and thus subject to their laws—then every citizen of Darkover can claim that privilege; and—"

"Perhaps there are many who do not consider it such a privilege—" Danilo began hotly, and Lerrys drawled, "Does it matter what such people think? Or, in denying them that privilege, are you simply demanding your own, Lord Danilo, as Warden of Ardais—"

But before Danilo could answer that, there was a commotion in the front room; then Dyan Ardais strode into the back room, where the few remaining senior officers, and the Comyn, were sitting. He came directly to their table.

"Greetings, kinsmen." He bowed slightly. Danilo, as befitting a foster-son in the presence of the Head of his Domain, rose and stood awaiting recognition or orders.

Dyan was tall and spare, mountain Darkovan from the Hellers; his features aquiline, his eyes steel-gray, almost colorless, almost metallic. Ever since Regis had known him, Dyan had affected a dress of unrelieved black, whenever he was not in uniform, or clad in the ceremonial colors of his Domain: it gave him a look of chilly austerity. Like many hillmen, his hair was not the true Comyn red, but coarse, curly and dark.

"Danilo," he said, "I have been looking for you. I might have known I would find you here; and Regis with you, of course."

Regis felt the little ironic flicker of telepathic touch, recognition, awareness, annoyingly intimate, as if the older man had taken some mildly unsuitable liberty in public, tousled his hair as if he were a boy of eight or nine; nothing serious enough so that he could object without loss of dignity. He knew Dyan liked to see him ill at ease and off balance; what he did not know was *why*. But the Ardais Lord's face was blank and indifferent.

He said, "Will you both dine with me? I have something to say to you, Danilo, which will affect your plans for Council season, and since I know your first move afterward would be to tell it to Regis, I might as well say it to both of you at once and save the time."

"I am at your orders, sir," said Danilo with a slight bow.

"Will you join us, cousin?" Lerrys asked, and Dyan shrugged. "One drink, perhaps."

Lerrys slid along the bench to make room for Dyan and for his young companion; Regis did not recognize the younger man, and Lerrys, too, looked questioningly at Dyan.

"Don't you know one another? Merryl Lindir-Aillard."

Dom Merryl was, Regis thought, about twenty; slender, red-haired, freckled, good-looking in a boyish way. With a mental shrug—Dyan's friends and favorites were no business of his, Aldones be praised—he bowed courteously to young Merryl. "Are you kin to *Domna* Callina, *vai dom?* I do not think we have met."

"Her step-brother, sir," Merryl said, and Regis could hear in the other young man's mind, like an echo, the question he was too diffident to ask: *Lord Dyan called him Regis, is this the Regent's grandson, the Hastur Heir, what is he doing here just like anyone else, like an ordinary person....* It was the usual mental jangle, wearying to live with.

"Are you to sit in Council this year, then?"

"I have that honor; I am to represent her in Council while she is held at Arilinn by her duties as Keeper there," he said, and the annoying telepathic jangle went on: *in any other Domain it would be my Council seat, but in this one, damn all the Council, rank passes in the female line and it is my damned bitch of a half-sister, like all women, coming the mistress over us all....*

Regis made a strong effort to barricade himself and the trickle of telepathic leakage quieted. He said politely, "Then I welcome you to Thendara, kinsman."

The dark, slender youngster sitting between Lerrys and Rafe Scott said shyly, "You are Callina's brother, *dom* Merryl? Why, then, I shall welcome you as kinsman too; Callina's half-sister Linnell was fostered with me at Armida, and I call her *breda*. She has spoken of you, kinsman."

"I'm afraid I don't know all of *Domna* Callina's relatives," Merryl returned, in the most indifferent formal mode. Regis winced at the direct snub he had given the boy, and suddenly knew who the other must be; Kennard's younger son, Marius, never acknowledged by the Council, and educated among the Terrans. Regis hadn't recognized Marius, but that wasn't sur-

prising; they moved in different orbits and he had not seen
the boy since he was the merest child. Now he must be all
of fifteen. He seemed indifferent to Merryl's snub; was he
merely so accustomed to insults that he had truly learned to
ignore them, or had he only learned not to seem to care? With
a little extra courtesy, Regis said, "Dom Marius; I did not
recognize you, cousin."

Marius smiled. His eyes were dark, like a Terran's."Don't
apologize, Lord Regis; there aren't many in Council
who do." And again Regis heard the unspoken part of that,
or would admit it if they did. Lerrys covered the small, awkward silence by pouring wine, passing it to Dyan with some
offhand comment about the quality of wine here not being
the best.

"But as a Guardsman, cousin, no doubt you've learned to
ignore that."

"One would never think, now, that you had worn a Guardsman's uniform, Lerrys," Dyan returned, affably enough.

"Well, I did my share of it for a Comyn son," Lerrys said,
with a grin, "as did we all. Though I do not remember seeing
you among the cadets, Merryl."

Merryl Lindir-Aillard said with a grimace, "Oh, I caught
one of the fevers about the time I should have done service
in the cadets, and my mother was a timid woman, she thought
I'd melt in the summer rains...and later, when my father
died, she said I was needed at home." His voice was bitter.
Danilo said, smiling, "My father felt so too; and he was old
and feeble. He let me go, willingly enough, knowing I should
better myself there; but he was glad to have me home again.
It's not easy to judge where one is needed most, kinsman."

"I think we have all had experience of that," said Dyan.

"You didn't miss anything," said Lerrys. "Zandru's hells,
kinsman, who needs sword practice and training at knife play
in this day and age? The Cadets—saving your presence, Lord
Regis—are an anachronism in this time, and the sooner we
admit it, and call them an honor guard in fancy dress, the
better off we'll be. The Guardsmen police the city, but we
ought to take advantage of the Terran offer to send Spaceforce
to teach them modern police techniques. I know you must
feel as if you missed what every Comyn kinsman should have,
Merryl, but I spent three years in the Cadets and two more
as an officer, and I could have done as well without it. As
long as you look handsome in a Guardsman's cloak—and I

can see by looking at you that you'll have no trouble with that—you already know all you'll need for *that*. As I'm sure Dyan's told you."

"There's no need to be offensive, Lerrys," Dyan said stiffly. "But I might have expected it of you—you spend more time on Vainwal exploring alien pleasures than here in Thendara doing your duty as a Comyn lord! It seems to be the climate of the day. I can't blame you; when the Altons neglect their duty, what can one expect of a Ridenow?"

"Are you jealous?" Lerrys asked. "On Vainwal, at least I need not conceal my preferences, and if the Altons can spend their time idling throughout the Empire, by what right do you criticize me?"

"I criticize them no less—" Dyan began hotly.

"Lord Dyan," said Marius Alton angrily, "I thought you at least were my father's friend—or friend enough not to judge his motives!"

Dyan looked him straight in the eye and drawled, "Who the hell are you?"

"You know who I am," Marius retorted, "even if it amuses you to pretend you do not! I am Marius Montray-Lanart of Alton—"

"Oh, the Montray woman's son," Dyan said, in the derogatory mode implying *brat* or *foundling*.

Marius drew a deep breath and clenched his fists. "If Kennard, Lord Alton, acknowledges me his son, it matters nothing to me who else does not!"

"Wait a minute—" Lerrys began, but Merryl Lindir said, "Must we listen to this even here in Thendara? I did not come here to drink with Terran bastards—and with Terran spies!"

Marius sprang angrily to his feet. "Terran spies? Captain Scott is *my* guest!"

"As I said, Terran spies and toadies—I did not come here for that!"

"No," retorted Marius, "it seems you came here for a lesson in manners—and I am ready to give you one!" He kicked the chair back, came around the table, his hand on his knife. "Lesson one: you do not criticize the invited guest of anyone—and I am here as the guest of the Lord Lerrys, and Captain Scott as mine. Lesson two: you do not come into Thendara and cast aspersions on any man's lineage. You will apologize to Captain Scott, and retract what you said about my father—

and my mother! And you too, Lord Dyan, or I shall call you
to account as well!"

Good for him, Regis thought, looking at the angry youngster, knife in hand, crouched into a stance of readiness for a
fight. Merryl blinked; then whipped out his knife and backed
away, giving himself room to move. He said, "It will be a
pleasure, Alton bastard—"

Lerrys tried to move toward them, laid a hand on Marius's
wrist. "Wait a minute—"

"Keep out of this, sir," Marius said, between gritted teeth.

*Good, the boy has courage! Good-looking, too, in his own
way! Zandru's hells, why didn't Kennard*— For a moment
Regis could not identify the source of the thought, then Dyan
said aloud, "Put your knife up, Merryl! Damn it, that's an
order! You too, Marius, lad. Council never acknowledged your
father's marriage, but it's not hard to see you're your father's
son."

Marius hesitated, then lowered the knife in his hand.
Merryl Lindir-Aillard snarled, "Damn you, are you afraid to
fight me, then, like all you coward Terrans—ready to kill
with your coward's weapons and guns from a distance, but
frightened of bare steel?"

Lerrys stepped between them, saying, "This is no place for
a brawl! In Zandru's name—"

Regis saw that the others in the tavern had drawn back,
making something like a ring of spectators. *When kinsmen
quarrel, enemies step in to widen the gap! Does it give them
pleasure to see Comyn at odds?* "Stop it, both of you! This is
not a house of bandits!"

"Get back, both of you," said a new, authoritarian voice,
and Gabriel Lanart-Hastur, Commander of the Guard, stepped
forward. "If you want to fight, make it a formal challenge,
and let's not have any stupid brawls here! Are you both
drunk? Lerrys, you are an officer, you know no challenge is
valid unless both challengers are sober! Marius—"

Marius said, fists clenched, "He insulted my father and
mother, kinsman! For the honor of the Alton Domain—"

Gabriel said quietly, "Leave the honor of the Domain in
my hands until you are older, Marius."

"I am sober enough to challenge him!" Marius said, angrily, "and here I call challenge—"

"Merryl, you damned fool—" Dyan said urgently, laying
a hand on his shoulder, "this is serious—"

"I'm damned if I'll fight a Terran bastard with honor,"
shouted Merryl, enraged, and rounded on Gabriel Lanart-
Hastur. He said, "I'll fight *you,* or your whole damned Domain—if I can get any of them back here on Darkover where
they belong! But your Lord Alton is no better than any of his
bastards, off gallivanting all over the Empire when they're
needed in Council—"

Gabriel took a step forward, but there was a glare of blue
fire and Merryl went reeling back staggering. The telepathic
slap was like a thunder in the minds of everyone there.

BRIDLE YOUR STUPID TONGUE, LACK-WIT! I HAVE LONG SUS-
PECTED THAT DOMNA CALLINA IS TRULY THE MAN OF YOUR
HOUSEHOLD, BUT MUST YOU PROVE IT HERE IN PUBLIC LIKE THIS?
ARE YOUR BRAINS ALL WHERE YOU CAN SIT UPON THEM? It was
followed by an obscene image; Regis saw Merryl cringe. He
felt it in Danilo's mind too; Danilo had known what it was
to be abused by Dyan, mercilessly, with sadistic strength,
until Danilo had cracked and drawn a knife on him.... Regis,
feeling Danilo cower, felt his friend's agony and stepped back,
blindly, to stand close to him. Merryl was dead white; for a
moment Regis thought he would weep, there before them all.

Then Dyan said aloud, coldly, "Lord Regis, Danilo, I believe we have an engagement to dine. *Dom* Lerrys, I thank
you for the drink." He nodded to Regis, then turned away
from them all. There was nothing Regis or Danilo could do
but follow him. Merryl was still numbly holding the knife;
he slid it into his sheath and went after them. With a swift
look backward, Regis saw the tension had evaporated; Gabriel was talking in an urgent undertone to Marius, but that
was all right; there was no malice, Regis knew, in his brother-
in-law; and after all, in Kennard's absence, Gabriel was Marius's guardian.

Outside, Dyan frowned repressively at Merryl. "I had intended to ask you to join us; I want you and Regis to know
one another. But you'd better stay away until you learn how
to behave in the city, boy! The first time I take you into the
company of the Comyn, you get yourself into a stupid brawl!"

Neither tone nor words need have been changed a fraction
if he had been speaking to a boy of eight or nine who had
bloodied his nose in a dispute over a game of marbles. Inex-
cusable as Merryl's behavior had been, Regis felt sorry for
the youngster, who stood, crimson, accepting Dyan's tongue-
lashing without a word. Well, he deserved it. Merryl said,

swallowing, "Was I to stand there and be insulted by Terrans and half-Terrans, kinsman?" He used the word in the intimate mode which could mean Uncle, and Dyan did not reprove him; he reached out and slapped him very lightly on the cheek.

"I think you did the insulting. And there's a right way and a wrong way to do these things, *kiyu*. Go think about the right way. I'll see you later."

Merryl went, but he no longer looked quite so much like a puppy that had been kicked. Regis, acutely uncomfortable, followed Dyan through the street. The Comyn lord turned into the doorway of what looked like a small, discreet tavern. Inside, he recognized the place for what it was, but Dyan shrugged and said, "We'll meet no other Comyn here, and I can endure to be spared the company of any more like the last!" The flicker of unspoken thought again, *if you value your privacy, lad, you might as well get used to places like this one,* was so indifferent that Regis could ignore it if he chose.

"As you wish, kinsman."

"The food's quite good," Dyan said, "and I have ordered dinner. You needn't see anything else of the place, if you prefer not to." He followed a bowing servant into a room hung with crimson and gilt, and talked commonplaces—about the decorations, about the soft stringed music playing—while young waiters came and brought all kinds of food.

"The music is from the hills; they are a famous group of four brothers," said Dyan. "I heard them while they were still in Nevarsin, and it was I who urged them to come to Thendara."

"A beautiful voice," said Regis, listening to the clear treble of the youngest musician.

"Mine was better, once," said Dyan, and Regis, hearing the indifference of the voice, knew it covered grief. "There are many things you do not know about me; that is one. I have done no singing since my voice broke, though when I was in the monastery for a time last winter, I sang a little with the choir. It was peaceful in the monastery, though I am not a *cristoforo* and will never be so; their religion is too narrow for me. I hope a day will come when you will find it so, Danilo."

"I am not a good *cristoforo*," Danilo said, "but it was my father's faith and will be mine, I suppose, till I find a better."

Dyan smiled. He said, "Religion is an entertainment for

idle minds, and yours is not idle enough for that. But it does
a man in public life no harm to conform a little to the religion
of the people, if the conformity is on the surface and does not
contaminate his serious thinking. I hold with those who say,
even in Nevarsin, *There is no religion higher than the truth.*
And that is not blasphemy either, foster-son; I heard it from
the lips of the Father Master. But enough of this—I had
something to say to you, Danilo, and I thought to save you
the trouble of running at once to pour it into Regis's ears. In
a word; I am a man of impulse, as you have known for a long
time. Last year I dwelt for a time at Aillard, and Merryl's
twin sister bore me a son ten days since. Among other business of the Comyn, I am here to have him legitimated."

Danilo said correctly, "My congratulations, foster-father."

Regis said a polite phrase also, but he was puzzled.

"You are surprised, Regis? I am a bit surprised myself. In
general, even for diversion, I am no lover of women—but as
I say, I am...a creature of impulse. Marilla Lindir is not a
fool; the Aillard women are cleverer than the men, as I have
reason to know. I think it pleased her to give Ardais a son,
since sons to Aillard have no chance of inheriting that Domain. I suppose you know how these things can happen—or
are you both too young for that?" he asked with a lift of the
eyebrows, and a touch of malice. "Well, so it went—when I
found she was pregnant, I said nothing. It might have been
a daughter for Aillard, rather than an Ardais son—but I took
the trouble to have her monitored and to be sure the child
was mine. I did not speak of it when we met at Midwinter,
Danilo, because anything might have befallen; even though
I knew she bore a son, she might have miscarried, the child
might have been stillborn or defective—the Lindirs have
Elhalyn blood. But he is healthy and well."

"Congratulations again, then," said Danilo.

"Do not think this will change anything for you," said
Dyan. "The lives of children are—uncertain. If he should
come to misfortune before he is grown, nothing will change;
and should I die before he is come to manhood, I should hope
you will be married by then and be named Regent for him.
Even so, when he leaves his mother's care, I am no man to
raise a child, nor would I care, at my age, to undertake it; I
should prefer it if you would foster him. I will soon apply
myself to finding you a suitable marriage—Linnell Lindir-
Aillard is pledged to Prince Derik, but there are other Lindirs,

and there is Diotima Ridenow, who is fifteen or sixteen now, and—well, there is time enough to decide; I do not suppose you are in any too great a hurry to be wedded," he added ironically.

"You know I am not, foster-father."

Dyan shrugged. "Then any girl will do, since I have saved you the trouble of providing an Heir to Ardais; we can choose one who is amiable, and content to keep your house and run your estate," he said. "A legal fiction, if you wish." He turned his eyes to Regis, and added, "And while I am about it, my congratulations are due to you, too; your grandfather told me about the Di Asturien girl, and your son—will he be born this tenday, do you suppose? Is there a marriage in the offing?"

Shock and anger flooded through Regis. He had intended to tell Danilo this in his own time. He said stiffly, "I have no intention of marrying at this time, kinsman. No more than you."

Dyan's eyes glinted with amused malice. He said, "Why, have I said the wrong thing? I'll leave you to make your peace with my foster-son, then, Regis." He rose and bowed to them with great courtesy. "Pray command anything here you wish, wine or food or—entertainment; you are my guests this evening." He bowed again and left them, taking up his great fur-lined cloak, which flowed behind him over his arm like a living thing.

After a minute Danilo said, and his voice sounded numb, "Don't mind, Regis. He envies our friendship, no more than that, and he is striking out. And, I suppose, he feels foolish; to father a bastard son at his age."

"I swear I meant to tell you," Regis said miserably, "I was waiting for the right time. I wanted to tell you before you heard it somewhere as gossip."

"Why, Regis, what is it to do with me, if you have love affairs with women?"

"You know the answer to that," said Regis, low and savage, "I have no *love affairs* with women. You know that things like this must happen, while I am Heir to Hastur. Comyn Heirs at stud in the Domains—that's what it amounts to! Dyan doesn't like it any better than you do, but even so, he spoke of getting you married off. And I am damned if I'll marry someone they choose for me, as if I were a stud horse! That's what it was, and that is *all* it was. Crystal di Asturien is a very nice young woman; I danced with her at half a dozen of the public dances, I found her friendly and pleasant to talk to, and—" He shrugged. "What can I say to you? She wanted to bear a Hastur son. She's not the only one. Do I have to apologize for what I must do, or would you rather I did not enjoy it?"

"You certainly owe me no apologies." Danilo's voice was cold and dead.

"Dani—" Regis pleaded, "are we going to let Dyan's malice drive a wedge between us, after all this time?"

Danilo's face softened. "Never, *bredhyu*. But I don't understand. You already have an Heir—you have adopted your sister's son."

"And Mikhail is still my Heir," Regis retorted, "but the Hastur heritage has hung too long on the life of a single child. My grandfather will not force me to marry—as long as I have children for the Hastur lineage. And I don't want to marry," he added. The unspoken awareness hung in the air between them.

A waiter came, bowing, and asked if the *vai domyn* had any other pleasure: wine, sweets, young entertainers....He weighted this last heavily, and Danilo could not conceal a grimace of distaste.

"No, no, nothing more." He hesitated, glancing at Regis. "Unless you—"

Regis said wryly, "I am a libertine only with women, Dani, but no doubt I have given you cause to think otherwise."

"If we have to quarrel," Dani said, with a gulp, "Let us at least do it in clean air and not in a place like this!"

Regis felt a great surge of enormous bitterness. Dyan had done this, damn it! He said, "Oh, no doubt, this is the place for lovers' quarrels of this kind—and I suppose if the Heir to Hastur and his favorite must quarrel, better here than in Comyn Castle, where all the Domains, sooner or later, will hear!"

And again he felt, it is more of a burden than I can bear!

Vainwal: Terran Empire
Fifth year of exile

CHAPTER TWO

Dio Ridenow saw them first in the lobby of the luxury hotel serving humans, and humanoids, on the pleasure-world of Vainwal. They were tall, sturdy men, but it was the blaze of red hair on the elder of them that drew her eyes; Comyn red. He was past fifty and walked with a limp: his back was bent, but it was easy to see that once he had been a large and formidable man. Behind him walked a younger man in nondescript clothing, dark-haired and black-browed, sullen, with steel-gray eyes. Somehow he had the look of deformity, of suffering, which Dio had learned to associate with lifetime cripples; yet he had no visible defect except for a few ragged scars along one cheek. The scars drew up one half of his mouth into a permanent sneer, and Dio turned her eyes away with a sense of revulsion; why would a Comyn lord have such a person in his entourage?

For it was obvious that the man was a Comyn lord. There were redheads in other worlds of the Empire, and plenty on Terra itself; but there was a strong facial stamp, an ethnic likeness; Darkovan, Comyn, unmistakable. And the older man's hair, flame-red, now dusted with gray. But what was he doing here? For that matter, who was he? It was rare to find Darkovans anywhere but on their home world. The girl smiled; someone might have asked her that question, as well, for she was Darkovan and far from home. Her brothers came here because, basically, neither of them was interested in political intrigue; but they had had to defend and justify their absence often enough.

The Comyn lord moved across the great lobby slowly limping, but with a kind of arrogance that drew all eyes; Dio framed it to herself, in an unfocused way; he moved as if he should have been preceded by his own drone-pipers, and worn high boots and a swirling cloak—not the drab, featureless Terran clothing he actually wore.

And having identified his Terran clothing, suddenly Dio knew who he was. Only one Comyn lord, as far as anyone knew, had actually married, *di catenas* and with full ceremony, a Terran woman. He had managed to live down the scandal, which in any case had been before Dio was born. Dio herself had not seen him more than twice in her life; but she knew that he was Kennard Lanart-Alton, Lord Armida, self-exiled Head of the Alton Domain. And now she knew who the younger man must be, the one with the sullen eyes; this would be his half-caste son Lewis, who had been horribly injured in a rebellion somewhere in the Hellers a few years ago. Dio took no special interest in such things, and in any case she had still been playing with dolls when it happened. But Lew's foster-sister Linnell Aillard had an older sister, Callina, who was Keeper in Arilinn; and from Linnell Dio had heard about Lew's injuries, and that Kennard had taken him to Terra in the hope that Terran medical science could help him.

The two Comyn were standing near the central computer of the main hotel desk; Kennard was giving some quietly definite order about their luggage to the human servants who were one of the luxury touches of the hotel. Dio herself had been brought up on Darkover, where human servants were commonplace and robots were not; she could accept this kind of service without embarrassment. Many people could not overcome their shyness or dismay at being waited on by people rather than servomechs or robots. Dio's poise about such things had given her status among the other young people on Vainwal, many of them among the new-rich in an expanding Empire, who flocked to the pleasure worlds like Vainwal, knowing little of the refinements of good living, unable to accept luxury as if they had been brought up to it. Blood, Dio thought, watching Kennard and the exactly right way he spoke to the servants, would always tell.

The younger man turned; Dio could see now that one hand was kept concealed in a fold of his coat, and that he moved awkwardly, struggling one-handed to handle some piece of their equipment which he seemed not to want touched by anyone else. Kennard spoke to him in a low voice, but Dio could hear the impatient tone of the words, and the young man scowled, a black and angry scowl which made Dio shudder. Suddenly she realized that she did not want to see any more of that young man. But from where she stood she could not leave the lobby without crossing their path.

She felt like lowering her head and pretending they were not there at all. After all, one of the delights of pleasure worlds like Vainwal was to be anonymous, freed of the restraints of class or caste on one's own home world; she would not speak to them, she would give them the privacy she wanted for herself.

But as she crossed their path, the young man, not seeing Dio, made a clumsy movement and banged full into her. Whatever he was carrying slid out of his awkward one-handed grip and fell to the floor with a metallic clatter; he muttered some angry words and stooped to retrieve it.

It was long, narrow, closely wrapped; more than anything else it looked like a pair of dueling swords, and that alone could explain his caution; such swords were often precious heirlooms, never entrusted to anyone else to handle. Dio stepped away, but the young man fumbled with his good hand and succeeded only in sending it skidding farther away across the floor. Without thinking, she bent to retrieve it and hand it to him—it was right at her feet—but he actually reached out and shoved her away from it.

"Don't touch that!" he said. His voice was harsh; raw, with a grating quality that set her teeth on edge. She saw that the arm he had kept concealed inside his coat ended in a neatly folded empty sleeve. She stared, open-mouthed with indignation, as he repeated, with angry roughness, "Don't touch that!"

She had only been trying to help!

"Lewis!" Kennard's voice was sharp with reproof; the young man scowled and muttered something like an apology, turning away and scrambled the dueling swords, or whatever the untouchable package was, into his arms, turning ungraciously to conceal the empty sleeve. Suddenly Dio felt herself shudder, a deep thing that went all the way to the bone. But why should it affect her so? She had seen wounded men before this, even deformed men; surely a lost hand was hardly reason to go about as this one did, with an outraged, defensive scowl, a black refusal to meet the eyes of another human being.

With a small shrug she turned away; there was no reason to waste thought or courtesy on this graceless fellow whose manners were as ugly as his face! But, turning, she came face to face with Kennard.

"But surely you are a countrywoman, *vai domna?* I did not know there were other Darkovans on Vainwal."

She dropped him a curtsy. "I am Diotima Ridenow of Serrais, my lord, and I am here with my brothers Lerrys and Geremy."

"And Lord Edric?"

"The Lord of Serrais is at home on Darkover, sir, but we are here by his leave."

"I had believed you destined for the Tower, mistress Dio."

She shook her head and knew the swift color was rising in her face. "It was so ordained when I was a child; I—I was invited to take service at Neskaya or Arilinn. But I chose otherwise."

"Well, well, it is not a vocation for everyone," said Kennard genially, and she contrasted the charm of the father with the sneering silence of the son, who stood scowling without speaking even the most elementary formal phrases of courtesy! Was it his Terran blood which robbed him of any vestige of his father's charm? No, for good manners could be learned, even by a Terran. In the name of the blessed Cassilda, couldn't he even *look* at her? She knew that it was only the scar tissue pulling at the corner of his mouth which had drawn his face into a permanent sneer, but he seemed to have taken it into his very soul.

"So Lerrys and Geremy are here? I remember Lerrys well from the Guards," Kennard said. "Are they in the hotel?"

"We have a suite on the nineteenth floor," Dio said, "but they are in the amphitheater, watching a contest in gravity-dancing. Lerrys is an amateur of the sport, and reached the semi-finals; but he tore a muscle in his knee and the medics would not permit him to continue."

Kennard bowed. "Convey them both my compliments," he said, "and my invitation, lady, for all three of you to be my guests tomorrow night, when the finalists perform here."

"I am sure they will be charmed," Dio said, and took her leave.

She heard the rest of the story that evening from her brothers.

"Lew? That was the traitor," said Geremy, "Went to Aldaran as his father's envoy and sold Kennard out, to join in

some kind of rebellion among those pirates and bandits there.
His mother's people, after all."

"I had thought Kennard's wife was Terran," Dio said.

"Half Terran; her mother's people were Aldarans," Geremy said. "And believe me, Aldaran blood isn't to be trusted."

Dio knew that; the Domain of Aldaran had been separated
from the original Seven Domains, so many generations ago
that Dio did not even know how long it had been, and Aldaran
treachery was proverbial. She said, "What were they doing?"

"God knows," Geremy said. "They tried to hush it up afterward. It seems they had some kind of super-matrix back
there, perhaps stolen from the forge-folk; I never heard it all,
but it seems Aldaran was experimenting with it, and dragged
Lew into it—he'd been trained at Arilinn, after all, old Kennard gave him every advantage. We knew no good would
come of it; burned down half of Caer Donn when the thing
got out of hand. After that, I heard Lew switched sides again
and sold out Aldaran the way he sold us out; joined up with
one of those hill-woman bitches, one of Aldaran's bastard
daughters, half-Terran or something, and got his hand
burned off. Served him right, too. But I guess Kennard
couldn't admit what a mistake he'd made, after all he'd gone
through to get Lew declared his Heir. I wonder if they managed to regenerate his hand?" He wiggled three fingers, lost
in a duel years ago and regenerated good as new by Terran
medicine. "No? Maybe old Kennard thought he ought to have
something to remember his treachery by."

"No," Lerrys said. "You have it wrong way round, Geremy.
Lew's not a bad chap; I served with him in the Guards. He
did his damnedest, I heard, to control the fire-image when
it got out of hand but the girl died. I heard he'd married her,
or something. I heard from one of the monitors of Arilinn,
how hard they'd worked to save her. But the girl was just too
far gone, and Lew's hand—" He shrugged. "They said he was
lucky to have gotten off that easy. Zandru's hells, what a
thing to have to face! He was one of the most powerful telepaths they ever had at Arilinn, I heard; but I knew him
best in the Guards. Quiet fellow, standoffish if anything, nice
enough when you got to know him; but he wasn't easy to
know. He had to put up with a lot of trouble from people who
thought he had no right to be there, and I think it warped
him. I liked him, or would have if he'd let me; he was touchy
as the devil, and if you were halfway civil to him, he'd think

he was being patronized, and get his back up." Lerrys laughed
soundlessly.

"He was so standoffish with women that I made the mistake of thinking he was—shall we say—one who shared my
own inclinations, and I made him a certain proposition. Oh,
he didn't *say* much, but I never asked him *that* again!" Lerrys
chuckled. "Just the same, I'll bet he didn't have a good word
for you, either? That's a new thing for you, isn't it, little
sister, to meet a man who's not at your feet within a few
minutes?" Teasing, he chucked her under the chin.

Dio said, pettishly, "I don't like him; he's rude. I hope he
stays far away from me!"

"I suppose you could do worse," Geremy mused. "He *is*
Heir to Alton, after all; and Kennard isn't young, he married
late. He may not be long for this world. Edric would like it
well if you were to be Lady of Alton, sister."

"No." Lerrys put a protecting arm around Dio. "We can
do better than that for our sister. Council will never accept
Lew again, not after that business with Sharra. They never
accepted Kennard's other son, in spite of the best Ken could
do; and Marius's worth two of Lew. Once Kennard's gone,
they'll look elsewhere for a Head of the Alton Domain—there
are claimants enough! No, Dio—" gently he turned her
around to look at him—"I know there aren't many young
men of your own kind here, and Lew's Darkovan, and, I suppose, handsome, as women think of these things. But stay
away from him. Be polite, but keep your distance. I like him,
in a way, but he's trouble."

"You needn't worry about that," Dio said. "I can't stand
the sight of the man."

Yet inside, where it hurt, she felt a pained wonder. She
thought of the unknown girl Lew had married, who had died
to save them all from the menace of the fire-Goddess. So it
had been Lew who raised those fires, then risked death and
mutilation to quench them again? She felt herself shivering
again in dread. What must his memories be like, what nightmares must he live, night and day? Perhaps it was no wonder
that he walked apart, scowling, and had no kind word or
smile for man or woman.

Around the ring of the null-gravity field, small crystalline
tables were suspended in midair, their seats apparently hanging from jeweled chains of stars. Actually they were all sur-

rounded by energy-nets, so that even if a diner fell out of his
chair (and where the wine and spirits flowed so freely, some
of them did), he would not fall; but the illusion was breath-
taking, bringing a momentary look of wonder and interest
even to Lew Alton's closed face.

Kennard was a generous and gracious host; he had commanded seats at the very edge of the gravity ring, and sent
for the finest of wines and delicacies; they sat suspended over
the starry gulf, watching the gravity-free dancers whirling
and spinning across the void below them, soaring like birds
in free flight. Dio sat at Kennard's right hand, across from
Lew, who, after that first flash of reaction to the illusion of
far space, sat motionless, his scarred and frowning face obliv-
ious. Past them, galaxies flamed and flowed, and the dancers,
half-naked in spangles and loose veils, flew on the star-
streams, soaring like exotic birds. His right hand, evidently
artificial and almost motionless, lay on the table unstirring,
encased in a black glove. That unmoving hand made Dio
uncomfortable; the empty sleeve had seemed, somehow, more
honest.

Only Lerrys was really at ease, greeting Lew with a touch
of real cordiality; but Lew replied only in monosyllables, and
Lerrys finally tired of trying to force conversation and bent
over the gulf of dancers, studying the finalists with unfeigned
envy, speaking only to comment on the skills, or lack of them,
in each performer. Dio knew he longed to be among them.

When the winners had been chosen and the prizes awarded,
the gravity was turned on, and the tables drifted, in gentle
spiral orbits, down to the floor. Music began to play, and
dancers moved onto the ballroom surface, glittering and
transparent as if they danced on the same gulf of space where
the gravity-dancers had whirled in free-soaring flight. Lew
murmured something about leaving, and actually half-rose,
but Kennard called for more drinks, and under the service
Dio heard him sharply reprimanding Lew in an undertone;
all she heard was "Damn it, can't hide forever—"

Lerrys rose and slipped away; a little later they saw him
moving onto the dance floor with an exquisite woman whom
they recognized as one of the performers, in starry blue cov
ered now with drifts of silver gauze.

"How well he dances," Kennard said genially. "A pity he
had to withdraw from the competition. Although it hardly
seems fitting for the dignity of a Comyn lord—"

"Comyn means nothing here," laughed Geremy, "and that is why we come here, to do things unbefitting the dignity of Comyn on our own world! Come, kinsman, wasn't that why *you* came here, to be free for adventures which might be unseemly or worse in the Domains?"

Dio was watching the dancers, envious. Perhaps Lerrys would come back and dance with her. But she saw that the woman performer, perhaps recognizing him as the contestant who had had to withdraw, had carried him off to talk to the other finalists. Now Lerrys was talking intimately with a young, handsome lad, his red head bent close to the boy. The dancer was clad only in nets of gilt thread, and the barest possible gilt patches for decency; his hair was dyed a striking blue. It was doubtful, now, that Lerrys remembered that there were such creatures as women in existence, far less sisters.

Kennard watched the direction of her glance. "I can see you are longing to be among the dancers, Lady Dio, and it is small pleasure to a young maiden to dance with her brothers, as I have heard my foster-sister and now my foster-daughters complain. I have not been able to dance for many years, *damisela,* or I would give myself the pleasure of dancing with you. But you are too young to dance in such a public place as this, except with kinsmen—"

Dio tossed her head, her fair curls flying. She said, "I do as I please, Lord Alton, here on Vainwal, and dance with anyone I wish!" Then, seized by some imp of boredom or mischief, she turned to the scowling Lew. "Yet here sits a kinsman—will you dance with me, cousin?"

He raised his head and glared at her, and Dio quailed; she wished she had not started this. This was no one to flirt with, to exchange light pleasantries with! He gave her a murderous glance, but even so, he was shoving back his chair.

"I can see that my father wishes it, *damisela.* Will you honor me?" The harsh voice was amiable enough—if you did not see the look deep in his eyes. He held out his good arm to her. "You will have to forgive me if I step on your feet. I have not danced in many years. It is not a skill much valued on Terra, and my years there were not spent where dancing was common."

Damn him, Dio thought, this was arrogance; he was not the only crippled man in the universe, or on the planet, or even in this room—his own father was so lame he could hardly put one foot before the other, and made no bones about saying so!

He did not step on her feet, however; he moved as lightly as a drift of wind,and after a very little time, Dio gave herself up to the music, and the pure enjoyment of the dance. They were well matched, and after a few minutes of moving together in the perfect rhythm—she knew she was dancing with a Darkovan, nowhere else in the civilized Empire did any people place so much emphasis on dancing as on Darkover—Dio raised her eyes and smiled at him, lowering mental barriers in a way which any Comyn would have recognized as an invitation for the telepathic touch of their caste.

For the barest instant, his eyes met hers and she felt him reach out to her, as if by instinct, attuned to the sympathy between their bodies. Then, without warning, he slammed the barrier down between them, hard, leaving her breathless with the shock of it. It took all her self-control not to cry out with the pain of that rebuff, but she would not give him the satisfaction of knowing that he hurt her; she simply smiled and went on enjoying the dance at an ordinary level, the movement, the sense of being perfectly in tune with his steps.

But inside she felt dazed and bewildered. What had she done to merit such a brutal rejection? Nothing, certainly; her gesture had indeed been bold, but not indecently so. He was, after all, a man of her own caste, a telepath and a kinsman, and if he felt unwilling to accept the offered intimacy, there were gentler ways of refusing or withdrawing.

Well, since she had done nothing to deserve it, the rebuff must have been in response to his own inner turmoil, and had nothing to do with her at all. So she went on smiling, and when the dance slowed to a more romantic movement, and the dancers around them were moving closer, cheek against cheek, almost embracing, she moved instinctively toward him. For an instant he was rigid, unmoving, and she wondered if he would reject the physical touch, too; but after an instant his arm tightened round her. Through the very touch, though his mental defenses were locked tight, she sensed the starved hunger in him.... How long had it been, she wondered, since he had touched a woman in any way? Far too long, she was sure of that. The telepath Comyn, particularly the Alton and Ridenow, were well-known for their fastidiousness in such matters; they were hypersensitive,

much too aware of the random or casual touch. Not many of
the Comyn were capable of tolerating casual love affairs.

There were exceptions, of course, Dio thought; the young
Heir to Hastur had the name of a follower of women; though
he was likely to seek out musicians or matrix mechanics,
women who were sensitive and capable of sharing emotional
intensity, not common women of the town. Her brother Lerrys, too, was promiscuous in his own way, though he too
tended to seek out those who shared his own consuming interests.... A quick glance told her that he was dancing with
the youngster in the gilded nets, a quick-flaring, overflowing
intimacy of shared delight in the dance.

The dance slowed, the lights dimming, and she sensed that
all around them couples were moving into each other's arms.
A miasma of sensuality, almost visible, seemed to lie like
mist over the whole room. Lew held her tight against him,
bending his head; she raised her face, again gently inviting
the touch he had rebuffed. He did not lower his mental barriers, but their lips touched; Dio felt a slow, drowsy excitement climbing in her as they kissed. When they drew apart
his lips smiled, but there was still a great sadness in his eyes.

He looked around the great room filled with dancing couples, many now entwined in close embraces. "This—this is
decadent," he said.

She smiled, snuggling closer to him. "Surely no more than
Midsummer festival in the streets of Thendara. I am not too
young to know what goes on after the moons have set."

His harsh voice sounded gentler than usual. "Your brothers would seek me out and call challenge on me."

She lifted her chin and said angrily, "We are not now in
the Kilghard Hills, *Dom* Lewis, and I do not allow any other
person, not even a brother, to tell me what I may or may not
do! If my brothers disapprove of my conduct, they know they
may come to me for an accounting of it, not to you!"

He laughed and with his good hand touched the feathery
edges of her hair. It was, she thought, a beautiful hand, sensitive and strong, without being over-delicate. "So you have
cut your hair and declared the independence of a Free Amazon, kinswoman? Have you taken their oath too?"

"No," she said, snuggling close to him again. "I am too
fond of men ever to do that."

When he smiled, she thought, he was very handsome; even

the scar that pulled his lip into distortion only gave his smile a little more irony and warmth.

They danced together much of the evening, and before they parted, agreed together to meet the next day for a hunt in the great hunting preserves of the pleasure planet. When they said good night, Kennard was smiling benevolently, but Geremy was sullen and brooding, and when the three of them were in their luxurious suite, he demanded wrathfully, "Why did you do that? I told you, stay away from Lew! We don't really want an entanglement with that branch of the Altons!"

"How dare you try to tell me whom I can dance with? I don't censure your choice of entertainers and singing women and whores, do I, Geremy?"

"You are a Lady of the Comyn! And when you behave so blatantly as that—"

"Hold your tongue!" Dio flared at him. "You are insulting! I dance one evening with a man of my own caste, because my brothers have left me no other dancing partner, and already you have me bedded down with him! And even if it were so, Geremy, I tell you once again, I will do as I wish, and neither you nor any other man can stop me!"

"Lerrys," Geremy appealed, "Can't you reason with her?"

But Lerrys stood regarding his sister with admiration. "That's the spirit, Dio! What is the good of being on an alien planet in a civilized Empire, if you keep the provincial spirit and customs of your backwater? Do what you like, Dio. Geremy, let her alone!"

Geremy shook his head, angry, but he was laughing too. "You too! Always one in mind, as if you had been born twins!"

"Certainly," said Lerrys. "Why, do you think, am I a lover of men? Because, to my ill-fortune, the only woman I have ever known with a man's spirit and a man's strength is my own sister!" He kissed her, laughing. "Enjoy yourself, *breda*, but don't get hurt. He may have been on his good behavior last night, or even in a romantic mood, but I suspect he could be savage."

"No." Suddenly Geremy was sober. "This is no joke. I don't want you to see him again, Diotima. One evening, perhaps, to do courtesy to our kinsmen; I grant you that, and I am sorry if I implied it was more than courtesy. But no more, Dio, not again. Lerrys said as much last night, when he wasn't devilling me! If you don't think I have your good at heart, certainly you know Lerrys does. Listen to me, sister; there are enough men on this planet to dance with, flirt with, hunt with—yes, damn it, and to lie with too, if that's your pleasure! But let Kennard Alton's half-caste bastard alone—do you hear me? I tell you, Dio, if you disobey me, I shall make you regret it!"

"Now," said Lerrys, still laughing, as Dio tossed her head in defiance, "you have made it certain, Geremy; you have all but spread the bridal bed for them! Don't you know that no man alive can forbid Dio to do anything?"

In the hunting preserve next day, they chose horses, and the great hawks not unlike the *verrin* hawks of the Kilghard Hills. Lew was smiling, good-natured, but she felt he was a little shocked, too, at her riding breeches and boots. "So you are the Free Amazon you said you were not, after all," he teased.

She smiled back at him and said, "No. I told you why I could never be that." *And the more I see him,* she thought, *the more sure I am of it.* "But when I ride in the riding-skirts I would wear on Darkover, I feel like a housecat in leather mittens! I like to feel free when I ride, if not, why not stay on the ground and embroider cushions?"

"Why not, indeed?" he asked, smiling, and in his mind, painless for once, she saw, reflected, a quick memory of a laughing woman, red-headed, riding bareback and free over the hills....The picture slammed shut; was gone. Dio wondered who the woman had been and felt a faint, quick envy of her.

Lew was a good rider, though the lifeless artificial hand seemed to be very much in his way; he could use it, after a fashion, but so clumsily that she wondered if, after all, he could not have managed better one-handed. She would have thought that even a functional metal hook would have been more use to him. But perhaps he was too proud for that, or feared she would think it ugly. He carried the hawk on a special saddleblock, as women on Darkover did, instead of holding it on his wrist as most hillmen did; when she looked at it, he colored and turned angrily away, swearing under his breath. Again Dio thought, with that sudden anger which Lew seemed able to rouse in her so quickly, *why is he so sensitive, so defensive, so self-indulgent about it? Does he think most people know or care whether he has two hands, or one, or three?*

The hunting preserve had been carefully landscaped and terraformed to beautiful and varied scenery, low hills which did not strain the horses, smooth plains, a variety of wild life, colorful vegetation from a dozen worlds. But as they rode she heard him sigh a little. He said, just loud enough for her to hear, "It is beautiful here. But the sun here—is wrong, somehow. I wish—" and he closed off the words, the way he could close off his mind, sharp and swift, brutally shutting her out.

"Are you homesick, Lew?" she asked.

He tightened his mouth. "Yes. Sometimes," he said, but he had warned her off again, and Dio turned her attention to the hawk on her saddle.

"These birds are very well trained."

He made some noncommittal remark, but she managed to catch his thought that birds which were well enough trained to be used by all comers were like whores, not at all interesting. All he said aloud was, "I would rather train my own."

"I like to hunt," she said, "but I am not sure I could train a bird from the beginning. It must be very difficult."

"Not difficult for anyone with the Ridenow gift, I should think," Lew said. "Most of your clan have sensitivity to all animals and birds, as well as the gift you were bred for, to sense and make contact with alien intelligences—"

She smiled and shrugged. "In these days there is little of that. The Ridenow gift, in its original form—well, I think it must be extinct. Though Lerrys says it would be very useful in the Terran Empire, to make communication possible with non-humans. Is it very difficult to train hawks?"

"It is certainly not easy," said Lew. "It takes time and patience. And somehow you must put your mind into touch with the bird's mind, and that is frightening; they are wild, and savage. But I have done it, at Arilinn; so did some of the women. Janna Lindir is a fine hawk trainer, and I have heard it is easier for women... though my foster-sister Linnell would never learn it, she was frightened of the birds. I suppose it is like breaking horses, which my father used to do... before he was so lame. He tried to teach me that, a little, a long time ago." Talking easily of these things, Dio thought, Lew was transformed.

The preserve was stocked with a variety of game, large and small. After a time they let their hawks loose, and Dio watched in delight as hers soared high, wheeled in midair

and set off on long, strong wings after a flight of small white
birds, directly overhead. Lew's hawk came after, swiftly
stooping, seizing one of the small birds in midair. The white
bird struggled pitiably, with a long, eerie scream. Dio had
hunted with hawks all her life; she watched with interest,
but as drops of blood fell from the dying bird, spattering them,
she realized that Lew was staring upward, his face white and
drawn with horror. He looked paralyzed.

"Lew, what is the matter?"

He said, his voice strained and hoarse, "That sound—I
cannot bear it—" and flung up his two arms over his eyes.
The black-gloved artificial hand struck his face awkwardly;
swearing, he wrenched it off his wrist and flung it to the
ground under the horse's hoofs.

"No, it's not pretty," he mocked, in a rage, "like blood, and
death, and the screams of dying things. If you take pleasure
in them, so much the worse for you, my lady! Take pleasure,
then, in this!" He held up the hideously scarred bare stump,
shaking it at her in fury; then wheeled his horse, jerking at
the reins with his good hand, and riding off as if all the devils
in all the hells were chasing him.

Dio stared in dismay; then, forgetting the hawks, set after
him at a breakneck gallop. After a time they came abreast;
he was fighting the reins one-handed, struggling to rein in
the mount; but, as she watched in horror, he lost control and
was tossed out of the saddle, falling heavily to the ground,
where he lay without moving.

Dio slid from her horse and knelt at his side. He had been
knocked unconscious, but even as she was trying to decide
whether she should go to bring help, he opened his eyes and
looked at her without recognition.

"It's all right," she said. "The horse threw you. Can you
sit up?"

He did so, awkwardly, as if the stump pained him; he saw
her looking, flinched and tried to thrust it into a fold of his
riding cloak, out of sight. He turned his face away from her,
and the tight scar tissue drew up his mouth into an ugly
grimace, as if he were about to cry.

"Gods! I'm sorry, *domna*, I didn't mean—" he muttered,
almost inaudibly.

"What was it, Lew? Why did you lose your temper and
rush off like that? What did I do to make you angry?"

"Nothing, nothing—" Dazed, he shook his head. "I—I can-

not bear the sight of blood, now, or the thought of some small
helpless thing dying for my pleasure—" he said, and his voice
sounded exhausted. "I have hunted all my life, without ever
thinking of it, but when I saw that little white bird crying
out and saw the blood, suddenly it all came over me again
and I remembered—oh, Avarra have mercy on me, I remembered.... Dio, just go away, don't, in the name of the merciful
Avarra, Dio—"

His face twisted again and then he was crying, great
hoarse painful sobs, his face ugly and crumpled, trying to
turn away so that she would not see. "I have seen...too much
pain...Dio, don't—go away, go away, don't touch me—"

She put out her arms, folded him in them, drawing him
against her breast. For a moment he resisted frantically, then
let her draw him close. She was crying too.

" I never thought," she whispered. "Death in hunting—I
am so used to it, it never seemed quite real to me. Lew, what
was it, who died, what did it make you remember?"

"Marjorie," he said hoarsely. "My wife. She died, she died,
died horribly in Sharra's fire—Dio, don't touch me, somehow
I hurt everyone I touch, go away before I hurt you too, I don't
want you to be hurt—"

"It's too late for that," she said, holding him, feeling his
pain all through her. He raised his one hand to her face,
touching her wet eyes, and she felt him slam down his defenses again; but this time she knew it was not rejection, only
the defenses of a man unbearably hurt, who could bear no
more.

"Were you hurt, Dio?" he asked, his hand lingering on her
cheek. "There's blood on your face."

"It's the bird's blood. It's on you too," she said, and wiped
it away. He took her hand in his and pressed the fingertips
to his lips. Somehow the gesture made her want to cry again.
She asked, "Were you hurt when you fell?"

"Not much," he said, testing his muscles cautiously. "They
taught me, in the Empire hospital on Terra, how to fall without hurting myself, when I was—before this healed." Uneasily he moved the stump. "I can't get used to the damned hand.
I do better one-handed."

She had thought he might. "Why do you wear it, then? If
it's only for looks, why do you think I would care?"

His face was bleak. "Father would care. He thinks, when
I wear the empty sleeve, I am—flaunting my mutilation.

Making a show of it. He hates his own lameness so much, I would rather not—not flaunt mine in his face."

Dio thought swiftly, then decided what she could say. "You are a grown man, and so is he. He has one way of coping with his own lameness, and you have another; it is easy to see that you are very different. Would it really make him angry if you chose another way to deal with what has happened to you?"

"I don't know," Lew said, "but he has been so good to me, never reproached me for these years of exile, nor for the way in which I have brought all his plans to nothing. I do not want to distress him further." He rose, went to collect the grotesque lifeless thing in its black glove, looked at it for a moment, then put it away in his saddlebag. He fumbled one-handed to pin his empty sleve over the stump; she started to offer, matter-of-factly, to help him, and decided it was too soon. He looked into the sky. "I suppose the hawks are gone beyond recall, and we will be charged for losing them."

"No." She blew the silver whistle around her neck. "They are birds with brains modified so they cannot choose but come to the whistle—see?" She pointed as two distant flecks appeared in the sky, growing larger and larger; spiraling down, then landing on the saddle blocks where they sat patiently, awaiting their hoods. "Their instinct for freedom has been burnt out."

"They are like some men I know," said Lew, slipping the hood on his bird. Dio followed suit, but neither of them moved to mount. Dio hesitated, then decided he had probably had far too much of politely averted eyes and pretenses of courteous unawareness.

"Do you need help to mount? Can I help you, or shall I fetch someone who can?"

"Thank you, but I can manage, though it looks awkward." Again, suddenly, he smiled and his ugly scarred face seemed handsome again to her. "How did you know it would do me good to hear that?"

"I have never been really hurt," she said, "but one year I had a fever, and lost all my hair, and it did not grow in for half a year; and I felt so ugly you couldn't imagine. And the one thing that bothered me worse was when everyone would say how nice I looked, tell me how pretty my dress or sash or kerchief looked, and pretend nothing at all was wrong with me. So I felt so bad about how miserable I was, as if I was making a dreadful fuss about nothing at all. So if I was—was really lamed or crippled, I think I would hate it if people made me go on acting as if nothing at all was wrong and there was nothing the matter with me. Please don't ever think you have to pretend with me"

He drew a deep breath. "Father flies into a rage if anyone seems to notice him limping, and once or twice when I have tried to offer him my arm, he has nearly knocked me down."

Yet, Dio thought, *Kennard used his lameness, last night, to manipulate me into dancing with Lew. Why?* She said, "That is the way he manages *his* life and *his* lameness. You are not your father."

Suddenly he started shaking. He said, "Sometimes—sometimes it is hard to be sure of that," and she remembered that the Alton gift was forced rapport. Kennard's intense closeness to his son, his deep ambition for him, was well-known on Darkover; that closeness must become torture sometimes, make it hard for Lew to distinguish his own feelings and emotions. "It must be difficult for you; he is such a powerful telepath—"

"In all fairness," said Lew, "it must be difficult for him too; to share everything I have lived through in these years, and there was a time when my barriers were not as strong as they are now. It must have been hell for him. But that does not make it less difficult for me."

And if Kennard will not accept any weakness in Lew... but Dio did not pursue that. "I'm not trying to pry. If you don't want to answer, just say so, but...Geremy lost three fingers in a duel. The Terran medics regrew them for him, as good as new. Why did they not try to do that with your hand?"

"They did," he said. "Twice." His voice was flat, emotionless. "Then I could bear no more. Somehow, the pattern of the cells—you are not a matrix technician, are you? It would be easier to explain this if you knew something about cell division. I wonder if you can understand—the pattern of the cells, the *knowledge* in the cells, that makes a hand a hand, and not an eye, or a toenail, or a wing, or a hoof, had been damaged beyond renewing. What grew at the end of my wrist was—" he drew a deep breath and she saw the horror in his eyes. "It was not a hand," he said flatly, "I am not sure just *what* it was, and I do not want to know. They made a mistake with the drugs, once, and I woke and saw it. They tell me I screamed my throat raw. I do not remember. My voice has never been right since. For half a year I could not speak above a whisper." His harsh voice was completely emotionless. "I was not myself for years. I can live with it now, because—because I must. I can face the knowledge that I am—am maimed. What I cannot face," he said, with sudden violence, "is my father's need to pretend that I am—am whole!"

Dio felt the surge of violent anger and was not even sure whether it was her own, or that of the man before her. She had never been so wholly aware of her own *laran;* the Ridenow gift, which was a sharing of emotions, full empathy, even with nonhumans, aliens.... She had never had much experience with it before. Now it seemed to shake her to the core. Her voice was unsteady. "Never pretend with me, Lew. I can face you as you are—exactly as you are, always, all of you."

He seized her in a rough grip, dragged her close. It was hardly an embrace. "Girl, do you know what you're saying? You can't know."

She felt as if her own boundaries were dissolving, as if somehow she was melting into the man who stood before her. "If you can endure what you have endured, I can endure to know what it is that you have had to endure. Lew, let me prove it to you,"

In the back of her mind she wondered, *why am I doing this?* But she knew that when they had come into each other's arms on the dancing floor last night, even behind the barriers of Lew's locked defenses, their bodies had somehow made a pact. Barricade themselves from the other as they would, something in each of them had reached out to the other and accepted what the other was, wholly and forever.

She raised her face to him. His arms went round her in grateful surprise, and he murmured, still holding back, "But you are so young, *chiya,* you can't know....I should be horsewhipped for this...but it has been so long, so long...." and she knew he was not speaking of the most obvious thing. She felt herself dissolve in that total awareness of him, the receding barricades... *the memory of pain and horror, the starved sexuality, the ordeals which had gone on past human endurance...the black encompassing horror of guilt, of a loved one dead, self-knowledge, self-blame, mutilation almost gladly accepted as atonement for living on when she was dead....*

In a desperate, hungering embrace she clasped him close,

knowing it was this for which he had longed most; someone who knew all this, and could still accept him without pretense, love him nevertheless. *Love; was this love, the knowledge that she would gladly take on herself all this suffering, to spare him another moment of suffering or guilt...?*

For an instant she saw herself as she was, reflected in his mind, hardly recognizing herself, warm, glowing, woman, and for a moment loved herself for what she had become to him; then the rapport broke and receded like a tide, leaving her awed and shaken, leaving tears and tenderness that could never grow less. Only then did he lower his lips to hers and kiss her; and as she laughed and accepted the kiss, she said in a whisper, "Geremy was right."

"What, Dio?"

"Nothing, my love," she said, lighthearted with relief. "Come, Lew, the hawks are restless, we must get them back to the mews. We will have our fee refunded because we have claimed no kill, but I, for one, have had full value for my hunt. I have what I most wanted—"

"And what is that?" he asked, teasing, but she knew he did not need an answer. He was not touching her now, as they mounted, but she knew that somehow they were still touching, still embraced.

He flung up one arm and called, "We may as well have a ride, at least! Which of us will be first at the stables?"

And he was off; Dio dug her heels into her horse's sides and was off after him, laughing. She knew as well as he did, how and where this day would end.

And it was only the beginning of a long season on Vainwal. It would be a long, beautiful summer.

Even though she knew there was darkness ahead, and that she moved into it, unafraid and willing, she was willing to face it. Beyond the darkness she could see what Lew had been and what he could be again...if she could have the strength and courage to bring him through. She raced after him, crying out "Wait for me—Lew, we'll ride together!" and he slowed his horse a little, smiling, and waited for her.

Lew Alton's narrative:
Vainwal: sixth year of exile

CHAPTER THREE

I thought I had forgotten how to be happy.

And yet, that year on Vainwal, I was happy. The planet is more than the decadent city of the pleasure world. Perhaps we would have left it altogether—though not, perhaps, to return to Darkover—but my father found the climate beneficial to his lameness, and preferred to stay in the city where he could find hot springs and mineral baths, and sometimes, I suspect, companionship he could tolerate. I've wondered, sometimes, about that; but, close as we were, there are some things we could not—quite—share, and that was one area of itchy privacy I tried, hard, to stay away from. I suppose it's hard enough with ordinary sons and their fathers.

When both father and son are telepaths, it becomes even more difficult. During my years in Arilinn, working in the telepathic relays as a matrix mechanic, I had learned a lot about privacy, and what it has to be when all around you are closer than your own skin. There used to be an old taboo preventing a mother and her grown son from working in the relays at the same time; or a father and his nubile daughter. My father could mask his thoughts better than most. Even so, I described that sort of thing, once, to somebody, as living with your skin off. During these years of exile, we'd been so close that there were times when neither of us was sure which thought belonged to whom. Any two solitary men are going to get on each other's nerves from time to time. Add to that the fact that one of them is seriously ill and at least (let me not pass too lightly over this) intermittently insane, and it adds another turn of the screw. And we were both extremely powerful telepaths, and there had been long periods of time when I had no control over what I was sending. By the time

58

I was even halfway sane again there were long periods of time where there was at least as much hate as there was love. We had been too close, too long.

Not the least of what I had to be grateful to Dio for was this; that she had broken that deadlock, broken into that unhealthy over-preoccupation with one another's every thought. If we had been mother and son, father and daughter, brother and sister, at least there would have been a taboo we could break. For a father and son there was no such dramatic exit from the trap; or it seemed to us that there was not, though I cannot swear it never entered either of our minds. We were both old enough to make such a decision, we were away from the world which had ingrained such taboos, and we were alone together in an alien universe, among the head-blind who would neither know nor care what levels of decadence we might choose to explore. Nevertheless, we let it alone; it was, perhaps, the only thing we never tried to share, and I think it may have been the only way we kept our sanity.

My father was quickly enchanted with Dio, too, and I think he was genuinely grateful to her; not least because she had come between our unhealthy preoccupation with one another. Yet, glad as he was to have some degree of freedom from my constant presence and to be free of fears for my continued sanity (and, though he had shielded them carefully from me, I was always aware of it, and a man watched constantly for signs of insanity will doubt his own sanity the more), the coming of Dio had left him alone. He could not admit his helplessness; Kennard Alton never would. Yet daily I saw him growing worse, and knew that a time would come, even if it had not come yet, when he needed me. He had always been there when I needed him, and I would not leave him alone, a prey to age and infirmity. So Dio and I found a home at the edge of the city, where he could call upon us when he needed us, and in the overflow of our own happiness, it was easy enough to spare him some time for companionship.

Well, we were happy. When I lost Marjorie, in the horror of that last night when Caer Donn had gone up in flames and we had tried, with our two lives thrust into the gap, to close the breach Sharra had made in the fabric of the world, we had both been ready to die. But it hadn't happened that way; Marjorie died, and I—lived on, but something had been destroyed in me that night. Not cut clean away, but, like my hand, rotting and festering and growing into terrifying inhuman shapes. Dio had gone unflinching into all that horror, and somehow, after that, I had healed clean.

Neither of us thought of marriage. Marriage *di catenas,* the ritual formalized marriage of the Domains, was a solemn joining of property, a mutual matter concerning two families, two houses, for the raising of children to inheritance and *laran.* What Dio and I had was so deeply personal that we had no wish or need to bring either family into it. With Marjorie, half my love for her had been a desire to see her as my wife, living with me at Armida, bringing up children we would share in common, the desire for the long quiet years of peace in our beloved home. With Dio it was something different. When Dio found herself pregnant, in the second year we were together, we were not really happy about it. But perhaps our bodies had spoken to what our minds refused to know. It lay deep in both of us, of course, a desire for continuity, something to come after us when we were gone, the deep-rooted desire for the only immortality anyone can ever know.

"I needn't have the child, if you don't want it," she said, curled up at my side in our living room, which was high above the lights of Vainwal, below us; colored lights, strung gaily in ribbons along the streets; there was always some kind of festival here, noise and gaiety and confusion and the seeking of pleasure.

She was close enough to me to feel my instinctual flinching. She said "You *do* want it—don't you, Lew?"

"I don't know, and that's the truth, Dio."

Truth; I resented the intrusion of our idyll by any third party, however beloved; someone who would inevitably destroy the deepest closeness between us; Dio would no longer be altogether preoccupied with my needs and wishes, and in that way, selfishly, I resented the knowledge that she was pregnant.

Truth, equally; I remembered with anguish that night— the very night before her death—when I knew that Marjorie was carrying the child she would not live long enough to bear. I had sensed the tentative life as I now sensed the new and growing seed of life in Dio and my very soul shrank from seeing it extinguished. Maybe it was only squeamishness. But, selfishly, I wished *this* child to live.

I said, "I want it and I do not. It is you who will have to

bear it; you must make the choice. Whatever you decide, I will try to be happy with your decision."

For a long time she watched the changing play of lights in the city below us. At last she said, "It will change my life in ways I can't even imagine. I'm a little afraid to change that much. It's you I want, Lew, not your child," and she laid her head on my shoulder. Yet I sensed she was as ambivalent as I. "At the same time, it's something that—that came out of our love. I can't help wanting—" She stopped and swallowed, and laid her hand, almost protectively, over her belly. "I love you, Lew, and I love your child because it's yours. And this is something that could be—well, different and stronger than either of us, but *part* of what we have together. Does that make any sense to you?"

I stroked her hair. At that moment she seemed so infinitely precious to me, more so than she had ever been before; perhaps more than she would ever be again.

"I'm frightened, Lew. It's too big. I don't think I have the right to decide something as big as that. Maybe the decision was made by something beyond either of us. I never thought much about God, or the Gods, or whatever there is. I keep feeling that there's something terrible waiting for us, and I don't want to lose even a minute of what happiness we could have together." Again the little gesture, holding her hand over her womb, as if to shield the child there. She said, in a scared whisper, "I'm a Ridenow. It's not just a *thing*, Lew, it's alive, I can feel it alive—oh, not moving, I won't feel it moving for months yet, but I can sense it there. It's alive and I think it wants to live. Whether it does or not, I *want* it to live—I want to feel it living. I'm scared of the changes it will make, but I want to have it, Lew. I want this baby."

I put my hand over hers, trying to sense it, feeling—maybe it was my imagination—the sense of something living. I remembered the depthless, measureless grief I had felt, knowing Marjorie would not live to bear me her child. Was it only the memory of *that* grief, or did I really sense deeper sorrow awaiting us? Perhaps it was at that moment that I fully accepted that Marjorie was gone, that death was forever, that there would be no reunion in this world or the next. But under my hand and Dio's was life, a return of hope, something in the future. We were not only living from day to day, grasping for pleasure wholly our own, but life went on, and there was always more life to live. I kissed her on the forehead and on the lips, then bent to kiss her belly too.

"Whatever comes of it," I said, "I do too, *preciosa*. Thank you.

My father, of course, was delighted; but troubled, too, and he would not tell me why. And now that we were not so close, he could shield his thoughts from me. At first Dio was well and blooming, quite free of the minor troubles which some women feel in pregnancy; she said she had never been happier or healthier. I watched the changes in her body with amusement and delight. It was a joyful time; we both waited for the child's birth, and even begun to talk about the possibility—which I had never been willing, before, to acknowledge—that someday we would return to Darkover together, and share the world of our birth with our son or daughter.

Son or daughter. It troubled me, not to know which. Dio had not a great deal of *laran* and had not been trained to use what little she had. She sensed the presence and the life of the child, but that was all; she could not tell which, and when I could not understand this, she told me with spirit that an unborn child probably had no awareness of its own gender, and therefore, not being aware of its own sex, she could not read its mind. The Terran medics could have taken a blood sample and a chromosome analysis and told us which, but that seemed a sick and heartless way to find out. Perhaps, I thought, Dio would develop the sensitivity to find it out, or if all else failed, I would know when the child was born. Whichever it might be, I would love it. My father wanted a son but I refused to think in those terms.

"This child, even if it is a son, will not be Heir to Armida. Forget it," I told him, and Kennard said with a sigh, "No, it will not. You have Aldaran blood; and the Aldaran gift is precognition. I do not know why it will not, but it will not." And then he asked me if I had had Dio monitored to make certain all was well with the child.

"The Terran medics say that all is well," I told him, defensively. "If you want her monitored, do it yourself!"

"I *cannot*, Lew." It was the first time he had ever confessed weakness to me. I looked at my father carefully for the first time, it seemed, in months, his eyes sunken deep in his face, his hands twisted and almost useless now. It seemed as if the flesh was wasting off his bones. I reached out to him and as I had often enough done to him, he rebuffed the touch, slam-

ming down barriers. Then he drew a long breath and looked
me straight in the eye. *"Laran* sometimes fails with age.
Probably it is no more than that. You are free from Sharra
now, are you not? You have Ridenow blood; you and Dio are
cousins. My father's wife was a Ridenow, and so was his
mother. A woman who bears a child with *laran* should be
monitored."

I sighed. This was the simplest of the techniques I had
learned in Arilinn; a child of thirteen can learn to monitor
the body's functions, nerves, psychic channels. Monitoring a
pregnant woman and her child is a little more complex, but
even so, there was no difficulty in it. "I'll—try."

But I knew he could feel my inner shrinking. The Sharra
matrix was packed away into the farthest corner of the farthest closet of the apartments I shared with Dio, and not
twice in ten days, now, did I think of that peculiar bondage.
But then, I did not use my own personal matrix, either, or
seek to use any *laran* except the simplest, that reading of
unspoken thoughts which no telepath can ever completely
blockade from his mind.

"When?" he insisted.

"Soon," I said, cutting him off.

*Get out! Get out of my mind! Between you and Sharra, I
have no mind of my own!* He winced with the violence of the
thought, and I felt pain and regret. In spite of all that had
been between us, I loved my father, and could not endure
that look of anguish on his face. I put my hand out to him.

"You are not well, sir. What do the Terran medics say to
you?"

"I know what they would say, and so I have not asked
them," he said, with a flicker of humor, then returned to the
former urgency. "Lew, promise me; if you find you cannot
monitor Dio, then promise me—Lerrys is still on Vainwal,
though I think he will soon leave for Council season. If you
cannot monitor her, send for Lerrys and make him do it. He
is a Ridenow—"

"And Dio is a Ridenow, and has *laran* rights in the estate,
and the legal right to sit in Council," I said. "Lerrys quarreled
with her because she had not married me; he said her children
should have a legal claim to the Alton Domain!" I swore, with
such violence that my father flinched again, as if I had struck
him or gripped his thin crippled hands in a vise-grip.

"Like it or not, Lew," my father said, "Dio's child is the

son of the Heir to Alton. What you say or think cannot change it. You can forswear or forgo your own birthright, but you cannot renounce it on your son's behalf."

I swore again, turned on my heel and left him. He came after me, his step uneven, his voice filled with angry urgency.

"Are you going to marry Dio?"

"That's *my* business," I said, slamming down a barrier again. I could do it, now, without going into the black nothingness. He said, tightening his mouth, "I swore I would never force or pressure you to marry. But remember; refusing to decide is also a decision. If you refuse to decide to marry her, you have decided that your son shall be born *nedestro,* and a time may come when you will regret it bitterly."

"Then," I said, my voice hard, "I will regret it."

"Have you asked Dio how she feels?"

Surely he must know that we had discussed it endlessly, both of us reluctant to marry in the Terran fashion, but even less willing to bring my father, and Dio's brothers, into the kind of property-based discussions and settlements there would have to be before I could marry her *di catenas.* It had no relevance here on Vainwal, in any case. We had considered ourselves married in what Darkovans called freemate marriage—the sharing of a bed, a meal, a fireside—and desired no more; it would become as legal as any *catenas* marriage when our child was born. But now I faced that, too; if our son was born *nedestro,* he could not inherit from me; if I should die Dio would have to turn to her Ridenow kin. Whatever happened, I must provide for her.

When I explained it that way, as a matter of simple and practical logic, Dio was willing enough, and the next day we went to the Empire HQ on Vainwal and registered our marriage there. I settled the legal questions, so that if I died before her, or before our child had grown to maturity, she could legally claim property belonging to me, on Terra or on Darkover, and our son would have similar rights in my estate. I realized, somewhere about halfway through these procedures, that both of us, without any prearrangement, had mutually begun referring to the child as "he." Father had reminded me that I was part Aldaran, and precognition was one of those gifts. I accepted it as that. And knowing that, I knew all that I needed to know, so why trouble myself with monitoring?

A day or two later, Dio said, out of a clear blue sky, as we sat at breakfast in our high room above the city, "Lew, I lied to you."

"Lied, *preciosa?*" I looked at her candid fair face. In general one telepath cannot lie to another but there are levels of truth and deceit. Dio had let her hair grow; now it was long enough to tie at the back of her neck, and her eyes were that color so common in fair-haired women, which can be blue or green or gray, depending on the health, and mood, and what she is wearing. She had on a loose dress of leaf-green—her body was heavy, now—and her eyes glowed like emeralds.

"Lied," she repeated. "You thought it was an accident— that I had become pregnant by accident or oversight. It was deliberate. I am sorry."

"But why, Dio?" I was not angry, only perplexed. I had not wanted this to happen, at first, but now I was altogether happy about it.

"Lerrys—had threatened to take me back to Darkover for this Council season," she said. "A pregnant woman cannot travel in space. It was the only way I could think of to make sure he would not force me to go."

I said, "I am glad you did." I could not, now, envision life without Dio.

"And now, I suppose, he will use the knowledge that I am married, and have a son," I said. It was the first time I had been willing to ask myself what would become of the Alton Domain, with both my father and myself self-exiled. My brother Marius was never accepted by the Council; but if there really was no other Alton Heir, they might make the best of a bad bargain and accept him. Otherwise it would probably go to my cousin Gabriel Lanart; he had married a Hastur, after all, and he had three sons and two daughters by his Hastur wife. They had wanted to give it, and the command of the Guards, to Gabriel in the first place, and my father would have saved a lot of trouble if he had permitted it.

It would all be the same in the end anyhow, for I would never return to Darkover.

Time slid out of focus. I was kneeling in a room in a high tower, and outside the last crimson light of the red sun set across the high peaks of the Venza mountains behind Thendara. I knelt at the bedside of a little girl, five or six years old, with fair hair, and golden eyes...Marjorie's eyes...I had knelt at Marjorie's side like this...and we had seen her to-

gether, our *child,* that *child...but it had never been, it would
never be, Marjorie was dead...dead...a great fire blazed,
surged through my brain...and Dio was beside me, her hand
on the hilt of a great sword....*

Shaken, I surfaced, to see Dio looking at me in shock and
dismay.

"Our child, Lew—? And on Darkover—"

I gripped at the back of a chair to steady myself. After a
time I said shakily, "I have heard of a *laran*—I thought it
was only in the Ages of Chaos—which could see, not only the
future, but many futures, some of which may never come to
pass; all of the things which *might* someday happen. Perhaps—perhaps, somewhere in my Alton or Aldaran heritage
there is a trace of that *laran,* so that I see things which may
never be. For I have seen that child once before—with Marjorie—and I thought it was *her* child." Dimly I realized that
I had spoken Marjorie's name aloud for the first time since
her death. I would always remember her love; but she had
receded very far, and I was healed of that, too. "Marjorie,"
I said again. "I thought it was our child, our daughter; she
had Marjorie's eyes. But Marjorie died before she could bear
me any child, and so what I thought was a true vision of the
future never came to be. Yet now I see it again. What does
it mean, Dio?"

She said, with a wavering smile, "Now I wish my *laran*
were better trained. I don't know, Lew. I don't know what it
means."

Nor did I; but it made me desperately uneasy. We did not
talk about it any more, but I think it worked inward, coloring
my mood. Later that day she said she had an appointment
with one of the medics at the Terran Empire hospital; she
could have found any kind of midwife or birth-woman in
Vainwal, which spanned a dozen dozen cultures, but since
she could not be tended as she would be on Darkover, the cool
impersonality of the Terran hospital suited her best.

I went with her. Now, thinking back, it seems to me that
she was very quiet, shadowed, perhaps, by some weight of
foreknowledge. She came out looking troubled, and the doctor, a slight, preoccupied young man, gestured to me to come
and talk with him.

"Don't be alarmed," he said at once. "Your wife is perfectly
well, and the baby's heartbeat is strong and sound. But there
are things I don't understand. Mr. Montray-Lanart—"my

father and I both used that name on Terra, for Alton is a
Domain, a title, rather than a personal name, and *Lord Armida* meant nothing here—"I notice your hand; is it a congenital deformity? Forgive me for asking—"

"No," I said curtly. "It was the result of a serious accident."

"And you did not have it regenerated or regrown?"

"No." The word was hard and final and this time he understood that I would not talk about it. I understand there are
cultures where there are religious taboos against that kind
of thing, and it was all right with me if he thought I was that
sort of idiot. It was better than trying to talk about it. He
looked troubled, but he said, "Are there twins in your family,
or other multiple births?"

"Why do you ask?"

"We checked the fetus with radiosound," he said, "and
there seems to be—some anomaly. You must prepare yourself
for the fact that there might be some—minor deformity, unless it is twins and our equipment did not pick up exactly
what we intended; twins or multiple births lying across one
another can create rather odd images."

I shook my head, not wanting to think about that. But my
hand was *not* a congenital deformity, so why was I worried?
If Dio was carrying twins, or something like that, it was not
surprising that we could not clearly identify male or female.

Dio asked, when I came out, what the doctor had said.

"He said he thought you might be carrying twins."

She looked troubled, too. She said, "He told me the pla-
centa was in a difficult position—could not see the baby's
body as clearly as he could wish," she said. "But it would be
nice to have twins. A boy *and* a girl, perhaps." She leaned
on my arm and said, "I'm glad it won't be long now. Not forty
days, perhaps. I'm tired of carrying him, or them, around—
it will be nice to let you hold him for a while!"

I took her home, but when we arrived we found a message
on the communicator which was an integral part of all Empire
apartments; my father was ill and asking for me. Dio offered
to go with me; but she was tired after the morning's excursion,
so she sent him loving messages, and begged his pardon for
not attending him, and I set off for the city alone.

I had expected to find him abed, but he was up and around,
his step dragging. He motioned me to a chair, and offered me
coffee or a drink, both of which I refused.

"I thought I'd find you laid up. You look as if you ought to be in bed," I said, risking his wrath, but he only sighed. He said, "I wanted to say good-bye to you; I may have to go back to Darkover. A message has come from Dyan Ardais—"

I grimaced. Dyan had been my father's friend since they were children together; but he has never liked me, nor I him. My father saw my expression and said sharply, "He has befriended your brother when I was not there to guard his interests, Lew. He has sent me the only news I had—"

"Don't you throw that up at me," I said sharply. "I never asked you to bring me here! Or to Terra, either."

He waved that aside. "I won't quarrel with you about that. Dyan has been a good friend to your brother—"

"If I had a son," I said deliberately, "I would want a better friend for him than that damned sandal-wearer!"

"We've never agreed on that, and I doubt we ever will," said my father, "but Dyan is an honorable man, and he has the good of the Comyn at heart. Now he tells me that they are about to pass over Marius, and formally give over the Alton Domain to Gabriel Lanart-Hastur."

"Is that such a tragedy? Let him have it! I don't want it."

"When you have a son of your own, you will understand, Lew. That time is not very far away, either. I think you should come back with me to Darkover, and settle things at this Council season."

He heard my refusal, like a shout of rage, before what I actually said, which was a quiet "No. I cannot and I will not. Dio is too pregnant to travel."

"You can be back before the child is born," he said reasonably. "And you will have settled his future properly."

"Would you have left my mother?"

"No. But your son should be born at Armida—"

"It's no good thinking about that," I said. "Dio is here, and here she must stay until the baby is born. And I will stay with her."

His sigh was heavy, like the rustling of winter leaves. "I am not eager for the journey, alone, but if you will not go, then I must. Would you trust me to stay with Dio, Lew? I do not know if I can bear the climate of the Kilghard Hills. Yet I will not let Armida go by default, nor let them pass over Marius's rights without being sure how Marius feels about it." And as he spoke I was overwhelmed with the flood of memories—Armida lying in the fold of the Kilghard Hills, flooded with sunlight, the great herds of horses grazing in the upland pastures, the streams rushing, or frozen into knotted and unruly floods, torrents arrested in motion and midair; snow lying deep on the hills, a line of dark trees against the sky; the fire that had ravaged us in my seventeenth year, and the long line of men, stooped over their fire-shovels in back-breaking work; camping on the fire-lines, sharing blankets and bowls, the satisfaction of seeing the fires die and knowing that our home was safe for another season... the smell of resins, and bloom of *kireseth,* gold and blue with the blowing pollen in a high summer... sunset over the roofs... the skyline of Thendara... the four moons hanging behind one another in the darkening sky of Festival... my home. My home, too, loved and renounced....

Get...out! Were even my memories not my own?

"There's still time, Lew. I won't leave for more than a tenday. Let me know what you decide."

"I've already decided," I said, and slammed out, not waiting for the concerned questions I knew would follow, his scrupulous inquiries about Dio, his kind wishes for her well-being.

The decision had been made for me. I would not return with my father. Dio could not go and so I would not go, it was as simple as that, I need not listen to the thousand memories that pulled me back....

It was that night that she asked me to monitor the child. Perhaps she sensed my agitation; perhaps, in that curious way that lovers share one another's preoccupations and fears (and Dio and I, even after the year and more we had spent together, were still very much lovers), she felt the flood of my memories and it made her eager for reassurance.

I started to refuse. But it meant so much to her. And I was free now, free of it for months at a time; surely a time would come when I was wholly free. And this was such a simple thing.

And what the Terran medic had said made me uneasy, too. Twins; that was the simplest answer, but when he had asked about congenital deformities, I knew I was uneasy, had been uneasy since the child was conceived.

"I'll try, love. I'd have to try sometime...."

One more thing, perhaps, to rediscover with Dio; one more healing, one more freedom, like the manhood I had rediscovered in her arms. I fumbled one-handed with the little leather bag around my neck, where the blue crystal hung in its shielded wrapping of pale insulating silks.

The crystal dropped into my hand. It felt warm and alive, a good sign, without the instant flare, blaze, fire. I cupped the blue stone in my palm, trying not to remember the last time I had done this.

It had been the other hand, the stone had burned *through* my hand... not my own matrix, but the Sharra matrix... *enough!* I forced the memories away, closing my eyes for a moment, trying to settle myself down to the smooth resting rhythm of the stone. It had been so long since I had touched the matrix. Finally I sensed that I had keyed into the stone, opening my eyes, glancing dispassionately into the blue depths where small lights flickered and curled like live things. Maybe they were.

I had not done monitoring for many years. It is the first task given to young apprentices in the Towers; to sit outside a matrix circle, and through the powers of the starstone, amplifying your own gifts, to keep watch on the bodies of the workers while their minds are elsewhere, doing the work of the linked matrix circles. Sometimes matrix workers, deep in rapport with one another through the starstones, forget to breathe, or lose track of things which should be under the control of their autonomic nervous systems, and it is the monitor's work to make sure all is well. Later, the monitor learns more difficult techniques of medical diagnosis, going *into* the complex cells of the human body... it had been a long time. Slowly, carefully, I made the beginning scan; heart and lungs were doing their work of bringing oxygen to the cells, the eyelids blinked automatically to keep the eye surfaces lubricated, there was stress on the back muscles because of the weight of pregnancy... I was running through surface things, superficial things. She sensed the touch; though her eyes were closed, I felt her smile at me.

I hardly believed this; that, once again, slowly, stumbling like a novice, I was making contact with the matrix stone after six years, though I had, as yet, barely touched the surface. I dared a deeper touch....

Fire. Blazing through my hand. Pain... outrageous, burning agony—in a hand that was not there to burn. I heard myself cry out... or was it the sound of Marjorie screaming... before my locked eyes the fire-form rose high, locks tossing in the firestorm wind, like a woman, tall and chained, her body and limbs and hair all on fire....
Sharra!

I let the matrix stone drop as if it had burned through my good hand; felt the pain of having it away from my body, tried to scrabble for it with a hand that was no longer part of my arm...*I felt it there, felt the burning pain through every finger, pain in the lines of the palm, in the nails burning*...Sobbing with pain, I fumbled the matrix into its sheath around my neck and wrenched my mind away from the fire-image, feeling it slowly burn down and subside. Dio was staring at me in horror.

I said, my mouth stiff and fumbling on the words, "I'm— I'm sorry, *bredhiya*, I—I didn't mean to frighten you—"

She caught me close to her, and I buried my head in her breast. She whispered, "Lew, it is I should beg forgiveness— I did not know that would happen—I would never have asked—Avarra's mercy, what was that?"

I drew a deep breath, feeling the pain tearing at the hand that was not there. I could not speak the words aloud. The fire-form was still behind my eyes, blazing. I blinked, trying to make it go away, and said, "You know."

She whispered, "But how..."

"Somehow, the damned thing is keyed into my own matrix. Whenever I try to use it, I see...only *that*." I swallowed and said thickly, "I thought I was free. I thought I was—was healed, and free of *that*..."

"Why don't you destroy it?"

My smile was only a painful grimace. "That would probably be the best answer. Because I am sure I would die with it...very quickly and not at all pleasantly. But I was too cowardly for that."

"Oh, no, no, no—" She held me close, hugging me desperately. I swallowed, drew several deep breaths, knowing this was hurting her more than me; Ridenow, empath, Dio could not bear any suffering...there were times when I wondered whether what she felt for me had been love, or whether she had given me her body, her heart, her comfort, as one soothes a screaming baby because one cannot bear his crying and will do anything, anything to shut him up....

But it had helped me, to know my pain hurt Dio and I must somehow try and control it. "Get me a drink, will you?" When she brought it, calming herself a little by the need to collect her thoughts and look for something, I sipped, trying to quiet my mind. "I am sorry, I thought I was free of that."

"I can't bear it," she said fiercely. "I can't bear it, that *you*

think you should apologize to *me....*" She was crying, too.
She laid her hand over the baby and said, trying to make a
joke of it, "Already he is troubled when he hears his mother
and father yelling at each other!"

I picked up on it at once and made a joke of it too, saying
with exaggerated humor, "Well, we must be very quiet and
not wake up the baby!"

She came and curled up next to me on the couch, leaning
against my breast. She said seriously, "Lew, on Darkover—
there are matrix technicians who could free you—aren't
there?"

"Do you think my father hasn't done his best? And he was
First at Arilinn for almost ten years. If he can't do it, it
probably can't be done."

"No," she said, "but you *are* better; it doesn't happen now
as often as it did in the first years—does it? Maybe, now,
they could find a way...."

The communicator jangled and I went to answer it. I might
have known it would be my father's voice.

"Lew, are you all right? I felt uneasy...."

I wasn't surprised. Every telepath on this planet, if there
were any others, must have felt that shock. Even the distant
voice of my father tried to reassure me. "It hasn't happened
for a long time, has it? Don't get discouraged, Lew, give yourself time to heal...."

Time? The rest of my life, I thought, holding the voice-
piece of the communicator under my chin with the stump of
my left hand, the fingers of my remaining hand nervously
smoothing the insulating silks over my matrix. Never again.
I would never touch the matrix again, not when—this—was
waiting for me. What I said to my father was surface noise,
mouthed platitudes of reassurance, and he must have known
it, but he did not press me; he probably knew I would have
slammed down the communicator and refused to answer it
again. All he said was, "In ten days there is a ship which will
touch at Darkover. I have booked a double passage; and a
reservation on the ship which leaves ten days after *that,* so
that if something should prevent my taking ship on the first,
I will be on the second, and your place is reserved too. I think
you should come; has this, tonight, not proved it to you, that
you must face it soon or late?"

I managed not to shout at him the furious refusal storming
in my mind. The distance, and the mechanical communicator,

blocked out thoughts; this was the best way to talk to my
father, after all. I even managed to thank him for his attempt
at kindness. But after I had refused him again and replaced
the communicator set, Dio said, "He's right, you know. You
can't live the rest of your life with this. It started on Darkover
and it should end there. You can't go through your life dragging that—that horrible link behind you. And I understand—you said something, once—that you cannot leave
it...."

I shook my head. "No. It—it *nags* me. Believe me, I've
tried."

I had tried to abandon it, when we left the lake cabin on
Terra where we had been living while my hand healed after
the final failure and the amputation. I had gone halfway
round the world and then...the fire-form behind my eyes,
blurring out all sight and sense....I had had to return, to
pack it among our luggage...to carry it with me, a monstrous
incubus, a demon haunting me; like my father's presence
within my mind, something of which I would never be free.

"The question's academic," I said, "You can't go, and I
won't leave you. That's what my father wanted."

"The baby might not be born for forty days, at least...you
could go and return...."

"I don't know about babies," I said, "but I do know they
come when they will and not when we expect them." But why
did the thought bring such anguish and fear? Surely it was
only the aftermath of Sharra's impact on my shattered nerves.

"What about the others? You were a whole matrix circle,
linked to the Sharra matrix—weren't you? Why didn't they
die?"

"Maybe they did," I said. "Marjorie did. She was our—
you'd have to say, our Keeper. And I took it from her when
she—when she burned out." I could talk about it, now, almost
dispassionately, as if I were talking of something that had
happened a long time ago to someone else. "The others were
not linked quite so tight to Sharra. Rafe was only a child.
Beltran of Aldaran—my cousin—he was outside the circle.
I don't think they would die when they lost contact with the
matrix, or even when it went offworld. The link was made
through me." In a matrix circle, where there is a high-level
matrix, it is the Keeper who links with the matrix, and then
with the individual matrix stones of the telepaths in her
circle. I was a high-level matrix mechanic; I had taught Mar-

jorie to make that link, so that in a very real sense, I had
been Keeper to the Keeper....

"And the others?" Dio persisted. I resented her dragging
it out of me this way, but I supposed I would have to think
of this sooner or later, or she would never believe I had really
explored all avenues to be free. And I owed her this; Sharra
had touched her too, now, although at a safe remove, and
even touched our child.

I said, "The others? Kadarin and Thyra? I don't know; I
don't know what happened to them, or where they were
when—when everything went up."

She persisted. "If you couldn't leave the matrix behind,
wouldn't they have died when the matrix went offworld?"

Again I grimaced when I tried to smile. I said, "I hope so,"
and even as I spoke, knew it was not true. Kadarin. We had
been friends, brothers, kinsmen, united in a shared dream
which would bring Darkover and Terra close together, heal
our shattered heritage...at least, that had been what we
shared at first. Without knowing I was doing it, I fingered
the scars on my face. He had given me those scars. And Thyra.
Marjorie's half-sister; Kadarin's woman. I had loved her,
hated her, desired her...I could not think that she was dead.
Somewhere, somehow, I knew she lived, and that Kadarin
lived. I could not explain it; but I knew.

*Reason beyond all reasons, the thousandth reason I could
never return to Darkover...*

After Dio was asleep I sat long in the outer room of the
apartment, looking down at the lights of the city below me,
the lights which were never extinguished, far into the night.
On Vainwal the pursuit of pleasure goes on, deepening and
growing more frantic as the day's rhythms subside, when
other people are sleeping. Down there, perhaps, I could find
some kind of forgetfulness. Wasn't that, after all, why I had
come to Vainwal, to forget duty and responsibility? But now
I had a wife and a child, and I owed them something. Dio's
little finger meant more to me than all the unexplored pleasures of Vainwal.

And my son....I had been angry when my father said it.
But it was true. He should be born at Armida; when he was
five years old I would take him out, as my father had taken
me riding on his shoulder, to see the great river of wild horses
flowing down through the valley....

No; that was gone, renounced. There would be other worlds

for my son. Dozens, hundreds of them, an Empire of them, and beyond. I went and laid myself down beside my sleeping wife and slept. But even through my sleep, uneasy dreams moved, I saw my hand again, the horror that had grown there...and it reached out, reached *into* Dio's body, clawing at the child, pulling it forth bloody, dripping, dying...I woke with my own shriek in my ears, and Dio staring at me in shock. I covered her carefully, kissed her and went to sleep in the other room where my nightmares would not disturb her dreams.

This time I slept peacefully without nightmares; it was Dio who woke me in the graying dawn, saying hesitantly "Lew, I feel so strange—I think the baby's coming. It's early—but I think I should go and be certain."

It was far too early; but the Terrans have made something of a specialty of this, artificial wombs for babes cast from their mothers too young, and most of them, in that artificial life-support, do quite well, though they are beyond the thoughts and tenderness of their mothers; I have wondered, sometimes, if this is why so many Terrans are headblind, without any traceable *laran,* the distance from that most intimate of contacts, where the mother teaches the little heart to beat, and all things in the unborn body to function as they should...the body can grow, artificially supported and nourished, but what of the mind and *laran?*

Well, if this should damage the unborn child's *laran,* so be it, if it saved his life...my own *laran* had done me little good. And surely it would not hurt this child to be away from our troubled thoughts and fears, and such torment as it had certainly overheard during my ill-fated attempt to monitor. That attempt had certainly brought on this premature labor, and Dio must have known it, but she did not reproach me, and once, when I spoke of it, she hushed me, saying, "I wanted it, too."

So I was cheerful as we made our way through the streets, from which all but a hardy few pleasure-seekers had vanished in these last gray hours before sunrise. The Terran hospital was pale and austere in the growing light, and Dio flinched as fast elevators swooped us upward to the highest floors, where they kept maternity cases; high above the sound and clamor of the noisy pleasure-world. I told them who I was and what was happening, and some functionary assured Dio that a technician would be there in a few moments to take her to a room.

We sat on characterless, comfortless furniture, waiting. After a time, a young woman entered the room. She was wearing Medic clothing, bearing the curious staff-and-serpents of Terran medical services; I had been told that it was an antique religious symbol, but the medics seemed to know no more than I about what it meant. But there was something in the voice that made me look up and cry out with pleasure.

"Linnell!"

For the girl in uniform was my own foster-sister. Avarra alone knew what she was doing on Darkover, or in that curious uniform, but I hurried to her, took her hands, repeating her name. I could have kissed her, and I nearly did, but the young nurse drew back in outrage.

"What—I don't understand!" she exclaimed, indignant, and I blinked, realizing I had made an insane blunder. But even now, staring, I could only shake my head and say, "It's amazing—it's more than just a resemblance! You *are* Linnell!"

"But I'm not, of course," she said, with a puzzled, chilly smile. Dio laughed. She said, "It's true, of course, you are very like my husband's foster-sister. Very, *very* like. And how strange to meet a double of a close relative, here on Vainwal, of all places! But of course Linnell would never have come here, Lew; she's too conventional. Can you imagine Linnell wearing that kind of outfit?"

And of course I couldn't; I thought of Linnell, in her heavy tartan skirt and embroidered over-tunic, her hair hanging in shining brown braids down her neck. This woman was wearing a white tunic and close-fitting trousers...a Darkovan in such costume would have feared incipient lung-fever, and Linnell would have died of outraged modesty. There was a little patch with a name written on it. I could read the Terran letters now, after a fashion, not well, but better than Dio. I spelled them out, slowly.

"K-a-t-h—"

"Kathie Marshall," she said, with a friendly smile. She even had the little dimple near the right corner of her mouth, and the small scar on her chin which she'd gotten when we'd gone riding in a forbidden canyon on Armida land and our horses had stumbled and fallen under us. I asked her, "If you don't mind, could you tell me where you got that scar?"

"Why, I've had it since I was ten," she said. "I think it was an accident with an air-sled; I had four stitches."

I shook my head, baffled. "My foster-sister has one just like it, in the same place." But Dio made a sharp movement, as of pain, and instantly the woman, familiar-strange, Linnell-Kathie, was all professional solicitude.

"Have you timed the contractions? Good. Here, I'll take you and get you into bed—" and as Dio turned to me, grabbing at my hand in sudden panic, she reassured, "Don't worry about it; your husband can come and stay with you, as soon as the doctor's had a look at you and seen what's going on. Don't worry," she said to me, and the expression on her face was exactly like Linnell's, sober and sweet and gentle. "She's very healthy, and we can do a lot, even if the baby is born too soon. Don't worry about your wife, or the baby either."

And within the hour they called me into her room. Dio was lying in bed in a sterile hospital gown, but the surroundings were pleasant enough in the Vainwal fashion, green plants everywhere, patterns of shimmering rainbows beyond the windows; laser holograms, I supposed, but pleasant to watch, distracting the mind of the prospective mother from what was going on.

"Our *coridom* behaves like this when a prize mare is about to foal," Dio said wryly. "Petting her and fussing over her and whispering reassuring words into her ears, instead of leaving her alone to get on with it. They're all over me with machines supposed to tell them everything about the baby including the color of his eyes, but they won't tell me anything."

They let me stay with her in the early stages, rubbing her back, giving her sips of water, reminding her of the proper breathing; but we all knew it was too soon, and I was afraid. And I sensed Dio's fear too, the tensing of fright, even through her careful attempts to relax, to cooperate with the inexorable process that was thrusting our child, unready, too soon into the world. We watched the rainbows, played a game or two with cards, but even I noticed one omission; neither of us discussed the future, or spoke of a name for the coming child. I told myself we were waiting until we knew whether we were really naming a son or daughter, that was all. Every hour or so they would send me out into the hall, while they came and examined her; and as the day moved on toward nightfall, after one of these intervals, the young nurse,

Kathie, said, "You'll have to stay down here, Mr. Montray;
they're taking her up to surgery. Things aren't going quite
as they should, and this baby will be *very* premature, so we
need all kinds of support for him, or her, right at hand the
minute he's born."

"But I want Lew with me—" Dio cried, almost in tears,
and clung, hard, to my good hand.

Kathie said gently, "I know. I'm sure it would comfort both
of you. But, you see, we have to think first of the baby. As
soon as the baby's born we'll let your husband come up and
stay with you again. But now now, I'm afraid. I'm sorry."

I held Dio close, trying to reassure her with my touch. I
knew how she felt, let myself sink into her body, into her
pain—on Darkover, no telepath, no Comyn, would have considered being apart from the woman who bore his child, sharing her ordeal, so that he too should know the price of a
child...but we were not on our home world, and there was
nothing to be done.

"He is frightened," Dio whispered, her voice shaken, and
it frightened me too, to see her cry; I had grown so accustomed
to her courage, her unflinching strength which had so often
supported my own fears. Well, it was my turn to be strong.

"They'll do the best for you that they can, *preciosa*." I tried
to send forth all kinds of soothing, calming thoughts, to enfold
Dio and the child in a wash of calm and comfort; under it I
saw the pain go out of her face, and she sighed and smiled
up at me.

"Don't worry about me, Lew; we'll be all right," she said,
and I kissed her again, and Kathie motioned to the other
nurse to stand aside so that I could lift Dio onto the rolling
bed they would use to take her away into their inner sanc-
tuaries. Her arms tightened around me, but I knew I had to
let her go.

I paced the halls, smelling the sharp hospital smells that
reminded me of my own ordeal, sharply aware of the phantom
pain in my missing hand. I would rather live in Zandru's
ninth and coldest hell than within the reach of those damnable smells. Blurred by distance, and my own growing weariness, I could feel Dio's fear, and hear her crying out for
me....I would have tried to fight my way to her side, but it
would have done no good, not here on this alien world. At
home, beneath our own red sun, I would have been sharing
her ordeal, in close mental rapport with her...no man could

allow his wife to go through childbirth alone. How, now, could
we share our child, when I, his father, had been isolated from
the birth? Even in the distance, I could feel her fright, bravely
concealed, her pain, and then it all went into the blurring of
drugs. Why had they done that? She was healthy and strong,
well prepared for childbirth, she should not have needed nor
wanted this unconsciousness, and I knew she had not asked
for it. Had they drugged her against her will? I berated myself, that my own distaste for the hospital surrounding, my
own revived horror at the memory of the Terran hospital
where they had tried, and failed, to save my hand, had prevented me from what I should have done. I should have stayed
in rapport with her mind, been present with her in every
moment, telepathically, even if I was prevented from being
physically present. I had failed her, and I was full of dread.

I tried to quiet my growing dismay. In a few hours, we
would have our son. I should have called my father, at some
time during this endless day. He would have come to the
hospital, kept me company here. Well, I would send him word
as soon as our son was born.

Could I be to my son such a father as Kennard had been
to me, fighting endlessly to have me accepted, trying to protect me from any insult or slight, fighting to have me given
every privilege and duty of a Comyn son? I hoped I would not
have to be as hard on my son as my father had been on me;
would have less reason. Yet I could understand now, a little,
why he had been so harsh.

What would we call the boy? Would Dio object if I wanted
to name him Kennard? My own name was Lewis-Kennard;
my father's older brother had been named Lewis. Kennard-
Marius, perhaps, for my brother and my father. Or would Dio
want, perhaps, to name him for one of her own brothers, her
favorite, Lerrys, perhaps? Lerrys had quarreled with me, perhaps he would not want his name given to my son... I played
with these thoughts to hide my own desperate unease, my
growing concern at the delay—why was I told nothing?

Perhaps I should go now—there was a communicator
screen in the lower lobby of the hospital—and call Kennard,
telling him where I was, and what was happening. He would
want to know, and I realized that at this moment I would
welcome his company. What would he think, I wondered, when
he saw the young nurse Kathie, who was so much like Linnell? Maybe he would not even see the resemblance, perhaps

I was simply in a hypernormal state which had exaggerated a slight likeness into a near-identity. After all, most young girls have a dimple somewhere and a small scar somewhere else. Nor is it unusual for a young woman of Terran ancestry—and whether we liked it or not, Darkover had been colonized from a single homogeneous stock, which accounted for our strong ethnic similarity—to be brown-haired, blue-eyed, with a heart-shaped face and a sweet husky voice. My own agitation had done the rest, and exaggerated. She was probably not at all like Linnell, and I would certainly see it, in the unlikely event that I could see them standing side by side...

Perhaps it was my own growing exhaustion, the effort I was making to hold sleep at bay; it seemed for a minute that I could see them standing side by side, Linnell in her Festival gown, and somehow Linnell looked older, worn, and Kathie, by her side, somehow was wearing Darkovan clothing too...and behind them, it seemed, there was a wavering darkness....

There was a soft sound and I turned to see the young nurse who looked so much like Linnell...yes, she *did* look like her, the resemblance was not an illusion; calling up Linnell's picture in my mind had made me surer than ever.

Ah, to be at home, in the hills near Armida, riding with Marius and Linnell over those hills, with the old Terran coridom Andres threatening to beat us for racing and riding at so breakneck a pace that Marius and I tore our breeches and Linnell's hair tangled in the wind too much for her governess to brush it properly...by now Linnell was probably married to Prince Derik, and Derik crowned, so that my foster-sister was a Queen....

"Mr. Montray?"

I whirled. "What is it? Dio? The baby? Is everything all right?" I thought she looked subdued, deeply troubled; and she would not meet my eyes.

"Your wife is perfectly all right," she said gently, "but Doctor DiVario wants to see you, about the baby."

The young doctor was a woman; I was grateful for that, glad Dio had been spared the indignity of male attendance. Sometimes a strong telepath or empath can transcend the difference of gender, but here among the head-blind, I knew Dio would prefer a doctor of her own sex. The woman looked tired and strained, and I knew that, if she had not empathy,

not in the strong sense of the Ridenow gift, she at least had
that rudimentary awareness that differentiates the indifferent doctor from the good one.

"Mr. Montray-Lanart? Your wife is well; you can see her
in a few minutes," she said, and I whispered a prayer of
thanks to the Mother Avarra, a prayer I had not known I
remembered. Then I said, "Our child?"

She bent her head and already I knew—I thought, the
worst. "Dead?"

"It was simply too soon," she said, "and we could do nothing."

"But," I protested, like a fool, "the life-support, the artificial wombs—babies born even more prematurely than this
have lived...."

She waved that aside. She looked strained. She said, "We
did not let your wife see. The minute we knew, we—drugged
her. I am sorry, but I felt it the safest way; she was very
agitated. She should be coming out of the anesthetic any
moment, now, and you should be with her. But first—" she
said, and looked at me with what I recognized, uncomfortably,
as pity, "you must see. It is the law, so that you cannot accuse
us of making away with a healthy child—" and I remembered
there was a thriving market in adoptive children, for women
who did not want to be bothered bearing their own. I sensed
the young doctor's distress, and somehow it made me remember a dream—I could not remember the details, something
about the doctor who had said to me here, a few days ago,
that I should be prepared for some degree of
deformity...something dreadful, blood, horror...

She took me into a small bare room, with cabinets and
closed doors and sinks, and a tray lying covered with a white
cloth. She said, "I am sorry," and uncovered it.

Once I came up through the veils of the drug and saw the
horror which had grown at the end of my arm. The messages,
deep within the cells, which bid a hand be a hand and not a
foot or a hoof or a bird's wing...

I had screamed my throat raw....

But no sound escaped me this time. I shut my eyes, and
felt the young doctor's compassionate hand on my shoulder.
I think she knew I was glad our child lay there, lifeless, for
I would surely—I could not have let it live. Not like that. But
I was glad it was not my hand which had....

...thrust through Dio's body and wrenched the child forth bloody, clawed, feathered, a horror past horror...

I drew a long breath and opened my eyes, looking stony-eyed at the dreadfully deformed thing lying lifeless before me. *My son. Had Kennard felt like this when he saw what Sharra had left of me?* For a moment I wished I could still take refuge in the darkness of insanity. But it was too late for that. I said meaninglessly, "Yes, yes, I see," and turned away from the thing. So the damage, cell-deep, had gone deeper than I knew, into the very germ plasm of my seed.

No son of mine would ever sit on my shoulder and watch the horses at Armida.... turned away, I still seemed to see the horror behind my eyes. Not even human. And yet, monstrously, it had been alive as recently as last night....

The Goddess has shown us mercy...

"Does Dio know?"

"I think she knows it was—too deformed to live," said the doctor gently, "but she does not know quite how, and if you are wise you will never tell her. Tell her some quite simple lie—she will believe you; women do not want to know, I think, beyond what they must. Tell her a simple truth, that the child's heart stopped." She led me out of that room, away from the thing I would see again and again in nightmares. She touched me again compassionately on the shoulder and said, "We could have— re-started the heart. Would you have wanted that? Sometimes a doctor must make such decisions."

I said, heartfelt, "I am very grateful to you."

"Let me take you to your wife."

Dio was lying in the bed where they had brought her, looking stunned and very small, like a child who had cried herself to sleep, with traces of tears still on her face. They had covered her hair with a white cap, and tucked her up warmly under blankets; one of her hands gripped the softness of the blanket like a child clutching a toy. I could smell the sharpness of the drug all around her; her skin smelled of it when I bent to kiss her.

"Preciosa..."

She opened her eyes and started to cry again.

"Our baby's dead," she whispered. "Oh, Lew, our baby, it couldn't live...."

"You're safe, darling. That's all that matters to me," I whispered, gathering her into my arms.

But behind my eyes it was still there, that thing, the horror, not human.... She reached in her weakness for the comfort of rapport, she who had always been the stronger of us two, reached for my mind....

I could feel her recoil from what she saw there, see it lying cold and impersonal in that cold bare room on a surgical tray, not human, terrible, nightmare....

She screamed, struggling away from me; she screamed and screamed, as I had screamed when I saw what had taken the place of my hand, screamed and screamed and fought to be free of me when I would have comforted her, struggled away from the horror....

They came and drugged her, afraid she would hurt herself again, and they sent me away from her. And when, having shaved and washed and eaten and made grotesque legal arrangements for the cremation of what should have been our son, I went back, resolved that if she wished to blame me I could bear it...she had lived with me through all of my horrors and nightmares....I could be strong for her now....She was not there.

"You wife checked out of the hospital hours ago," the doctor told me, when I made a scene and demanded to know what they had done with my wife. "Her brother came, and took her away."

"She could be anywhere," I said, "anywhere in the Empire."

My father sighed, leaning his head on his thin distorted hand. "She should not have done that to you."

"I don't blame her. No man should do that to any woman...." and I clenched my teeth against the flood of self-blame. If I had been able to barricade my thoughts. If I had had myself monitored to be sure there was no such damage to the germ plasm...I could have known; I *should* have known, seeing that my hand had not grown back as a hand, but as a nightmare—the pain in the arm was nightmarish now, distant, dreadful, welcome, blurring the pain of losing Dio. But I did not blame her. She had borne so much for me already, and then this...no. If I had been Dio I would not have stayed for a tenday, and I had had her presence, her comfort, for a year and a half....

"We could have her found," my father said. "There are detectives, people who specialize in tracing the lost; and citizens of Darkover do not find it exactly easy to blend into the general citizenry of the Empire...."

But he had spoken diffidently, and I shook my head.

"No. She is free to come and go. She is not my prisoner or my slave." If the love between us had crashed in the wake of tragedy, was she to blame? Even so I was grateful to her. Two years ago, something like this would have broken me, sent me into a tailspin of agony and despair and suicidal self-pity. Now I felt grief immeasurable, but what Dio had given me could not be destroyed by her absence. I was not healed—I might never heal—but I was alive again, and I could live with whatever happened. What she had given me was a part of me forever.

"She is free to go. Someday, perhaps, she may learn to live with it, and come back to me. If she does, I will be ready. But she is not my prisoner, and if she returns it must be because she wishes to return."

My father looked a long time at me, perhaps expecting me to break again. But after a time, perhaps, he believed that I meant what I said, and began to talk of something else.

"There is no reason, now, why you should not come with me to Darkover, to settle what remains of the Alton heritage—"

I thought of Armida, lying in a fold of the Kilghard Hills. I had thought of going there with my son on my shoulder, showing him the horses, teaching him what I had been taught, watching him grow up there, do his first fire-watch duty at my side...no. That had been a mad hope. Marius was undamaged; it would be *his* sons that would carry on the Alton lineage, if there was one. I no longer cared; it no longer had anything to do with me. I was transplanted, cut off from my roots, exiled...and the pain of that was less than the pain of trying to return. I said, "No," and my father did not try to persuade me. I think he knew I was at the end of endurance, that I had borne enough, had no further strength to struggle.

"You don't want to go back to the place you shared with Dio, not yet," he said, and I wondered how he knew. It was too full of memories. Dio, curled in my arms, looking down with me at the lights of the city. Dio, her hair down her back, in her night-dress, gigglingly playing at a domesticity which was new and amusing to us both. Dio....

"Stay here a few days," he said.

If she comes back, wants me...

"She will know where to find you," he said. And as he spoke I knew she would not come back.

"Stay here with me a few days. Then I will be taking ship for Darkover...and you can return to your own place, or come and stay here alone. I won't—" he looked at me with a pity he was too wise to speak aloud, and said, "I won't—intrude." For the first time in my life, I felt my father spoke to me as to an equal, to another man, not to his child. I sighed and said, "Thank you, Father. I'd be glad to come."

I did not think again of the Sharra matrix, wrapped and insulated and packed away in the farthest corner of the farthest closet of the apartment I had shared with Dio at the very outskirts of the city. Nor did either of us speak of it again, in those days, the final ten days we spent in that apartment. He was not on the first of the outbound ships. I think he wanted to spend that remaining time with me, that he would not leave me wholly alone on a planet which had become as strange to me as if I had not lived there for the best part of two years.

There were still five days to go before the second of the ships on which he had tentatively booked passage would depart from the Vainwal spaceport. Not many ships had a final destination at Cottman IV, as the Terrans called Darkover. But many ships touched down there; it was located between the upper and lower spiral arms of the Galaxy, a logical transfer point. Around midday, my father asked me, rather tentatively it is true, if I cared to accompany him to one of the great pleasure palaces of the city, one whose main attraction was a giant bath, modeled after that of some famous old Terran city which had raised bathing to a fine art.

My father had been crippled for years; one of my earliest memories was of the hot springs at Armida, and soaking, after an icy day in the saddle, neck-deep in the boiling water. It was not only the lame or infirm who enjoyed that. But all over the Empire, and more especially on pleasure-worlds where nothing is taboo, bathhouses serve as a gathering place for those whose interest is in something other than hot water and soothing mineral baths. Maybe the atmosphere of relaxed nudity contributes to the breakdown of inhibitions. Many sorts of entertainment are offered there which have little to do with bathing.

My father's infirmity and his noticeable lameness gave him the most obvious and respectable reasons for being there;

also, he found masseurs who could give his aching muscles considerable ease. I seldom visited such places—there had been a time when it was agony to me to be in the midst of such things, and the women who gathered there seeking men whose inhibitions had been loosened by the atmosphere of the baths were not, to put it mildly, the kind of women who attracted me much. But my father seemed more lame than usual, his steps more uneasy. He could have called to summon a masseur who would have accompanied him there, or even someone to carry him in a sedan chair—on Vainwal you can have literally any kind of attention or care, for a price—but in his present condition I would not leave him to hired attendants. I accompanied him to the bathhouse, took him to the door of the hot pools, and went off to the restaurant for a drink. There I sat watching a group of dancers doing the most astonishing things with their anatomy, later waved away the women—and men—who went round afterward trying to find clients sufficiently roused by the display to pay for a more private exhibition. Later I watched another entertainment, this time in hologram, a musical drama telling an ancient legend of the love and revenge of the fire-God; one of his fellow-Gods had had his wife stolen, ravished away by a third, and the fire-God had declared her chaste, though the one who had lost his wife was jealous and would not accept assurances. But the illusion of flames surrounding the actor who mimed the fire-God made me nervous, and I rose and uneasily left the restaurant. I went into one of the bars for another drink, and there my father's masseur found me.

"You are Lewis-Kennard Lanart—"

Quickly, I was troubled, knowing something was wrong, braced for more tragedy. "My father—what is wrong with my father?"

"He is not in danger now," the masseur said, fidgeting with the towel in his hands, "but the heat of the steam room was too much for him, and he collapsed. I sent for a medic," he added defensively. "They wanted to take him to the Terran hospital, but he would not go. He said all he wanted was a few minutes of rest, and for you to come and take him home."

They had sent for a valet to help him dress, and he was sipping a glass of strong brandy. He looked very pale, thinner than I had noticed. Pain and compunction struck me. I said, "Let me take you home, Father," and sent for one of the little skycabs which lifted us directly to the roof-platform of our own building.

I had not felt his distress, nor his collapse; I had been watching the stupid dancers!

"It's all right, Lew," he said gently. "You're not my keeper." And somehow that made me feel raw-edged too, troubled. For once, instead of staying on his feet, he was willing to lie down on a piece of furniture, a soft flotation couch in the apartment, though he would not go to bed.

"Father, you're not planning, surely, to travel to Darkover in five days? You'll never be able to endure the trip! And the climate of Thendara—"

"I was born there," he said tightly. "I can endure it. And I have no choice, unless you choose to go and save me the trouble."

I said, anger and pity fighting in me, "That's not fair! You can't ask it—!"

"I do ask it," he said. "You're strong enough, now, to do it. I didn't ask it of you before you were ready. But now there is no reason you should not—"

I considered it. Or tried to. But everything in me flinched away. Return; walk back on my own two feet into that corner of hell where I had found death and mutilation, rebellion, love and treachery....

No. No. Avarra's mercy, no....

He sighed, heavily. "You'll have to face it some day, Lew. And I don't want to face the Council alone. I can count on only one ally there—"

"Dyan," I said, "and he'll do more for you if I'm not there. He hates my guts, Father."

My father shook his head. "I think you're mistaken. He promised—" and then he sighed. "Still, be that as it may, you'll have to go back some day...."

You cannot live like this, Lew. On Darkover there are some experts in matrix technology who might be able to find a way to free you from Sharra....

"They tried," I said. "You told me they tried before you brought me offworld, and they couldn't; which is why we had to bring the matrix offworld, you couldn't separate me from it without killing me—"

"You were weaker then. That was years ago. "You could survive it, now."

A thousand regrets, terrors, agonies flooded me; if it had

not been for my ill-fated attempt to monitor her, perhaps Dio would not have gone into premature labor...

And that monstrous horror might have lived, breathed...

But Dio might have understood. Might not have—loathed me. Might not have shrunk in horror from the monster I had fathered, the monster I had become....

Free of Sharra, might the damage somehow have been reversed? The link with that giant matrix which had somehow damaged my very cells...if I had had the courage to endure it, being freed of Sharra, perhaps the horror would not have reached out and touched our child...at least I could have been monitored, to know enough, beforehand, avoid fathering a child...could have warned Dio, so she need not have suffered that loss....

"I don't think it would have made any difference. The damage was done before ever I met Dio." I knew he shared the image in my mind, of that monstrous failure with my hand...but we would never be sure.

"Some day. Some day. Maybe."

He started to speak; then shut his mouth, and although I could hear the words he did not speak, clearly in his mind...*I need you, Lew, I cannot go alone*...I was grateful that he did not use that last weapon, his weakness, to persuade me. I felt guilty that I did not offer it, unasked. But I could not, *I could not....*

He shut his eyes. "I would like to rest." I went out and left him alone.

I paced the apartment, debating whether or not I should go down into the multiformed world of the pleasure planet below me, get myself blind drunk; too drunk to know or care what horrors pulled at my mind, what guilt and self-blame. My father needed me; he had done, unsparing, whatever I needed when I was sick and helpless, and now I would not, could not force myself to give to him as generously as he had given to me. But I would not leave him alone. I could not do what he wished of me; but I would do what I could.

I do not know how long it was before I heard his voice, that cry of terrible pain, ringing and echoing in my mind and crashing through the rooms. I know, now, that there was no cry, it had been so swift that he could never have uttered a sound, but it was a scream of agony. Even as I ran toward his room, stumbling in haste, his voice crashed through my mind as it had done in that first rapport where he had shocked my *laran* awake when I was eleven years old; pain like death and the harsh command, inflexible, that I could not shut out.

LEW! YOU MUST GO, I CANNOT—YOU MUST GO BACK TO DARKOVER, FIGHT FOR YOUR BROTHER'S RIGHTS AND FOR THE HONOR OF ALTON AND THE DOMAIN—YOU MUST GO BACK AND FREE YOURSELF FROM SHARRA—LEW, I COMMAND YOU. IT IS MY DYING WISH, THE LAST WISH—

And then a flood of love and tenderness and a moment of pure joy.

"Elaine," he cried out in my mind. *Yllana. Beloved.*

Then I broke into his room, and he lay there, quite dead. But on his face was a tender smile of happiness.

BOOK TWO:

The Form of Fire

Darkover. The end of exile

CHAPTER ONE

There was someone at the door. Regis Hastur struggled up through confused dreams and found himself in his own rooms in Comyn Castle, his body-servant arguing in dogged whispers with someone who stood at the door, insisting. Regis threw a furred bedgown about his shoulders and went to see what it was.

"*Vai dom,* this—this *person* is insisting on seeing you, even at this godforgotten hour...."

"Well, I'm awake now anyhow," he said, blinking. For a moment he did not recognize the sturdy, dark-eyed youngster who stood there, and the youngster's wry smile told Regis that he knew it.

"We haven't met many times and I don't think we've ever been formally introduced," he said. "Not since I was eight or nine years old, anyhow. My name is Marius, and I won't argue about the rest of it when I'm here to ask a favor of you."

Now Regis recognized Kennard's younger son. He had seen him, briefly, somewhere in Thendara, about three years ago; perhaps in the company of Lerrys Ridenow? He said, "Of course I remember you, kinsman." And when he had spoken that word, *kinsman,* a formal recognition as to an equal, he thought, tardily, how vexed his grandfather would have been. The Council, after all, had gone to considerable lengths to avoid extending that formal recognition to Kennard's younger son.

Yet they had placed Regis himself in Kennard's hands for fostering between the ages of nine and twelve. Regis and Lew had been *bredin,* sworn brothers. How could he now refuse that recognition to Kennard's son and Lew's brother, who, by all standards of honor and decency, was Regis's foster-brother too. But he had neglected that obligation. Even now, his body-servant was staring at Marius as if the youngster were something with a hundred legs which the man had found in his porridge-bowl.

Regis said, "Come in, Marius; what can I do for you?"

"It's not for me," Marius said, "but for my friend. I have been living, this season, in my father's town house in Thendara. I haven't been made to feel exactly welcome in Comyn Castle."

"I know, and I'm sorry, Marius. What can I say? I don't make Council decisions, but that doesn't mean I agree with them, either. Come in, won't you? Don't stand here in the hallway. A drink? Erril, take his cloak."

Marius shook his head. "There's no time for that, I'm afraid. My friend—you know him; he told me, once, you were prisoners together at Aldaran, and you know something of—" Marius fidgeted, lowered his voice as if he spoke a gutter obscenity— "of *Sharra.*"

Now Regis remembered his dream, the monstrous fire-form flaring and ravaging in his nightmare, ships bursting in flame....."I remember," he said, "all too well. Your friend—Rafe Scott, isn't it?" He remembered, too, that he had seen them together in Thendara. Yes; in the company of Lerrys Ridenow, who liked the society of Terrans. "What's happened, Marius?"

And yet his mind was running quick counterpoint, *this can't happen, all these years I have not even dreamed of Sharra, and now...this is more than coincidence.*

"He was my guest," Marius said, "and the servants heard him crying out and came and wakened me; but when I went to him he didn't know me, just kept crying out, raving about Sharra....I couldn't make him hear me. Could you—could you come?"

"What you want is a healer," Regis said. "I don't have any skill at that kind of thing..." and he found himself wondering if Danilo, who had been prisoner with him during those weeks at Aldaran, who also had been touched by the fire-form, had wakened in terrifying nightmares of Sharra. And what did it mean?

"Lord Regis," said the body-servant in outrage, "you're not thinking of going out with this—at this hour of night, at the beck and call of just anybody?"

Regis had been thinking of refusal. What Marius needed was a healer or a licensed matrix technician. Regis had spent a season in a Tower, learning to manage his own *laran* so that it would not make him ill or drive him mad, but he had none of the advanced skills for matrix healing of mind or body, and what he knew of Sharra was very little. Only that for all that time his own matrix had been overshadowed, so that he could not touch it without seeing that ravaging form of fire.... but the servant's words made him angry again.

"I don't know if I can help you very much, Marius, and I don't know the Scott youngster at all. I haven't seen him since then, not to speak to. But I'll come as a friend," he said, disregarding his servant's look of outrage. "Get me my clothes, Erril, and my boots. If you'll excuse me while I get dressed—"

Hurrying into his clothes, he thought that he was perhaps the only telepath still in the Domains who had had even that much indirect experience with Sharra. What little he knew of it did not tempt him to learn more.

But what can this mean? The matrix is not even on Darkover! It went with Lew and Kennard into exile...

He splashed his face with icy water, hoping to clear his confusion. And then he realized what could have happened...

I am responsible for this. I sent the message, and my grandfather will be very angry when he finds out that it was I. And already I am suffering the consequences of my actions.

It flashed through his mind, relived in an instant as it had happened. It had been a score of tendays ago; and he had, as Heir to Hastur, been privy to a decision made by the *cortes,* the ruling body of Thendara. He was in honor bound not to discuss their decisions with any outsider; *but what to do when honor conflicts with honor?* And in the end he had gone to the one man on Darkover who might have a stake in reversing this decision.

Dyan Ardais had heard him out, a faint smile playing ironically over his lips, as if he could sense how Regis hated this...the necessity that he, Regis, should come as a suppliant, begging favors of Dyan. Regis had concluded, angrily, "Do you want to see them do this to Kennard?"

Dyan had frowned, then, and made him go all over it again. "What exactly are they intending to do?"

"At the first session of Council, this year, they are going to declare Kennard's estates forfeit because he has abandoned Darkover; and they are going to give Armida into the hands of Gabriel Lanart-Hastur! Just because he commands the Guards and because he's married to my sister!"

"I don't see what choice they have."

"Kennard *must* come home," Regis said angrily. "They shouldn't do this behind his back! He should have a chance to protest this! And Kennard has another son!"

After a long silence, Dyan had said, "I'll make certain that Kennard knows, at least. Then, if he chooses not to return and press his claim—well, I suppose the law must take its course. Leave it to me, Regis. You've done all you can."

And now, weeks later, hurrying to join Marius, Regis wondered about that. Even if Kennard had returned, he would not be fool enough to bring the Sharra matrix back to Darkover, would he?

Perhaps, he thought, perhaps it is only nightmare...perhaps it is not the frightening coincidence I think. Perhaps Rafe's nightmare reached out to the one person in Thendara who had been touched by Sharra and so I, too, dreamed....

He slung his cloak about his shoulders and said to Marius, "Let's go. Erril, call my bodyguard." He didn't want the man; but he also knew, even at this hour, he could not walk the streets of Thendara wholly unattended; and even if he could, he had been forced to promise his grandfather that he would not.

I am past twenty and a grown man. Yet as my grandfather's Heir, the Heir to Hastur, I am forced to do his will.... He waited for the man in Guardsman's uniform to come, and went down through the hallways of Comyn Castle and down into the empty streets of Thendara, Marius moving quietly at his side.

It had been many years since Regis had entered Kennard Alton's Thendara town house. It stood at the edge of a wide cobbled square, and tonight it was all dark except for a single light at the back. Marius led him to a side door; Regis said to the Guardsman, "Wait here." The man argued a little in an undertone—the *Vai Dom* should be careful, it might be a trap—but Regis said wrathfully that such a statement was an offense to his kinsman, and the Guardsman, who had, after all, known Kennard as his Commander, and probably Lew too as cadet and officer, growled and subsided.

But after he had left them Regis thought he would have been glad of the man's company after all. He tended to trust Marius, but Rafe Scott was a Terran, and they were noted for their indifference to codes of honor. And Rafe was also blood kin somehow, to that arch-traitor Kadarin, who had been Lew's sworn friend, but had betrayed him, beaten and tortured him, drugged him and forced him, unwilling, to serve Sharra....

From inside the darkened house rose a cry, a scream, a howl of terror, as if no human throat could quite compass that cry. For a moment, behind Regis's eyes he felt the blaze of fire—the primal terror of the fire-form, raging, ravening....then he shut it out, knowing it was the terror in the other's mind that he picked up and read. He managed to barrier his mind, and turned to Marius, white with dread, at his side. He wondered if the younger man had enough *laran* to pick up the image, or whether it was Rafe's distress that troubled him.

Kennard had proved to the Council that Lew had the Alton gift and they had accepted him. They had not accepted Marius; did that mean that Kennard's younger son was wholly without laran?

"Remember, Marius, I don't know if I can do anything at all for him. But I ought to see him."

Marius nodded, and led the way into an inner room. A frightened servant stood shaking by the door, afraid to go in. "There hasn't been any change, *dom* Marius. Andres is with him."

Regis just flicked the barest glance of recognition at the burly, graying man in Darkovan clothing—though Regis knew he was a Terran—who had been chief *coridom*, or steward, at Armida when Regis was there as a child. Rafe Scott was sitting bolt upright, staring at nothing Regis could see, and as Regis came into the room, again there was that infernal, animal howl of terror and dread. Even through his strong barriers, Regis could sense the blaze of heat, fire, torment...a woman, locks of fiery hair blazing, tossing....

Regis felt the hair on his forearms, every separate hair on his body bristling and standing upright; like some animal in the presence of a primordial enemy. Marius had asked Andres something in a low, concerned tone, and the man shook his head. "All I could do was hold him so he wouldn't hurt himself."

"I wish Lerrys was in the city," Marius said. "The Ridenow are trained to deal with alien intelligences—presences that aren't on this dimension at all."

Regis looked at the terrified face of the young man before him. He had seen Rafe only once, and that briefly; he remembered him best as a child, a boy of thirteen, at Aldaran. He had thought, then, that the boy was young to be admitted into one of the matrix circles. He must be nineteen or twenty now—

Not a boy, then. A young man. But, living among Terrans, he has not had the training which would teach him to cope with such things.

... but Lew was trained at Arilinn, and the best they could do could not keep him unburned by the fires of Sharra....

It would do no good to send for an ordinary matrix technician. They could do many things—unfasten locks without a key, trace lost objects through clairvoyance matrix-amplified, set truthspell for business dealings where ordinary trust would not serve, diagnose obscure complaints, even perform simple surgery without knife or blood. But Sharra would be beyond their knowledge or their competence. For better or for worse, Regis, who knew little, knew as much of Sharra as anyone.

He felt the most terrible revulsion against touching that horror; but he reached out, steadying his mind by gripping the matrix around his neck, and tried to make a light contact with Rafe's mind. At the strange touch, Rafe convulsed all over, as if in the grip of horror again, and cried out, "No! No, Thyra! Sister, don't—"

For just a fraction of a second Regis saw and recognized the picture in Rafe's mind, a woman, not the flame-haired horror that was Sharra, but a woman, red-haired, red-lipped, with eyes of a curious golden color....

And then Rafe blinked and in the twinkling of an eye it was gone and he looked at Regis with intelligence in his eyes. Regis noted, with mild surprise, that his eyes too were golden, like the woman he had seen. Rafe said, "What's the matter, why are you staring at me? What are you doing here—" He blinked again and looked round him wildly. "Marius, what happened?"

"You tell *me* that," said Marius angrily. "All I know is that you wakened the whole house screaming and raving of—of—" Again the hesitation and Rafe finally, matter-of-factly, supplied the word. He said "Sharra," and Regis was relieved, obscurely, as if a deadlock had been broken.

Marius said, "I couldn't make you hear me; you didn't know me."

Rafe frowned and said, "I'm sorry for having disturbed

you—in hell's name, did you go and fetch the Hastur out of
bed at this hour of the night?" He looked at Regis in apology
and dismay. "I'm sorry. It must have been a bad dream, no
more."

Outside the dawn was graying into pale light. Marius said,
embarrassed, "Will you honor my house, Lord Regis, and take
some breakfast here? It is a poor apology for disturbing your
rest—"

"It will be my pleasure, cousin," Regis said, using the word
just a trace more intimate than the formal *kinsman*, not quite
as intimate as *foster-brother*. His grandfather would be very
angry when he heard; but all the smiths in Zandru's forges
can't mend a broken egg, and done was done. Marius gave
orders to Andres, and Regis added, "Ask the servants to feed
my Guardsman in the kitchens, will you?"

When the servants were gone, Marius said, "What happened, Rafe? Or don't you really know?"

Rafe shook his head. "I don't think it was a dream," he
said. "I saw my sister Thyra, and she—she turned into Sharra
again. I was afraid—"

Regis demanded, "But why should it happen now, of all
times, when nothing like it has happened for six years?"

Rafe said, "I'm almost afraid to find out. I thought Sharra
was gone—dormant, at least here on Darkover—"

"But it isn't here on Darkover," Regis said, "The Altons
took it offworld; perhaps to Terra. I've never known
why—"

"Perhaps," Rafe said, "because, here on Darkover, it could
never be controlled and might do more harm—" and he was
silent, but Regis, seeing the picture in his mind, remembered
that the old Terran spaceport at Caer Donn, in the mountains,
had gone up in flames. "If it had been here, Kadarin might
have gotten it back."

"I didn't know he was still alive," said Regis.

Rafe sighed. "Yes. Though I haven't seen either of them
for years. They were—in hiding for a long time." He seemed
about to say something more, then shrugged and said, "Under
ordinary circumstances, I would have been glad to know that
Thyra was still alive, but now—"

With shaking fingers he fumbled at the matrix around his
neck. "I was only a child when the Sharra circle was broken,
and then I—I was in shock. I was ill for a long time. When
I recovered, they told me Marjorie was dead, that Lew had

taken the matrix offworld and would never return, and I—I found I could not use my starstone; I had been part of it, and when the link with the Sharra matrix was broken, my own starstone was—was burned out, I thought. But now I am not sure...."

He unwrapped the stone. It was, Regis thought dispassionately, a very small one, a blue jewel, faceted, flawed. He bent his eyes on it; it flamed crimson within, so clearly that even Regis and Marius could see the form of fire. He put the stone away, with fingers that wobbled as he tried to draw the strings of the little leather pouch.

"What does it mean?" he asked in a whisper.

"There's only one thing it can mean," Regis said. "It means that Kennard has come home. Or Lew. Or both. And that, for some reason or other, they have brought the Sharra matrix home with them."

On the first day of Council season, Regis Hastur came early to the Crystal Chamber. He debated, for a moment, going in through the Hastur entrance—in the hallway around the Chamber, there was a private entrance for each Domain, and a small antechamber to each railed-off segment, so that the members of the Domain might meet privately for a moment before making formal appearance in Council—but then shrugged, and, pausing for a friendly word with the Guardsman at the door, went into the main entrance.

Outside it was a day of brilliant sun, and the light streamed through the prisms in the ceiling which gave the chamber its name; it was like standing at the multicolored heart of a rainbow. The Crystal Chamber was eight-sided, and spacious—at least, Regis thought, it seemed spacious now; at the height of Comyn powers it must have seemed small for all those who had Domain-right in the Comyn. Where Regis stood was a central dais, the wide double doors at the back protected by trusty Guardsmen; the other seven sides were allotted, each to one of the Domains, and each was a section divided off by wooden railings and lined with benches, boxes, and a few curtained-off enclosures so that the lords and ladies of each Domain might watch unseen or maintain their privacy until the time came for the full Council session. One segment was empty, and had been empty since Regis, or any of his living relatives, could remember; and he remembered that his grandfather had told him once, when he was a boy, that the Domain of Aldaran had been untenanted since *he*, or any of *his* relatives, could remember. The old Seventh Domain, Aldaran, had been exiled from the Comyn for so long that no one could remember why; the reasons, if indeed there were reasons, had been lost in the Ages of Chaos. He had seen it every year since he was old enough to attend Council; empty, dusty benches and seats, a bare space on the wall where once the double-eagle banner of Aldaran had hung.

The curtains were drawn around the Alton Domain's enclosure too. It had been empty for the last five seasons; now, at the beginning of the sixth, Regis supposed that either Lew or Kennard or both would be there, to head off the threatened action—to declare the Alton Domain vacant and place it formally in the hands of Gabriel Lanart-Hastur as Warden of the Domain. But had either of them returned? He could not believe that Kennard would return without paying at least a courtesy call on Lord Hastur, and there had been no such call. On the other hand, if Lew had returned, Regis found it unlikely that he would not have sent some word to Regis himself.

We were friends. I think Lew would have let me know.

But there had been no word, and Regis was beginning to be troubled. Perhaps Lew and Kennard had decided to let the Domain go by default. In the days that were inevitable, a feudal lordship over an enormous Domain might have no meaning. Marius was well-to-do; Kennard owned a good deal of property aside from the Great House at Armida. Perhaps, Regis thought, he was better spared that kind of feudal Wardenship of the ancient Domain, as Regis himself would as soon have been spared the changes that were certainly coming in Darkovan society; let Gabriel have the thankless task of dealing with them.

He looked around the Chamber. He could see someone stirring behind the partially closed curtains of the Ridenow enclosure; perhaps Lord Edric's wife or any of her grown daughters. Well, there were enough Ridenow sons and daughters; they were not, apparently, cursed by the barrenness which plagued some of the older Domains. The direct line of the Aillard was extinct; a collateral line, the Lindir-Aillard family, ruled that house, with Lady Callina as formal head of the Domain; she had a younger sister Linnell, who had been another of Kennard's fosterlings, and a brother who was one of Dyan Ardais's circle, though Regis was not sure (and did not care) whether the boy was Dyan's lover and favorite, or simply a hanger-on. Latterly, Merryl Lindir-Aillard had been seen more often in the company of young Prince Derik Elhalyn. On one occasion Regis's grandfather, Danvan, Lord Hastur, had expressed some distress at the company the prince kept.

"I don't think you need to worry, sir," Regis had said, a little wryly. "No matter what Merryl is, Derik's a lover of women. Merryl flatters him, that's all."

And because of what he was, telepath—and, although there were telepathic dampers all around the Crystal Chamber, they had not yet been set or adjusted—Regis was not surprised to hear the Guardsman at the door, his voice changed from the friendly, though respectful tone he had used with Regis to a flat deference.

"No, *vai dom*, you have come early; there is no one here but the Lord Regis Hastur."

"Oh, good," said the high voice of the young prince. "I haven't seen Regis since last season," and Regis turned and bowed to Derik Elhalyn. But Derik disregarded that and came to give Regis a kinsman's embrace.

"Why have you come so early, cousin?"

Regis smiled and said, "I might ask the same of you, my lord. I wasn't aware I was all that early—I hadn't expected to be the first one here." There were one or two, even in the Comyn, to whom he might have said, forthrightly, *Grandfather was badgering me again about letting my marriage be arranged this season, and I walked out because I didn't want to quarrel with him again.* But, although Derik was three years older than Regis himself, tall and good-looking, such adult affairs seemed out of place when talking to Derik.

The Domain of Elhalyn had once been a Hastur sept—although, in fact, all the Domains had once been descended from the legendary Hastur and Cassilda, the Elhalyn had retained their kinship to Hastur longer than the rest. A few hundred years ago, the Hastur kings had ceded their ceremonial functions, and the throne itself, to the Hasturs of Elhalyn. Regis's mother had been a sister of King Stephen, and so the "cousin" was not courtesy alone. Regis had known Derik since they were little children; but by the time Regis was nine years old, it was already apparent that Regis was quicker and more intelligent, and he had begun to treat Derik almost as a younger brother. The adult Regis wondered sometimes if that was why they had separated them and sent Regis to be fostered at Armida, so that the young prince might not feel his inferiority too much. As they all grew older, it had become painfully obvious that Derik was dull-witted and slow. He might have been crowned at fifteen, the age at which a boy was legally a man; at that age, Regis had been declared Heir to Hastur, and given all the responsibilities that went with that position; but Derik's crowning had been delayed, first until he was nineteen, then till he should reach twenty-five.

And what then, Regis wondered. *What will my grandfather do when it becomes painfully obvious that Derik is no readier to rule at five-and-twenty than he was at fifteen?* Most likely he would crown the youngster, retaining the unofficial Regency in the eyes of all Darkover, as many Hasturs had done over the centuries.

"We should have a new banner when I am crowned," said Derik, standing outside the rails of the Elhalyn enclosure. "The old one is threadbare."

Merryl Lindir-Aillard, standing behind him, said softly, "But the old one has seen the crowning of a hundred Elhalyn kings, sir. It holds all the tradition of the past."

"Well, it's time we had some new traditions around here," said Derik. "Why aren't you in uniform, Regis? Aren't you in the Guards anymore?"

Regis shook his head. "My grandfather needs me in the *cortes*."

"I don't think it was fair that they never let me serve in the cadets as all the Comyn sons do," said Derik. "There are so many things they don't let me do! Do they think I haven't the wit for them?"

That, of course, was exactly what they thought; but Regis had not the heart to say so. He said, "My grandfather told me once that he was cadet-master for a few seasons, but they had to replace him because all the young cadets were too much in awe of him as a Hastur."

"I'd have liked to wear a cadet uniform, though," said Derik, still sulky, and Merryl said smoothly, "You *wouldn't* have liked it, my prince. The cadets resent having Comyn among them—they made your life miserable, didn't they, Dom Regis?"

Regis started to say, *only during the first year, only until*

*they knew I wasn't trying to use the privileges of rank to get
special favors I hadn't worked for.* But he supposed that was
beyond Derik's understanding. He said, "They certainly gave
me a lot of trouble," and left it at that.

"Even if they've delayed my crowning, they won't delay
my marriage again," said Derik. "Lord Hastur said that he
would speak to Lady Callina about announcing the be-
trothal with Linnell at this Council. I think I should ask
you instead, Merryl. *You* are her guardian—aren't you?"

Merryl said, "As the Comyn is now arranged, sir, the Aillard line is ruled by the female line. But Lady Callina is very
busy with her work in the Towers; perhaps it can be arranged
so that the lady need not be troubled with such minor matters
as this."

Regis asked, "Is Callina still Keeper at Neskaya—no—
Arilinn, *Dom* Merryl?" He used the formal address, annoyed
by the way in which the youngster was planting the thought
in Derik's mind that perhaps he, Merryl, should be consulted
before the rightful Warden of the Domain. Merryl scowled
and said, "No, I believe she has been brought here to serve
as Keeper to work with the Mother Ashara."

"Merciful Avarra, is old Ashara still alive?" Derik asked.
"She was a bogey for my nurse to frighten me with when I
was six years old! Anyway, Callina won't be there long, will
she, Merryl?" He smiled at his friend, and Regis thought
there was some secret understanding there. "But I've never
seen Ashara, and I don't think anyone else has—my great-
aunt Margwenn was under-Keeper for her a long time ago,
before I was born; she said *she* had hardly seen her. Ashara
must be as old as Zandru's grandmother!"

Regis was trying to remember what he had heard of the
ancient Keeper of the Comyn Tower. "I think we would have
heard if she was dead," he said. "But surely she is too old to
take any real part in Comyn affairs. Is she Hastur, or Elhalyn? I don't think I ever knew."

Derik shook his head. "For all I know," he said, "she could
have been foster-sister to the Cassilda of the legends! I suppose she has *chieri* blood—I have heard they are incredibly
long-lived."

"I have never seen a *chieri*," Regis said. "Nor has anyone,
I think, in our lifetimes; though Kennard told me once that
once, on a journey into the mountains with his foster-brother,
he had been guested in a *chieri* dwelling; he was not out of

his teens then. For that matter, our grandfather seems likely
to live as long as a *chieri*," and he smiled. "That is fine as far
as I am concerned—may his reign be long! I am not at all
eager to take over the Domain of Hastur!"

"But I am ready for the Domain of Elhalyn," said Derik
sullenly. "My first act will be to find you a noble wife, Regis."

But before they could pursue it further, there was a stir
in the Ardais sector, and Dyan Ardais came in through the
entrance at the back of the Ardais section, and went into one
of the private boxes. Danilo was with him, and Regis went
to speak to him, briefly, while he saw Derik and Merryl separate and go to their individual Domains.

"Dom Regis." As always before strangers, Danilo was ex-
cessively formal. "Is your Heir to sit in Council today?"

"No; Mikhail's only eleven. Time enough for that when
he's declared a man," said Regis. Six years ago, under the
spur of danger, he had adopted the youngest son of his sister
Javanne for his Heir.

*Mikhail is eleven. In two more years he will be old enough
for the Cadet corps, and then for all the responsibilities of a
Comyn son. Javanne's elder sons, Gabriel and Rafael, are in
the cadets now—fifteen and fourteen. If their father, the older
Gabriel, is made Warden of the Alton Domain, will they be
Alton or Hastur? Rank follows the higher parent; they are
Hastur, then...*

He glanced at Dyan Ardais. Today the Ardais lord wore,
not his usual unrelieved black, but the glimmering black and
silver of his Domain, somber and elegant. He said to Dyan,
not quite a question:

"There is no one in the Domain of Alton—"

Dyan, if anyone, would know if Kennard had returned—

*Perhaps I should tell him about—about what happened
two nights ago, about Marius, and Rafe Scott—and Sharra.*

But Dyan said, "Regis, the Domain will not fall unchallenged into the hands of the Hasturs. I promise you that."
And Regis, looking at the flat, metallic eyes of the Ardais
lord, unreadable as if shuttered, knew he could not ask Dyan
exactly what he had arranged. He bowed and went to his own
place in the railed-off section, beneath the blue and silver fir-
tree banner of the Hasturs.

Other men and women were coming in now, arranging
themselves under the banners of the different Domains. A
faint distant hum told him that someone was setting the

telepathic dampers; when the Comyn Castle and the Crystal Chamber were built, it had been assumed that everyone here, everyone with blood-right in the Domains, was *laran*-gifted, and by tradition there were telepathic dampers set all about the Chamber at strategic intervals, to prevent involuntary (or voluntary) telepathic eavesdropping.

Everyone here, Regis thought, *is my kinsman, or should be.* Everyone in the Comyn held descent from the legendary seven sons of Hastur and Cassilda. Legend, all of that; legend called Hastur a god, son of Aldones who was Lord of Light. Hastur the god, so they said, had put off his godhead for love of a mortal woman. Whatever truth might lie behind the legend was veiled in time and prehistory, before ever the Ages of Chaos came down to split the country of the Domains into a hundred little kingdoms, and at the end of those ages, though the Hastur-kin had reclaimed their powers, all but a few Towers lay shattered and the *laran* of the Comyn had never recovered.

And yet, he thought, *the Terrans claim, and say they can prove it that we here on Darkover, Seven Domains, Comyn and all, are descended from a colony ship which crashed here, Terran colonists. What is the truth?* Even more, what does the truth mean? Whence came the legends? If we are all Terrans, where had the *laran* come from, the Comyn powers? In the Ages of Chaos, Regis knew from the history he had read at Nevarsin, there had been a time of great tyranny, when the Comyn Council had ruled over a breeding program which would fix the gifts of each Domain into their sons and daughters; matrix technology had reached its height, even meddling with the genes of the Comyn children.

And we are suffering still from that great inbreeding and genetic meddling. Look at Derik. And many of the Ardais are unstable; Dyan's father was mad for decades before his death, and there are those in Council who think Dyan himself is none too sane.

Javanne Lanart-Hastur, with her husband, Gabriel, came in through the rear doors of the Hastur enclosure. She embraced Regis, in a flurry of scent, curls, ruffles, and took her seat. Gabriel—tall burly, wearing the uniform of the Castle Guard as Commander—nodded good-naturedly to Regis as he took his place. Their oldest son, Rafael, a scrawny, dark-haired youngster of fifteen, who reminded Regis of his own mirrored face at that age, bowed to Regis and sat down on one of the back benches. He wore cadet uniform and side-arms.

Two more years and I will be expected to enroll Mikhail in the cadet corps. And in the name of Aldones, Lord of Light, and Zandru, lord of all the hells, what sense does it make for me to send the Heir to Hastur into the cadets, as I was sent, as Javanne is dutifully sending her sons? Yes, of course, if Mikhail is one day to inherit the power and might of the Hasturs—and I have never seen the woman I wish to marry, so it's likely Mikhail will inherit—he must learn to command himself, and others. But with the Empire on Darkover, with the inevitability of an interstellar empire at our very door-step, surely there is a better way to educate the Heir to Hastur than sending him to be schooled in swordplay and the code duello, and taught unarmed combat and the best way to keep drunks off the streets! Regis sighed, thinking of the inevitable outcry it would cause if he, Heir to Hastur, should choose to have his son given the Terran education which Marius, Ken-nard's son, had had.

And where was Marius? Surely he should have come into the Alton Domain's enclosure! He was old enough, now, and if he wished to lay claim to the Domain, before it was declared vacant, surely it should be now!

Perhaps he too has bowed to the inevitable, or decided he would rather leave the Wardenship of the Domain to Gabriel. Again, Regis sighed, remembering a time when he had told his grandfather that he would as soon leave the Domain to Javanne's sons.

One, at least, of my sons, should have a Terran education. If not Mikhail, he thought, then his son by Crystal di As-turien. It was early to think about that—the boy was a hearty toddler not yet two years old, and Regis had seen him fewer than a dozen times. He had two other children, too, daughters, through similar liaisons. *Terrans educate their daughters. I will see that the girls, at least, are educated, though I suppose there will be trouble about it; their mothers are conventional enough to think it an honor to bear a child to a Hastur Heir.* He knew perfectly well the women had not had much interest in him aside from that, and his undoubted good looks—women pursued him for that and it grew a little wearying.

At this point his train of thought was interrupted by a loud cry from the Guardsmen at the door.

"Danvan Hastur of Hastur, Warden of Hastur, Regent of Elhalyn and of the Comyn!"

Regis rose with the rest as his grandfather—Hastur of Hastur, an aging man, his light hair still retaining some gold among the gray, clad in the ceremonial blue and silver of the Hasturs—came into the Crystal Chamber and went slowly to his seat. He seated himself in the front row and looked round the Crystal Chamber.

"Kinsmen, nobles, *Comynari,*" he said, in his rich voice. "I welcome you to Council. Highness—" he bowed to Derik— "will it please you to call the roll of the Domains?"

So Lord Hastur had decided that he must give Derik some privileges and responsibilities, however empty and ceremonial! Derik rose and came forward; like the Hasturs, he was wearing blue and silver with the golden crown of the Elhalyns across the fir-tree emblem.

"I speak for Hastur of Elhalyn," he said. "Hastur of Hastur?"

Danvan Hastur rose and bowed. He said, "I am here at your service, my lord Derik."

"Ardais?"

Dyan Ardais stood up and bowed. "Dyan-Gabriel, Warden of Ardais."

"Aillard?"

There was a small stir behind the curtains of one of the boxes in the enclosure of the Aillards, and Callina Aillard, thin and pale, in the formal gray and crimson draperies of the Aillards, said quietly, *"Para servirte, vai dom."* Regis saw Merryl, looking sullen, in a seat somewhat below his half-sister; then a handful of loosely related families, Lindir, Di Asturien, Eldrin. Regis did not know most of them by sight at all.

"Ridenow of Serrais."

This was out of order, Regis thought; the Alton Domain was higher in rank than the Ridenow. But perhaps he was giving them ample time to answer.

"I speak for Ridenow, and I am here at your command, *vai dom,*" said Edric Ridenow. An enormously fat man, well into middle age, he sat with his half-grown sons and a small herd of his brothers; Regis recognized Lerrys, and Auster who had been in the Guards as officers. There were others he didn't know. There were a few women behind the curtains in the private boxes; the Ridenow lived at the very borders of the

Dry Towns and were of Dry-town blood, and while they did not follow Dryland customs and chain their women, they did keep them in somewhat greater seclusion than most of the mountain Domains.

"Alton?" Derik called, and for some reason he looked pleased.

Silence.

"Alton of Armida, Alton of Mariposa—"

Gabriel Lanart-Hastur rose within the Hastur enclosure and said, "For the sixth time I answer for the Domain of Alton, as Regent during the absence of the rightful claimants."

Derik bowed and then he turned toward Lord Hastur. He asked, "Do I ask him now?"

Regis saw his grandfather flinch slightly. But he nodded and Derik said, "This answer has been acceptable for five years. On the sixth year it is time to declare the Domain of Alton of Armida vacant, and accept the claim of the next Heir. Gabriel Lanart-Hastur of Edelweiss, come forward."

Regis tightened his lips. Gabriel, or Old Hastur himself, had put Derik up to this; the young prince had not the wit to think it out for himself. Gabriel stood up and went forward into the center of the room, the rainbow lights playing over him. He was, Regis thought, a reasonable claimant. He was an honorable man; he was the grandson of one of the sisters of Kennard's father, giving him Ridenow and Alton blood; he had commanded the Guards for six years in Kennard's absence; he was married and had fathered several sons.

Dyan promised it should not go unchallenged. What is he waiting for? Regis looked over at the Ardais enclosure, but Dyan sat without moving, unsmiling, his face blank and grim.

Danvan Hastur made his way slowly down into the central area and stood before Gabriel. Regis could see that Javanne was hugging herself with excitement.

"Gabriel Lanart-Hastur, Alton of Mariposa," said Hastur quietly, "for six years you have ruled the Domain of Alton in the absence of Kennard-Gwynn Lanart-Alton of Armida, and of his lawful heir Lewis-Kennard. In the continuing absence of these two, I call upon you to relinquish the state of Regent-Heir to the Domain, and assume that of Warden of Alton and Lord Alton of Armida, over the entire Domain of Alton and those who owe them loyalty and allegiance. Are you prepared to assume wardship over your people?"

"I am prepared," said Gabriel quietly.

"Do you solemnly declare that to your knowledge you are fit to assume this responsibility? Is there any man who will challenge your right to this solemn wardship of the people of your Domain?"

Gabriel made the correct ritual answer: "I will abide the challenge."

Ruyven di Asturien, second-in-command of the Guardsmen, commander of the Honor Guard, strode to Gabriel's side and drew his sword. He cried out in a loud voice, "Is there any here to challenge the worth and rightful wardship of Gabriel-Alar, Lord Alton?"

There was a minute of silence. Regis looked at Dyan, but he was as impassive as ever. Young Gabriel, on the back benches of the Hastur enclosure, was watching his father with excitement. Regis wondered, will Gabriel declare young Gabriel his Heir? Or will he do the decent thing and declare himself willing to adopt Marius as his Heir, giving him Council recognition? I swear by the Lord of Light, if he does not, I shall do so myself....

Then, from two corners of the room, there were two answers.

"I challenge."

"And I."

Slowly, Marius came forward from the curtained box in the empty Alton enclosure. He said, "None could challenge my cousin Gabriel's worth, my lords; but I challenge his rightful wardship. I am Marius-Gwynn Lanart Alton y Aldaran, son of Kennard Alton, and his rightful Heir in the absence of my elder brother, Lewis-Kennard, and I claim the Domain of Alton and the household of Armida."

And from the rear of the Ardais enclosure came a man Regis did not recognize: a tall, broad-shouldered man with flaming red hair just touched with gray. He came slowly down the steps and said, "I challenge Gabriel-Alar Lanart-Hastur, worth and wardship; he is Regent, not Heir. I can rightfully claim the Domain of Alton, though many years ago I renounced it in favor of Kennard Alton: now I claim it as Regent for Kennard, since Dom Gabriel has violated his Regency by making claim to the Domain on his own part."

Danvan Hastur said formally, "I do not recognize you; state the nature of your claim." Yet Regis knew from the look on his grandfather's face that he knew the man, or at least knew who he was. A quick look at Dyan, and in spite of the telepathic dampers he picked up the thought, *you see, Regis, I promised you the Domain should not go unchallenged, and now I have confused them with not one claimant but two.*

The strange red-haired man said, "My mother was Cleindori Aillard; my father was Lewis Lanart-Alton, elder son of Valdir, Lord Alton. And my name, though I have never used it, in all my years at Arilinn, is Damon Lanart-Aillard; and for twenty years I have been Second in the Arilinn Tower as Technician and *tenerézu.*" He used the archaic word which could mean Keeper or Guardian. "I can claim Council-right, both through my mother and my father; and I was married to Elorie Ardais, daughter of Lord Kyril, and half-sister to Lord Dyan."

"We do not recognize this man as Aillard!" shouted Merryl, half leaping down the steps almost into the central space. "He is a Terran imposter!"

"Silence, sir!" said Lord Hastur sharply. "You do not speak for your Domain! Lady Callina?"

She said quietly, "I have known Jeff—*Dom* Damon—for many years at Arilinn. His heritage is Alton and Aillard; if he had had a daughter, she would stand where I stand now. It is true that he was fostered on Terra; yet he has come within the Veil at Arilinn and I am here to witness that he has the Alton gift in full measure."

"Are we going to let a woman testify about this kind of thing?" demanded Merryl. And Derik said, "*Dom* Merryl has the right to speak for Aillard—"

"Not in the presence of Lady Callina, but only in her absence," said Hastur sharply. "So here we have two claimants to Alton, and the day when such claims could be settled by the sword is over forever." Regis, unwilling, remembered the last time such a challenge had been made in this room; Dyan had been challenged, and he, a superb swordsman, could have settled it at once that way; but he had wisely refused to do so. It seemed that Dyan had set a precedent. "For Gabriel's claim we have his Regency of the affairs of the Domain for the last six years, and his command of the Castle Guard, and certainly there is none can say he has commanded unworthily. Marius Lanart-Montray—" he said, turning to Marius and speaking directly to him, and Regis reflected that this was the first time Lord Hastur had admitted that Marius existed. He had not given him his title claimed as Kennard's heir, Lanart-Alton, but he had acknowledged his existence, and that was more than he had ever done before. "Marius Lanart-Montray, since you have appealed to justice here before Comyn, we are required by law to hear the nature of your claim."

Marius had dressed himself in the green and black of his Domain; he wore a ceremonial cloak bearing the device of the Altons and their standard. He had, Regis noticed, Kennard's own sword. No doubt Andres had kept it for him till this day.

He said, and his voice was not entirely steady, "I declare that I am the true and lawful son of Kennard, Lord Alton, and Elaine Aldaran-Montray."

Hastur said, "We do not recognize the Domain of Aldaran as having any claims among the Comyn."

"But that is due to change," said Prince Derik, stepping forward, "for on this day I have betrothed the sister of my dear friend and cousin and loyal paxman, Merryl Lindir-Aillard, to Lord Beltran of Aldaran; and through his marriage to the Lady Callina, who will be my sister-in-law after my marriage to Linnell Lindir-Aillard, the Domain of Aldaran will be restored to the Comyn."

Callina made a short, sharp exclamation; Regis realized that she had been told nothing of this! Merryl was grinning like a housecat which has just devoured a cagebird and is pretending to lick nothing more than cream from his whiskers. Dyan leaned forward, with a dismayed stare.

Danvan Hastur said, and he could not keep the reproach from his voice, "My prince, you should have informed me privately about this!"

"Why?" Derik demanded, not even trying to conceal his insolent stare. "You have delayed my crowning well past the age when every other King in Thendara has taken his throne, my Lord Hastur, but you cannot refuse me the right to make a good marriage for my loyal paxman."

Hastur muttered something under his breath. It sounded like an oath—or was it a prayer? He could not openly refuse the Heir to the throne, and, Regis thought, it serves him right for never facing the fact that Derik simply is not fit to be crowned—and that he should have tried to have him legally set aside.

He said, sharply reproving, "We will speak of this later,

my prince; may I venture to remind you that it is the Alton
Domain now at stake?"

"But Marius is part Aldaran, and the Aldaran claim is
legitimate now—" said Derik, insisting. Hastur was at a point
where he was, Regis could see, ready to tell Derik that if he
did not sit down and be quiet, he would have him removed,
and that, Regis realized, would blow the pretense of Derik's
competence sky-high. But Linnell Aillard, leaning over the
railing, said something softly to Derik, and he fell silent.

Marius was obviously trying to collect his thoughts. He
said, "I challenge Gabriel's wardship; he has not the Alton
gift and he has not arranged to have me tested to prove
whether or not I have it."

Gabriel asked, staring directly at Marius, *"Do* you claim
to have the Alton gift?"

"I don't know," said Marius. "I have not been tested. Do
you claim to have it?"

Gabriel said, "In these days—" but was interrupted by a
cry of surprise from the Guardsman at the door.

"Gods above! Is it you, sir?"

And then a tall, gaunt man strode into the Crystal Chamber. He was wearing Terran clothing; one arm ended in a
folded sleeve at his wrist. His dark hair, thick and curling,
was streaked with gray, and his face was scarred and ema-
ciated.

"I am Lewis-Kennard, Lord Alton, Warden of Armida," he
said in a harsh voice that sounded raw and strained, "and
I claim your indulgence, my lords, for coming late to this
assembly; as you can see, I have but just landed here, and
have come at once without even delaying to clothe myself in
the ceremonial colors of my Domain."

General uproar, exploding in all directions from the walls
of the Crystal Chamber. In the middle of it, Old Hastur's
voice crying out uselessly for order; and finally he spoke urgently to Gabriel, who bellowed in his best drill-sergeant
voice, "Council is recessed for half an hour! We will reconvene
then and make some sense out of all this!"

Lew Alton's narrative

CHAPTER TWO

I'm no good at handling crowds; no telepath is, and I'm worse than most. Within seconds after Hastur called a recess, they were all around me, and despite the telepathic dampers, the blend of curiosity, horror, shock—malice from some-where—was more than I could take. I elbowed a way into the corridor outside, and moments later, Marius was beside me.

"Lew," he said, and we hugged each other. I stood back a little to look at him.

"I wouldn't have recognized you. You were just a skinny little tadpole—" I said. Now he was tall, almost as tall as I, sturdy, broad-shouldered—a man. I could see the shock in his eyes as he took in the scars on my face, the arm that ended in the folded sleeve. I don't know what, if anything, my father had told him—and he had only been a child when it happened—but God only knows what gossip he had heard in the Comyn. Well, I was used to that shock in people's faces when they saw me first; I only had to remember the first time I'd looked in a mirror after it all happened. They got used to it, and if they didn't, they weren't likely to stay around in my life long enough for it to matter. So I didn't say anything except, "It's good to see you, brother. Where's Andres?"

"Home," Marius said. "Waiting. I wouldn't let him come with me this morning. Whatever happened, I didn't want him mixed up in it. He's not as young as he used to be." I caught the unspoken part of that, too. He didn't want it thought that the claimant for the Alton Domain wanted, or needed, a Ter-ran bodyguard. I never thought of Andres as Terran anymore; he'd been a second father to me, and all the father Marius had had during these crucial years between boy and man.

That had been my fault, too. Then, angrily, I put that thought aside. No law had required our father to spend all his attention on his elder son. It was not my doing, but Marius had been neglected for me, and I wondered, even as we embraced, just how much he resented it. Even now, he might feel that I had turned up just in time to snatch the Domain from his hands.

But there were those in the Comyn who would see nothing in Andres but his Terran background and name. Andres was one of the half dozen or less people here on Darkover that I cared to see.

One of the others was waiting quietly behind Marius until our embrace loosened and we stood back from each other. I said, "Well, Gabriel?"

"Well, Lew?" he replied, in almost the same inflection. "You certainly picked one hell of a moment to walk in!"

"I'm sure you'd have preferred him to wait a day or two, until you had the Domain neatly tied up in your own wallet," Marius retorted sharply.

"Don't be a fool, youngster," Gabriel said without heat, and I remembered that Gabriel's oldest son must be close to Marius's own age; a bit younger, perhaps, but not much. "What was I to think, with no word from Kennard? And by the way, Lew, where is the old man? Not well enough to travel?"

I hadn't wanted Marius to find it out that way, but Gabriel picked it up from my mind before I spoke and so did Marius. Gabriel said something shocked and sympathetic, and Marius began to cry. Gabriel put an arm around him as Marius struggled for self-control. He was still young enough to be ashamed of weeping in public. But behind him my other kinsman made no attempt to conceal the tears streaming down his face.

I hadn't seen him since I'd left Arilinn, and there, though everyone knew that he was the son of my father's elder brother and could have been the rightful claimant, before my father or me, to Armida, he had made a great thing, a point of honor, of bearing the name of his Terran foster-father; he was *Lord Damon* only on ceremonial occasions. The rest of the time we knew him—and thought of him—only as Jeff Kerwin. As he looked at me, tears falling down his face, I remembered the close ties among the Arilinn circle. It was the only time, perhaps, I had been truly happy, truly at peace, in my entire life. He asked now, "Did you—did you at least bring him home to rest here on Darkover, cousin?"

I shook my head. "You know the Terran law," I reminded him. "I came as soon as I had—had buried him."

Jeff sighed and said, "He was like a father to me, too, or

an elder brother." He turned to Marius, embracing him, and said, "I have not seen you since you were a child—a baby, really."

"So here we have all four claimants for the Alton Domain," said a harsh, musical voice behind us. "But instead of disputing manfully for the Domain as one would expect of hillmen, they are indulging in a love-feast! What a touching spectacle, this reunion!"

Marius whirled on him and said, "Listen, you—" His fists clenched, but I touched his arm with my good hand. "Let it go, brother. He doesn't know. Lord Dyan, you were my father's friend, you'll want to know this. He is buried on Vainwal. And on the last day of his life, a few minutes before his death—which was very sudden and unexpected—he spoke kindly of you and said you had been a good friend to my brother."

But as I spoke of that last day, remembering—my head was ringing.

—My last command! Go back, Lew, go back and fight for your brother's rights—

With that final command still ringing in my mind, drowning out everything else, I was even prepared to be civil to Lord Dyan.

Dyan stared straight ahead, his jaw tight, but I saw the muscles in his throat move. At that moment I came closer to liking Dyan Ardais than ever before, or ever again. Somehow his struggle not to weep, as if he were a boy still young enough to be ashamed of tears, touched me as no display could have done. Jeff actually dared to lay a compassionate hand on Dyan's shoulder. I remembered that Jeff had been married to Dyan's half-sister—I had never seen her; she had died before I came to Arilinn—and watching them, I knew how Jeff had been persuaded to leave Arilinn and come here, when Jeff had about as much interest in the Regency of Alton—or the politics of the Comyn—as he had in the love life of the banshee. Less, really; he might have had some intellectual curiosity about the banshee.

The silence stretched.

...back and fight for your rights, your brother's rights...last command...

Endless, a never-ending loop battering my mind... It seemed, for a moment, impossible that they did not hear.

Gabriel said finally, "All my life he's been there; bigger than
life. I simply can't believe he's gone."

"Nor I," said Jeff. Abruptly he looked at me, and I saw my
face mirrored in his mind and was shocked. "Zandru's hells,
Lew! Did you come here directly from the spaceport?" I nodded
and he asked, "When did you eat last?"

I thought about that and said at last, "I can't remember.
They shot me so full of drugs aboard ship...I'm still fuzzy."

...*My last command...go back*... it was to drown that
unending clamor in my mind, that I put my hand to my head,
but Jeff put his hand under my arm. He said, "You can't
think straight in this condition, and thinking straight is the
first thing you have to be able to do. Besides, you ought not
to appear before Council wearing Terran clothes. It made a
dramatic point, perhaps, for a few minutes, but it would start
people thinking the wrong things. Dyan—?"

The Ardais lord nodded, and Jeff said, "I am guested here
in the Ardais quarters—I don't know who, if anyone, is living
in the Alton ones—"

"Caretakers," said Gabriel, with a wry twist of his mouth.
"I may be presumptuous, but not *that* presumptuous!"

"Come along," Jeff said. "We can find you something to
eat, and some decent clothes—"

Dyan said, "Yours would go round him twice, Jeff." He
looked me up and down. "You're thinner than you used to be.
Tell them to find something of mine for him."

Jeff led me quickly along the corridor; I was glad to get
away, for some others of the Comyn and the others in the
Crystal Chamber had come out into the hallway. I saw someone wearing Ridenow colors, and the flash of golden and green
made me think of Dio.

*Was she here, would she confront me at any moment,
shrieking* Monster! *Would she think I had come to force her
back as if the Terran ceremony had made her my prisoner?* ...

*Her touch, her understanding...it might even have quieted
the shrieking in my mind...yet the love between us had not
been strong enough to hold through tragedy. How could I ask
it...that horrible thing...no man had any right to do that
to a woman...*

"Steady," said Jeff. "There in a minute. Sit down." He
shoved me onto a piece of furniture. It was dreamlike, *déjà
vu*, for I could not remember ever being in the Ardais apartments before. Yet my father had known them well, I sup-

posed, Dyan had been his closest friend when they were young....*Zandru's hells, would I never again be sure which thoughts, feelings, emotions were mine, which my father's? The forced rapport which had wakened my Alton gift when I was eleven years old had been bad enough, but that last dying death-grip on my mind...*I shuddered, and when Dyan thrust a drink into my hand I leaned for a moment against his shoulder, letting him support me. Memories of a younger Dyan flooded me with an affection warm, almost sensual, which shocked me to the bone, and I slammed the barrier shut, straightening up and easing free of his support. I drained the glass without noticing the taste. It was the strong *firi* cordial of the Kilghard Hills.

"Thanks. I needed that, but some soup would be better, I suppose, or something solid—"

"If I remember rightly," Dyan said, "your father was allergic to the Terran drugs too." He used the Terran word "allergic"; there wasn't one in *casta*. "I wouldn't try to eat anything solid for a few hours, if I were you. They'll bring you something to eat in a few minutes, but you don't really have that much time. We could call for a day or two delay, if you want." He looked around, saw Marius hovering, and asked, "Where's Gabriel?"

Marius said, "He's honor guard there; he had to go back, he said."

"Damn." Jeff scowled. "We need a family conference of some kind."

Dyan's lip curled. "Keep Gabriel out of it," he said. "He's a Hastur lackey. I've always suspected that's why old Hastur married him to the girl...his granddaughter. I don't suppose you had sense enough to get yourself married and father a son, did you, Lew?"

With an effort that made me tremble, I slammed down a barrier. It was enough that I would never be free of the memory of that inhuman *thing* which should have been my son. If it were ever to be shared, it would not be with Dyan. He might have been my father's chosen friend and confidant; he was not mine. I shrugged off his supporting arm as I rose.

"Let's see about those clothes. No, I don't mind wearing Ardais colors..."

But it turned out Marius had sent a servant at a run to the townhouse, with orders to fetch a cloak and Domain colors for me. I glanced in the mirror, saw myself transformed. And

I could hide the missing hand in a fold of the cloak, if I wished.
Marius gave me my father's sword and I fastened it at my
side, trying not to think of the Sharra matrix.

It wasn't too far; I could tolerate that much distance...

*I had tried, again, to leave it on Vainwal. Had thought,
this time, I could be free...and then the burning, the blurring
clamor...I had nearly missed the ship because I had realized
I could not abandon it, to abandon it would be death...not
that I would have minded death...better dead than enslaved
this way...*

"At least now you look proper Comyn," said Jeff. "You
have to fight them on their own ground, Lew."

I hurried with the tunic-laces, making a little extra display
of my one-handed skill because I was still damnably sensitive
about Marius watching. Dyan's eyes flicked over the empty
sleeve.

"I told Kennard that hand would have to come off," he
said. "They should have had it off at Arilinn. He kept on
hoping the Terrans could do something. Terran science was
one of the few things he kept on believing in, even after he
lost faith in damned near everything else."

The silence stretched, came to a full stop. Jeff, who had
seen the hand at Arilinn, and had tried to save it, would have
spoken, but I mentally commanded him to be silent. I might
manage to discuss it, some day, with Jeff; but not with Dyan;
and not with anyone here, not yet.

Dio had accepted it...I cut off that train of thought, afraid
of what it would lead to.

*Sooner or later, I supposed, I would see her again, and I
would have to make it clear...she was free, not my prisoner
or slave, not bound to me....*

There was a tentative knock at the door, and one of
Hastur's servants, liveried in blue and silver, came in to
convey the Regent's compliments and request that the Ardais
and Alton lords would return to Council.

Dyan said, with a faint curl of his lip, "At least there is
now no reason to declare the Domain vacant."

That was true. At first there had been no rightful claimant;
now there were four. I asked Marius, as we went down the
hallway toward the Crystal Chamber, "Do you have the Alton
Gift?"

Marius had the dark eyes of our Terran mother. I have
always thought dark eyes were expressionless, unreadable.

"I haven't the faintest idea," he said. "What with one thing and another, I've been given to understand that it would be...insufferable insolence...to try and find out. I'm fairly sure Gabriel doesn't, though."

"The reason I asked," I said, exasperated, "is that they'll be badgering me to declare an Heir." And I knew he could pick up the part of that I did not speak aloud; that I would prefer to assume he had it, without the shock tactics my father had had to use on my own Gift.

"It's probably irrelevant," Dyan said. "Everyone knew I didn't have the Ardais Gift; it didn't stop them from declaring me as Heir and Regent to my father." The Ardais gift—catalyst telepathy, the gift of awakening latent *laran*—had been thought extinct, until it had been discovered in Danilo. That made me think about Regis, and wonder why he had not come to greet me. Well, if there was a plot to take the Alton Domain under Hastur wardship, I wasn't surprised he didn't care to face me just yet.

...*fight for your brother's rights...last command...*

I shook my head to clear it of the insistent jangling, and, between my kinsmen, walked back into the Crystal Chamber.

Some kind of hurried conference was going on behind the curtained enclosure of the Hastur Domain. For once in my life I was glad of the telepathic dampers, which lessened the jangle in my head to a manageable ache. When they called us to order again, Danvan Hastur rose and said, "From having no rightful claimant to the Alton Domain, we now have four, and the situation must be investigated further. I ask that we delay the formal investiture of Lord Alton for another seven days, until the period of Council mourning for Kennard Alton is finished."

I could hardly protest it, that they should give my father his due.

Marius had taken a seat beside me in the Alton enclosure; I noticed that Gabriel's wife, Javanne Hastur, had seated herself among the Hasturs, with a dark, slender boy who looked like Gabriel and was, I supposed, Gabriel's elder son. Gabriel himself, down with the honor Guard, was thus spared any confusion about whether he should seat himself among Hasturs or Altons, and I supposed he had planned it that way. I had always liked Gabriel; I preferred to think that he meant precisely what he said. My own whereabouts and my father's being unknown, he had claimed the Domain on Hastur's orders. I didn't think I needed to worry about Gabriel. My eyes sought old Hastur, a small squarish unbending figure, graying, upright, like the rock of the castle itself, and just as unchanging. Was this the real enemy I must face?

And why? I know he had never cared much for me, but I had done him the courtesy, before this, to believe it was not personal; I was simply an uncomfortable reminder of my father's stubbornness in marrying the wrong woman, and he had acted as if my Terran and Aldaran blood were simply a mistake for which I was not to blame. But now all was in confusion; Hastur was behaving like my enemy, and Dyan, who had always disliked me, as a kinsman and friend. I couldn't figure it out. Near the back of the Hastur enclosure I saw Regis. He did not seem to have changed much; he was taller, and his shoulders somewhat broader, and the fresh boyish face was now shadowed by faint reddish beard, but he still had the Hastur good looks. The change must have been inside; I would have expected him to come and greet me, and the boy I had known would have done it, even more quickly than Marius. I had, after all, been closer to Regis than to the little brother from whom six years had separated me.

Hastur was calling us all to order again, and I saw Prince Derik, in the Elhalyn enclosure with some people whom I did not know. I supposed they were his elder sisters and their families, or some of the Elhalyn connections: Lindirs, perhaps, Di Asturiens, Dellerays. Mentally I counted on my fingers; why had Derik not been crowned? I remembered that he had been somewhat too immature at sixteen, but now he must be well into his twenties. There was so much I did not know; I was being thrown into Council without any time to find out what had happened! Why, in the name of all the probably nonexistent Gods of the Comyn, had I agreed to come?

*....last command....fight for your brother's rights....*despite the dampers, the mental command kept reverberating in my mind till I began seriously to wonder, as I had done several times on the ship which brought me from Vainwal, if there had been damage to the brain! The unbridled anger of an Alton can kill—I had always known that; and my father's mental Gift was unusually powerful. Now, when he was dead and I should have been free of that dominating voice in my

mind, I seemed more bound than ever, more hag-ridden. Would I ever be free of it?

Marius saw the nervous gesture, hand to head, and leaned close to whisper, "What's wrong, Lew?" But I shook my head restlessly and muttered, "Nothing." I had that eerie sense of being *watched* from somewhere. Well, I had always had that, in Council. I tried to pull myself together and focus on what was going on.

Hastur said gravely, "My lord Derik, before the Council was interrupted—" I could *hear* him saying what he had started to say, *disrupted*, "—by the arrival of an unexpected Heir to Alton—" *at least he admitted I was that*—"you had spoken of an alliance which you had made. Will it please you to explain it to us, *vai dom?*"

"I think I should let Merryl do that," Prince Derik said, "since it concerns the Aillards."

Merryl came down slowly from the enclosure; but was stopped by a clear feminine voice.

"I object to this," said the voice, which I recognized. *"Dom* Merryl does not speak for the Aillards." And I looked up and saw my cousin Callina coming slowly down the center of the enclosure. She paused at the rails and waited. That clear voice troubled me; I had heard it last when Marjorie...died. She had died in Callina's arms. And I... once again it seemed that I could feel the old agony in my wounded hand, tearing through every nerve and finger and nail which had been long gone...This was madness; I caught at vanishing self-control and listened to what Callina was saying.

"In courtesy, Lord Hastur, if something concerns the Domain of the Aillards, I should be asked to give my consent before *Dom* Merryl speaks."

She was slight and slender; she wore the ceremonial regalia and the crimson veils of a Keeper in Council, and I, who had spent years on Vainwal seeing women who looked as if they were free and alive, thought that she looked like a prisoner, with the heavy robes, the ceremonial ornaments weighing down her slight body so that she appeared fettered, like a child trying to wear the garments of an adult. Her hair was long and dark as spun black glass, what little I could see of it shining through the veil.

Merryl turned on her, with a look of pure hatred. He said, "I have been left to manage the affairs of the Domain while you were isolated at Neskaya and then at Arilinn, my lady;

am I now to turn all these things over to you again at your whim? I think my management of the Domain speaks for my competence; what of yours?"

"I do not question your competence," she said, and her voice was like molten silver. "But where your arrangements for the Domain alliances concern me, I have a legitimate right to question, and if need be, to veto. Answer what Hastur has asked you, my brother." She used the most formal and distant mode of that word. "I cannot comment until I know what is being proposed."

Merryl looked disconcerted. I didn't know him; I didn't know most of the younger Aillards, even though Callina's younger sister Linnell was my foster-sister. Now he stood shifting nervously from foot to foot, glanced at Derik, who was grinning and gave him no help, and finally said, "I have made arrangements that the Lady Callina should consolidate a new alliance by marriage with *Dom* Beltran of Aldaran."

I saw shock come over Callina's face, but I could not keep silent. I burst out, "You people must all have gone mad! Did you say—alliance with Aldaran? Beltran of Aldaran?"

Hastur glanced repressively at me, and Derik Elhalyn said, "I see no reason against it." He sounded defensive, very young. "The Aldarans are already allied to one major Domain by marriage, as you of all people should know, *Dom* Lewis. And in this day and age, with the Terrans at our very doorstep, it seems well to me that we should take this opportunity to line up their allegiance with the Comyn."

He repeated this as a child repeats his lesson. I wondered who had schooled him in that theory. Glancing at Merryl, I decided that the answer was not far to seek.

But—*ally with Aldaran? With that damned renegade clan—?*

Callina said, "When before this has a Keeper been subjected to the whims of the Council? I am the head of the Aillard Domain in my own right; and not subject to *Dom* Merryl. I think there need be no further discussion of this—" I could almost hear her sorting through her mind for an inoffensive adjective, and she finally compromised—"this ill-advised plan. I am sorry, my prince; I refuse."

"You—refuse?" Derik turned to stare at her. "On what grounds, lady?"

She made an impatient gesture; her veil fell back, revealing dark hair braided with gems. She said, "I have no will to marry at this time. And if I should, and when I do, I shall, no doubt, be capable of finding myself a husband who will be suitable. And I do not think I will look for him among the Aldaran Domain. I know more of that Domain than I wish to know, and I tell you, we might as well hand ourselves over here and now to the accursed Terrans than ally with that—" again the mental sorting, the visible search for a word—"with that renegade, exiled Domain."

Dyan said, "*Domna,* you have been misinformed." His voice held that exquisite, indifferent courtesy which he always had when speaking to women. "The Aldaran are no longer in the laps of the Terrans. Beltran has broken that alliance to Terra, and for that reason, if for no other, I do not think we can afford to hold aloof from Aldaran." He turned to the Council and explained: "Alliance with Aldaran would give us more strength, and that is what we need now, to stand united against the pull of the Terran Empire. Granted, there are those among us who would turn us over to the Terrans—" His eyes moved toward the Ridenow enclosure—"but there are also those who remain loyal to our world and to the old ways. And of these, I am convinced, Beltran of Aldaran is one. Our forefathers—for reasons which seemed good to them, no doubt—cast out the Domain of Aldaran from the Comyn. But there were seven Domains; there should be seven Domains again, and this move, I am sure, would catch the imagination of the common people."

She said, "I am a Keeper—"

He shrugged and said, "There are others. If Beltran has asked for alliance to the Aillard Domain—"

"Then I say for the Aillards that we will have none of it," said Callina. And, unexpectedly she turned to me.

"And here sits one who can prove the truth of what I say!"

"You damned, incredible fools!" I heard my own voice, and as Hastur turned to me, there was first a stir of voices, then a mutter, then a clamor, and I realized that once again I had disrupted Council, that I had jumped head-first into an argument I really knew nothing about. But I had started and I must go on.

"The Terrans are bad enough. But what the Aldarans got us into—" I fought for control. I would not, I *would not* speak the name of that ravening terror, which had flared and raged in the hills, which had sent Caer Donn up in flames, which had burned away my hand and my sanity....

"You ought to be in favor of this alliance," said Derik.
"After all, if we recognize the Aldarans, there won't be so
much question about whether you are legitimate or not, will
there?"

I stared at him, wondering if Derik were really this much
of a fool, or whether the statement had a profundity that
somehow escaped me; no one else seemed inclined to question
it. It was like some nightmare, where perfectly ordinary people said the most outrageous things and they were taken for
granted.

Dyan Ardais said bluntly, "There's no question of legitimacy. Council accepted Kennard's eldest son, and that's that.
Sit down and listen, Lew. You've been away a long time, and
when you know what's been happening while you were away,
you may change your mind. It might not change your status,
but it could change your brother's."

I glanced at Marius. It was certain that the recognition
of Aldaran would do a great deal to alter his legitimacy or
otherwise. But did Dyan honestly think that would make the
rest of the Council overlook his Terran blood? Dyan went on,
his rich musical voice persuasive and kind, "I think it's your
hate speaking, not your good sense. Comyn—" he said, looking around, "I think we can all agree that *Dom* Lewis has
reason for prejudice. But it was a long time ago. Listen to
what we have to say, won't you?"

There was a general murmur of approval. I could have
dealt with hostility from Dyan, but this—! Damn him! He had
hinted—no, he had said right out—that I was to be pitied,
a cripple with an old grudge, coming back and trying to take
up the old feud where I left off! By skillfully focusing all the
unspoken feelings, their pity, the old admiration and friendship for my father, he had given them a good reason to disregard what I said.

The worst of it was, I wasn't sure he was wrong. The
rebellion at Aldaran, in which I had played so disastrously
wrong-headed a part, had been, like all civil wars, a symptom
of something seriously wrong in the culture; not an end in
itself. The Aldarans were not the only ones on Darkover who
had been lured by the Terran Empire. The Ridenow brothers
had almost given up pretending loyalty to the Comyn...and
they were not the only ones. The Comyn, officially at least,
had stood out almost alone against the lure of the Terran
Empire, promising a world made easier, simpler, with Terran

technology and a star-spanning alliance. I had been an easy scapegoat for both sides, with my Terran blood on the one hand and, on the other, the fact that Kennard, educated on Terra, had nevertheless turned his back on the Empire and become one of the staunchest supporters of the Comyn conservatives. Maybe all sons rebel against their fathers as a matter of course, but few can have had their personal rebellion escalated into such tragedy, or brought down such disaster on their own heads or their families'. I had been drawn into the rebellion, and my tremendous *laran,* trained at Arilinn, had been put to the service of Beltran's rebellion and to...even now I flinched and could not say the name to myself. My good hand clutched at the matrix and let it go as if it burned me.

Sharra. Ravening, raging, a city in flames...

What the hell was I doing here, twice haunted, hag-ridden by my father's voice...

Lerrys Ridenow stood up, turning to Lord Edric for formal permission to speak; Edric gave him the slightest gesture of recognition. He said, "By your leaves, my lords, I would like to say that perhaps this whole argument is futile. The day is past when alliances can be cemented by marriages with unwilling women. Lady Callina is a Keeper, and the independent head of a Domain. If Aldaran wishes to marry into Comyn—"

"You'd like that, wouldn't you?" said Merryl. "Make this fine alliance for one of your own, and line Aldaran up with the rest of the toadies licking Terran arses—"

"Enough!" Callina spoke sharply, but I could see the faint stain of color etching her cheek. She was too old, and too well-bred, to reprove him for the obscenity directly, but she said, "I did not give you leave to speak!"

"Zandru's hells," shouted Merryl. "Will you silence that woman, Lord Hastur? She knows nothing about this—she has spent her life shut up in one Tower after another—now she is here as a puppet of old Ashara, but are we to keep up this nonsensical farce that a cloistered professional virgin knows anything at all about the conduct of her Domain? Our world is on the edge of destruction. Are we going to sit and listen to a girl squalling that she doesn't want to marry this one or that?"

Callina was white to the lips; she stepped forward, her hand clasped at her throat where I knew her matrix was

concealed. She said, very low, but her voice carried to the
heights of the Crystal Chamber, "Merryl, the rulership of the
Domain is not at issue here. A time may come when you wish
to dispute it. I cannot keep it by force of arms, perhaps—but
I shall keep it by any means I must." She laid her hand on
the matrix, and it seemed to me that somewhere there was
a dim rumble as of distant thunder. Without taking the
slightest notice, she turned her face to Gabriel and said, "My
lord commander, you are charged with keeping peace in this
chamber. Do your duty."

Gabriel laid his hand on Merryl's arm and spoke to him,
in a low, urgent voice. Despite the telepathic dampers, I had
no trouble in following the general import of what Gabriel
said: that if Merryl didn't sit down and shut up, he would
have him carried out by force. Teeth clenched, Merryl glanced
at Dyan Ardais, as if for support, then at Prince Derik.

Derik said uneasily, "Come, come, Merryl, that's no way
to talk before ladies. We'll discuss it later, my dear fellow.
Let's have peace and quiet here, by all means."

Merryl sank into a seat, glowering.

Callina said quietly, "As for this marriage, I think everyone here knows that it is not marriage which is being discussed. It is *power*, my lords, power in the Comyn. Why should
we not call things by their right names? The question before
us, and I think my brother knows it as well as I do, is this:
do we want to put that kind of power within Comyn in the
hands of the Aldarans? I think not. And there sits one who
can attest to the truth of what I say. Would you like to tell
them, *Dom* Lewis, why it would be—unwise—to put that
much power in the hands of Aldaran, or to trust him with
it."

I felt my forehead breaking out in cold sweat. I knew I
should explain myself, calmly and quietly, how at one time
I had trusted Beltran, and how I had been—betrayed. Now
I must speak calmly, without undue emotion.

Yet, to drag it all out here, in Council, before all those
kinsmen who had tried to deny me my very place in this
room...I could not. My voice failed me, I felt it strangle in
my throat, and knew if I spoke aloud I would crack completely. My father's voice, the ravening flames of Sharra, the
continuous unrhythmic waves of the telepathic jangle—my
head was pandemonium. Yet Callina was standing there,
waiting for me to speak, and I opened my mouth, trying to

force myself to find words. I heard only a raw meaningless croak. I finally managed to say, "You—know. You were there at Arilinn—"

And I cringed before the pity in her eyes. She said, "I was there when Lew came to Arilinn with his wife, after they both risked their lives to break the link with Sharra."

"Sharra is not relevant here," said Dyan harshly. "The link was broken and the matrix controlled again. We are talking now of Beltran of Aldaran. And he, too, has a strong interest in seeing that nothing like that ever happens again. As for Lew—" his eyes turned on me. "I am sorry to say this, kinsman, but those who meddle with forces as strong as Sharra should not complain if they are—hurt. I cannot but think that Lew brought his trouble upon himself, and he has had his lesson—as Beltran has had his."

I bent my head. Perhaps he was right, but that made it no easier. I had learned to live with what had happened, after a fashion. That did not mean I was willing to hear Dyan lecture me about it.

Regis Hastur rose to his feet within the Hastur enclosure. He said, not looking at me, "I cannot see that Lew was so much to blame. But whether or nor, I do not think we can trust Beltran. It was Beltran's doing, and Kadarin's. And Lew was Beltran's kinsman, his guest and under the safeguard of hospitality. He imprisoned him; he imprisoned me; he kidnapped Danilo and attempted to force him to use his *laran* for the Sharra circle. And if Beltran did *this* to a kinsman—" he turned and gestured, with what seemed mute apology for turning all eyes to me—"how could anyone trust him?"

I could read the horror in the eyes turned on me; even through the telepathic damper their horror surged into my mind, the shock and horror... *the scars on my face, the arm ending abruptly at the wrist, the horror that had surged into my mind from Dio when she saw in my mind the horror that had been our child...Merciful Avarra, was there no end to this agony?* I dropped my forehead on my arms, hiding my face, hiding my mutilated arm. Marius laid his hand on my shoulder; I hardly felt it there.

Danilo's voice, shaken with emotion, took up the tale where Regis had left off.

"It was Beltran's doing; he had Lew tied and beaten. He stripped him of his matrix. All of you Comyn who have been in a Tower know what that means! And why? Because Lew begged him to use caution with Sharra, to turn it over to one of our own Towers and see if a safe way could be found for its harnessing! And look at Lew's face! This—this torturer is the man you want to invite courteously into Comyn, to marry the head of a Domain and Ashara's Keeper?"

Dyan's voice lashed. "I did not give you leave to speak!"

Danilo turned to him. He was very pale. "My Lord, with all respect, I am testifying only to the truth of what I witnessed with my own eyes. And it is relevant to what is being discussed in the Comyn. I have Council-right; am I to sit silent?"

Hastur said, his displeasure evident in his voice, "It seems this is the day for all the unruly younger members of the Domains to speak in Council without leave of their elders!" His eyes rested on Merryl, on Danilo, then on Regis, and the younger man drew a deep breath.

"By your leave, sir, I can only repeat what my paxman said: I am testifying to what I myself saw and witnessed. When we see our elders and—and our betters, about to take a step which they could not honorably take if all the facts were known to them, then, for the—" again he hesitated, almost stammering—"for the honor of the Comyn, we must bring it to the light. Or are we to believe, sir, that the Comyn consider it of no importance that Beltran was capable of betraying, and torturing, a kinsman?" The words were impeccably courteous, and the tone; but his eyes were blazing.

"All this," said Dyan, "took place a long time ago."

"Still," said Regis, "before we bring Beltran of Aldaran into Comyn itself—whether by marriage-right or any other way—should we not first assure ourselves that he has come to think otherwise about what has happened?" And then he said what I knew I should have said myself. "In the names of all the Gods, do we want the kind of thing that happened in Caer Donn to happen in Thendara? Do we want—Sharra?"

Lerrys Ridenow came down to the center of the dais. I had not seen him since shortly after my marriage to Dio; but he had not changed: slender, elegant, dressed now in Darkovan clothing, the green and gold of the Ridenow Domain, but exhibiting the same foppish grace as he had had in the clothing he had worn on the pleasure world.

He said, "Are you going to raise the bogey of Sharra again? We all know the link was broken and the matrix controlled again. The Sharra matrix is no trouble to anyone now—or rather," he said, raising his head and cocking it a little to one side with a calculating glance at me, "it may be very grave trouble to Lew Alton, but he asked, after all, for his trouble."

How could he have known that? Dio must have told him! How could she...how could she have betrayed to him what was so personal to me? And what else had she told him, what else had she betrayed? I had trusted her implicitly.... My hand clenched and I bit back a rising surge of nausea. I did not want to believe that Dio could have betrayed me this way.

But next to me, Marius rose to his feet. I was startled, almost turned to him to remind him sharply that he had no voice here—then I remembered. He was one of the official claimants for the Alton Domain; they could no longer refuse to acknowledge his existence.

He said, and his voice was only a shred of sound. "That's not true, *Dom* Lerrys. The matrix is—is active again. Lord Regis, tell that what you saw...in my father's house, not three days ago."

"It's true," Regis said, and he was very pale. "The Sharra matrix is alive again. But I did not know, at that time, that Lew Alton had returned to Darkover. I think he must have brought it back with him."

I had had no choice, but there was no way I could tell them that. While Regis spoke, I listened, transfixed with horror. I clutched at Marius's sleeve and said, "Rafe. He is in Thendara...."

But I hardly heard Marius's reply.

Rafe was in Thendara.

That meant Kadarin and Thyra were—somewhere.

And so was the Sharra matrix.

And so—all the Gods of Darkover be merciful—so was I.

CHAPTER THREE

Even as he told the story of what he had seen in Kennard's house the night Marius had come in panic to summon him, Regis watched Lew, thinking that he would hardly have known the older man, who had been like a brother in his childhood. Lew looked, he formed the thought without volition, like something hung up in a field to scare the birds! Not so much the gauntness, though he was thin enough, and looked worn, nor even the dreadful scars. No, it was something in the eyes, something haunted and terrible.

In six years, has he found no peace?

Surely it was only that Lew was travel-worn, still suffering with the shock of his father's sudden death. Regis knew that when he could stop to think, he too would mourn the kindly and genial man who had been foster-father and friend, who had trained him in swordplay and given him the only family and home he had ever known. But this was no time for mourning. Tersely, he completed the tale.

"...and when I tried to look within my own matrix, it was as it had been in the Hellers, during that time when Sharra was freed and Lew was—enslaved. I saw nothing but the Form of Fire."

From his place among the Altons, the big red-headed man who had come from Arilinn, and who was one of Lew's kinsmen—Regis had only heard his name briefly and did not remember it—said, "I find this disturbing, Lord Regis. For look, my own matrix is free of any taint." With the big fingers which looked better suited to the hilt of a sword—or to a blacksmith's hammer—he deftly untwisted the silk about the cord at his neck; briefly, Regis saw a glow of pallid blue before the man covered it again.

"And mine," said Callina quietly but without moving. Regis assumed that, as a Keeper, she would know the condition of her matrix without touching it. Sometimes he wished he had chosen to remain in a Tower, to be trained in the skills of using all of his latent *laran*, whatever it was. Usually, when this wish came upon Regis, it was when he saw a trained

131

technician working with a matrix. It had not been strong
enough to hold him in a Tower against the other claims of
clan and caste, and he supposed that for a true mechanic or
technician, that call must supersede other claims and needs.

Callina said quietly to Lew, "What of yours?"

He shrugged, and to Regis it seemed like the last hopeless
movement of a man so defeated that there was no longer
strength in him to fight this ultimate shame and despair. He
wanted to cry out to Callina, *Can't you see what you are doing
to him?* At last Lew said tonelessly, "I have never been—free
of it."

But the others in the Crystal Chamber were growing restless. Already the quality of the light had altered, as the
Bloody Sun beyond the windows sank toward the horizon and
was lost in the evening mists; now the light was cold, chill and
austere. At last someone, some minor noble somewhere
within the Ardais Domain, called out, "What has this to do
with the Council?"

Callina said in her sombre voice, "Pray to all the Gods you
never find out how much this can have to do with us, *comynari*. There is nothing that can be done here, but we must
investigate this...." She looked at Lew's kinsman from Arilinn and said, "Jeff, are there any other technicians here?"

He shook his head. "Not unless the mother Ashara can
supply some." He turned back to the Hasturs and addressed
himself to Regis's grandfather.

"Vai Dom, will you dismiss the Council for a few days,
until we can look into this and find out why there has been
this—this outbreak of a force we thought safely controlled."

Hastur frowned, and Derik said shrilly, "It is too late to
stop this alliance, Lord Hastur, and anyway I don't think.
Beltran has anything to do with the Sharra people—not now.
I think he's had his lesson about that! Don't you think so,
Marius?"

Regis saw Lew start and stare in dismay at Marius, and
wondered if Lew had not known about the ties between his
brother and Rafe Scott—ties that probably meant with the
Aldarans too. Well, they were Marius's kinsmen, his mother's
people. *We made a great mistake,* he thought drearily, *we
should have kept Marius allied to us in bonds of friendship,
kin-ties. We cast him out; where could he turn, save to the
Terrans, or Aldarans, or both? And now it seems we must
deal with him as Heir to Alton.* It seemed fairly obvious that

Lew was in no shape to take upon himself the rulership of the Alton Domain, even if the Council could be brought to accept him there.

There was once a laran *which could foretell the future,* Regis thought, *and it was among the Hasturs. Would that I had some of that gift!*

He had missed what Marius had said, but his grandfather looked distressed. Then he said, "There can be no question of alliance with Aldaran until we know something of this—" he hesitated and Regis saw the old man's lip curl in fastidious distaste—"this—reappearance of Sharra."

"But that's what I am trying to tell you," said Derik in exasperation. "We have sent the message to Beltran, and he will be here on Festival Night!" And, as he read the anger and dismay in old Hastur's face, Derik added, defensive, petulant, like a small boy who has been caught at some mischief, "Well, I am Lord of Elhalyn! It was my right—wasn't it?"

Danvan Hastur took the cup of warmed spiced wine that his body-servant had set in his hand, and propped his feet up on a carven footstool. Around him the servants were moving quietly, lighting lamps. Night had fallen; the same night after which he had had no choice but to dismiss the Council.

"I should send a message to see how Lew does," Regis said, "or go and greet him. Kennard was my friend and foster-father; Lew and I were *bredin*."

Hastur said with asperity, "You could surely find yourself a less dangerous friend in these days. That alliance won't do you any good."

Regis said angrily, "I don't choose my friends for their political expediency, sir!"

Hastur shrugged that away. "You're still young enough for the luxury of friendships. I remained convinced that Kennard was a good friend—perhaps for too long." As Regis stirred, he said, "No, wait. I need you here. I have sent for Gabriel and Javanne. The question before us is this: what are we going to do about Derik?" As Regis looked blank he said impatiently, "Surely you don't still think we can have him crowned! The boy's not much better than a halfwit!"

Regis shrugged. "I don't see what choice you have, Grandfather. It's worse than if he were a halfwit; then everyone would agree that he can't be crowned. The trouble is that Derik has nine-tenths of his wits, and he's missing only the most important tenth." He smiled, but knew there was no mirth in the joke.

But Danvan Hastur did not smile, he said, "In some lesser walk of life—even as the ordinary Head of a Domain—it wouldn't be so important; he's going to marry Linnell Lindir-Aillard, and she's no fool. Derik loves her, he's grown up with the knowledge that the Aillard women are the Heads of Council in their own right, and he would let himself be guided by her. I remember when my father married off one of the less stable Ardais to an Aillard woman; Lady Rohana was the real head of that clan well into Dyan's time. But—to wear the crown of the Hasturs of Elhalyn—" he shook his head slowly, "and in the days that are coming now? No, I can't risk it."

"I don't know that you have the power to risk it or not risk it, sir," Regis pointed out. "If you had faced the fact, years ago, that Derik would never be fit for his crown, perhaps when he was twelve or fifteen, and instead had him put under Guardianship and had him set aside—who is the next Heir to Elhalyn?"

Danvan Hastur scowled, lines running down sharply from his jaw to his chin. "I can't believe you are *that* naïve, Regis."

"I don't know what you mean, Grandfather."

Danvan Hastur sighed and said heavily, as if he were explaining a thing to a child with the use of colored pictures, "Your mother, Regis, was King Stephen's sister. His only sister." Just in case Regis might have missed the implications of *that*, he added baldly, "You are nearest to the crown—even before the sons of Derik's sisters. The oldest of those sons is three years old. There is also an infant at the breast."

"Aldones! Lord of Light!" Regis muttered, and the imprecation was nevertheless a prayer. Words he had said, joking, to Danilo years before, came back to him now. *"If you love me, Dani, don't wish a crown upon me!"*

"If I had had him set aside," his grandfather said, "who would have believed that I was not simply trying to consolidate power in my own hands? Not that it would have been such a bad thing, in these days—but it would have lost me the popular support that I needed to keep order in a crownless realm. I delayed, hoping it would become clear to everyone that Derik was really unfit."

"And now," said Regis, "everyone will think that you are

trying to depose Derik the first time he makes a decision contrary to yours."

"The trouble is," his grandfather said, and he sounded despondent, "this proposed alliance with Aldaran might not be such a bad idea, if we could be absolutely certain that the Aldarans are once and for all out of the Terran camp. What happened during that Sharra business seemed to have broken off the closeness between Terrans and Aldaran. If we could get the Aldarans firmly on our side—" he considered for a moment.

"Grandfather, do you honestly think that the Terrans are going to pack up their spaceport and go away?"

The old man shook his head. "I want us to turn our backs on them completely. I think my father made a very great mistake when he allowed Kennard to be educated on Terra, and I think I compounded that mistake when I recognized Lew for Council. No, of course the Terran Empire won't go away. But the Terrans might have respected us, if we hadn't kept looking over the wall. We should never have let the Ridenow go offworld. We should have said to the Terrans, 'Build your spaceport if you must, but in return for that, let us alone. Leave us with our own way of life, and go about your business without involving us.'"

Regis shook his head. "It wouldn't have worked. You can't ignore a fact, and the Terran Empire is a fact. It's *there*. Sooner or later it's going to affect us one way or the other, no matter how strictly we try to pretend it doesn't exist. And you can't ignore the fact that we are Terran colonists, or that we were once—"

"What we were once doesn't matter," Danvan Hastur said. "Chickens can't go back into eggs."

"The very point I'm trying to make, sir. We were cut off from our roots, and we found a way of life which meant we accepted ourselves as belonging to this world, compelled to live within its restrictions. That worked while we were still isolated, but once we had come back into contact with a—" he stopped, and considered—"with an empire which spans the stars, and takes world-hopping for granted, we can't pretend to continue as we were."

"I don't see why not," Hastur said. "The Terrans have nothing that we want."

"Nothing *you* want, perhaps, sir." Regis made a point of not staring markedly at the silver coffee service on his grand-

father's table, but the old man saw his look anyhow and said,
"I am willing to do without any Terran luxuries, if it will
encourage the rest of our people to do likewise."

"Once again, sir, won't work. We had to turn to the Terrans
during the last epidemic of Trailmen's fever. There's some
evidence the climate's changing, too, and we need some tech-
nological help there. People will die if they don't see an alternative, but if we let them die when Terran medicine can
help them, are we anything but tyrants? Sir, one thing no
one can control is *knowledge*. We can use it or misuse it—
like *laran*," he added grimly, remembering that his own laran
had brought him such unendurable self-knowledge that, at
one time, he would willingly have had it burned forever from
his brain. "But we can't pretend it's never happened, or that
it's our destiny to stay on this one world as if it was all there
would ever be in the universe."

"Are you trying to say that we must inevitably become
part of the Terran Empire?" his grandfather asked, scowling
so furiously that Regis wished he had never started this.

"I am saying, sir, that whether we join into it or not, the
Terran Empire is now a fact of our existence, and whatever
decisions we make, must be made in the full knowledge that
the Terrans are *there*. If we had refused them permission to
build their spaceport, at first, they might—I say they *might*,
not that they *would*—have turned their backs, gone away
and built it somewhere else. I doubt it. Most likely they would
have used just enough force to stop our open rebellion against
it, and built it anyhow. We could have tried to resist—and
perhaps, if we still had the weapons of the Ages of Chaos, we
might have been able to drive them away. But not without
destroying ourselves in the process. You remember what happened in a single night when Beltran turned *Sharra* against
them—" He stopped, shivering. "That is not the worst of the
Ages of Chaos weapons, but I pray I will never see a worse
one. And we do not, now, have the technology of the Ages of
Chaos, so that those weapons, are uncontrollable. And even
you, sir, don't think we can drive away the Terrans with the
swords of the Guardsmen—not even with every swordsman
on Darkover under arms."

His grandfather sat silent, head on hands, for so long that
Regis wondered if he had said the unforgivable, if the next
thing Danvan Hastur did would be to disown and disinherit
him as a traitor.

But everything I said was true, and he is honest enough to know it.

"That's right," said Danvan Hastur, and Regis was, guiltily, startled; he had grown used to the knowledge that his grandfather was only the most minimal of telepaths, and never used mindspeech if he could possibly help it; so little, in fact, that sometimes he forgot there was any *laran* they shared.

"I should be as witless as Derik if I tried to pretend that Darkover alone could stand out against anything the size of the Terran Empire. But I absolutely refuse to let Darkover become a Terran colony, and nothing more. If we can't retain our integrity in the face of Terran culture and technology, perhaps we don't deserve to survive at all."

"It's not that bad," Regis pointed out. "That's one reason Kennard was educated on Terra in the first place—to point out that our way of life is viable, even for us, and that we don't need the worst of their technology—that we needn't adopt it, for instance, to the level where our own ecology suffers. We can't support the kind of technology they have on some of the city worlds, for instance; we're metal-poor, and even too-intensive agriculture would strip our topsoil and forests within two generations. I was brought up with that fact and so were you. The Terrans know it, too. They have laws against world-wrecking, and they're not going to give us anything we don't demand. But with all respect, Grandfather, I think we've gone too far in the other direction and we're insisting that we keep our people in a state—" he groped for words—"a state of barbarism, a feudal state where we maintain hold over people's very minds."

"They don't know what's good for them," Hastur said despairingly. "Look at the Ridenow! Spending half their time on places like Vainwal—deserting our people when they most need responsible leadership! As for the common people, they look at the luxuries Terran citizenship would give them—they think—and forget the price that would have to be paid."

"Maybe I trust people more than you do, sir. I think that if we gave them more education, more knowledge—maybe they'd know what they were fighting and know why you were refusing it."

"I've lived longer than you have," pointed out the old man dryly, "long enough to know that most people want what's going to give them the most profit and the least effort, and they *won't* think about the long-range consequences."

"That's not always true," said Regis. "Look at the Compact."

Hastur said, "That was forced on the people by one singleminded fanatic, when they were already frightened and exhausted by a series of suicidal wars. And it was kept only because the keepers of those old weapons destroyed them before they could be used again, and took the knowledge to their graves. Look how it's been kept!" His lip curled. "Every now and then someone digs up an old weapon and uses it—or so they say—in self-defense. You're not old enough to remember the time when the catmen darkened all the lands of the Kilghard Hills, or when some of the forge-folk—I suppose—raised Sharra against some bandits a couple of generations ago. If the weapons are *there*, people are going to use them, and to hell with the long-range consequences! Your own father was blown to pieces by smuggled contraband weapons from the Terran Zone. So much for the strength of our way of life against the Terrans!"

"I still think that could have been avoided if people had been dully warned against the consequences," Regis said, "but I'm not saying we must become a Terran colony. Even the Terrans aren't demanding that."

"How do you know what they want?"

"I've talked with some of them, sir. I know you don't really approve, but I feel it's better to know what they're doing—"

"And as a result," said his grandfather coldly, "you stand here and defend them to me."

Regis fought back a surge of exasperation. He said at last, "We were speaking of Derik, Grandfather. If he can't be crowned, what's the alternative? Why can't we just marry him to Linnell and rely on her to keep him within bounds?"

"Linnell's too good for him," Danvan Hastur said, "and I hate to see him come any further under the influence of Merryl. I don't trust that man."

"Merryl's a fool and a hothead," said Regis, "and dangerously undisciplined. But I imagine Lady Callina can help there—if you don't tie her hands by letting Merryl marry her off. I don't, and won't, trust the Aldarans. Not with Sharra loose again."

"I cannot go directly against the heir to the Throne, Regis.

If I cause him to lose *kihar*—" deliberately, Danvan Hastur used the untranslatable Dry-Town word meaning personal integrity, honor, dignity—less and more than any of these, "before the Council. How can he ever rule over them after that?"

"He can't anyway, Grandfather. Will you let him marry off Callina to save his face before Council? If you have to crown him—and I think perhaps you do—you must let him know *before* he's crowned that the Council can always veto his decisions, or you'll have him playing the tyrant over us in all kinds of foolish ways. Callina Lindir is Head of a Domain in her own right, and has been Keeper of Neskaya and Arilinn, and now here under Ashara. What about *Callina's* loss of *kihar?*"

His grandfather scowled; Regis knew, though it was not—quite—telepathy, that Hastur was reluctant to allow Callina also that much Council power.

Not unless he's sure she'll support him and his isolationist notions. Otherwise he'll marry her off just to get her out of the Council!

"I don't suppose you'd be willing to marry her yourself?"

"Callina?" he asked in horror, "She must be twenty-seven!"

"Hardly senile," said the old man dryly, "but I was speaking of Linnell. She's too good for that fool Derik."

Evanda's mercy, is the old man harping on that string again? "Sir, Derik and Linnell have been sweethearts since Linnie's hair was too short to braid! And you've encouraged it. She's the only woman Derik would, perhaps, consent to be ruled by. You'd break both their hearts! Why separate them now?"

"I'd like to be firmly allied to the Aillards—"

"We're that already, sir, with Linnell handfasted to Derik. But we won't be if you alienate them by losing face for Callina by marrying her off against her will—and to Aldaran," Regis said. "And you're forgetting the most important thing, Grandfather."

"What's that?" The old man snorted, getting up and pacing the room restlessly. "All this business about Sharra?"

"Don't you see what's happening, Grandfather? Derik did this behind our backs, and Beltran will be here on Festival Night. Which means he's already on the road, unless he's patched things up enough with the Terrans to get an aircraft or two, and it's not very easy to fly through the Hellers." He remembered someone telling him that they had been, profanely, dubbed worse things than that by the only Terrans to try to fly over them in anything slower and lower than a rocketplane; they were a nightmare of updrafts, down-drafts and wild thermal patterns. "So when he gets here, what do you say? *Please, Lord Aldaran, turn around and go home again, we've changed our minds!*"

Old Hastur grimaced. "Wars have been fought for a lot less than that on Darkover."

"And the Aldarans haven't always observed the Compact that well," Regis pointed out. "Either we have to let him marry Callina—or we have to insult Beltran by saying, maybe in public, 'Sorry, Lord Aldaran, the woman won't have you,' or by telling him that our Prince and Ruler is a ninny who can't be entrusted even with the making of a marriage for his paxman! Either way, Beltran will have a grievance! Grandfather, I find it hard to believe you couldn't have foreseen this day!"

Hastur came and dropped in his carved and gilded presence-chair. He said, "I knew Derik couldn't be trusted to make any important decision. I said again and again that I didn't like him going about with Merryl! But could I have foreseen that Merryl would have the insolence to speak for the head of his Domain—or that Aldaran would listen?"

"If you had faced the fact that Derik was witless—well, not witless, not a ninny who should be in leading-strings with a he-governess to look after him, but certainly without the practical judgment of a boy of ten, let alone the presumptive Heir to the Throne—" Regis began, then sighed. He said, "Sir, done is done. There's no point in arguing what we should have done. The question now is, how do we get out of this without a war?"

"I don't suppose Callina would consent to marry him, just to go through the ceremony as a formality—" Hastur began, but broke off as his servant entered and stood near the door.

"Yes?"

"*Domna* Javanne Lanart-Hastur and her consort, Dom Gabriel."

Regis went to kiss his sister's hand and draw her into the room. Javanne Hastur was a tall, handsome woman, well into her thirties now, with the strong Hastur features. She glanced at both of them and said, "Have you been quarreling with

Grandfather again, Regis?" She spoke as if reproving him for climbing trees and tearing his best holiday breeches.

"Not quarreling," he said lightly. "Simply exchanging views on the political situation."

Gabriel Lanart grimaced and said, "That's bad enough."

"And I was reminding my grandson and Heir," said Danvan Hastur sharply, "that he is old to be unmarried, and suggesting that we might even marry him to Linnell Aillard-Lindir, if that will convince him to settle down. In Evanda's name, Regis, what are you waiting for?"

Regis tried to control the anger surging up in him and said, "I am waiting, sir, to meet a woman with whom I can contemplate spending the rest of my life. I'm not refusing to marry—"

"I should hope not," his grandfather snorted. "It's—undignified for a man your age, to be still unmarried. I don't say a word against the Syrtis youngster; he's a good man, a suitable companion for you. But in the times that are coming, one of the things we don't need is for anyone to name the Heir to Hastur in contempt as a lover of men!"

Regis said evenly, "And if I *am,* sir?"

His grandfather was denying too many unpalatable facts this evening. Now let him chew on this one. Javanne looked shocked and dismayed. Granted, it was not the right thing to say before one's sister, but after all, Regis defended himself angrily, his grandfather knew perfectly well what the situation was.

Danvan Hastur said, "Nonsense! You're young, that's all. But if you're old enough to have such pronounced views, and if I'm supposed to take them seriously, then you ought to be willing to convince me you're mature enough to be worth hearing. I want you married, Regis, before this year is out."

Then you will be in want for a long time, Grandfather, Regis thought, but he did not say it aloud. Javanne frowned, and he knew that she, who had somewhat more telepathic sensitivity than his grandfather, had followed the thought. She said, "Even Dyan Ardais has provided his Domain with an Heir, Regis."

"Why, so have I," said Regis. "Your own son, Javanne. Would it not please you if he were Hastur-lord after me? And I have other sons by other women, even though they are *nedestro.* I am perfectly capable of—and willing—to father sons for the Domain. But I do not want a marriage which will simply be a hoax, a sham, to please the Council. When I meet a woman I wish to marry, I wish to be free to marry her." And as he spoke, it seemed to him that he walked side by side with someone, and the overpowering emotion that surged up in him was like nothing he had ever felt, except in the first sudden outpouring of love and gratitude when Danilo had awakened his *laran* and he had allowed himself to accept it, and himself. But although he knew there was a woman by his side, he could not see her face.

"You are a romantic fool," said Javanne. "Marriage is not like that." But she smiled and he saw the kindly look she gave Gabriel. Javanne was fortunate; she was well content in her marriage.

"When I find a woman who suits me as well as Gabriel suits you, sister, then I will marry her," he said, and tried to keep his voice light. "And that I pledge to you. But I have not found such a woman yet, and I am not willing to marry just because it would please the Council, or you, or grandfather."

"I don't like hearing it said," Javanne said, frowning, "that the Heir to Hastur is a lover of men. And if you do not marry soon, Regis, it will be said, and there will be scandal."

"If it is said, it will be said and there's an end to it," Regis said, in exasperation. "I will not live my life in fear of Council tongues! There are many things that would trouble me more than Council's speculation on my love life—which, after all, is none of their affair! I thought we came here to discuss Derik, and the other troubles we had in Council! And to have dinner—and I've seen no sign of food or drink! Are we to stand about wrangling over my personal affairs while the servants try to keep dinner hot, afraid to interrupt us while we are quarreling about when to hold my wedding?"

He was ready to storm out of the apartments, and his grandfather knew it. Danvan Hastur said, "Will you ask the servants to set dinner, Javanne?" As she went to do it, he beckoned a man to take Gabriel's cloak. "You could have brought your son, Gabriel."

Gabriel smiled and said, "He has guard duty this night, sir."

Hastur nodded. "How does he do in the cadets, then? And Rafael, he's in the first year, isn't he?"

Gabriel grinned and said, "I'm trying hard not to notice Rafael, kinsman. He's probably having the same trouble any

lad of rank does in the cadets—young Gabe last year, or
Regis, or Lew Alton—I still remember having to give Lew
some extra skills in wrestling. They really had it in for him,
they made his life miserable! I suppose Kennard himself had
the same trouble when he was a first-year cadet. I didn't, but
I was out of the direct line of Comyn succession." He sighed
and said, "Too bad about Kennard. We'll miss him. I'll go on
commanding the Guardsmen until Lew is able to make decisions—he's really ill, and this business of Sharra hasn't
helped. But when he recovers—"

"You certainly don't think Lew's fit to rule the Alton Domain, do you?" Hastur asked, shocked. "You saw it as well
as I did! The boy's a wreck!"

"Hardly a boy," Regis said. "Lew is six years older than
I, which means he is halfway through his twenties. It's only
fair to wait until he's recovered from the loss of his father,
and from the journey from Vainwal. Kennard told me, once,
that most long passages have to be made under heavy se-
dation. But when he recovers from that—"

Hastur opened his mouth to speak, but before he could say
anything, Javanne said, "Dinner is on the table. Shall we go
in?" and took her husband's arm. Regis followed, with his
grandfather. Dinner had been laid on a small table in the
next room, with elegant cloths and the finest dishes and gob-
lets; Javanne, at her grandfather's nod, signaled for service
and poured wine. But Gabriel said, as he spread his napkin
on his knees, "Lew's sound enough, I think."

"He has only one hand; can he command the Guards as
a cripple?"

"Precedent enough for that too," said Gabriel. "Two or
three generations ago, Dom Esteban—who was my great-
grandfather and Lew's too, I think—commanded the Guards
for ten years from a wheelchair after he lost the use of his
legs in the Catmen's War. For that matter, there was Lady
Bruna, who took up her sword and made a notable commander, once, when the Heir was but a babe—" he shrugged.
"Lew can dress himself and look after himself one-handed—
I saw him. As for the rest—well, he was a damned good
officer once. And if he wants me to go on commanding the
Guards—well, he's the head of my Domain, and I'll do what
he says. And the boys coming up—and there's Marius. He
hasn't had military training, but he's perfectly well-edu-
cated."

"Terran education," Hastur said dryly.

Regis said, "Knowledge is knowledge, Grandfather." He remembered what he had been thinking in Council, that it made more sense to have Mikhail, perhaps, instructed under the Terrans than to shove him into the cadets for military discipline and training in swordplay. "Marius is intelligent—"

"And has some unfortunate Terran friends," said Javanne scornfully. "If he hadn't involved himself with the Terrans, he wouldn't have brought out all that business about Sharra today at Council!"

"And then we wouldn't know what was going on," said Regis. "When a wolf is loose in the pastures, do we care if the herdsman loses a night's sleep? And whose fault is it that Marius was not given cadet training? I'm sure he would have done as well there as I did. We chose to turn him over to the Terrans, and now, I'm afraid, we have to live with what we have made of him. We made certain that one Domain, at least, would remain allied to the Terrans!"

"The Altons have always been too ready to deal with the Terrans," said Hastur. "Ever since the days when Andrew Carr married into that Domain—"

"Done is done," Gabriel said, "there's no need to hash it over now, sir. I didn't see any signs that Lew was so happy among the Terrans that he can't rule the Altons well—"

"You're acting as if he were going to be Head of the Domain," said Hastur.

Gabriel laid down his spoon, letting the soup roll out on the tablecloth. "Now look here, Grandfather. It's one thing for me to claim the Domain when we had no notion whether Lew was alive or dead. But Council accepted him as Kennard's Heir, and that's all there is to it. It's up to him, as head of the Domain, to say what's to be done about Marius, but I suppose he'll name him Heir. If it were Jeff Kerwin I might challenge—he doesn't want the Domain, he wasn't brought up to it—"

"A Terran?" asked Javanne in amazement.

"Jeff isn't a Terran. I ought to say, *Dom* Damon—he has no Terran blood at all. His father was Kennard's older brother. He was fostered on Terra and brought up to think he was Terran, and he bears his Terran foster-father's name, that's all," Gabriel explained, patiently, not for the first time. "He has less Terran blood than I do. My father was Domenic

Ridenow-Lanart, but it was common knowledge that he was fathered by Andrew Carr. Twin sisters married Andrew Carr and Damon Ridenow—"

Danvan Hastur frowned. "That was a long time ago."

"Funny, how a generation or two wipes out the scandal," said Gabriel with a grin. "I thought that had all been hashed over, back when they tested Lew for the Alton Gift. He had it, I didn't, and that was that."

Danvan Hastur said quietly "I want you at the head of the Alton Domain, Gabriel. It is your duty to the Hastur clan."

Gabriel picked up his spoon, frowned, rubbed it briefly on the napkin and thrust it back into his soup. He took a mouthful or two before he said, "I did my duty to the Hastur clan when I gave them two—no, three—sons, sir, and one of them to be Regis's Heir. But I swore loyalty to Kennard, too. Do you honestly think I'm going to fight my cousin for his rightful place as Alton Heir?"

But that, Regis thought, watching the old man's face, *is exactly what Danvan Hastur does think. Or did.*

"The Altons are allied to Terra," he said. "They've made no secret of it. Kennard, now Lew, and even Marius, have Terran education. The only way we can keep the Alton Domain on the Darkovan side is to have a strong Hastur man in command, Gabriel. Challenge him again before the Council; I don't even think he wants to fight for it."

"Lord of Light, sir! Do you honestly think—" Gabriel broke off. He said, "I can't do it, Lord Hastur, and I won't."

"Do you want a half-Terran pawn of Sharra at the head of the Alton Domain?" Javanne demanded, staring at her husband.

"That's for him to say," said Gabriel steadily. "I took oath to obey any lawful command you gave me, Lord Hastur, but it isn't a lawful command when you bid me challenge the rightful Head of my Domain. If you'll pardon my saying so, sir, that's a long way from being a lawful command."

Old Hastur said impatiently "The important thing at this time is that the Domains should stand fast. Lew's unfit—"

"If he's unfit, sir—" and Gabriel looked troubled—"it'll be apparent soon enough."

Javanne said shrilly, "I thought they had deposed him as Kennard's successor after the Sharra rebellion. And now both he and his brother are still tied up with Sharra—"

Regis said, "And so am I, sister; or weren't you listening?"

She raised her eyes to him and said, disbelieving, "You?"

Regis reached, with hesitant fingers, for his matrix; fumbled at taking it from its silk wrapping. He remembered that Javanne had, years ago, taught him to use it, and she remembered too, for she raised her angry eyes and suddenly softened, and smiled at him. There was the old image in her mind, *as if the girl she had been—herself motherless, trying to mother her motherless baby brother—had bent over him as she had so often done when he was small, swung him up into her arms*—For a moment the hard-faced woman, the mother of grown sons, was gone, and she was the gentle and loving sister he had once known.

Regis said softly, "I am sorry, *breda*, but things don't go away because you are afraid of them. I didn't want you to have to see this." He sighed and let the blue crystal fall into his cupped hand.

Raging, flaming in his mind, the form of fire...a great tossing shape, a woman, tall, bathed in flame, her hair rising like restless fires, her arms shackled in golden chains...Sharra!

When he had seen it six years ago at the height of the Sharra rebellion, his *laran* had been newly waked; he had been, moreover, half dead with threshold sickness, and Sharra had been only another of the horrors of that time. When he had seen it briefly in Marius's house, he had been too shocked to notice. Now something cold took him by the throat; his flesh crawled on his bones, every hair on his body rose slowly upright, beginning with his forearms, slowly moving over all his body. Regis knew, without knowing how he knew, that he looked upon a very ancient enemy of his race and his caste, and something in his body, cell-deep, bone-deep, knew and recognized it. Nausea crawled through his body and he felt the sour taste of terror in his mouth.

Confused, he thought, *but Sharra was used and chained by the forge-folk, surely I am simply remembering the destruction of Sharra loosed, a city rising in flame...it is no worse than a forest fire*—but he knew this was something worse, something he could not understand, something that fought to draw him into itself....*recognition, fear, a fascination almost sexual in its import...*

"Aaahh—" It was a half-drawn breath of horror; he heard, saw, *felt* Javanne's mind, her terror reaching out, entangled. She clutched at the matrix under her own dress as if it had burned her, and Regis, with a mighty effort, wrenched his mind and his eyes from the Form of Fire blazing from his matrix. But Javanne clung, in terror and fascination....

And something in Regis, long dormant, unguessed, seemed to uncoil within him; as a skilled swordsman takes the hilt in his hand, without knowing what moves he will make, or which strokes he will answer, knowing only that he can match his opponent, he felt that strangeness rise, take over what he did next. He *reached out* into the depths of the fire, and delicately picked Javanne's mind loose, focusing so tightly that he did not even touch the Form of Fire... as if she were a puppet, and the strings had been cut, she slumped back fainting in her chair, and Gabriel caught her scowling.

"What did you do?" he demanded, "What have you done to her?"

Javanne, half-conscious, was blinking. Regis, with careful deliberation, wrapped up his matrix. He said, "It is dangerous to you too, Javanne. Don't come near it again."

Danvan Hastur had been staring, bewildered, as his grandson and granddaughter stared in terror, paralyzed, then, as they withdrew. Regis remembered, wearily, that his grandfather had little *laran*. Regis himself did not understand what he had done, only knew he was shaking down deep in the bones, exhausted, as weary as if he had been on the fire-lines for three days and three nights. Without knowing he was doing it, he reached for a plateful of hot rolls, smeared honey thickly on one and gobbled it down, feeling the sugar restoring him.

"It was Sharra," Javanne said in a whisper. "But what did you do?"

And Regis could only mumble, shocked, "I haven't the faintest idea."

Lew Alton's narrative

CHAPTER FOUR

I've never been sure how I got out of the Crystal Chamber. I have the impression that Jeff half-carried me, when the Council broke up in discord, but the next thing I remember clearly, I was in the open air, and Marius was with me, and Jeff. I pulled myself upright.

"Where are we going?"

"Home," said Marius, "The Alton town-house; I didn't think you'd care for the Alton apartments, and I've never been there—not since Father left. I've been living here with Andres and a housekeeper or two."

I couldn't remember that I'd been to the town house since I was a very young child. It was growing dark; thin cold rain stung my face, clearing my mind, but fragments of isolated thought jangled and clamored from the passersby, and the old insistent beat:

...*last command....return, fight for your brother's rights*...Would I never be free of that? Impatiently I struggled to get control as we came across the open square; but I seemed to see it, not as it was, dark and quiet, with a single light somewhere at the back, a servant's night-light; but I saw it through someone else's eyes, alive with light and warmth spilling down from open doors and brilliant windows, companionship and love and past happiness...I realized from Jeff's arm around my shoulders that he was seeing it as it had been, and moved away. I remembered that he had been married, and that his wife had died long since. He, too, had lost a loved one....

But Marius was up the steps, calling out in excitement as if he were younger than I remembered him.

"Andres! Andres!" and a moment later the old *coridom* from Armida, friend, tutor, foster-father, was staring at me in astonishment and welcome.

"Young Lew! I—" he stopped, in shock and sorrow, as he

148

saw my scarred face, the missing hand. He swallowed, then
said gruffly, "I'm glad you're here." He came and took my
cloak, managing to give my shoulder an awkward pat of affection and grief. I suppose Marius had sent word about
father; mercifully, he asked no questions, just said "I've told
the housekeeper to get a room ready for you. You too, sir?"
he asked Jeff, who shook his head.

"Thank you, but I am expected elsewhere—I am here as
Lord Ardais's guest, and I don't think Lew is in any shape
for any long family conferences tonight." He turned to me
and said, "Do you mind?" and held his hand lightly over my
forehead in the monitor's touch, the fingers at least three
inches away, running his hand down over my head, all along
my body. The touch was so familiar, so reminiscent of the
years at Arilinn—the only place I could remember where I
had been wholly happy, wholly at peace—that I felt my eyes
fill with tears.

*That was all I wanted—to go back to Arilinn. And it was
forever too late for that. With the hells in my brain that would
not bear looking into, with the matrix tainted by Sharra . . . no,
they would not have me in a Tower now.*

Jeff's hand was solid under my arm; he shoved me down
in a seat. Through the remnant of the drugs which had destroyed my control, I felt his solicitude, Andres's shock at my
condition, and turned to face them, clenching my hand, aware
of phantom pain as by reflex I tried to clench the missing
hand too; wanting to scream out at them in rage, and realizing
that they were all troubled for me, worrying about me, sharing my pain and distress.

"Keep still, let me finish monitoring you." When he finished Jeff said, "Nothing wrong, physically, except fatigue
and drug hangover from that damned stuff the Terrans gave
him. I don't suppose you have any of the standard antidotes,
Andres?" At the old man's headshake he said dryly, "No, I
don't suppose they're the sort of thing that one can buy in an
apothecary shop or an herb-seller's stall. But you need sleep,
Lew. I don't suppose there's any *raivannin* in the house—"

Raivannin is one of the drugs developed for work among
Tower circles, linked in the mind of a telepathic circle. . . . There
are others: *Kirian,* which lowers the resistance to telepathic
contact, is perhaps the most common. *Raivannin* has an action almost the opposite of that of Kirian. It tends to shut
down the telepathic functions. They'd given it to me, in Ar-

ilinn, to quiet, a little, the torture and horror which I was
broadcasting after Marjorie's death...quiet it enough so that
the rest of the Tower circle need not share every moment of
agony. Usually it was given to someone at the point of death
or dissolution, or to the insane, so that they would not draw
everyone else into their inner torment....

"No," Jeff said compassionately. "That's not what I mean.
I think it would help you get a night's sleep, that's all. I
wonder—There are licensed matrix mechanics in the City,
and they know who I am; First in Arilinn. I will have no
trouble buying it."

"Tell me where to go," said a young man, coming swiftly
into the room, "and I will get it; I am known to many of them.
They know I have *laran*. Lew—" he came around and stood
directly before me. "Do you remember me?"

I focused my eyes with difficulty, saw golden-amber eyes,
strange eyes...Marjorie's eyes! Rafe Scott flinched at the
agony of that memory, but he came up and embraced me. He
said, "I'll find some *raivannin* for you. I think you need it."

'What are you doing in the city, Rafe?" He had been a child
when I had drawn him, with Marjorie, into the circle of
Sharra. Like myself, he bore the ineradicable taint, fire and
damnation....*no!* I slammed my mind shut, with an effort
that turned me white as death.

"Don't you remember? My father was a Terran, Captain
Zeb Scott. One of Aldaran's tame Terrans." He said it wryly,
with a cynical lift of his lip, too cynical for anyone so young.
He was Marius's own age. I was beyond curiosity now;
though I had heard Regis describing what he had seen,
and knew that he was Marius's friend. He didn't stay, but
went out into the rainy night, shrugging a Darkovan cloak
over his head.

Jeff sat on one side of me; Marius on the other. We didn't
talk much; I was in no shape for it. It took all my energy for
me to keep from curling up under the impact of all this.

"You never did tell me, Jeff, how you came to be in the
city."

"Dyan came to bring me," he said. "I don't want the Domain and I told him so; but he said that having an extra
claimant would confuse the issue, and stall them until Kennard could return. I don't think he was expecting you."

"I'm sure he wasn't," Marius said.

"That's all right, brother, I can live without Dyan's affec-

tion," I said. "He's never liked me..." but still I was confused
by that moment of rapport, when for a moment I had seen
him through my father's eyes...

*...dear, cherished, beloved, sworn brother...even, once or
twice, in the manner of lads, lovers...*I slammed the thought
away. In a sense the rejection was a kind of envy. Solitary
in the Comyn, I had had few *bredin,* fewer to offer such affection even in crisis. Could it be that I envied my father
that? His voice, his presence, were a clamor in my mind....

I should tell Jeff what had happened. Since Kennard had
awakened the latent Alton gift, the gift of forced rapport, by
violence when I was hardly out of childhood, he had been
there, his thoughts overpowering my own, choking me, leaving me all too little in the way of free will, till I had broken
free, and in the disaster of the Sharra rebellion, I had learned
to fear that freedom. And then, dying, his incredible strength
closing over my mind in a blast I could not resist or barricade...

*Ghost-ridden; half of my brain burnt into a dead man's
memories...*

*Was I never to be anything but a cripple, mutilated mind
and body? For very shame I could not beg Jeff for more help
than he had given me already...*

He said neutrally, "If you need help, Lew, I'm here," but
I shook my head.

"I'm all right; need sleep, that's all. Who is Keeper at
Arilinn now?"

"Miranie from Dalereuth; I don't know who her family
was—she never talks about them. Janna Lindir, who was
Keeper when you were at Arilinn, married Bard Storn-Ley-
nier, and they have two sons; but Janna put them out to
foster, and came back as Chief Monitor at Neskaya. We need
strong telepaths, Lew; I wish you could come back, but I
suppose they'll need you on the Council—"

Again I saw him flinch, slightly, at my reaction to that.
I knew the state I was in, as well as he did; every transient
emotion was broadcasting at full strength. Andres, Terran
and without any visible *laran,* still noticed Marius's distress;
he had, after all, lived with a telepath family since before I
was born. He said stolidly, "I can find a damper and put it
on, if you wish."

"That won't be—" I started to say, but Jeff said firmly,
"Good. Do that." And before long the familiar unrhythmic

pulses began to move through my mind, disrupting it. It blanked it out for the others—at least the specific content— but for me it substituted nausea for the sharper pain. I listened with half an ear to Marius telling Andres what had happened at the Council. Andres, as I had foreseen, understood at once what the important thing was.

"At least they recognized you; your right to inherit was challenged, but for once the old tyrant had to admit you existed," snorted Andres. "It's a beginning, lad."

"Do you think I give a damn—" Marius demanded. "All my life I haven't been good enough for them to spit on, and suddenly—"

"It's what your father fought for all his life," Andres said, and Jeff said quietly, "Ken would have been proud of you, Marius."

"I'll bet," said the boy scornfully. "So proud he couldn't come back even once—"

I bent my head. It was my fault, too, that Marius had had no father, no kinsman, no friend, but was left alone and neglected by the proud Comyn. I was relieved when Rafe came back, saying he had found a licensed technician in the street of the Four Shadows, and he had sold him a few ounces of *raivannin*. Jeff mixed it, and said, "How much—"

"As little as possible," I said. I had had some experience with the chemical damping-drugs, and I didn't want to be helpless, or unable to wake if I got into one of those terrible spiraling nightmares where I was trapped again in horrors beyond horrors, where demons of fire flamed and raged between worlds....

"Just enough so you won't have to sleep under the dampers," he said. To my cramping shame, I had to let him hold it to my lips, but when I had swallowed it, wincing at its biting astringency, I felt the disruptions of the telepathic damper gradually subsiding, mellowing, and slowly, gradually, it was all gone.

It felt strange to be wholly without telepathic sensitivity; strange and disquieting, like trying to hear under water or with clogged ears; painful as the awareness had been, now I felt dulled, blinded. But the pain was gone, and the clamor of my father's voice; for the first time in days, it seemed, I was free of it. It was there under the thick blankets of the drug, but I need not listen. I drew a long, luxurious breath of calm.

"You should sleep. Your room's ready," Andres said. "I'll

get you upstairs, lad—and don't bother fussing about it; I carried you up these stairs before you were breeched, and I can do it again if I have to."

I actually felt as if I could sleep, now. With another long sigh, I stood up, catching for balance.

Andres said, "They couldn't do anything about the hand, then?"

"Nothing. Too far gone." I could say it calmly now; I had, after all, before that ghastly debacle when Dio's child was born and died, learned to live with the fact. "I have a mechanical hand but I don't wear it much, unless I'm doing really heavy work, or sometimes for riding. It won't take much strain, and gets in my way. I can manage better, really, without it."

"You'll have your father's room," Andres said, not taking too much notice. "Let me give you a hand with the stairs."

"Thanks. I really don't need it." I was deathly tired, but my head was clear. We went into the hallway, but as we began to mount the stairs, the entry bell pealed and I heard one of the servants briefly disputing; then someone pushed past him, and I saw the tall, red-haired form of Lerrys Ridenow.

"Sorry to disturb you here; I looked for you in the Alton suite in Comyn Castle," he said. "I have to talk to you, Lew. I know it's late, but it's important."

Tiredly, I turned to face him. Jeff said, "Dom Lerrys, Lord Armida is ill." It took me a moment to realize he was talking about me.

"This won't take long." Lerrys was wearing Darkovan clothing now, elegant and fashionable, the colors of his Domain. In the automatic gesture of a trained telepath in the presence of someone he distrusts, I reached for contact; remembered: I was drugged with *raivannin*, at the mercy of whatever he chose to tell me. It must be like this for the headblind. Lerrys said, "I didn't know you were coming back here. You must know you're not popular."

"I can live without that," I said.

"We haven't been friends, Lew," he said. "I suppose this won't sound too genuine; but I'm sorry about your father. He was a good man, and one of the few in the Comyn with enough common sense to be able to see the Terrans without giving them horns and tails. He had lived among the Terrans long enough to know where we would eventually be going." He sighed, and I said, "You didn't come out on a rainy night to give me condolences about my father's death."

He shook his head. "No," he said, "I didn't. I wish you'd
had the sense to stay away. Then I wouldn't have to say this.
But here you are, and here I am, and I do have to say it. Stay
away from Dio or I'll break your neck."

"Did she send you to say that to me?"

"I'm saying it," Lerrys said. "This isn't Vainwal. We're in
the Domains now, and—" He broke off. I wished with all my
heart that I could read what was behind those transparent
green eyes. He looked like Dio, damn him, and the pain was
fresh in me again, that the love between us had not been
strong enough to carry us through tragedy. "Our marriage
ceremony was a Terran one. It has no force in the Domains.
No one there would recognize it." I stopped and swallowed.
I had to, before I could say, "If she wanted to come back to
me, I'd—I'd welcome it. But I'm not going to force it on her,
Lerrys, don't worry about that. Am I a Dry-towner, to chain
her to me?"

"But a time's coming when we'll all be Terrans," Lerrys
said, "and I don't want her tied to you then."

It was like struggling under water; I could not reach his
mind, his thoughts were blank to me. Zandru's hells, was this
what it was like to be without *laran,* blind, deaf, mutilated,
with nothing left but ordinary sight and hearing? "Is this
what Dio wants? Why doesn't she tell me so herself, then?"

Now there was blind rage exploding in Lerrys's face; it
needed no *laran* to see that. His face tightened, his fists
clenched; for a moment I braced myself, thinking he would
strike me, wondering how I could manage, with one hand, to
defend myself if he did.

"Damn you, can't you see that's what I want to spare her?"
he demanded, his voice rising to hysteria. "Haven't you put
her through enough? How much do you think she can stand,
you—you—you damned—" His voice failed him. After a time
he got control of it again.

"I don't want her to have to see you again, damn you. I
don't want her left with any memory of what she had to go
through!" he said, raging. "Go to the Terran HQ and dissolve
your marriage there—and if you don't, I swear to you, Lew,
I'll call challenge on you and feed your other hand to the
kyorebni!"

Through the drugs I was too dulled to feel sorrow. I said
heavily, "All right, Lerrys. If that's what Dio wants, I won't
bother her again."

He turned and slammed out of the house; Marius stood staring after him. He said, "What, in the name of all the Gods, was that all about?"

I couldn't talk about it. I said, "I'll tell you tomorrow," and, blindly, struggled up the stairs to my father's room. Andres came, but I paid no attention to him; I flung myself down on my father's bed and slept like the dead.

But I dreamed of Dio, crying and calling my name as they took her away from me in the hospital.

When I woke my head was clear; and I seemed, again, to be in possession of it alone. It had assumed the character of any family reunion; Marius came and sat on my bed and talked to me as if he were the young boy I'd known, and I gave him the gifts I'd remembered to bring from Vainwal, Terran lensed goods: binoculars, a camera.

He thanked me, but I suspected he thought them gifts for a child; he referred to them once as "toys." I wondered what would have been a proper gift for a man? Contraband blasters, perhaps, in defiance of the Compact? After all, Marius had had a Terran education. Was he one of those who considered the Compact a foolish anachronism, the childish ethic of a world stuck in barbarism? I suspected, too, that he felt little grief for our father. I didn't blame him; father had abandoned Marius a long time ago.

I told them I had business at the Terran HQ, without telling them much about it.

"You've got seven days, after all," Jeff pointed out to me after breakfast. "They deferred the formal transfer of the Domain until ritual mourning for Kennard was completed. And now it's only a formality—they accepted you as his Heir when you were fifteen."

There was the question as to whether they would accept Marius.

"Stupid bigots," Andres grumbled, "to decide a man's worth on the color of his eyes!"

Or the color of his hair; I could feel Jeff thinking that, remembering a time when, in Arilinn, most Comyn had had hair of the true Comyn red. I said, only half facetiously, "Maybe I should dye mine—and Marius's—so we'll look more like Comyn."

"I couldn't change my eyes," Marius said dryly, and I thought, with a pang, of the changeable sea-colors in Dio's

eyes. But Dio hated me now, and that was all past; and who
could blame her?

"They'll challenge me," I said. "And if they do—hell, I
can't fight them with one hand."

"Stupid anachronism in this day and age," Marius said
predictably, "to settle anything as important as the Heirship
of a Domain with a sword."

Andres—we had demanded he sit with us at table; *coridom*
or no, he had been guardian and foster-father much of our
lives—asked, with equal dryness, "Would it make more sense
to fight it out with blasters or invade each other's Domains
and fight a war over it?"

Jeff was leaning back in his chair, a half-empty cup in
front of him. "I remember hearing, in the Tower, why it was
that the formal challenge with swords was instituted. There
was a time when a formal challenge for the rulership of a
Domain was made with the Gift of that Domain—and the
one whose *laran* was the stronger won it. There was a day
when the Domains bred men and women like cattle for these
Gifts—and the Alton Gift, full strength, can kill. I doubt
Gabriel wants to try *that* kind of duel against you."

"I'm not so sure, after last night, that I could win it if he
did," I said. "I had forgotten where Comyn immunity came
from." At Arilinn, matrix mechanics and technicians in training sometimes fought mock battles with *laran*, but I had been
taught control since I was into my teens; real battles with
laran were forbidden.

*The Compact was not invented to ban blasters and firearms,
but the older* laran *weapons which were as dreadful as anything the Terran empire could produce...*

"I don't think Gabriel will challenge you," Andres said.
"But they'll ask why, at your age, you're not married, and
whether you have a legitimate child for an Heir."

I felt the scars at my mouth pull as I grimaced. "Married,
yes, but not for long; that was what Lerrys came here about,"
I said. "And no children, nor likely to have."

Marius started to ask questions; Jeff stared him down. He
knew what I was talking about. "We were afraid, at Arilinn,
that would happen, but the technique of cell-monitoring at
that level was lost sometime in the Ages of Chaos. Some of
us are working to master it again—it's quicker and safer
than some of the DNA work they do in the Empire. I don't
suppose you fathered any bastards before you went offworld?"

There had been adventures in my youth, but if I had fathered a child—I put it bluntly to myself—the girl involved would have been proud to tell me so. And Marjorie had died, her child unborn.

"They'd accept Marius if I tested him for the Alton Gift, perhaps," I said. "They might have no choice. Comyn law says there *must* be an Heir named, a succession insured. By letting Kennard take me offworld, they gave tacit consent for Marius as presumptive Heir, I'd think. The law is clear enough." I didn't want to test Marius for the Alton Gift—not by the shock tactics my father had used on me, and I knew no others. Not now. And with my matrix in the shape it was in... about all I could do would be to give a demonstration of the powers of Sharra!

It wanted me, the fires sought to call me back....

But there were other things to think about now.

"Marius should be tested before the formal challenge," I said. "You're First at Arilinn; you can do that, can't you?"

"Certainly," Jeff said. "Why not? I suspect he has some *laran*, perhaps Ridenow gift—there's Ridenow in the Alton lineage, and Ardais, too; Kennard's mother was Ardais and I always suspected he had a touch of catalyst telepathy."

Marius had been tearing a buttered roll to pieces. He said now, without looking up, "What I have, I think, is—is the Aldaran Gift. I can see—ahead. Not far, not very clearly; but the Aldaran Gift is precognition, and I—I have that."

That he would have had from our half-Terran mother. In these days the gifts were entangled anyhow, bred out by intermarriage between the Domains. But I stared at him and demanded, "How would you know about the Aldaran Gift?"

He said impatiently, "The Aldarans are all the kin I have! And hell, Lew, the Comyn weren't very eager to claim me as kin! I spent one summer with Beltran—why not?"

This was a new factor to be reckoned with.

"I know he didn't treat you well," Marius went on, defensively, "but your quarrel was a private one, after all. What do you expect, that I should declare blood-feud for three generations because of that? Are we the barbarians the Terrans call us, then?"

There was no answer to that, but I didn't know what to say.

"We could all use some information about the future," I said. "If you've got *that* Gift, for the love of Aldones tell me what's going to happen if I claim the Domain? Will they accept you as my Heir?"

"I don't know," he confessed, and once again he seemed young, vulnerable, a boy half his age. "I—I tried to find out. They told me that sometimes that happened, you couldn't see too clear for yourself or anyone close to you..."

That was true enough, and since it was true, I wondered, not for the first time, what good that Gift was to anyone. Perhaps, in the days when Aldarans could see the fate of rulers, kingdoms, even of the planet...and that was another disquieting thought. Maybe the Aldarans, with their foresight, saw that Darkover would go the way of the Terran Empire and that was why they had joined forces, for so long, with Terra. I wondered if Beltran had entirely broken with them after the Sharra rebellion.

Well, there was one way to find out, but there was no time for it now. I strode restlessly to the window, looked out across the bustle of the cobbled square. Men were leading animals to the market, workmen going about carrying tools; a quiet familiar bustle. Because of the season, there was only a light thin powdering of snow on the stones; Festival, and High Summer, were upon us. Still it seemed cold to me after Vainwal and I dressed in my warmest cloak. Let the Terrans call me *barbarian* if they liked, I was home again, I would wear the warm clothes my own world demanded. The fur lining felt good even at this season as I drew it round me. Both Marius and Jeff offered to accompany me; but this was private business and I must attend to it by myself, so I refused.

It was a bright day; the sun, huge and red—the Terrans called it Cottman's Star, but to me it was just the sun, and just the way a sun should be—hung on the horizon, coming free of layers of morning cloud, and there were two small shadows in the sky where Liriel and Kyrddis were waning. Once I could have told you what month we were in, and what tenday of which month, by the position of the moons; as well as what to plant, in season, or what animals would be rutting or dropping their young; there is a month called Horse Month because more than three-quarters of the mares will foal before it fades, and there are all kinds of jokes about Wind Month because that is when the stallions and chervines and other animals run in rut; I suppose, where people live very close to the land, they work too hard to have much time for rutting,

like the stallions, except at the proper season, and it becomes
an uneasy joke.

But all that land...knowledge was only a dim memory,
though I supposed, as I lived here longer, it would come back
to me. As I strode through the morning streets, I felt comfortable under morning light and shadowed moons, something in my brain soothed and fed by the familiar lights. I've
been on several planets, with anywhere from one to six
moons—with more than that, the tides make the place uninhabitable—and suns yellow, red and blazing blue-white;
at least I knew this one would not burn my skin red or brown!

So Marius, in addition to a Terran education, had the
Aldaran Gift. That could be a dangerous combination, and
I wondered how the Council would feel when they knew.
Would they accept him, or would they demand that I adopt
one of Gabriel's sons?

It was a fairly stiff walk from the quarter of the city where
my father and his forefathers had kept their town house, to
the gates of the Terran Zone. A high wind was blowing, and
I felt stiff. I wasn't used to this kind of walk, and for six years
I had lived on a world, Terra or Vainwal, where urgent business could be settled by mechanical communicators—anywhere in the Empire I could have settled the formalities for
the dissolution of a marriage by communicator and video-
screens—and where, if personal appearance had really been
necessary, I could have all kinds of mechanical transport at
a moment's notice. Darkover has never had much interest in
roads—it takes either machine labor, man-hours or matrix
work to build good roads, and our world has never wanted
to pay the price of any of those three. I'd spent my share of
time in a Tower, providing the kind of communication you
can get through the relays, telepathically operated; and I'd
done my share of mining, too, and chemically purifying min-
erals. I'd monitored, and trained monitors. But I knew how
hard it was to find enough talent for the matrix work, and
it was no longer required of my caste, who had *laran*, that
they spend their lives behind Tower walls, working for the
people they served.

Were we Comyn the rulers of our people, because of our
laran...or were we their slaves? And which was which? A
slave is a slave, even if, for his laran work, the people he serves
surround him in every luxury and bow to his every word. A

*protected class quickly becomes an exploited and exploiting
class. Look at women.*

The gates of the Terran HQ, stark and sombre, loomed
before me, a black-leathered spaceman at their gates. I gave
my name and the guard used his communicator; they admitted I was on legitimate business, and let me in. My father
had gone to some trouble to arrange double citizenship for
me, and the Terrans claimed that Darkover was a lost Terran
colony anyhow, which meant it was part of their policy to
grant citizens rights to anyone who went to the trouble of
applying for them. I had never troubled to vote for a representative in the Imperial Senate or Parliament, but I had a
shrewd suspicion that Lerrys always did. I don't have much
faith in parliamentary governments—they tend to pick, not
the best man, but the one who appeals to the widest mass
temperament, and, in general, majorities tend to be always
wrong—as the long history of culture and the constant return
of certain types of slavery and religious bigotry show us. I
didn't trust the Empire to make decisions for Darkover, and
why in all of Zandru's nine hells—or the four hundred known
and inhabited worlds of the Empire—should the Darkovans
have any voice in making decisions for such worlds as Vainwal? Even in small groups—such as Comyn Council—poli-
ticians are men who want to tell their fellows what to do; and
thus criminal at heart. I seldom thought about it much, and
preferred it that way. My father had tried, many times, to
point out the flaws in that reasoning, but I had better things
to do with my life than worry about politics.

Better things? Had I anything to do with my life at all? At
the back of my brain it seemed there was a familiar mutter.
I kept my thoughts resolutely away from it, knowing that if
I focused on it, it would be the clamor of my father's voice,
the nag of the Sharra matrix at my brain.... no, I wouldn't
think of it.

The marriage was a line in a computer, hardly more than
that. My occupation? When I went offworld, drugged and only
half alive after being seared in Sharra's fires, my father had
had to name his occupation and he had put both his and mine
down as *Matrix mechanic.* What a joke that was! He could
have called himself *rancher*—Armida produces about a twentieth of the horses traded in the Kilghard Hills—or, because
of his post as commander of the Guards, *soldier;* or, for that
matter, because of his Council seat, claimed equal rank with

a Senator or Parliamentarian. But, knowing the mystique the Terrans attach to our matrix technology, he had called himself, *Matrix Technician,* and me, *mechanic.* What a joke that was! I couldn't monitor a pebble from the forge-folk's cave! Not with my matrix still overshadowed by Sharra....

There were technicians and Keepers on Darkover still. Perhaps I could be freed...but later, later. The business at hand was trouble enough. Lewis-Kennard Montray-Lanart, Lord Alton, resident of Cottman Four—which is what the Empire calls Darkover—occupation, matrix mechanic, residence, Armida in the Kilghard Hills, temporary residence—I gave them the name of the street and the square of the town house. Damned if I wanted Comyn Castle brought into this! Wife's name: Diotima Ridenow-Montray. Wife's middle name. I didn't think she had any, I said. I was sure she did, and probably didn't use it; half the Ridenow of Serrais named their daughters *Cassilda,* perhaps because there was some doubt about their status as genuine descendants of Hastur and Cassilda, who probably never existed anyhow. Wife's residence. Well, she was certainly in the custody of her brother, so I gave the estate of Serrais, where the Ridenow ought to live, and I heartily wished they were all out there. Reason for dissolution of marriage?

Here I stopped, not sure what to say, and the clerk, who acted as if loves like this were disrupted a hundred times a day, and in the anthill population of the Empire they probably were, told me irritably that I must state a reason for dissolving the marriage. Well, I could hardly say that her brother threatened to murder me otherwise!

The clerk prompted: "Barrenness if you both wish for children; impotence; irreconcilable differences in life-styles; desertion..."

That would do; she had certainly deserted me.

But the clerk was yammering on.

"Allergy to the other's planet or residence; failure to support the children of the marriage; inability to father viable offspring if both wish for children..."

"That will do," I said, though I knew in principle that this, or barrenness, were seldom actually cited for divorces; usually they cited less offensive reasons by mutual consent, such as desertion or irreconcilable difference of life-styles. But Dio had asked for it, and I would state the real reason.

Slowly he put it into the computer in code; now it was on

record that I was incapable of fathering viable offspring. Well, they must have it somewhere in the records of that Terran hospital on Vainwal.... what had been born to Dio on that night of disaster. I smothered an agonized picture of Dio, smiling up at me as she talked about our son...no. It was over. She wanted to be free of me, I would not cling to a woman who had every reason to despise me.

While the clerk was finishing up the details, a communicator beeped somewhere, and he answered it, looked up.

"Mr. Montray, if you will stop at the Legate's office on your way out—"

"The Legate?" I asked, raising my eyebrows. I had seen the Terran Legate once, a stuffy functionary named Ramsay, when he attended a conference where I had been Honor Guard; I was still one of my father's officers, then. Perhaps he too wished to pay courtesy condolences after my father's death, the sort of meaningless social formality not limited to Darkover *or* to Terra. The clerk said, "That's finished, then," and I saw our marriage, and our love, reduced to meaningless lines of print, stored somewhere in a computer. The thought filled me with revulsion.

"Is that all there is to it?"

"Unless your wife contests the divorce within a tenday," said the clerk, and I smiled bitterly. She wouldn't. I had caused enough havoc in her life; I could not blame her if she wanted no more.

The clerk pointed me in the direction of the Legate's office, but when I got there, (wishing, because of the stares, that I had worn my hand) I found the Legate was not the man I remembered, but that his name was Dan Lawton.

I had known him briefly. He was actually a distant relative of mine, though closer kin to Dyan—who was, after all, my father's cousin. Lawton's story was something like mine; only reversed, Terran father, a mother who was a kinswoman of Comyn. He could have claimed a seat in Comyn Council if he had chosen; he had chosen otherwise. He was tall and lean, his hair nearer to Comyn red than my own. His greeting was friendly, not over-hearty, and he did not, to my great relief, offer to shake hands; it's a custom I despise, all the more since I had no longer a proper handshake to offer. But he didn't evade my eyes; there are not many men who can, or will, look a telepath full in the eyes.

"I heard about your father," he said. "I suppose you're sick of formal condolences; but I knew him and liked him. So you've been on Terra. Like it there?"

I said edgily, "Are you implying I should have stayed there?"

He shook his head. "Your business. You're Lord Armida now, aren't you?"

"I suppose so. It's up to Council to confirm me."

"We can use friends in Council," he said. "I don't mean spies; I mean people who understand our ways and don't automatically think all Terrans are monsters. Danvan Hastur arranged for your younger brother to be educated here at the Terran HQ; he got the same education a Senator's son would have had: politics, history, mathematics, languages— you might encourage him to go in that direction when he's old enough. I always hoped your father would apply for a place in the Imperial Senate, but I had no chance to persuade him. Maybe your brother."

"That would be one direction for Marius, if the Council won't accept him as my formal Heir," I said, temporizing. It did make more sense than putting him at the head of the Guards. Gabriel wanted *that* and would be good at it. "I'll talk to him about it."

"Before he would be eligible for Imperial Senate," he said, "he must live on at least three different planets for a year apiece, and demonstrate understanding of different cultures. It's not too soon to start arranging it. If he's interested, I'll put him in the way of a minor diplomatic post somewhere— Samarra, perhaps. Or Megaera."

I did not know if Marius was interested in politics. I said so, adding that I would ask him. It might be a viable alternative for my brother.

And I need not test him for the Alton Gift, need not risk his death at my hands...as my father had risked mine...

"Is he, too, a matrix mechanic?"

I shook my head. "I don't think so. I don't even know how much of a telepath he is."

"There are telepaths on some worlds," he said. "Not many, and this is the only culture where they're really taken for granted. But if he'd be more comfortable on a world where the population accepted telepathic and psi powers as a matter of course—"

"I'll ask him." I hoped that when I broached the subject Marius wouldn't think I was trying to get rid of him. In history, brothers were allies; in fact they had all too often been rivals. Marius ought to know how little I cared to dispute with him for the Domain! I made a move to rise. "Was there anything else?"

"As a matter of fact," Lawton said, "there was. What do you know about a man named Robert Raymon Kadarin?"

I flinched. I knew too much about the accursed traitor Kadarin, who had—once—been friend, almost brother; who had brought the Sharra matrix from its forges, given it over to me, given me these scars, forced Marjorie to the pole of Sharra's power.... *no!* I made myself stop thinking about that; my teeth clenched. "He's dead."

"We thought so too," said Lawton. "And even in the course of nature and time, he *ought* to be dead. He was on Terran Intelligence considerably before I was born—hell, before my grandfather was born, which means he's probably about a hundred, or older."

I remembered the gray eyes, colorless.... there was *chieri* blood in the Hellers, as there had been in Thyra, in Majorie herself and her unknown mother. And the mountain men with the half-human *chieri* blood were abnormally long-lived, as some of the old Hastur kings had been.

"He's dead anyway if he crosses my path," I said. "His life is mine, where, as and how I can; if I see him, I warn you, I will kill him like a dog."

"Blood-feud—?" Lawton asked, and I said, "Yes." He was one of the few Terrans who would understand. Unsettled blood-feud outweighs any other obligation, in the hills....I could, if need be, stall the formal proceedings for claiming the Alton Domain by speaking of blood-feud in the old way.

I should have killed him before....I thought he was dead. I had been offworld, forgetting my duty, my honor....I thought him dead already.... and a voice whispered in my mind, but ready to roar again, *my last command...return to Darkover, fight for your brother's rights....* the Alton Domain could not survive with the stain of unsettled blood-feud....

"What makes you think he's alive?" I asked. "And why do you ask me about him anyway? I've been offworld, in any case, even if I hadn't, he'd hardly be likely to hide himself under my cloak!"

"Nobody accused you of sheltering him," Lawton pointed out. "I understood, though, that you and he were allies during the rebellion and the Sharra troubles, when Caer Donn burned...."

I said quickly, to ward off questions, "No doubt you've heard some of the story from Beltran—"

"I haven't. I've never met the present Lord Aldaran," Lawton said, "though I saw him once. Did you know there's a very strong resemblance? You're cousins, aren't you?"

I nodded. I have seen twins who were less like than Beltran and I; and there had been a time when I had been glad of that resemblance. I said, touching the scars on my face, "We're not so much alike now."

"Still, at a quick look, anyone who knew you both might take either of you for the other," Lawton said. "Half a gram of cosmetic would cover those scars. But that's neither here nor there... what did Kadarin have to do with Beltran, and with you?"

I gave him a brief, bald, emotionless outline of the story. Spurred on by Beltran of Aldaran, when old Lord Aldaran— who was my great-uncle—lay dying, the old man who called himself Kadarin had brought the Sharra matrix from the forge-folk.

"The name Kadarin is just defiance," I said. "In the Hellers, any—bastard—is known as a 'son of the Kadarin' and he adopted it."

"He was one of our best intelligence men, before he left the Service," Lawton said, "or so the records say. I wasn't out of school then. Anyhow, there was a price on his head—he'd served on Wolf; nobody knew he'd come back to Darkover until the Sharra trouble broke out."

I fought against a memory: Kadarin, lean, wolfish, smiling, telling me of his travels in the Empire; I had listened with a boy's fascination. So had Marjorie. Marjorie.... *time slid, for a moment, I walked the streets of a city which now lay in burned ruins, hand in hand with a smiling girl with amber eyes... and we shared a dream which would bring Terran and Darkovan together as equals.*

I told the story flatly, as best I could.

"Beltran, with Kadarin, had a plan, to form a circle around one of the old, high-level matrixes; show the Terrans that we had a technology, a science, of our own. It was one of the matrixes that could power aircraft, mine metals—we thought, when we learned to handle it, we could offer it to the Empire in return for some of the Empire sciences. We formed a circle—a Tower circle, but without a Tower; a mechanic's circle—"

"I'm no expert at matrix technology," said Lawton, "but I know something about it. Go on. Just you and Kadarin and Beltran, or were there others?"

I shook my head. "Beltran's half-sister Thyra; her mother was said to be part of *chieri*, a foundling of the forest-folk. She—the *chieri* woman, I don't remember her name—also had two children by one of Lord Aldaran's Terran officers, a Captain Scott."

"I know his son," said Lawton. "Rafael Scott—do you mean to tell me he was one of you? He wouldn't have been more than nine or ten years old, would he? You'd take a *child* into a thing like that?"

"Rafe was twelve," I said, "and his *laran* was awake, or he couldn't have been one of us. You know enough about Darkover to know that if a child's old enough to function as a man—or a woman—then he's old enough, and that's all there is to it. I know you Terrans tend to keep young men and women in the playroom long after they're grown; we don't. Do we have to debate social customs now? Rafe was one of us. And so was Thyra, and so was Rafe's sister Marjorie." And then I stopped. There was no way I could talk about Marjorie; not now, with old wounds torn fresh.

"The matrix got out of control. Half of Caer Donn went up in flames. I suppose you know the story. Majorie died. I—" I shrugged, moving the stump of my arm slightly. "Rafe didn't seem much the worse when I saw him last. But I thought Kadarin, and Thyra, were both dead."

"I don't know about the woman," Lawton said. "I haven't heard. Wouldn't know her if she walked into this office. But Kadarin's alive. He was seen in Thendara, less than a tenday ago."

"If he's alive, she's alive," I said. "Kadarin would have died before letting her be hurt." Guilt clawed me again; *as I should have died before Marjorie, Marjorie*... and then I had a disquieting thought. Thyra was Aldaran as well as *chieri*. Had she foreseen the return of Sharra to Darkover... and come to Thendara, drawn by that irresistible pull, even before I knew, myself, that I would bring it back?

Were we nothing more than pawns of that damned thing?

Lawton said, "What *is* Sharra? Just a matrix—"

"It's that, certainly," I said. "A very high-level one; ninth or tenth," and I forestalled his question. "In general, a ninth-level matrix is a matrix which can only be operated or controlled by at least nine qualified telepaths of mechanic level."

"But I gather it's more—"

"Yes," I said. "It's probably—I'm not sure what it is. The forge-folk thought it was the talisman controlling a Goddess who brought fire to their forges..."

Lawton said, "I was not asking for an account of Darkovan superstitions about Sharra. I've heard the stories of the flame-hair—"

"They're not stories," I said. "You weren't there when Caer Donn burned, were you? Sharra *appeared*—and struck fire down on the ships—"

He said restlessly, "Hypnotism. Hallucination."

"But the fire was real," I said, "and believe me, the Form of Fire is real." I shut my eyes as if I could see it there, as if my matrix was keyed to the burning in that older, larger matrix—

Lawton may have had a touch of *laran;* I have never been sure. Many Terrans do, not knowing what it is or how to use it. He asked, "Do you suppose he came to Thendara because you were here—to try and recover the Sharra matrix?"

That was what I feared. Above all, that was what I feared; the matrix in the hands of Kadarin again...

and I unwilling slave to the matrix, burning, burning, sealed to the form of fire... "I would kill him before that," I said.

Lawton's eyes dwelt a moment past courtesy on my one hand. Then he said, "There is a price on his head in the Empire. And you are an Empire citizen. If you like, I will issue you a weapon, to protect yourself against a known criminal under sentence of death, and give you the legal right to execute him."

To my eternal shame, I considered it; I was afraid of Kadarin. And the ethics of the Compact—my father said it cynically once—crumble in the face of fear or personal advantage. Regis Hastur's father had died, twenty years ago, leaving the Domains to be ruled by an unborn son, because some band of rebels had accepted contraband weapons with what, I am sure, they thought were reasons important enough to overthrow their allegiance to Compact.

Then I said, with a shudder, "Forget it. I may not be much good with a sword just now, but I doubt if I can shoot well enough to make it worth the trouble. I'll fight him if I must. He'll have the Sharra matrix only over my dead body."

"Your dead body wouldn't do any of us a damned bit of good if Kadarin had the Sharra matrix," said Lawton impatiently, "and I'm not concerned at this moment with your honor or the Compact. Would you consider moving the matrix—and yourself—into the Terran Zone so that we could protect you with effective weapons?"

This was a Darkovan affair. Should I hide behind the hem of a Terran's robe, guarded by their guns and blasters, coward's weapons?

"Stubborn damned fool," Lawton said without heat. "I can't force you, but be careful, damn it, be careful, Lew." It was the first time he had called me by my name, and even through my anger, I was warmed; I needed friends, even Terran friends. And I respected this man. He said, "If you change your mind, or want a gun, or a bodyguard with a gun, tell me. We need friends in Council, remember."

I said reluctantly, "I can't promise to be your friend, Lawton."

He nodded and said, "I understand. But—" he hesitated and looked me straight in the eye, "I can promise to be yours. Remember that if you need it. And my offer stands."

I thought about that, as I went out, and down the long elevators and lifts to the ground level. Outside the wind was chilly, and the sky was covered with cloud; later it would snow. I was amazed how quickly my weather skills returned to me. Snow, at high summer! Not unprecedented. Once a summer snow had saved Armida, in a terrifying forest fire when half our buildings had gone up in the backfire. But not common, either, and perhaps an omen of ill-luck. Well, that would be no surprise.

I didn't tarry to look at the starships. I had seen enough of them. Quickly, drawing my cloak close about my shoulders against the chill, I walked through the streets. I should move as quickly as possible, back into the Alton apartments in Comyn Castle, establish possession; show that I regarded myself as legitimate head of the Alton Domain, Lord Armida. The Sharra matrix too, left alone in the town house, safeguarded only by the fact that no one knew where it was—it too would be safer in Comyn Castle. Better yet, take it to the Comyn Tower and ask my cousin Callina, who was Keeper now for the incredibly ancient keeper there, old Ashara, to put it in the Tower matrix laboratory under a matrix lock. Kadarin could break into the town house, he might even manage to break into the Castle, but I did not believe he could break into a matrix-locked laboratory in Comyn Tower, in the hands and under the wardship of a Keeper. But if he could do that, then we were all dead anyhow and it did not matter.

Having made this resolve, I felt better. It was good to breathe, not the mechanical smells of the Terran Zone, but the clean natural smells of my own part of the city; spices from a cookshop, heat from a forge where someone was shoeing a string of pack animals; a group of Renunciates, their hair cut so short it was hard to tell whether they were men or women, dressed in bulky trail clothing, readying an expedition into the hills; a shrouded and heavily veiled lady in a sedan chair in the midst of them. The clean smell of animals, fresh smells of garden plants. Thendara was a beautiful city, though I would rather have been out in the Kilghard Hills....

I could go. I owned estates that needed me. Armida was mine now...my home. But it was Council season and I was needed here....

Across a square I heard a soft call and challenge; a patrol of young Guardsmen. I looked up, and Dyan Ardais left the patrol and came striding toward me, his military cloak flying briskly behind him.

This encounter was the last thing I wanted. As a boy I had detested Dyan with a consuming hatred; older, I had wondered whether a part of my dislike might not be that he had been my father's friend, and I, bastard, lonely, friendless, had envied every attention that my father had paid to anyone else. The unhealthy closeness between my father and myself had not all been his doing, and I knew that now. In any case, Kennard was dead and, one way or another, I must free myself of his influence, the real or imagined voice in my mind.

Dyan was my kinsman, he was Comyn, and he had befriended my brother and my father. So I greeted him civilly enough, and he returned the formal greeting, Comyn to Comyn, the first time in my life that he had greeted me as an equal.

Then he dropped formality and said, "I need to talk to you, cousin." The word, a degree more intimate than "kinsman," seemed to come as hard to him as to me. I shrugged, though I wasn't pleased. The talk with Lawton had made me, even

more than before, desperately uneasy about the Sharra matrix; I wanted it put into a safe place before anyone—for
anyone read *Kadarin,* who was the only one I knew who could
get it—could know its presence on Darkover through the
reawakening of his matrix—and if that had happened to my
matrix, it would certainly have happened to his. And once
he knew the matrix was back on Darkover, what would he
do? I didn't have to ask; I knew.

"There's a tavern; will you drink with me? I need to talk
with you, cousin,"

I hesitated; I'm not that much of a drinker at any time.
"It's early for me, thank you. And I am rather in a hurry.
Can it wait?"

"I'd rather not," said Dyan. "But I'll walk with you, if you
like." Too late I realized: it had been meant as a friendly
gesture. I shrugged. "As you like. I don't know this end of
the city so well."

The tavern was clean enough, and not too dark, though
my spine prickled a little as I went into the unlighted room,
Dyan behind me. He evidently knew the place, because the
potboy brought him a drink without asking. He poured some
for me; I put out my hand to stop him.

"Only a little, thanks." It was more a ritual than anything
else; we drank together, and at the back of my mind I thought,
if my father knew, he would have been pleased to see me
drinking in all amiability with his oldest friend. Well, I could
do that much homage to his memory. He caught my eye and
I knew he shared the thought; we drank silently to my father's
peace.

"We'll miss him in Council," Dyan said. "He knew all the
Terran ways and wasn't seduced by them. I wonder—" and
his eyes dwelt on me a moment past courtesy, looking at the
scar, the folded sleeve. But I was enough used to that. I said,
"I'm not exactly enthralled by the Terran—more strictly, by
the Empire ways. Terra itself—" I shrugged. "I suppose it's
a beautiful world, if you can stand living under a yellow sun
and having the colors all wrong. There's a certain—status—
in being of old Terran stock, or living there, but I didn't like
it. As for the Empire—"

"You lived on Vainwal a long time," he said, "and you're
not a decadent like Lerrys, bound on pleasure and—exotic
entertainment."

It was half a question. I said, "I can live without Empire

luxuries. Father found the climate good for his health. I—"
I broke off, wondering just why I had stayed. Inertia, deadly
lassitude, one place no worse than another to me, until I met
Dio, and then any place as good as another, as long as she
was with me. If Dio had asked me, would I have come back
to Darkover? Probably, if the subject had been broached before it became impossible for her to travel. Why had we not
come before she became pregnant? At least, here, she could
have been monitored, we would have had some forewarning
of the tragedy—I stopped myself. Done was done; we had
done the best we could, unknowing, and I would not carry
that burden of guilt along with all the rest.

"I stayed with Father. After he died, he wanted me to come
back; it was his dying wish." I said it gingerly, afraid the
clamor in my mind would begin again, once invoked, but it
was only a whisper.

"You could hold Kennard's place in Council," he said, "and
have the same kind of power he held."

My face must have flinched, because he said half angrily,
"Are you a fool? You are needed in Council, provided you
don't take the part of the Ridenow and try to pull us all into
the Empire!"

I shook my head. "I'm no politician, Lord Dyan. And—
without offense—I'd like a little time to size it up on my own,
before being told what to think by each of the interested
parties!"

I had expected him to fly into a rage at the rebuke, but
he only grinned, that fierce and wolfish grin which was, in
its own way, handsome. "Good enough; at least you're capable
of thinking. While you're sizing up the situation, try and take
the measure of our prince. There's precedent enough—Council knew my own father was mad as a *kyorebni* in the Ghost
wind, and they took care to draw his fangs."

They had appointed Dyan his father's regent, and in one
of the old man's lucid intervals, old Dom Kyril had agreed
to it. But I said, "Derik has no near kinsman; isn't he the
only adult Elhalyn?"

"His sisters are married," Dyan said, "though not, perhaps,
as near to nobility as they would have been if we had known
one of their husbands might have to be regent of the Elhalyns.
Old Hastur wants to set Regis up in Derik's place, but the
boy's kicking about that, and who can blame him? It's enough
to rule over Hastur, without a crown as well. A crown is

nonsense in these days, of course; what we need is a strong Council of equals. And there's the Guard—not that a few dozen men carrying swords can do much against the Terrans, but they can keep our own people on the right side of the wall."

"Who's commanding the Guard now?" I asked, and he shrugged.

"Anybody. Nobody. Gabriel, mostly. I took it myself for the first two years—Gabriel seemed a bit young." I remembered Dyan had been one of the best officers. "After that it went to him."

"He's welcome to it," I said. "I never had much taste for soldiering."

"It goes with the Domain," Dyan said fiercely. "I suppose you would be willing to do your duty and command it?"

"I'll have to get my bearings first," I said, and then I was angry. "Which is more important? To get someone who's competent at commanding the Guards, and likes it, or to get someone who has the right blood in his veins?"

"They're both important," he said, and he was deadly serious. "Especially in these times. With the Hasturs gobbling up one Domain after another, Gabriel's *exactly* the wrong man to command the Guards; you should force the issue and take them away from him as soon as possible."

I almost laughed. "Force the issue? Gabriel could tie me up into a bow for his wife's hair, and do it with one hand tied—" I broke off; that particular figure of speech was, to say the least, unfortunate. "I could hardly fight a duel with him; are you suggesting assassination?"

"I think the Guard would be loyal to you for your father's sake."

"Maybe."

"And if you don't take over the Guard? What are you intending to do? Go back to Armida and raise horses?" He put all his scorn into the words. Pain flooded through me, remembering how I had wanted to take my son there. "I could probably do worse."

"Just sit at home and attend to your own affairs while Darkover falls into Empire hands?" he asked scornfully. "You might as well hide behind Tower walls! Why not go back with Jeff to Arilinn—or did they burn *that* out of you too?"

Rage flooded through me. How dared Dyan, under the pretense of kinship and his friendship for my father, probe old, unhealed wounds this way? "I was taught at Arilinn," I said deliberately, "to speak of such matters only to those who were concerned in them. Are you monitor, mechanic, or technician, Lord Dyan?"

I had always thought that the phrase *black with rage* was only a manner of speaking; now I saw it, the blood rising dark and congested in Dyan's face until I thought he would fall down, stricken by a stroke. Too late, I remembered; Dyan had been briefly in a Tower, and no one, not even my father, knew why he had left it. What I had meant as a freezing rebuke, a way of telling him to keep his distance, had been interpreted as deadly personal insult—an attack on his weakest spot.

"Neither monitor, mechanic nor technician, damn you," he said at last, his chair going over backward as he rose, "nor power-pole for the forces of Sharra, you damned insolent bastard! Go back to Armida and raise horses, or to a Tower if they'll have you, or back to the Empire, or to hell if Zandru will take you in, but stay out of Council politics—hear me?"

He turned and strode away, and I stared after him, in shock and dismay, knowing I had made, from a man who had been ready to befriend me, the most dangerous of enemies.

CHAPTER FIVE

The Comyn Tower rose high above the Castle, part of the great sprawling mass that looked down on Thendara, and yet apart from it, older than any part of it; immeasurably old, built of an ancient reddish sandstone which, otherwise, appeared only in the oldest, ruined houses of the Old Town. Regis had never come here before.

He said to the nonhuman servant, "Will you ask the *Domna* Callina Lindir-Aillard if she will receive Regis Hastur?"

It surveyed him for a long moment, the dark eyes alert and responsive; a humanlike form, a humanlike intelligence, but Regis could not dismiss the feeling that he had been speaking to a large and not altogether friendly dog. He had seen the silver-furred *kyrri* during his brief training session in Neskaya Tower; but he had never grown used to them. The thing stared at him longer, he thought, than a human would have done. Then it gave a brief graceful nod of its sleek silver head and glided noiselessly away.

Regis wondered, remotely and at the edge of awareness, how the *kyrri* would deliver its message to Callina. The origin of the *kyrri* was lost in the Ages of Chaos—had they, after all, been part of that monstrous breeding program which the Hastur-kin had carried on for centuries to fix the Comyn gifts in the families of the Seven Domains? Stranger games than the *kyrri* had been played with genetics modified by *laran* power and matrix technology.

Or did they go back further yet, part of the prehistory of Cottman's star before a lost Terran colony came to call it Darkover? He suspected that even in the Towers they were not sure what the *kyrri* were or how they had come to be traditional servants of the Tower. He took them for granted, had learned to stay out of range of the painful electric shocks they could give when they were excited or threatened, had been tended by their odd thumbless hands when it would have been unendurable to have near him human telepaths who could read his mind or reach it.

174

But all this was with the surface of his mind and had nothing to do with the underlying unease which had brought him here; and for a moment he wondered if he should have sought out Callina in the Aillard suite, presuming somewhat on his acquaintance with Linnell—who, like himself, had been fostered at Armida and was foster-sister to Lew and Marius. He had never spoken more than a dozen words to Callina, and those formal and ceremonious. He could have talked to Linnell as to a kinswoman, but Callina was something else again...Keeper at Neskaya and then at Arilinn, then sent here to be under-Keeper in the oldest of the Towers, long inactive, but still sheltering the ancient Ashara, who had not been seen outside the Tower in living memory—nor, Danvan Hastur had told him once, in the living memory of anyone *he* had ever known; and his grandfather was nearing his hundredth year. He supposed Ashara's own circle, if she had one, and her attendants, must see her sometime....

She must have been an ordinary woman once; at least as ordinary as any of the Comyn could be said to be ordinary; and not immortal, only long-lived as some of the Hasturs were long-lived. There was *chieri* blood mixed with the blood of the Domains. Regis knew little of the *chieri,* but they were said to be immortal and beautiful, still dwelling somewhere in a remote valley where humankind never came. But his own grandfather showed signs of being one of those Hasturs whose reign could span generations...*it was a lucky thing for the Comyn, that Danvan Hastur had been there to reign as Regent during these troubled years*...Regis found his thoughts sliding into unexpected channels, as if some other mind had briefly touched his own; he started, blinked as if he had fallen asleep on his feet for a moment; his skin crawled, and something *touched* him.... Regis felt a faint nausea deep in his body. A shadow had fallen across the doorway and Callina Aillard was standing there.

He had not seen her come. *Lord of Light!* Regis swore to himself, sweating; had he stood there, sound asleep on his feet, an idiot's grin on his face, his clothing disarranged or worse? He felt exposed, desperately uncomfortable; Callina was a Keeper, and uncanny. He managed to get out a formal, *"Su serva, Domna..."*

She was not now wearing the formal crimson robes she had worn in the Crystal Chamber, the traditional garb which marked out a Keeper as apart, untouchable, sacrosanct. Instead she had on a long, fleecy gown of blue wool, close-cut, high-necked. It was girdled with a copper belt, squared plaques of the precious metal, a large blue semi-precious stone at the center of each plaque; and her hair, coiled low on her neck, was caught into a priceless clasp of copper filigree.

"Come through here, and then we can talk if you wish. Hush; do not disturb the relays." Her voice was so low it barely stirred the air between them, and Regis followed on tiptoe, as if a normal step would be like a shout. They passed through a large silent chamber, bare, with relay screens staring blank and glassy blue, and other things which Regis did not recognize; before one of the screens a young girl was curled up on a soft seat. Her face had the strange, not-quite-present look of a telepath whose mind was fixed in the relays communicating with other Towers, other telepaths. Règis did not know the girl and Callina of course did not notice her in any way; in fact, only her body was there in the room with them at all.

Callina opened a noiseless door at the far end of the room, and they went through into a small, comfortable private room, with low divans and chairs, and a high window with colored glass, throwing prism lights across the room; but it was dark outside, and if it had not been high summer Regis would have thought it might be snowing. Callina shut the door soundlessly behind them, gestured him to a seat and curled up in one of them herself, tucking her feet under her, and drawing the hem of the blue gown over them. She said in her stilled voice, "Well, Regis, did Old Hastur send you to me to ask if I'd go through the marriage ceremony with Beltran, just to save the Council some embarrassment?"

Regis felt his face burning; had she read his mind while he stood there, asleep on his feet like a gaby? He said truthfully, "No, he didn't, though he did mention it to me at dinner last night. I don't think he would have the arrogance actually to ask it, Lady Callina."

Callina said, sighing, "Derik is an accursed fool. And I had no idea what that foolish brother of mine was doing behind my back, or that Derik was stupid enough to listen to him. Linnell loves Derik; it would break her heart to separate them now. How she can care for such a fool—!" Callina shook her head in exasperation. "Merryl's never reconciled himself to being born an Aillard, and subject to the female Head of the Domain. And I doubt he ever will."

"Grandfather did suggest that you might go through the ceremony—no more than that—as a matter of form," Regis said.

"It might be easier than telling Beltran what he otherwise must say to him," Callina said, "that this marriage was contrived by a young man greedy for power and a prince too dull to see how he's being manipulated."

"Don't forget," Regis said dryly, "a Regent too lazy or forgetful to keep a strong hand over his not-too-intelligent princeling."

"Do you really think it was only laziness or forgetfulness?" Callina asked, and Regis said, "I don't like to think my grandfather would have plotted against the Head of a Domain...."

Then he remembered a conversation he had had with Danilo three years ago, as fresh as today: *so Domain after Domain falls into Hastur hands; the Elhalyn is already under Hastur Regency, then the Aillard with Derik married to Linnell,* Regis thought, all the easier if Callina was married off and exiled in distant Aldaran. And he had watched his grandfather's machinations against the Altons.

"No, he couldn't plot it," Callina said, and a faint smile stirred her lips, "but he could sit back while Merryl and that fool of a Derik create such a situation that I must fall into place or seriously embarrass the Comyn."

"Callina, even Hastur cannot marry off the Head of a Domain without her own consent. And you are Keeper for Ashara; what will she say to that?"

"Ashara..." Callina was silent for a moment, as if the very sound of the name stirred unease in her calm face. She looked troubled. "I seldom see Ashara. She spends much of her time in meditation. I could hold all her power in the Council, but I am afraid—" she stopped herself in mid-sentence. "You are not Tower-trained, Regis?"

He shook his head. "I had enough training so that I could manage my Gift without becoming ill, but I'm not that powerful a telepath, and Grandfather needed me in Thendara, he said."

"I think you are more of a telepath than you believe, kinsman," Callina said, with a skeptical look.

The quiet, assured statement somehow made him uneasy;

he frowned, ready to protest. "I'm useless in the relays, and they couldn't teach me much about monitoring—"

"That may be," she said. "In the Towers we test only for those gifts which are useful to their functions; monitoring, the skill to stay in rapport with a matrix screen for mining and manipulating power.... in this day and age, that seems the only kind of *laran* the Towers find useful. But you are finding out that there is more to your *laran* than you believed—is it not so, cousin?"

Regis flinched as if she had put her fingers directly on a bruise he did not know he had.

"You had better tell me about it," she said, "I saw how you had picked up the presence of Sharra, in Council. Let me see your matrix, Regis."

Apprehensively, Regis touched the small velvet bag, undid the strings, tilted the small blue crystal into his palm. It lay there blue and placid, small distant lights glimmering inside the stone; no sign of fire, no sign of the ravening Form of Fire...

"It's gone!" he said in surprise.

"And you expected it to be there," Callina said. "Really, I think you had better tell me everything about it."

Regis was still staring at his matrix in disbelief. After a moment he managed to blurt out something about it; how Javanne had been trapped by the image, how he had, without thinking about it, freed her mind from the matrix.

"It was like—I watched her, once, unpicking a design that had gone wrong in her tapestry—I think it must have felt like that, though I don't know how to do tapestry...."

"I do," Callina said, "and that's just what it would have felt like."

"What did I do?" Regis had not known how frightened he was until he heard his own voice trembling. "How could I do that? I thought—it would take a powerful telepath, perhaps a Keeper—to match resonances like that—"

"There have been male Keepers in history," Callina said abstractedly. "Good ones, powerful ones. Only for the last few hundred years have Keepers been women. And until a few generations ago, they were locked up, treated like sorceresses, sacred virgins, ritual objects of great power and veneration." Her face was cool, ironic. "Now, of course, in these enlightened days, we know better...a Keeper today need be no more than centerpolar—the center of their matrix circles, the one

who holds the energon rings. Regis, have you had enough
Tower training to have the faintest idea what I'm talking
about?"

"I think so. I know the language, though I don't think I
really understand it all. They never thought I had had enough
strength as a telepath to let me work in a circle, and besides,
I was needed here. But if I wasn't even able to work as a
monitor, I couldn't have done a Keeper's work, not completely
untrained, not like that, could I?" His voice cracked, but he
was not quite so afraid; Callina had talked about it as a
technical problem, not some strange and terrifying flaw in
himself.

"But a Keeper's work, in these days, is no more than any
well-trained technician can do, as I said," she told him. "Kennard was a technician, and he could do almost everything
Elorie of Arilinn could do, except actually hold the center of
a circle. I think Jeff could do that if he had to, if tradition
would let him. And you're a Hastur, and your mother was
Hastur of Elhalyn—what do you know about the Hastur Gift,
Regis?"

"Not much," he said frankly. "When I was a boy, a *leronis*
told me I had not even the ordinary *laran*." The memory of
that, as always, was multiple layers of pain, the sense that
he was unworthy to follow in the steps of the forefather Hasturs who had come before him; and at the same time freedom,
freedom from the path laid out for the Hastur sons, a path
he must walk whether he would or no...

"But your laran wakened..." she said, half a question, and
he nodded. Danilo Syrtis, friend, paxman, sworn brother, and
the last known to hold the almost-extinct gift of catalyst
telepathy—Danilo had wakened Regis's *laran,* given him the
heritage of the Comyn; but it was not altogether a blessing,
for it had meant the loss of his freedom. Now he must shoulder
the burden, take up the heritage of all the Hasturs, and
abandon his dream of freedom from those unendurable
bonds....

*I have been a good Heir to the Hasturs; I have done my
duty, commanded in the Guard, sat in the Council, adopted
the son of my sister for an Heir in turn. I have even given sons
and daughters to the Hastur clan, even though I would not
marry the women who bore them to me....*

"I know something of those bonds," she said, and it seemed
to him that her passionless voice was sympathetic. "I am a

Keeper, Regis, not a Keeper in the new way, only a highly specialized technician, but Keeper in the old way; I was trained under Elorie of Arilinn. She was Dyan's half-sister, you know...Cleindori, Dorilys of Arilinn, freed the Keepers by reducing the old superstition to what they now call the science of matrix mechanics, and now the Keepers need not give up their lives, and live cloistered, virgin...but I had been trained in the old fashion, Regis, and after I had served at Arilinn and Neskaya, then I came here, just *because* I was the only woman in the Domains who had been trained in the ancient way. Ashara demanded it, and I, who had had the ancient training and was still virgin, because I had never felt any wish to marry, or leave my post even for a few years to marry or take a lover...." her smile was faint, almost absent. "I was content with my work, nor had I ever met any man who would tempt me to leave my calling. So I was sent, willy-nilly, to serve under Ashara, I who was ruler of a Domain in my own right...simply because I was what I was." For a moment it seemed that there was terror in her eyes, and he wondered: *is she so afraid of Ashara?* Fear seemed an unlikely emotion for a Keeper.

What had women to be afraid of? They didn't have to fight in the coming wars, they would be safe and protected....

She said, "What do you know of the Hastur Gift?" again, insistently.

"Not much, as I told you. I grew up thinking I didn't even have ordinary *laran*...."

"But whatever it may be, it's latent in you," she mused.

He asked her point-blank, "Do *you* know what the Hastur Gift is?"

She said, biting her lip, "Ashara must know..." and he wondered what that had to do with it. As if speaking to herself, she said, "The Ardais Gift; catalyst telepathy, the ability to awaken *laran* in others. The Ridenow make the best monitors because they are empaths...the Gifts are all so muddled, now, by inbreeding, by marriage with non-telepaths, it's rare to find the full strength of any of the old Gifts. And there is so much superstition and tradition cluttering any clear knowledge of the Gifts...there is a tradition that the original Gift of the Hasturs may have been what was trained into the Keepers: the ability to work with other matrixes, without the elaborate safeguards a Keeper must have. Originally the word Keeper—" she used the casta, *tenerésteis—*

"meant *one who holds, one who guards*...a Keeper, in the simplest terms, putting aside a Keeper's function of working at the center of the energon rings, is one who keeps the other matrixes in the group resonating together; it's a special skill of working with other matrixes, not just her own. As I say, some high-level technicians can do it. I wonder..." she hesitated a little, then said, "Hasturs, in general, are long-lived and mature late. Ordinary *laran* waked in you late—you were fifteen, weren't you? And perhaps that was only a first stirring of the *laran* you will eventually have. How old are you now? Twenty-one? That would mean your matrix was wakened at about the time as the Sharra troubles—"

"I was in the mountains then; and my matrix was overshadowed, like all the matrixes in the vicinity of the Sharra matrix," Regis said.

And he had, furthermore, been going through an intolerable personal crisis with the wakening of his heritage; his decision to accept himself as he was, and not as his grandfather and the Comyn wanted him to be; to accept self-knowledge and the unwanted burden of the Hasturs, or to bury it all, live a life without either, an uncomprehending, unburdened life without *laran*, without responsibility. But now there was this new dimension to his *laran*, and he could not even guess what further burdens it would demand of him.

"Let me be sure about this," Callina said. "While you were in the mountains during the Sharra rebellion, your matrix was overshadowed; you could not use it because of—of what I saw in Lew's at that time: the Form of Fire. But later, when Sharra was offworld—"

"It was clear," he said, "and I learned to use it, my matrix I mean, without any sign of Sharra. Only when Lew brought the Sharra matrix back to Darkover—"

She nodded. "And yet, you cleared your matrix," she said. "It will be easy enough to see if you have natural talent for a Keeper's skills." She unrolled her own from the tiny leather bag at her throat. She held it naked on her palm and said, "Can you match resonances and touch it without hurting me?"

Regis looked away, gulping; his mind was full of that day in Castle Aldaran, when he had seen Kadarin strip away Lew's matrix and send Lew to the floor in violent convulsions, a shrieking mindless wreck... He muttered, "I wouldn't know where to start. And I'd be afraid to try. I could—I could kill you."

She shook her head. "No, you couldn't, not here, not safeguarded as I am," she said. "Try it."

Her voice was low and indifferent, but it was a command, and Regis, sweating, tried to think himself into the blue crystal that lay in Callina's palm. He tried to remember how he had gone into Javanne's mind, reaching out to unpick her mind from the matrix as if it were interwoven threads of tapestry....He felt a strange, unpleasant force against his mind and moved squeamishly against it. *Was that Callina?* He glanced up, hesitant, unable to reconcile that cold stony force with the smiling, gentle woman before him.

"I—can't," he said.

"Forget about me! Match resonances with the matrix, I said!"

This is foolish. I have known Callina most of my life. It is absurd to be afraid of her! He reached out again, tentative, feeling the pulsing life-force, her guarded thoughts—she had the strongest barrier he had ever touched; he supposed it had something to do with being a Keeper. He caught only fragments, the light hurting her eyes from a window, subliminal awareness of him, Regis, *he's a good-looking boy,* how tired he was of that reaction from women....Again he felt the pulsing of the matrix, tried to match his breathing against it....A face sketched itself lightly on his mind, cold, distant, making him shiver as if he stood naked in frost...beautiful, terrible, alien....He banished that, too, and the fear, and forced himself into the matrix, feeling the resonance, the cold life of stone, the glowing lights in tune with his breathing, the blood in his veins...He felt himself reach out, not conscious of movement, and closed his fingers over it, lifting it lightly from her hand....distant cold eyes, gray and colorless as metal....Cold seas washing over his mind....

Pain splintered through Callina's head and Regis quickly let the matrix go, tilting it back into her hand. She blinked and he felt her controlling the stab of pain. She said, "Well, you have the talent for that...but I don't know how much further it goes. I saw something, like a vision..." She was fumbling for words; she felt him share the fumbling and stopped it cold.

It was not at all like his contact with Javanne; it was not at all like the contact he had had with any of the women who had briefly been his lovers.... was it because she was a Keeper, that cold stony alien thing in her mind, a *leronis* of the old kind, vowed to virginity, to touch no man with even a hint of sexuality? *Or had it been Callina at all?* His own head was aching.

She said, "If you can do that, and if you could clear a matrix which had touched Sharra...." She bit her lip and he saw the pain move across her face again. "You have a gift we don't know about. Maybe it can be helpful..." and he picked up the words she was hesitant to speak, *perhaps it could help to control the Sharra matrix, free Kennard's son from the domination of that—that terrible thing....*

A second of terror; something greedy, ravenous, reaching out...

Then it was gone, or had it ever been there? "Go and tell Lew Alton that he should bring the Sharra matrix here, where it will be safe.... there is no time to lose. Perhaps you can help to free him..."

"I'd be afraid to try," he said, shaking.

"But you must not be afraid," she said, demanding. "If you have such a Gift as that..." and Regis felt she was not seeing him as a human being, not as Regis at all, just as a Gift, a strange and puzzling problem for a matrix technician, something to be solved and unraveled. It troubled him; for a moment he wanted to force her to see him as a human, a man standing before a woman; she was all cool aloofness, the woman in her subdued, her features cold and static, and for an instant Regis remembered the curious stony face that had briefly crossed his mind like a vision in the matrix.... *Was that Callina too? Which was real?* Then, so swiftly he could not be sure of it, it was gone, and Callina was only a frail-looking woman, slender, troubled, in a fuzzy blue robe, looking up at him and pressing her temples with her two hands as if they hurt her.

She said, "You must go now, but make sure the Sharra matrix is brought here..." and opened the door into the relay chamber. But as they went through, the young girl curled up before the relay screen raised her head and beckoned, and Callina, motioning Regis to go out into the outer chamber, stole on silent feet to her side. After a few minutes she joined him in the outer chamber. Her face was white, and she looked dazed.

"It is worse than I thought," she said. "Lilla has had word

from the relays.... Beltran has set forth. And he is traveling
with an escort so great that it could be called an army. He
will be here by Festival Night, here at our gates in Thendara.
Merciful Avarra," she whispered, "this will mean war in the
Domains! How could Hastur allow this to happen? How could
even Merryl do this to me? Does he really hate me that
much?"

And Regis had no answer for her.

Because there was nothing else to do, he went back to his
own rooms, half intending to face his grandfather, to tell him
that Derik's plan had borne unexpected fruit; that it could
indeed mean war in the Domains if Callina refused to do
their will. But his grandfather's steward told him that the
Regent had gone to confer with the *cortes,* and Regis set out
for the Alton town house. At least he could convey the message that the Sharra matrix would be safer in the Comyn
Tower.

But as he neared the house, he saw a familiar figure in
the green and black of the Alton Domain. Lew had changed
in the intervening years; Regis had barely recognized him in
Council; but his walk was unchanged, and Regis recognized
him now, though his back was turned. Regis walked faster
to catch up with him, hesitant about reaching out for the old
touch of minds.

But Lew must have sensed a presence behind him, for he
turned and waited for Regis to come up with him.

"Well, Regis, it's been a long time."

"It has, cousin," said Regis, and took him into a kinsman's
embrace, pressing his cheek to the scarred face. He stood back
and smiled. "I was coming to find you, and here you are in
my pathway... where are you going so early?"

"Not as early as all that," Lew said, looking into the sky
with a practiced eye. "Not too early for Dyan to offer me a
drink, or for a quarrel—damn him!"

"Dyan's not a good man to quarrel with," said Regis soberly, "How did you get into that?"

Lew sighed. "I hardly know. Something he said to me—I
suppose what he really meant was, *go to hell,* some version
of, *you've offended me,* but it sounded like a declaration of
war. I—"he broke off, troubled. "Will you walk with me to
my house? I'm uneasy, for no reason at all. But I wanted to
talk to you."

"And I had a message for you from the *leronis*," Regis said. He started to speak, then stopped, overcome by an overpowering conviction that he should not speak that ill-omened name, *Sharra*, here in the street. That was for privacy, and a well-shielded room. Instead he said, "You should move back into the Comyn Castle, into the Alton suite. It's expected at Council season, and if you're actually inhabiting the proper quarters, they'll have a harder time challenging your rights..."

"I've thought of that," Lew said, "The Terrans have a saying; possession is nine points of the law. Though I don't think I have to worry about Jeff, and the main problem may be to get them to accept Marius as my Heir. I don't know if he's even had the regular testing when he was thirteen or so—we haven't had any time to talk about such things."

"It may not mean anything," Regis said, "even if he has; remember, they told me I had no *laran* at all." Briefly, there was an old memory of bitterness. "At least if Marius turns out *not* to have laran, you won't send him to Nevarsin, will you, to be brought up there?"

"Not unless he wants to go," Lew said amiably. "A lad who's of a scholarly turn and wants a good education might enjoy the chance to study there, but Marius, I've heard, has already had the best education the Terrans could give. I owe your grandfather thanks for arranging that."

"He didn't do it to please you. On the contrary." It had been, and they both knew it, a way of emphasizing that Marius must seek his destiny among Terrans, not his father's people. "While you were away, I suppose you learned much of what the Terrans had to offer...."

"Not as much as I'd have liked to; I was in hospitals a good deal of the time," Lew said, and behind his scarred face Regis sensed much of what Lew would never tell him, pain and final acceptance of mutilation. "But while I was convalescing, yes, I'd have gone mad without something to do. I tried some surveying, map-making; there are parts of the Kilghard Hills, and most of the Hellers, that have never been properly mapped. Better to do it ourselves than to let the Terrans do it because we can't be bothered to teach our own people measurements. It seems preposterous, that *they* have a Mapping and Survey unit on Darkover, and we don't!"

Regis said, "I've thought of having my sons educated by the Terrans. Though, I suppose, I'd have to fight grandfather every step of the way. It might be better to have someone

who's had a Terran education—like Marius, or you—educate
them, instead of sending them offworld, or into the Trade
City—"

Lew said, with that sudden irradiating smile which made
Regis, finally and forever, forget the gargoyle scarring of the
face, "I've lived in the Empire too long; you seem young to
me to have a family. But you're twenty-one now, I should
have known Hastur would have married you off long since.
I'd be proud to foster your sons. Who is your wife? How many
children—"

Regis shook his head. "That's been a constant argument
with Grandfather, too. But I adopted my sister's son, just
before you went offworld—" He paused, hesitant, remembering; Lew had been in no state to remember that. But Lew
nodded and said, "I remember. You told me at Aldaran."

"I have a *nedestro* son and two daughters," Regis said.
"The oldest is past three; in a couple more years, I shall bring
him before the Council. And Mikhail is already eleven. When
he is twelve, I shall bring him to Thendara and take his
education into my own hands." He grinned and said, "I've
had a lot of experience fighting Grandfather on that subject;
I suppose I can supervise my son's education. I won't let him
grow up ignorant."

"You're right, we've kept to the old ways too long," Lew
said. "I remember my father saying that when he was fifteen,
he was an officer in the Guards, but he could neither read
nor write, and was proud of it; when he went among the
Terrans, they thought him an idiot because no one with a
sound mind is allowed to let it lie fallow—"

"The monks at Nevarsin deplore it just as much as a Terran would," Regis said. "I ought to be grateful to Grandfather
that he made certain I had that much education at least." In
Nevarsin monastery, he had at least learned to read and
write, done some elementary ciphering, and read such Darkovan history as was available, which wasn't much.

"Kennard had me taught to read and write, though I must
admit I wasn't tremendously apt at either," Lew said. "Lying
in the hospital, I made up for lost time; but boys are still
being brought up as if it was unmanly—I imagine it's because
a scholar hasn't enough time to master weapons, and of course
when the Domains were one constant battleground year after
year, that was the most important thing in a boy's education,
to be good with a sword and weapons. Even when I was a boy,

there were bandits enough in the Kilghard Hills. For centuries Armida had to be kept like an armed camp. Kennard would never have been criticized, if he'd kept me there to defend his lands instead of sending me into a Tower...."

Regis picked up the unspoken part of that too: that Lew's work in the Arilinn Tower, his skill at matrix technology, had led to the Sharra rebellion, and to the sword that was not a sword, the sword which concealed *Sharra*.... .

And he saw it growing, blossoming behind Lew's eyes, the look of horror that slid over Lew's face, felt his own hair rising as the flames flared in his mind....*Sharra!* He looked at Lew. The smiling man, the kinsman with whom he had been calmly discussing the merits of Darkovan versus Terran education, was gone; Lew's face was dead white, so that the scars stood out like crimson brands, and his eyes were—blank horror, staring at nothing Regis could see. But they could both see it, the raging, ravening form of the fire-Goddess, straining against the chains, fire-locks tossing high against the sky...She was not in the quiet street around them, she was not in this world at all, but she was there, *there* in their minds, horribly present for both of them....

Regis breathed hard, forcing himself to control the trembling of his hands, reached out for Lew's mind, tried to do what he had done with Javanne's, to pick the fire-form out of the texture of Lew's thoughts...and found something he had never touched. Javanne had seen Sharra only in his mind; Rafe had only seen the matrix...this was something else, something more dangerous; he saw a face, lean, wolfish, colorless hair, colorless gray eyes, and a woman's face like a restless flame....

"Kadarin—" he gasped, and never knew whether he had spoken aloud or not. The frozen, static horror left Lew's eyes. He said grimly, "Come on. I've been afraid of this—"

He began to run, and Regis, following, could feel the jolting pain, like fire in Lew's hand—a hand that was not there, a phantom fire...but real enough to make sweat stand out on Lew's forehead as he ran, jolting, uneven, his good hand gripping a dagger in his belt....

They turned into an open square, heard shrieks, cries. Regis had never been inside the Alton town house, though he had seen it from the outside. Half a dozen of the uniformed City Guard were fighting in the center of the square; Regis could not see who they were fighting. Lew cried out, "Marius!"

and ran up the steps. The door suddenly burst open, and at the same time Regis saw flames shooting from an upper window. One of the Guardsmen officers was trying to organize people into a fire-fighting line, water being passed from hand to hand from the nearest well and from a smaller well in the garden behind the house, but it was utter confusion.

Lew was fighting, on the steps, with a tall man whose face Regis could not see, fighting one-handed with his knife. *Gods! He has only one hand!* Regis ran, whipping his sword from its sheath; saw Andres struggling with a bandit who wore the garb of the mountains... *but what are mountain men doing here in Thendara?* The Guards flowed up the steps, an officer shouting to rally them. It was hard, in the press, to tell friend from foe; Regis managed to get himself back to back with Lew, covering him, and for a moment, as his sword went up, he saw a face he recognized....

Gaunt, gray-eyed, lips drawn back in a feral scowl....The man Kadarin looked older, more dangerous. His face was bleeding; Lew had somehow slashed him with his dagger. Behind Regis there was a great cracking roar, like an explosion; then Guardsmen were hurrying everyone down the steps, shouting urgently, and the house buckled slowly and erupted skyward. Regis was driven to his knees by the force of the blast. And then there was a high, clear call, in a woman's voice, and suddenly the bandits were gone, melting away across the square, evaporating like mountain mist into the labyrinth of streets. Dazed, Regis picked himself up, watching the Guardsmen struggling with the remains of the burning house. A cluster of scared servant women were crying in a corner of the garden. Andres, his jacket unlaced, his face streaked and grimed with smoke, one boot unlaced, limped down the stairs and bent over Lew. Jeff came and helped Lew to sit up.

Lew said in a sick, dazed voice, "Did you see him?"

Regis bent and pressed him back. "Don't try to sit up." Blood was flowing down Lew's face from a cut on his forehead; he tried to wipe it out of his eyes with his good hand. Lew said, "I'm all right," and tried to struggle to his feet. "What happened?"

Jeff Kerwin stared at the knife in his hand. It was not even bloody. "It all happened so fast. One minute all was quiet, the next, there were bandits all over the place and one of the serving-women shouted that the house was on fire...and

I was fighting for my life. I haven't held a knife since my first year in Arilinn!"

Lew said urgently, "Marius! Gods of hell, Marius! Where is my brother?" Again he started up, disregarding Andres's restraining hands. The horror was in his eyes again, and Regis could see in his mind the great flaming image, Sharra, rising higher and higher over Thendara...but there was nothing there. The street was quiet, the Guardsmen had the fire out; though there had been something like an explosion in the upstairs floors and there was a great gaping hole in the roof. Regis thought, with wild irrelevancy, that now Lew had no choice but to move into the suite in Comyn Castle which had, from time out of mind, been reserved for the Alton Domain. Jeff was touching, with careful hands, the cut on Lew's head.

"Bad," he said, "it will need stitches—"

But Lew struggled away from them. Regis grabbed him; laid his hand urgently over his eyes, and reached out with his mind, struggling to banish the ravening form of fire from his mind....slowly, slowly, the flames died in Lew's mind and his eyes came back to reality; he staggered, letting himself lean on Jeff's arm.

"Did you see him?" he asked again urgently. "Kadarin! It was Kadarin! *Do they have the Sharra matrix?*"

Regis, staggering with that thought, compelled by Lew's horror, suddenly knew this was what Callina had feared. Lew demanded, "Marius! Marius—" and stopped, his voice strangling and catching in a sob.

Merciful Gods! Not this too! My brother, my brother... He collapsed on the steps like a puppet whose strings are cut, his shoulders shaking with grief and shock. Jeff came and held him as if he were a child; with Andres, somehow they got him up the steps. But Regis stood still, looking at horror beyond horror.

Kadarin had the Sharra matrix.

And Marius Alton lay dead somewhere inside the burning house, with a Terran bullet through his heart.

Lew Alton's narrative

CHAPTER SIX

"Here." Jeff shoved a mirror into my hand. "Not as good as a Terran medic might have done—I'm out of practice—but it's stopped the bleeding, anyhow, and that's what counts."

I shoved the mirror away. I could—sometimes—make myself look at what Kadarin had left of my face; but not now. But none of it was Jeff's fault; and he had done his best. I said, trying to be flippant, "Just what I needed—another scar, to balance the top and the bottom of my face."

He had gone all over me very carefully, to make sure that the blow to the head had left no aftereffects; but the cut was only a surface wound and fortunately had missed my eye. I had a headache roughly the size of Comyn Castle, but otherwise there seemed to be no damage.

Through it all was the haunting cry that would not be silenced, like a roaring in my mind;... *to Darkover, fight for your brother's rights....* and now would never be stilled. Marius was gone, and my grief was boundless; not only for the little brother I had lost, for the man he was beginning to be, that I would never, now, know. Grief, and guilt too, for while I had stayed away, Marius was neglected, perhaps, but alive. He might have lost the Domain; but as a Terran he might have made a good life somewhere, somehow. Now life and choice were gone. (And beneath grief and guilt a deeper layer of ambivalence I would not let myself see; a trickle of relief, that I need never, now, risk that frightful testing for the Alton gift, never risk death for him as my father had risked it for me...)

"You have no choice, now, but to move into the Alton apartments in Comyn Castle," Jeff said, and I nodded, with a sigh. The house, at least for the moment, was uninhabitable. Gabriel had come, with the final crew of Guards who had gotten the fire out. He offered to arrange for men to guard the ruins and prevent looting until we could get workmen to repair the roof and make the place weatherproof again. Every room was filled with smoke, furniture lying blackened and ruined. I tried without success to close my eyes and nostrils to the sight and smell. I have...a horror of fire, and now, I knew, somewhere at the back of my mind, if I gave it mental lease, the form of fire was there, raging, ravening, ready to destroy....and destroy me with it.

Not that I cared a damn, now....

Andres looked twenty years older. He came to me now and said, hesitantly, "Where—where shall we take Marius?"

It was a good question, I thought; a damned good question, but I didn't know the answer. There had never been any room for him in the Comyn Castle, not since he was old enough to notice his existence; they had never noticed it, in life, and now, in death, they would not care.

Gabriel said quietly, "Have him carried to the chapel in Comyn Castle." I looked up, startled and ready to protest, but he went on: "Let him have that much in death, kinsman, even though he didn't have it in life."

I looked on his dead face only once. The bullet that had smashed out his life had somehow left his face unmarked; and he looked, dead, like the little brother I remembered.

Now indeed I was alone. I had laid my father to rest on Vainwal, near my son, who had never lived except in the dreams I had shared with Dio before his birth. Now my brother would lie in an unmarked grave, as the custom was, on the shores of the Lake of Hali, where all the Hastur-kin were laid to rest. A thousand legalities separated me from Dio.

I should never have come back here! I stared at the lightly falling snow in the street outside, and realized that it did not matter where I was, here or elsewhere. Andres, crushed and old; Jeff, who had left his adopted world behind for Darkover; and Gabriel, who had his own family, but who, now, in default of any other, was Alton. Let him have the Domain; I should have sent for Marius, taken him away before it came to this....

No. That way lay only endless regret, a time when I would listen and hunger for my father's voice in my mind because it was all I had left of the past, live complacently with ghosts and grief and guilt...no. Life went on, and someday, perhaps,

I would give a damn.... for now there were two things that must be done.

"Kadarin is somewhere in the City," I said to Gabriel. "He must be found. I can't possibly emphasize it enough—how dangerous he is. Dangerous as a banshee, or a wolf maddened by hunger...."

And he had the Sharra matrix! And somehow he might manage to raise it again, the raging form of fire which would break the Comyn Castle and the walls of Thendara like kindling-sticks in a forest fire...

And there was worse...I too had been sealed to Sharra...

I could not speak of that to Gabriel. Not even to Jeff. I tried to tell myself; Kadarin could do nothing, nothing alone. Even if he managed to raise the Sharra forces, alone or with Thyra... who must, somehow, be alive too.... the fires would turn on them and consume them, as they had burned and ravaged me. I could feel my hand burning again, burning in the fires of Sharra.... could feel it now, the burning that the Terran medics had called *phantom pain*.... haunted, I told myself at the edge of hysteria, haunted by the ghost of my father and the ghost of my hand.... and stopped myself, hard. That way I could go mad, too. I said grimly to Andres, "Get me something to eat, find us all some dinner. Then we will take Marius to the chapel at Comyn Castle, and go there for the rest of the Council. The caretakers there will be Alton men; they'll know me as my father's Heir. And there's one more person who has to be told. Linnell."

Andres's eyes softened. "Poor Linnie," he muttered. "She was the only person in Comyn who cared about him. Even when no one else remembered he was alive, he was always her foster-brother. She sent him Festival gifts, and went riding with him on holidays.... She had promised him, when they were children, that if he married first she would be his wife's bride-woman and if she married first he should give her away. She came here last not a tenday ago, to tell him that her wedding with Derik had been set, and they were laughing together and talking about the wedding—" and the old man stopped, quite overcome.

I had not seen Linnell to speak to since I came back. I had thought, when I went to speak with Callina about making the Sharra matrix safe, I would pay Linnell my respects.... she was nearer to Marius's age, but we had been friends, brother and sister. But there had been no time. Now time was running out for us; and I must speak with Callina too, not only as kinswoman but as Keeper.

I too had been sealed to Sharra . . . they could draw me into that unholy thing, at any moment. . . .

I bent over Marius's body; took the little dagger from his waist. I had given it to him when he was ten years old; I had not realized that he had borne it all these years. In the years on Vainwal, I had not remembered to wear side-arms. I slipped it into the empty sheath in my boot, startled at how easily the gesture came after all these years.

Before Sharra can draw me again into itself, this dagger will find my heart. . . .

"Take him to the Castle," I said, and followed slowly behind the small, weary procession through the lightly falling summer snow. I was almost glad for the roaring pain in my head, which kept me from thinking, too much, about Linnell's face when I must tell her of this death.

Marius rested that night in the Comyn Castle, in the chapel, beneath the old stone arches, the paintings on the wall; from her silent niche the blessed Cassilda, clad in blue and with a starflower in her hand, watched forever over her children. My father had cared little for the Gods, and brought me up the same way. Marius in death was closer to the Comyn than ever he had been in life. But I looked up at the Four Gods portrayed at the four corners of the Chapel—Avarra, dark mother of birth and death, Aldones, Lord of Light, Evanda, bright mother of life and growth, Zandru, the dark lord of the Nine Hells. . . . and, like pressing a sore tooth, felt the burning touch of Sharra somewhere in my mind. . . .

Sharra was bound in chains, by Hastur, who was the son of Aldones, who was the Son of Light. . . .

Fables, fairy tales to frighten children or console them in the dark. What had the Gods to do with me, who bore Sharra's fires like a raging torrent that might some day burn out my brain . . . *as she had burned my hand away. . . .*

But as I went out of the Chapel, I thought: the fire is real, real enough to burn away the city of Caer Donn, real enough to destroy Marjorie, to sear my hand to scars that would never heal; and in the end to destroy me, cell-deep, so that even the child I fathered came forth a monstrous, nonhuman *thing.* . . . that much is no fable. *Something* must lie behind the legends. If there is any answer anywhere under the four moons, it must be known to the Keepers, or it will not be known anywhere. As I came out, I looked up at the night sky, which had cleared somewhat, and at the darkness of the Tower behind the Castle. Ashara, oldest of the Keepers on Darkover, might know the answer. But first I would see my brother buried. And I must go and tell his foster-sister, so that she could weep for him the tears I could no longer shed.

Marius was buried two days later. It was a small procession that rode to Hali; Gabriel and I, Linnell, Jeff and Andres; and, to my surprise, Lerrys Ridenow. At my questioning look he said roughly, "I was fond of the boy. Not as you might think, damn you, but he was a good lad, and he didn't have many kinsmen who'd give him such a kind word as they'd throw to a dog. We needed him as Heir to Alton; he would have had some sense on the Council, and all the Gods know, in these days we can use some plain good sense!"

He said something like that at the graveside, where it was traditional to speak good memories of the dead; words that would transcend grief and give everyone something else to remember of the one who was buried. I remembered my father's bitterness when my mother had not been buried here; it was almost my first memory. *Elaine gave two sons to the Comyn, and yet they would not let her body rest among the children of Hastur.* Now, standing by the grave of my mother's son, who had been accepted in death though never in life, I found myself remembering my father's dying cry, ripping through my mind; but afterward...afterward, too, I had heard his last thought, the surprised cry of joy; *Elaine! Yllana...beloved!* Had his dying mind seen a vision, was there that kind of mercy in death, or was there, somehow, something beyond death? I had never thought so; death was the end. Yet, though my father had never believed, either, but in his last moments he had cried out to greet *someone, something,* and his last emotion had been astonishment and joy. What was the truth? Marius, too, even though his death had been terribly sudden, had looked peaceful.

Perhaps, then, somewhere, in spite of the galaxy of stars that lay between, somewhere beyond time and space, Marius knew that my father's last thought had been of him...*fight for your brother's rights*...or even that now, somewhere, he was with the mother whose life he had taken in birth....

No, this was morbid nonsense, fables to comfort the bereaved.

Yet, that cry of joy, delight....

I thought, cynically, *Well, I will know when I am dead, or I will never know the difference.*

Lerrys finished his short speech and stepped back. I could not bring myself to speak, save for a brief sentence or two. "My father's last words or thoughts were of his younger son. He was greatly loved, and it is my sorrow that he never knew it."

Linnell wore a dark cloak, thick gray, almost too heavy for her slight body. She said, in a voice thick with tears, "I never knew my own brothers; they were fostered away from me. When Marius and I were very little, before we knew we were boy and girl, or what that means, he said to me once, "Linnie, I'll tell you what, you can be my brother and I'll be your sister." Even weeping, she laughed through it.

No doubt, I thought, Marius was more a brother to her than that arrogant young scamp Merryl!

It was near noon; the red sun stood high in the sky, casting sharp shadows across the clouds which covered the surface of the Lake of Hali. Here on this shore, so legend among the Comyn said, the forefather of all the Comyn, Hastur, son of the Lord of Light, had fallen to earth, and here he had met with Cassilda the Blessed, and here she had borne the son who had fathered all of the Comyn...what was the truth of the legend? The hills rose beyond Hali, distant, shadowed, and above them a small shadow of moon, pale blue in the colored sky. And on the far shore the chapel of Hali, where rested the sacred things of the Comyn, from the days when the fullest powers of their minds were known...we were a shadow; a remnant; an echo of the powers that had been known in the Seven Domains in the old days. Once many Towers had risen over the Domains, telepaths in the relays had sped messages back and forth more quickly than the mechanical signals of the Terran Empire; the powers of mind allied to matrix had flown air-cars, brought metal to the ground from deep within the core of the planet, look deep within the body and cure disease, heal wounds, control the minds of animals and birds, look deep within the cell plasm and know whether the unborn child would be gifted with *laran* of a specific kind...yes, and in those days there had been wars fought with strange and terrible weapons, ranging into other dimensions, and of these weapons Sharra was one of the least...somewhere within the white gleaming walls of that chapel were there other weapons, one which could be effective against *Sharra*...?

I would never know. In the days of the Compact, knowledge of those weapons had been destroyed, too, and perhaps it was as well that it should be so. Who could have foreseen, in those days, that descendants of the Comyn should somehow discover the ancient talisman of Sharra, and raise that raging fire?

I looked around the shores of the Lake with a sudden shiver.

Kadarin! Kadarin had the Sharra matrix, and he would try, perhaps, to force me back within it....

In the old days at Aldaran, Kadarin and Beltran had raised dozens of fanatical believers, ready to let their own raw emotion rage forth, be drawn into the raging fires of Sharra, feeding all that raw hungry mind power into the destroying flames to be loosed on the city...could he bring such a force to Thendara, could he recapture me to loose that destroying power in my mind?...I trembled, looking at the hills, feeling that somehow I was being *watched,* that Kadarin lurked somewhere, waiting to seize me, force me back to the power-pole of Sharra, *feeding* that unholy flame!

And Sharra will rise and destroy and burn me wholly away in fire...all my hate, all my rage and torment...

Rafe Scott was not at the graveside. Yet he had been one of my brother's few friends. *Had Kadarin seized him too, drawn him back into Sharra?* Dizziness seized me, I saw men riding, an army on the road, marching on Thendara....

Andres's hand on my shoulder steadied me. "Easy, Lew," he muttered. "There's not much more. We'll be away from here soon, and then you can rest."

Rest be damned! With all this closing in on us, Sharra's matrix free and in Kadarin's hands once more, there would be no rest for me for some time.

Hoofbeats! I tensed, my hand gripping the hilt of the light ceremonial sword I had been persuaded to wear for this occasion. Kadarin with his rabble, ready to capture me and drag me into slavery to Sharra once more? But the riders came slowly to the graveside, and I saw they wore the uniform of the Castle Guard. Regis Hastur slid from his horse and came slowly to the graveside. I had wondered what had happened to him; he had been there when Marius died and the house was burned....

He stood for a moment over the grave and said quietly,
"I did not know.Marius well, and it is my sorrow. But once
I heard him speak, in a tavern, the kind of words which we
need in Council. His death is upon all our heads here; and
here I promise that I will have the courage to speak the words
he never had a chance to say in Council."

He looked up expectantly, and behind Regis I saw the tall,
lean figure of Dyan Ardais, in the ceremonial gray and black
of his Domain. He came to the graveside, and looked at the
open grave; but he did not speak, merely picked up a handful
of soil and cast it quietly into the grave. Then, after a long
silence, he said, "Rest well, kinsman; and may all the folly
and wrong which brought you to birth rest here with you."
He turned away from the grave and said, "Lord Regis persuaded me that it was well to guard you; in these days there
are enemies and Comyn should not ride unguarded. We will
escort you in safety back to the Castle."

In silence, then, I turned from my brother's grave, and we
went to our horses. As Lerrys mounted, I said quietly, "It was
good of you to come, kinsman. Thank you."

His fair face darkened and he said fiercely, "It wasn't for
you, damn you, it was for Marius!" He turned his back on me,
pulling himself up, with a dancer's agile movement, into the
saddle. He wore Darkovan dress and was heavily cloaked
against the fierce cold of the hills, in wool and leather, not
the elegant silks and synthetics of the pleasure worlds.

I hauled myself, awkwardly, one-handed, into the saddle.
Regis said from his horse, "I would have come sooner. But I
felt it necessary to get leave to bring guards. I never had a
chance to tell you; Beltran is on the road, and he brings what
could almost be called an army. Beltran has no love for you.
And if Kadarin's at large—"

I said, grimacing, "Don't tell me Hastur wouldn't be relieved if Beltran caught up with me—or I broke my neck!"

He looked down at his saddlehorn. Then he said very quietly, "I am Hastur too, Lew. My grandfather and I have had
differences before this, and we will have them afterward. But
you must believe me: he would not wish you to fall into Kadarin's hands. That would be true no matter what he felt
about you personally. And he bears you no ill will. He was
stupid and wrong-headed about Marius, perhaps. But whatever he may have felt, you are Lord Armida, and head of the
Alton Domain, and there is nothing he can do about that;

and he will accept it with such grace as he must. Your father was his friend."

I looked away across the hills. Danvan Hastur had never been unkind to me. I took up the reins, and we rode, side by side, for a little while. Mist from the Lake of Hali floated in wisps on our trail, covered Marius's silent grave, where he lay among the Comyn before him. Their troubles were over; mine lay ahead of me, on the trail. My hand was busy about the reins; I could not let it go to grip at the hilt of my sword, and I felt uneasy, as if somewhere at the back of my mind I could *see* Kadarin, surrounded by his fanatics, could see Thyra's strange golden eyes so much like Marjorie's. Where was Rafe? Had Kadarin seized on him too? Rafe feared Sharra, almost as much as I, but could he stand against Kadarin?

Could I? Would I let them force me back again into those fearful fires? I had not had the courage to die, before.... Would I live, craven, in Sharra, without courage to die...?

Gabriel was riding at the head of the Guards, and in the small detachment I noticed he had brought both his sons; the slender, dark, gray-eyed Rafael, like a younger, darker Regis, and sturdy young Gabriel, whose reddish hair made me think of my father. I supposed that sooner or later I would have to adopt one of them as my Heir, since I would father no more sons....

I heard Regis speaking and realized I had drifted very far away.

"Do you know if Marius had a son, Lew?"

"Why, no," I said. "If he did, he never told me...." But there had been so many things he had never had any time to tell me. He had not been a boy, though Lerrys had called him so; when he died he was twenty, and at that age I had been three years at Arilinn, three years as cadet and officer in the Guard, had sold myself into slavery and fire in Sharra. "I suppose it's possible. Why?"

"I'm not sure," Regis said. "But my foster-son, Mikhail—Javanne's son—told me that his brother Gabriel said something about a rumor going round among the Guards, just before Council. Everybody knew, of course, that the Alton Domain was to be declared forfeit, and—forgive me, Lew—that they wouldn't hear of Kennard's younger son taking it, because of his Terran education. But that the Council, or somebody, had found an Alton child, and they were going to declare it Head of the Domain, under Hastur Regency. Something of that sort. You know what sort of rumors get around in the cadet corps; but this seemed more persistent than most."

I shook my head. "I suppose it's not impossible Marius could have fathered a son. Or, for that matter, that my father might have left a bastard or two; he didn't tell me everything about his life. Though, I should think, I would have known—"

"It's possible that someone might have had his child, from a casual love affair, and not told anyone till he was gone," Regis said, and I caught the unspoken part of that, that there were women enough who would enjoy the status of bearing a *laran* child to Comyn, he should know. . . .

"And," I finished, "no woman would dare lie about it, not to a telepath, not to Comyn. But I'd think if it were true, your grandfather would have acted before this."

"I'd think so too," Regis said, and raised a hand to motion to Gabriel Lanart-Hastur to ride beside us. I think I myself would have questioned the boys, who had passed the rumor around, but perhaps Regis thought it beneath his dignity to interrogate boys in their teens. When Gabriel came riding close to us he said, "Brother-in-law, what's this tale going about in the cadets about an Alton child?"

"I don't know anything about it, Regis. Rafael said something, and the way I heard it, it was some bastard son of my own," said Gabriel good-humoredly, while I found myself thinking: if I had a sharp-tongued wife like the lady Javanne, I would make damned sure she never found out anything about any bastard child I had fathered! Gabriel's smile was rueful. "I could assure my son that it was none of mine, but there are other Alton kinsmen in the Domains. No doubt, if there's anything to it, whoever's backing him will bring the child forward when Council meets again." His eyes apologized to me as he said, "You're not all that popular anymore, Lew. The Guardsmen would follow you to hell—they still talk about how good an officer you were—but that's a long way from being Warden of Alton."

And for a moment I was heartily sick of the whole business. It occurred to me that the best thing to do, when I reached Thendara, was to come to some understanding with Gabriel about the Domain, then find a ship and take passage out, away from Darkover and Sharra and all of it . . . but I thought

of Armida, far in the Kilghard Hills, and my homeland there.
And I remembered, like a pain gripping me in the vitals.
*Kadarin had the Sharra matrix. Twice I had tried to leave
it behind, on another planet. Twice I had been drawn back to
it....I was slave and exile for Sharra and it would never let
me go, and somehow I must fight it and destroy it...fight
Kadarin, too, if need be, and all his wild-eyed madman and
followers....*
*Fight them? Alone? As soon face, with my single ceremonial
sword, and my one hand, all of Beltran's armies...and I was
no legendary Comyn hero, armed with a magical spell-sword
out of legend!*

I twisted my head, looking back toward the Lake of Hali
and the low, gleaming chapel on the shore. I could feel Regis
and Gabriel thinking that I was saying farewell to the last
resting place of my brother. But instead I was wondering if,
in all the history of the Comyn, there was a weapon against
Sharra.

Ashara must know. And if she knew, perhaps, my kinswoman Callina would know.

I said, "Gabriel, Regis, excuse me, I must go and speak to
Linnell. She loved Marius and she is crying again." I rode
forward, feeling the prickling again in my back as if I were
being watched, and I *knew*, that from somewhere, whether
with some small band of ruffians or through the matrix, Kadarin was watching me...but because Regis and Dyan had
brought a detachment of the Guard, with swordsmen, he
would not, quite, dare attack us now.

He had access to Terran weapons. Marius had died with
a bullet through his head. But even so, he could not face a
whole detachment of Guardsmen...so for the moment I was
safe.

Maybe.

Disregarding the pricking of warning, I rode forward to
speak to Linnell, to try to comfort my foster-sister.

Linnell's eyes were red and her face blotched, but she had
begun to look peaceful again. She tried to smile at me.

"How your head must ache, Lew—it's a bad cut, isn't it?
Jeff told me he put ten stitches in it. You should be in bed."

"I'll manage, little sister," I said, using the word *bredilla*
as if she were the child she had been. But Linnell must be
two or three and twenty now, a tall poised young woman,

with soft brown hair and blue eyes. I supposed she was pretty; but in every man's life there are two or three women—his mother, his sisters—who simply don't register on his mind as women. Linnell was, always, no more to me than my little sister. Before her big, sympathetic eyes, I wished suddenly that I could tell her about Dio. But I would not burden her with that dreadful story; she was still sick with grief about Marius.

She said, "At least he was buried as a full member of the Comyn, with all honors; even Lord Ardais came to do him honor, and Regis Hastur." I started to say something bitter—what good is the honor of the dead?—then held my peace; if Linnell could find comfort in that, I was glad. Life went on.

"Lew, would you be very upset if Derik and I were married soon after Festival?"

"Upset? Why, *breda*? I would be glad for you." That marriage had been in the air since Linnie put away her dolls. Derik was slow-witted and not good enough for her, but she loved him, and I knew it.

"But—I should still do mourning for—for Kennard, and for my brother—"

I reached over, clumsily, letting go of the reins for a moment, to pat her on the shoulder. "Linnie, if Father or Marius is anywhere where they can know about it—" which I did not believe, at least not most of the time, but I would not say that to Linnell—"do you think their ghosts could be jealous of your happiness? They loved you and would be glad to see you happy."

She nodded and smiled at me.

"That's what Callina told me; but she is so unworldly. I wouldn't want people to think I wasn't paying proper respect to their memory—"

"Don't you worry about that," I said. "You need kinsmen and family, and now more than ever; without foster-father or brother, you should have a husband to look after you and love you. And if anyone says anything suggesting you are not properly respecting them, you send that person to me and I will tell them so myself."

She blinked back tears and smiled, like a rainbow through cloud. "And you are the Lord of the Domain now," she said, "and it is for you to say what mourning shall be held. And Callina is Head of my Domain. So if both of you have given permission, then I will tell Derik. We can be married the day after Festival. And at Festival, Callina's to be handfasted to Beltran—"

I stared at her, open-mouthed. In spite of all, was the Council still bent on this suicidal madness?

I must certainly see Callina, and there was no time for delay.

Andres asked me, as we rode through the gates of the city, if I would come and speak to the workmen who had been hired to repair the town house. I started to protest—I had always obeyed him without question—and suddenly I recalled that I need not, now, even explain myself.

"You see to it, foster-father," I said. "I have other things I must do."

Something in my voice startled him; he looked up, then said in a queerly subdued voice, "Certainly, Lord Armida," and inclined his head in what was certainly a bow. As he rode away, I identified what had been in his tone; he had spoken to me as he had always spoken to my father.

Linnell's eyes were still red, but she looked peaceful. I said, "I must see Callina, sister. Will she receive me?"

"She's usually in the Tower at this time, Lew. But you could come and dine with us—"

"I would rather not wait that long, *breda*. It's very urgent." Even now I could still feel the prickling, as if Kadarin were watching me behind some clump of trees or from some dark and narrow alleyway. "I will seek her out there."

"But you can't—" she began, then stopped, remembering: I had spent three years in a Tower.

I had never been in the Comyn Tower before, though I had come to the Castle every summer of my life except for the Arilinn years. I had spoken to the technicians in the relays, but I did not think there were many living telepaths who had actually stepped through the insulating veils. And even among those who kept the relays going, I did not think there were many who had ever seen the ancient Keeper, Ashara. Certainly my father said she had not been seen in the memory of anyone he had ever known. Maybe, I thought, there was no such person!

Perhaps Callina knew I was coming; she met me and beckoned me softly through the relay chamber—I noted that there was a young girl at the screen, but I did not recognize her—and through an inner chamber into what must have been the ancient matrix laboratory—at least that is what we would have called it at Arilinn. I could believe it had been built long before that, in the Ages of Chaos or before; there were matrix monitor screens, and other equipment the use of which I had not the foggiest notion. I found I did not like to think of the level of matrix it would have taken to use some of these things. I could feel the soothing vibrations of a specially modulated telepathic damper which filtered out telepathic overtones without inhibiting ordinary thought. There was an immense panel about whose molten-glass shimmer I could not even make guesses; it might have been one of the almost-legendary psychokinetic screens. Among all these things were the ordinary prosaic tools of the matrix mechanic's art; cradles, lattices, blank crystals, a glass-blower's pipe, screwdrivers and soldering irons, odd scraps of insulating cloth. Beyond them she motioned me to a seat.

"I've been expecting you," she said, "ever since I heard that they got away with the Sharra matrix. I suppose it was Kadarin?"

"I didn't see him," I said, "but no one else could have touched it without killing me. I'm still here—worse luck!"

"You're still keyed into it, then? It's an illegal matrix, isn't it?"

"It's not on the screens at Arilinn," I said. They had found that out when Marjorie died. But this was an older Tower; some memory of it might linger here. She said, "If you can give me the pattern, I'll try to find it." She led me to the monitor screen, flashing with small glimmers, one for every known and licensed matrix on Darkover. She made a gesture I remembered; I fumbled one-handed with the strings of the matrix crystal around my neck, averted my eyes as it dropped into her hand, seeing the crimson fires within.... It still resonated to the Sharra matrix; it was no good to me.

And while I bore it, anyone with the Sharra matrix could find me...and it seemed, though it could have been my imagination, that I could feel Kadarin, watching me through it....

She took it from me, matching resonances so carefully that there was no shock or pain, and laid it in a cradle before the screen. The lights on the screen began to wink slowly; Callina leaned forward, silent, intent, her face shut-in and plain. At last she sighed. "It's not a monitored matrix. If we could monitor and locate it, we might even destroy it—though destroying a ninth-level matrix is not a task I am eager to attempt, certainly not alone. Perhaps Regis—" she looked thoughtfully at my matrix, but she did not explain and I wondered what Regis had to do with it. "Can you give me the pattern? If the others—Kadarin, Thyra—were using matrixes which resonated to Sharra—"

"Thyra, at least, was a wild telepath. I don't know where she got her matrix, but I'm sure it's not a monitored one," I said. I supposed she had it from old Kermiac of Aldaran; he had been training telepaths back in those hills since before my father was born. If he had lived, the whole story of the Sharra circle would have been different. I tried to show her the pattern against the blank screen, but only blurs swirled against the blue surface, and she gestured me to take up my own matrix and put it away.

"I shouldn't have let you try that, so soon after a head injury. Come through here."

In a smaller, sky-walled room, I relaxed, in a soft chair, while Callina watched me, aloof and reflective. She said at last, "Why did you come here, Lew? What did you want from me?"

I wasn't sure. I did not know what, if anything, she could do about the ghost-voice in my mind, my father's voice. Whether a true ghost or a reverberation from brain-cells injured in his dying grip on my mind, it would fade away at last; of that I was certain. Nor could she do anything much about the fact that the Sharra matrix was in the hands of Kadarin and Thyra, and that they were here in Thendara. I said harshly, "I should never have brought it back to Darkover!"

"I don't know what choice you had," she pointed out reasonably. "If you are keyed into it...."

"Then I shouldn't have come back!"

And this time she did not argue with me, only shrugged a little. I was here on Darkover and so was the matrix. I said, "Do you suppose Ashara knows anything about it? She goes back a long way..." and paused, hesitant. Callina's voice rebuked: "No one asks to see Ashara!"

"Then maybe it's time they did."

Her voice was still, stony and remote. "Perhaps she would consent to see you. I will inquire." For a moment she was nothing like the girl I had known, my cousin and kinswoman. I was almost afraid of her.

"There must have been a time when telepaths knew how to handle things like the Sharra matrix. I know it was used by the forge-folk to bring metal to their forges; and it was used as a weapon. If the weapon wasn't destroyed, why would they have destroyed the defenses against it?"

Callina started a little, as if she had been very far away and the sound of my voice had brought her back from whatever distance she had inhabited. I remembered that look on Marjorie's face, the heart-breaking isolation of a Keeper, alone even at the center of a great circle. Somehow it made me lonely for my days at Arilinn. Callina and I had not been there at the same time, but she was part of it, she remembered, we were comfortable together.

"What can Kadarin *do* with the matrix?" she asked.

"Nothing, himself," I said, "but he has Thyra to control it." Even at the beginning, he had wanted Thyra to control the matrix; she was more pliant to his will than Marjorie, who had, at the last, rebelled and tried to close the gate into that other world or dimension from which Sharra came into this world in raging fire...I said, "If he wanted to, he could burn Thendara around the heads of the Comyn, or go to the Trade City and bring one of their damned spaceships down out of the sky! The matrix is that powerful; and the thing is, he doesn't have enough telepaths to control it as if it were a proper ninth-level matrix. Which it isn't: it's something unholy, a weapon, a force—" I stopped myself. Like Callina I had been Tower-trained, I should know better. Old tales made matrixes magical, called them gates to sorcery and alien magic. I knew the science of which they were a part. A matrix is a tool, no more good or evil than the one who uses it; a device to amplify and direct the *laran,* the special hyper-developed psychic powers of the Comyn and those of their blood. The superstitious might speak of Gods and magical powers. I knew better. And yet the form of fire blazed in my mind, a woman, tall and imposing, overshadowing...and now she bore Marjorie's face. Marjorie, competent and unafraid in the midst of the rising illusion-flames of Sharra, and then—then crumpling, screaming in agony as the flames struck inward—my hand burning like a torch beneath the matrix....

Callina reached out one hand, lightly touched my forehead, where Jeff had stitched the sword cut. Under her touch the fire went out. I found that I was kneeling at her feet, my head bent under the weight of it.

She said "But would he dare? Surely no sane man—"

I said, hearing the bitterness in my own voice, "I'm not sure he's a man—and I'm even less sure he is sane."

"But what could he hope to accomplish, unless he is simply mad for destruction?" she asked. "Surely he would not risk the woman—Thyra, you called her?—She was his—" she hesitated, and I shook my head. I had never understood the relationship between Kadarin and Thyra. It was not the ordinary relationship of lovers, but something at once less and more. I bent my head; I too had been glamored by the dark, glowing beauty of Thyra, so like and so unlike Marjorie. I had chosen. And Marjorie had been destroyed....I turned on her in rage. She said softly, "I know, Lew. I know."

"You know! Thank the Gods you *don't* know—" I flung at her, in a blind fury. What could she know of that, that raging fire, that fury, ravening between the worlds....

But under her steady eyes my rage dissolved. Yes, she did know. On that dreadful day when I had turned on Kadarin with the desperation of a man who knows himself already condemned to death, smashed the gate between the worlds and closed away Sharra from this world, I had thrust forth with my last strength and brought Marjorie and myself *between* the world-gates. The Terrans called it teleportation. I had brought us both to the matrix chamber in Arilinn, both of us terribly wounded, Marjorie dying. Callina had fought to save her; Marjorie had died in her arms. I bent my head, haunted again by that memory burned into my brain; Callina, holding Marjorie in her arms, the moment of peace that had descended in that last minute over her face. Yes, she knew.

I said, trying to think about it calmly without going into the horror again, "I don't think, if he was sane, he would risk Thyra; but I'm not sure he understands the danger, and if the matrix has them both in its grip....I don't know if he would have any choice." I knew how the matrix could control a worker, how it had seized control even from our carefully balanced circle, going forth to do its ravening work of destruction.

"It—wants to destroy," I said unsteadily. "I think it was made in the Ages of Chaos, to burst forth from control, to kill as much as it could, burn, destroy....I don't think anyone alive now knows how to control it." For years, I knew, the

Sharra matrix had lain harmlessly on the altars of the forge-folk, a talisman invoking their fire Goddess, to light their altars. To bring fire to their forges and fires, and the Goddess within, content with her worshippers and their fires, had not been roused into this world....

And I had loosed it on Darkover; I, a complacent puppet in Kadarin's hands. And he had used my own rage, my own lust, my own inner fires...

This was superstitious nonsense. I drew a deep breath and said, "In the Ages of Chaos there were many such weapons, and somewhere there must be defenses, or the memory of defenses against them. Maybe, then, Ashara would know." But would she care, if she had withdrawn so far from the world?

Callina picked up the unspoken question and said, "I do not know. I—I am afraid of Ashara—" I could see her shaking. She said, "You think I am here, safe, isolated—out of the troubles in the Council and the Comyn—Merryl hates me, Lew, he will do anything to keep me from having power in Comyn Council. And now there is this alliance with Al-daran—you do know Beltran is bringing an army to the very gates of Thendara, and if at the last, they refuse him this alliance—do you suppose *he* knows about Sharra, or will use it as a weapon?"

I didn't know. Beltran was my kinsman; there had been a time when I had trusted him, even as I had trusted and liked Kadarin. But Sharra had seized on him, too, and I still felt that was why he had this lust for power... and he, too, would have been alerted to its presence.

I said, "They *can't* marry you off to Beltran, just like that! You are Head of a Domain and Keeper...."

"So I thought," she said dispassionately. "But if I were not Head of a Domain, he would not want me—I do not think it is me he wants. If he simply wanted to marry into the Comyn, there are other women as close to the center of power; Derik's sister Alanna was widowed last year. As for my being Keeper—I do not think the Council wants a Keeper in power there, either. And if I marry—" she shrugged. "There's the end of that."

I remembered the old stories that a Keeper maintains her power only through her chastity. It's drivel, of course, su-perstitious rubbish, but like all superstitions, it has a core of truth. *Laran,* in a Comyn telepath, is carried in the same channels as the sexual forces of the body. The main side effect, for men, is that prolonged or heavy work in the matrixes temporarily closes off the channels to sex, and the man undergoes a prolonged period of impotence. It's the first thing a man, working in the Towers, has to get used to, and some people never learn to handle it. I suppose for many people it would seem a high price to pay.

A woman has no such physical safeguard. While a woman is working at the center of a circle, holding the tremendous forces of the amplified linked matrixes, she must keep the physical channels clear for that work, or she can burn up like a torch. A three-second backflow, when I was seventeen years old, had burned a scar in my hand that had never really healed, the size of a silver coin. And the Keeper is at the very center of those flows. While she is working at the center of the screens, a Keeper remains chaste for excellent and practical reasons which have nothing to do with morality. It's a heavy burden; few women want to live with it, more than a year or two. In the old days, Keepers were vowed to hold their office lifelong, were revered and treated almost as Goddesses, living apart from anything human. In this day and age, a Keeper is simply required to retain her chastity while she is actively working as a Keeper, after which she may lay down her post, conduct her life as she pleases, marry and have children if she wishes. I had always assumed that Callina would elect to do this; she was, after all, the female Head of the Domain, and her oldest daughter would hold the Domain of Aillard.

She followed my thoughts and shook her head. She said wryly, "I have never had any wish to marry, nor met any man who would tempt me to leave the Tower. Why should I bear a double burden? Janna of Arilinn—she was your Keeper, was she not?—left her post and bore two sons, then fostered them away, and came back to her work. But I have served my Domain well; I have sisters, Linnell will soon be married, even Merryl, I suppose, will some day find a woman who will have him. There is no need..." but she sighed, almost in despair. "I might marry if there was another who could take my place.... but not Beltran. Merciful Avarra, not Beltran!"

"He's not a monster, Callina," I said. "He's very like me, as a matter of fact."

She turned on me with wild anger, and her voice caught

in her throat. "So you'd have me marry him too? A man who would bring an army against Thendara, and blackmail my kinsmen into giving him the most powerful woman in the Council for his own purposes? Damn you! Do you think I am a *thing,* a horse to be sold in the market, a shawl to be bartered for?" She stopped, bit her lip against a sob, and I stared at her; she had seemed so cold, remote, dispassionate, more like a mechanical doll than a woman; and now she was all afire with passion, like a struck harp still vibrating. For the first time I knew it; Callina was a woman, and she was beautiful. She had never seemed real to me, before this; she had only been a Keeper, distant, untouchable. Now I saw the woman, trapped and frantic behind that barricade, reaching out— reaching out to me.

She dropped her face into her hands and wept. She said, through her tears, "They have put it to me that if I do not marry Beltran it will plunge the Domains into war!"

I could not stop myself; I reached out, drew her into my arms.

"You shall *not* marry Beltran," I said, raging. "I will kill him first, kinswoman!" And then, as I held her against me I knew what had happened to us both. It was not as kinswoman that I had vowed to shelter and protect her. It went deeper than that; it went back to the time when she had been the only woman in the Comyn who understood my rebellion against my father, to the time when she had fought to save Marjorie's life and had shared my agony and despair. She was Tower-trained, she was a memory of the one good time in my entire life, she was home and Arilinn and a time when I had been happy and real and felt my life worthy; a time when I had not been damned.

I held her, trembling with fright, against me; clumsily, I touched her wet eyes. There was something else, some deeper, more terrible fear behind her.

I murmured, "Can't Ashara protect you? She is Keeper of the Comyn. Surely she would not let you be taken from her like this." '

We were deeply in rapport now; I felt her rage, her dread, her outraged pride. Now there was terror. She whispered, her voice only a thread, as if she feared that she would be heard, "Oh, Lew, you don't know—I am afraid of Ashara, so afraid...I would rather marry Beltran, I would even marry him to be free of her..." and her voice broke and strangled. She clung to me in terror and despair, and I held her close.

"Don't be afraid," I whispered, and felt the shaking tenderness I had thought I would never know again. Burned and ravaged as I was, scarred, mutilated, too deeply haunted by despair to lift my one remaining hand to save myself—still, I felt I would fight to the death, fight like a trapped animal, to save Callina from that fate.

... still there was something between us. I dared not kiss her; was it only that she was still Keeper and the old taboo held me? But I held her head against my breast, stroking her dark hair, and I knew I was no longer rootless, alone, without kin or friends. Now there was some reason behind my desperate holding on. Now there was Callina, and I promised myself, with every scrap of will remaining to me, that for her sake I would fight to the end.

CHAPTER SEVEN

"There's only one good thing about Council season," said Regis sleepily, "I get to see you now and then."

Danilo, barefoot and half-dressed at the window, grinned back at him. "Come now, is that the spirit in which to face the final day of Council?"

Regis groaned and sat up. "I suppose you had to remind me. Shall I send for breakfast?"

Danilo shook his head, rubbing his chin thoughtfully. "I can't stay; Lord Dyan asked me to dine with him last night, he even said I could bring you if I wished; but I told him I'd be engaged elsewhere." He smiled at his friend. "So he said breakfast would do. I suppose, too, that I'll have to wear Council robes." He made a wry face. "Without disrespect to our worthy forefathers, did you ever see any robes as ugly as full Council ceremonial dress? I am sure the cut and fashion have not changed since the days of Stephen the Fourth!"

Regis chuckled, swinging his feet out of bed. "Longer than that, surely—I am certain they were designed by Zandru's great-grandmother."

"And she made him wear them as punishment when he was more wicked than usual," laughed Danilo. "Or do you suppose they were designed by *cristoforos,* so that while we sit at Council we will be doing suitable penance for our sins?"

"Sitting in Council is penance enough," said Regis glumly.

"And the Ardais colors—gray and black, how dismal! Do you suppose that is why Dyan is so morose—the result of wearing black and silver in Council for so many years? If I were no more than your paxman, at least I could wear blue and silver!"

"We shall have to design you a special robe for your divided loyalties," said Regis, mock-serious. "Patchwork of black and blue. Suitable enough, I suppose, for anyone who comes under Dyan's influence—like my ribs when he was my arms-master!" After all these years, Regis could make a joke of it. But Danilo frowned.

"He spoke again of my marriage, a day or two ago. It seems

his *nedestro* son is three years old, and looks healthy, and likely to live to grow up; he wants me to foster the boy, he said. He has neither time nor inclination to bring him up himself—and to do this I must have a household and wife. He said that he understood why I was reluctant—"

"He should, after all," said Regis dryly.

"Nevertheless, he said it was my duty, and he would take care to find me a wife who would not trouble me too much."

"Grandfather speaks in the same vein—"

"I think," Danilo said, "that I shall take one who will find herself a devoted Lady-companion; and after I have given her a child or two to raise, she will not weep if I absent myself from her bed and fireside. Then we should both be content."

Regis pulled on tunic and breeches, slid his feet into indoor boots. "I must breakfast with Grandfather; time enough to haul myself into ceremonials later. There seems little sense in attending Council—most of the speeches I will hear today I could say over from memory!"

Danilo sighed. "There are times when I think Lord Dyan—and some others I could mention—would rather see the Ages of Chaos come again than wake up to realities! Regis! Does your grandsire really think the Terrans will go away if we pretend they are not there?"

"I don't know what my grandfather thinks, but I know what he will say if I do not breakfast with him," Regis said, fastening his tunic-laces. "And now that I think of it, Council may not be so predictable as all that—it seems we are to have seven Domains again, after all. Did you know Beltran has brought and quartered an army above Thendara?"

"I heard he was calling it an honor-guard," said Danilo. "I would not have thought, when were were his *guests*—" he gave the word an ironic inflection,—"at Aldaran, that he had so much honor as all that to guard."

"I would say, rather, he needs an army to keep what little honor he has from escaping him," said Regis, remembering the time when he and Danilo had been imprisoned in Castle Aldaran. "Are they really going to accept him in Council, I wonder?"

"I don't think they have much choice," said Danilo. "Whatever his reasons, I don't like it."

"Then, if you are given a chance to speak in Council you had better say so," Regis said. "Dyan is expecting you, and Grandfather, no doubt, awaiting me. You had better go."

"Is this the hospitality of the Hasturs?" Danilo teased. But he gave Regis a quick, hard hug, and went. Regis stood in the door of his room, watching Danilo cross the outer hallway of the suite, and briefly come face to face with Lord Hastur.

Danilo bowed and said cheerfully, "A good morning to you, my lord."

Danvan Hastur scowled in displeasure, grunting the barest of uncivil greetings; it sounded like "H'rrumph!" He went on without raising his head. Danilo blinked in surprise, but went out the door without speaking. Regis, his mouth tightening with exasperation, went to comb his hair and ask his valet to lay out his ceremonial garb for Council.

Through the window the fog was lifting; high across the valley he could see the Terran HQ, a white skyscraper reddened with the glint of the red sun. His body-servant was fussing with the robes. Regis looked at them in distaste.

I am weary of doing things for no better reason than that the Hasturs have always done them that way, he thought, and the man flinched nervously as if Regis's uneasy thoughts could reach him. Maybe they could.

He stared morosely at the skyscraper, thinking: if his grandfather had been wise, he should have had the same kind of Terran education as poor Marius. If his grandfather indeed perceived the Terrans as the enemy, all the more so, then— a wise man will take the measure of his enemy, and know his powers.

Regis stopped, the comb halfway to his hair. Suddenly he knew why Danvan Hastur had not done just that.

Grandfather is sure that anyone who had a Terran education would, of necessity, choose the ways of Terra. He does not trust me, or the strength of what I have been taught. Are the Terrans and their ways so attractive, then?

His grandfather, in the little breakfast room, was still scowling as Regis drew up his chair. Regis said a polite good morning and waited until the servant had gone.

"Grandsire, if you cannot be courteous to my sworn man, I will find quarters elsewhere."

"Do you expect me to approve?" asked the old man in frigid displeasure.

"I expect you to admit I am a grown man with the right to choose my own companions," Regis said hotly. "If I brought a woman here for the night, and she was any sort of respectable woman, you would show her civility, at least. Danilo is as well born as I—or you yourself, sir! If I spoke like that to one of *your* friends, you would say I deserved a beating!"

Old Hastur clamped his lips tight, and even a non-telepath could have read his thoughts: *that was different.*

Regis said angrily, "Grandfather, it is not as if I were carousing in common taverns, disgracing the Hastur name by letting myself be seen in brothels and such places as the Golden Cage, or keeping a perfumed minion as the Dry-towners do—"

"Silence! How dare you speak of such things to me?" Hastur clamped his lips in anger. He gestured to the breakfast table. "Sit down and eat; you will be late for Council." As Regis hesitated he commanded dryly, "Do as you are told, boy. This is no time for tantrums!"

Regis clenched his fists. The quick wave of anger almost dizzied him. He said icily, "Sir, you have spoken to me as if I were a child for the last time!" He turned and went out of the room, disregarding his grandfather's shocked "Regis!"

As he walked through the labyrinthine corridors of Comyn Castle, his fists were clenched, and he felt as if a weight were pressing inward on his chest. It had been only a matter of time; this quarrel had been building for years, and it was just as well it should be in the open.

In all save this I have been an obedient grandson, I have done everything he asked of me; I am sworn to obey him as the Head of the Domain. But I will not be spoken to as if I were ten years old—never again. When he entered the Ardais apartments he was still fighting back a wholly uncharacteristic fury. The servant who let him in said an automatic, *"Su serva, dom..."* and broke off to ask, "Are you ill, sir?"

Regis shook his head. "No—but ask Lord Danilo if he will see me at once."

The message was carried, but answered by Danilo himself coming to the outer room. "Regis! What are you doing here?"

"I came to ask if I may join you at breakfast," said Regis, more calmly than he felt, and Dyan, appearing in the doorway, already in the ceremonial black and silver of Council, said quickly, "Yes, come and join us, my dear fellow! I wanted a chance to speak with you, in any case."

He went back toward the breakfast room, and Danilo murmured in an undertone, "What's wrong?"

"I'll tell you later, if I may. Grandfather and I had words," Regis muttered, "Leave it for now, will you?"

"Set another place for Dom Regis," Dyan ordered. Regis took a seat. Danilo looked at him, a swift questioning look, as he unfolded a napkin, but asked nothing aloud, and Regis was grateful.

He must know that I quarreled with Grandfather, and why. But he said nothing more, except for a complimentary remark about the food. Dyan himself ate sparingly, a little bread and fruit, but he had provided an assortment of hot breads, broiled meat and fried cakes; when Danilo commented on this, Dyan said, with a comical emphasis, "I am quite experienced at judging the—appetites—of young men." He caught Regis's eye for a moment, and Regis looked at his plate.

When they had finished and were idling over some fruits, Dyan said, "Well, Dani, I'm glad Regis joined us; I really wanted to talk to both of you. Most of the business of the Council has finished; this will be the final session, and because of the mourning for Kennard, everything's been put off to this last session. And there's much to be done. The heritage of Alton has to be settled—"

"I thought it was settled when Lew came back," Regis said, his heart sinking as he realized what Dyan was driving at.

Dyan sighed. "I know he is your friend, Regis, but look at realities, will you, without sentiment? It's a pity Kennard died without formally disinheriting him—"

"Why would he do that?" Regis asked, resentfully.

"Don't be a fool, lad! If he hadn't been mortally wounded and ill, you know as well as I that he'd have stood trial before the Comyn for treason, for that Sharra business, and been formally exiled. I don't have any ill will toward him—" but Dyan's glance slid uneasily away as Regis faced him, "and I've no desire to see Kennard's son cast out or stripped of wealth and power. Lew has no son, nor is likely to have, from something I heard—no, don't ask me where. A compromise might be worked out whereby he could have Armida, or its revenues, or both, for his lifetime, but—"

"I suppose you want to set up Gabriel in his place," Regis said. "I heard that song from Grandfather; I didn't think you would sing it too!"

"With Marius dead, it seems reasonable, doesn't it? I have no wish to see Alton heritage in Hastur hands. But there *is* an Alton child. Fostered in a good, loyal Domain—perhaps even in the care of Prince Derik and Linnell—that child could be trusted to bring back the honor of the Alton Domain."

"A child of Marius? Or of Kennard?"

"I'd rather not say anything about it until arrangements have been made," Dyan evaded, "but I give you my word of honor, the child's an Alton, and with potential *laran*. Regis, you are Lew's friend; can't you persuade him to step down and hand over the Domain in return for an assurance that during his lifetime he'll have Armida unquestioned? What do you think of that plan?"

It stinks to high heaven, Regis thought, but he cast about for some more diplomatic way of saying it. "Why not put it up to Lew? He's never been ambitious, and if this child is an Alton, he might perfectly well agree to adopt him and name the youngster his Heir."

"Lew's too damned much of a Terran," Dyan said. "He's lived in the Empire for years. I wouldn't trust him, now, to bring up a Comyn Heir."

"Kinsman," said Danilo, in the most formal mode; then he paused and walked restlessly to the window. Regis and Danilo were lightly in rapport, and Regis could see, through his friend's eyes, the view of the high mountain pass above Thendara and the scattered watch-fires of Beltran's army. Abruptly Danilo swung around and said to Dyan angrily, "You pretend to be afraid of Lew because of his Terran education and because of Sharra! Have you forgotten that Beltran, out there, was part of the Sharra rebellion too? And *that's* the man you're trying to bring into the Comyn as full partner?"

"Beltran's devoted himself to undoing what his father did. Kermiac was a Terran lackey; but when Beltran became Lord Aldaran, he renounced that—"

"And renounced honor, decency and the laws of hospitality," said Danilo angrily. "You weren't there, sir, when he last decided to take action! I saw Caer Donn burning!"

Dyan shrugged slightly. "A Terran city. What a pity he didn't burn one or two more while he was at it! Don't you see, Beltran can use Sharra against the Terrans, to give us the upper hand if they continue to—encroach—on our good will and our world."

Regis and Danilo stared at him in horror. Finally Regis said, "Kinsman, I think you speak this way because you do not know much about Sharra. It cannot be tamed that way, and used as a weapon—"

"We would not have to use it," Dyan said. "The Terrans,

too, remember Caer Donn and the burning of the spaceport there. The threat would be enough."

Why should we need such a threat against the Terrans? We live in the same world! We cannot destroy them without destroying ourselves!

Dyan asked angrily, "Have you too, Regis, been seduced by the Empire? I never thought to see the day when a Hastur would speak treason!"

"I think what you say is worse than treason, Dyan," Regis said, struggling for calm. "I cannot believe that you would do what you censured Lew for doing—make compromise with Beltran to bring back all those old terrors out of the Ages of Chaos! I know Beltran. You do not."

"Don't I?" asked Dyan, his eyes glinting strangely.

"If you do, and you still wish this alliance—"

"Look here," said Dyan harshly, interrupting him, "what we face now is the very survival of the Comyn—you know that. We need a strong Comyn, firmly allied against those who would hand us over to the Terrans. The Ridenow have already gone over—or haven't you heard Lerrys's favorite speech? Write off the Ridenow. Write off Lew—a cripple, half Terran, with nothing to lose! Write off the Elhalyn—" and as Danilo began a formal protest he gestured him imperatively to silence. "If you don't know that Derik's a halfwit, you're the only one in Council who doesn't. Forget about the Aillard—*Domna* Callina is a sheltered woman, a Keeper, a Tower-dweller; she can't do much, but I do have some influence, praise to Aldones, on *Dom* Merryl." His grin was wolfish. "What does that leave? The three of us in this room, Merryl, and your grandfather—who's over a hundred, and although he's still sharp-witted enough, he can't go on forever! In the name of all of Zandru's frozen hells, Regis, need I say anything more?"

And this is the burden of being a Hastur, Regis thought wearily. *This is only the beginning. More and more they will come to me for such decisions.*

"You think that means we must make an alliance with Aldaran, even at the cost of betraying the legitimate Heads of two Domains?" he asked.

"Two Domains? Lew would have been exiled six years ago, and it seems to me we are being generous with him," Dyan said.

"And *Domna* Callina? Is a Keeper nothing more than a woman to be married off for a political alliance?"

"If she wished to remain a Keeper," said Dyan savagely, "she should have remained within her Tower and refrained from trying to meddle in Council affairs! Tell me, Regis, will you stand with me in Council, or are you going to side with the Ridenow and hand us over to the Terrans without making a fight for Darkover?"

Regis bent his head. Put starkly like that, it seemed to give him no choice. Dyan had neatly mousetrapped him into seeming to agree, and either way, he betrayed someone. Lew was his sworn friend from childhood. Painfully he remembered the years he had spent at Armida, running about like a puppy at Lew's heels, wearing his outgrown clothes, riding, hawking, fighting at his side in the fire-lines when the Kilghard Hills went up in flame; remembered a tie even stronger, even older than that with Danilo; the first fierce loyalty of his life. Lew, his sworn friend and foster-brother.

Maybe this was best after all. Lew had said, again and again, that he wants no power in Comyn. Certainly Regis could not allow Dyan to believe that he would side against the Hasturs, and for the Terrans. Regis swallowed hard, trying to weigh loyalties. For all of Dyan's harshness, he knew that the older man was a shrewd judge of political reality. The thought of Darkover and the Domains in the hands of the Terrans, one more colony in a star-spanning Empire, came hard. But there seemed no middle way.

"I will never compromise with Sharra," he said wearily. "I draw the line there."

"If you stand firmly with me," said Dyan, "we will never need to use it. If we take a firm line, the threat is enough—"

"I don't believe that," said Danilo. "Sharra—" he stopped and Regis knew Danilo was seeing what he saw, the monstrous form of fire, blanking every matrix in the vicinity, drawing power even from those who hated it...death, destruction, burning!

Dyan shook his head. "You were children then, both of you, and you had a scare. The Sharra matrix is no more than a weapon— a mighty weapon. But nothing worse. Surely—" he grinned his wolfish grin—"you do not believe that it is a God from some other dimension, or the old legends that Hastur bound Sharra in chains and that she should be loosed only at the end of the world—or maybe you do" Dyan grinned again, "and maybe, Regis, you will have to be the Hastur to bind her this time!"

He is making fun of me, Regis knew it, and yet a terrifying chill made every hair on his body stand again on end.

Hastur the God, father and forefather of all the Hastur-kin, bound Sharra in chains....and I am Hastur. Is this my task?

Shaking his head to clear it, he reached out to pour himself another cup of *jaco*, and sipped it slowly, hardly tasting the bitter-chocolate fragrance. He told himself angrily not to be superstitious. The Sharra matrix was a matrix, a mechanical means of amplifying psychic powers; it had been made by human minds and hands, and by other human minds and hands it could be contained and made harmless. In Beltran's hands—and Kadarin's—it would be a fearful weapon, but then, there was no reason Beltran should be allowed to use it. Kadarin was human; and both Comyn and Terran had put a price on his head. Surely it was not as bad as he feared.

He said steadily to Dyan, "On the word of a Hastur, kinsman, I will never sit by and see our world handed over to the Terrans. We may not agree on the methods taken to avoid this; but we are in agreement otherwise."

And as he said it, he realized that he was trying to placate Dyan, as if he were still a boy and Dyan his cadet-master.

Dyan and his grandfather were on the same side, aiming at the same goal. Yet he had quarreled with his grandfather; and he was trying hard to agree with Dyan. Why? he wondered. Is it only because Dyan understands and accepts me as I am?

He said abruptly, "Thank you for a fine breakfast, cousin, I must go and get myself into those damnable Council ceremonials, and try to persuade my grandfather that Mikhail is still too young to sit through an entire Council session, Heir to Hastur or no—he is nevertheless only a boy of eleven! Dani, I will see you in the Crystal Chamber," and he went out of the room.

But it was Lerrys who caught up with him on the threshold of the Crystal Chamber. He was wearing the colors of his Domain, but not the full ceremonial robes, and he looked mockingly at Regis.

"Full fancy dress, I see. I hope Lew Alton has sense enough to turn up this morning wearing something like Terran clothes."

"I wouldn't call that very sensible," Regis said. "They

wouldn't fit the climate, and it would just offend people without any reason. Why should it matter what we wear to Council?"

"It doesn't. That's the point. That's why it makes me so damnably angry to see a dozen or so grown men and women behaving as if it made a difference whether we wore one kind of dress or another!"

Regis had been thinking something rather like this himself, as he got into the cumbersome and archaic robes, but for some reason it exasperated him to hear Lerrys say it. He said, "In that case, what are you doing wearing your clan colors?"

"I'm a younger son, if you remember," said Lerrys, "and neither Head nor Heir to Serrais; if I did it, all they'd do would be to send me away for not following custom, like a horrid small boy who's dressed up for the fun of it. But if you, Heir to Hastur, or Lew, who's head of Armida by default— there's literally no one else now—should refuse to follow that custom, you might be able to change things...things which will never be changed unless you, or somebody like you, has the brains and the guts to change them! I heard that Lord Damon, what-do-they-call-him, Jeff, went back to Arilinn. I wish he'd stayed. He'd been brought up on Terra itself, and yet he was telepath enough to become a technician at Arilinn—that would have let some fresh air into Arilinn, and I think it's time to break a few windows in the Crystal Chamber, too!"

Regis said soberly, ignoring the rest of Lerrys's long speech, "I wish I were as sure as you that they'd accept Lew by default. Have you heard anything about a rumor that they've found a child of one of the Altons and they're going to set it up, like a figurehead, in Lew's place?"

"I know there's supposed to be such a child," said Lerrys. "I don't know all the details. Marius knew, but I don't think he ever got the chance to tell Lew. You got him first, didn't you?"

Regis stared at him in dismay and anger. "Zandru's hells! Are you daring to say that *I* had anything to do with Marius's death?"

"Not you personally," said Lerrys, "but I don't think we'd have to look too far for the murderer, do you? It's just too convenient for that group of power-mad old freaks in Council."

Regis shuddered but tried not to let Lerrys see his consternation. "You must be mad," he said at last. "If my grandsire—and I suppose it's Lord Hastur you're accusing—had intended to send assassins to deal with Marius, why would he have waited this long? He arranged it with the Terrans to have Marius given the best education they could provide, he always knew where Marius was—why in all the hells should he send anyone round to murder him now?"

"You're not going to tell me a boy Marius's age had any personal enemies, are you?" Lerrys demanded.

Not in the Comyn—no more than he had any personal friends there, Regis thought, and said stiffly, "That touches the honor of Hastur, Lerrys. I warn you not to repeat that monstrous slander beyond this room, or I will—"

"You'll what? Whip out your little sword and cut me to pieces with it? Regis, you're acting like a boy of twelve! Do you honestly believe all this stable-sweepings about the honor of Hastur?" Even through his rage, something in Lerrys's voice got through to Regis. His hand had gone to his dagger, without being fully aware of it; now he let go the hilt, and said, "Don't mock that honor, Lerrys, just because you don't know anything about it."

"Regis," said Lerrys, and now his voice was deadly serious, "believe me, I'm not implying that you are personally anything but a model of integrity. But it wouldn't be the first time that a Hastur had stood by and watched someone murdered, or worse, because that person didn't fit into the Comyn plan. Ask Jeff sometime who murdered his mother, because she dared to hint that a Comyn Keeper was not a sacrosanct virgin locked up in Arilinn to be worshipped. He himself had two or three narrow escapes from being murdered out of hand because the Council didn't find him too convenient to their long-range plans. We can't even blame the Terrans—assassination has been a favorite weapon here on Darkover since the Ages of Chaos. Do you know what the Terrans think of us?"

"Does it matter what the Terrans think of us?" Regis evaded.

"Damn right it matters! Whether you like it or not—" he broke off. "Ah, why should I waste this on you? You're no better than your grandfather, and why should I give you the full speech I'm going to try to make in Council, if they don't

shut me up first?" He started to push on by Regis, who caught
his arm and held him.

"My grandfather may not have mourned very much for
Marius," he said, "but I'd swear with my hand in the fires of
Hali that he had nothing to do with his murder! I was there
when the Alton's town house was burned. Marius was killed
by men trying to get the Sharra matrix—and they did get
it, you know. You don't think my grandfather had anything
to do with *that*, certainly?"

Lerrys stared at him for a moment; then said contemp-
tuously, "You're worse than Lew—or you've been talking to
him. He sees *Sharra* as the bogeyman under every bed!
Damned convenient, isn't it?" He pushed past Regis and went
into the Council Chamber.

Thoughtfully, Regis followed. Most of the Council members were inside their railed enclosures, and his grandfather
had already risen for the roll call of the Domains. He scowled
at Regis, seeing him enter almost with Lerrys Ridenow, but
they parted and went to their separate enclosures.

Was Marius's death not the accidental death he had
thought, killed in defending his father's house and home
against invaders searching for something he did not even
know about? Certainly Marius knew nothing about the
Sharra matrix except its danger—he thought of the night
Marius had come to seek his help for Rafe Scott.

*I wonder where he is? Maybe Lew would know. If I were
young Scott, I think I would be hiding inside the Terran Zone
and never put my nose outside it while Kadarin is loose with
the Sharra matrix; and I think if Lew had any sense he would
do the same.* But Lew is not that kind of person. *Terrans are
cowards,* he thought, his mind sliding over what he had taken
for granted all his life; his own father had been killed in a
war because some coward had trusted to Terran weapons
which kill at a distance; and then he stopped and began to
think about that.

*They can't all be cowards, any more than all Comyn lords
are honorable and proud....* he thought. And, as Derik began
to call the roll of the Domains, he thought: *I will have to go
to the Terran Zone and find out what Rafe Scott knows about
the Sharra matrix. Unless he's joined forces with Kadarin—
and that was not the idea I got of Rafe Scott!*

One by one, from their enclosures, the Comyn of the Seven
Domains answered for their Houses. When "Alton" was

called, Regis saw Lew, dressed in the ceremonial robes of his
house, step forward, and answer, "I am here for Alton of
Armida." Regis had been braced for a challenge, but it did
not come, not even from where Dyan sat beside Danilo beneath the Ardais banner. Was the challenge to be more insidious than this, simply pressure on Lew to remain quietly
at Armida and adopt the Alton son they had found somewhere? Were they allowing him to keep the nominal leadership of Alton in return for some other concession? Regis
discovered that he could not even guess. And why was Dyan
so certain that Lew would have no children?

*Even Dyan himself, who is a lover of men, has a son; and
he lost another in childhood. I have fathered several children.
Why should Lew not marry and have as many children as he
wants?* He turned to look at Lew, and saw, as Callina Aillard
rose to answer for her Domain, that Lew was watching her
intently, so intently that it seemed, even through the thick
disturbance of the telepathic dampers in the Crystal Chamber, that for an instant he could read Lew's thoughts.

*But Callina is a Keeper. Nevertheless, she would not be the
first Keeper to lay down her high office and marry....not the
first nor the last. She would have to train her successor first,
but Lew is not an impulsive boy; he could wait long enough
for that. I think they might even be happy.* It would be good
to see Lew happy again.

They had finished the roll-call of the Domains, without
reference to Aldaran. It seemed to Regis that there was someone in that enclosure, behind the curtains, and he wondered
at that, but Derik, his task finished, had stepped back, and
Hastur was taking his place to preside over the session. Supposedly, this final session of Council was to complete any
unfinished matters, anything left unsettled during the Council season. In actuality, Regis knew, any small time-consum-
ing triviality would be brought up, anything to fill time until
weariness, or even hunger, brought Council to an end; after
which, the matter would be closed till next year. He supposed
that was why Hastur had not challenged Lew when he spoke
for Armida; the real problem of the Alton heritage would be
settled quietly by personal pressures, behind the scenes, not
argued out in Council.

He had seen those tactics used before. And now, ignoring
Dyan's signal, Hastur gestured to Lerrys Ridenow, who had
risen for recognition.

Lerrys came down into the central space where the rainbows from the prisms in the roof cast colored lights over the pale floor and walls. He bowed, and Regis thought, dispassionately, that the young man was beautiful as a cat; red-haired, slender, lithe, with the delicate chiseled features of the Ridenow; more beautiful, he thought, than any of the women in the Crystal Chamber. He wondered why he was noticing this in this solemn setting.

"My lords," Lerrys said, "I've heard a lot in this Chamber since Council began. All of you—" with one of those quick catlike movements, he swiveled his head to look around the room, "have been talking about such serious matters as marriages, and heritages, and repairs to the Castle roof—oh, not literally, perhaps, but that's what it amounts to, discussing things seriously which could be settled in three minutes by a little common sense. I want to know when we are going to talk about serious things. For instance—" and this time the sweep of his eyes around the Chamber was hard and challenging, "when are we going to send our proper representative to the Empire Senate? When are we going to appoint a Senator with proper credentials? I want to know when, or if, we are going to launch a *real* investigation of who murdered Marius Alton and burned the Alton house over his head? And I want to know when we are going to take our part as an equal in the Empire Senate, instead of being under a Terran protectorate as a primitive, barbarian world with a feudal culture which mustn't be touched, as if we were savages just evolving to the point where we rub two sticks together and worship the god of fire who makes the spark!"

The contempt in his voice was scathing.

"They let us alone, when they ought to be honoring us as the first and most prestigious of their colonies!"

"That kind of honor—" it was a whiplash from Dyan— "we can well do without!"

Lerrys turned on him. He said, "What in hell do *you* know about the Terrans? Have you ever gone far enough to take a walk inside the Terran Zone and go through one of their buildings? Have you ever done *anything* in the Terran Zone except visit one of their exotic whorehouses? With all due respect—which isn't much, Lord Dyan—you ought to shut your mouth until you know what you're talking about!"

"I know you are trying to make us all Terrans—" said Dyan, and Lerrys said, "*Make* us Terrans? Hell! We *are* Ter-

rans, or has that significant fact been kept from you by your
crazy father, and all our forefathers? If there's anyone here
who doesn't know that we were a Terran colony once, it's
time that sheltered idiot learned the truth!"

Danvan of Hastur said repressively, "This matter has been
discussed before, by your elders, Dom Lerrys. We are all in
agreement that we want no part of Terra—"

"You are all in agreement," mocked Lerrys. "How many
of you are in agreement—all fifteen or sixteen of you? What's
the population of Thendara, at the last census, or have we
been too backward to number our people? What do you think
they would say, if you asked them whether they wanted to
go on worshipping you aristocrats as *the Hastur-kin, the children of Gods,* and all that balderdash? Or whether they preferred to be free citizens of the Empire, with a voice in their
own government, and no need to bow down to you lofty Comyn? Just ask them sometime!"

Edric Ridenow, Lord Serrais, rose ponderously from his
seat. He said, "We have ruled these lands from time out of
mind and we know what our people want. Get back to your
place, Lerrys; I did not give you leave to speak!"

"No, you didn't," retorted Lerrys at white heat, "and I
spoke anyway. It needs saying! I am a citizen of the Empire,
I want some real voice in what's happening!"

"Do you really believe that will give you such a voice?"
inquired Lord Hastur. Regis thought he sounded genuinely
curious. "You have accused Lord Dyan of speaking without
real knowledge of the Terrans. Can you accuse me of the
same? I have dealt with the Terrans during most of my long
life, Lerrys, and I can assure you, they have nothing worth
wanting. But I cannot sit here and let you speak out of turn
in Council. I beg you, sit until your brother and lord gives
you leave to speak."

"Who in all of Zandru's hells gave him godship over my
voice?" demanded Lerrys in a rage. "I am Comyn, though you
may not want to admit it, and I have a right to be heard—"

"Gabriel," said Hastur quietly, "your duty."

Regis said, "Let him speak, Grandfather. I want to hear
what he has to say." But he was shouted down, and Gabriel,
drawn sword of the honor-guard in hand, strode to Lerrys
and said quietly, "Sit, *dom* Lerrys. Silence."

Lerrys said, "Like hell—"

"You leave me no choice, sir. Forgive me," Gabriel gestured to the Guardsmen, who collared Lerrys roughly; he

elbowed and shoved, but he was lightly built and the Guards were two huge hefty men, and they had no trouble at all in restraining him. They frog-marched him toward his seat. Abruptly, with a swift kick or two well-placed, he managed to free himself, and stood defiant.

"Never mind. I'm not going to upset your precious fool's Council any more," he said. "You're not worth it. Now have me assassinated as you did with Marius Alton, because I'm on the wrong side of the political fence! Damned fools, all of you, and murderers, because you're afraid to listen to the facts! You're a damned bloody anachronism, all of you, sitting there playing at lords and ladies with a star-spanning Empire at your feet! All right, damn it, go to hell in your own way, and I'll stand there and watch while you do it!" He laughed, loud and mocking, swirled with a great flying toss of his cape and his long light hair, and turned his back, striding out of the Council Chamber.

Regis sat there, aghast. Lerrys had voiced the thoughts he had never dared, before, to voice—and he had sat there, like a lump, not daring to speak aloud, not challenging Gabriel. *Damn it, I should have stepped down there beside him and demanded some of those answers! I am Heir to Hastur, they could not have silenced me so easily!*

He told himself that he had had no choice; that Lerrys had been excluded because of his disregard of Council custom and courtesies, not because of what he was saying.

He all but accused them of murder, and no one spoke to deny it, Regis thought, with a sudden shiver. Was it only because they felt it too ridiculous to answer? He did not like to think about the alternative.

One of the lesser nobles, a Di Asturien from the shores of Lake Mirien—Regis knew him slightly; he had had a brief affair with one of the man's daughters—rose and gestured to Lord Hastur for recognition. Hastur nodded, and the man came down to the speaker's place.

"My lords," he said, "I do not question your wisdom, but I feel it needs explaining. In these days, when we in Council are so few, why should Prince Derik be married inside of Comyn? Their children will be divided between the two Domains involved; would it not be better for Prince Derik to marry outside the Council, and thus bring in a strong alliance? Linnell Lindir-Aillard, too, should be married to some man who will bring new blood into Council. I also wish to point out that the two of them are very closely akin. With all respect, sir, I point out that the inner circle of Comyn has already been thinned overmuch by inbreeding. I'm not asking that we go back to the old days of keeping stud-books on *laran*, my lord, but any horse-breeder can tell you that too much inbreeding brings out bad things in the blood lines."

Yes, it does, Regis thought, looking at Callina, who looked so frail it seemed a puff of air would waft her off her feet; at Derik's shallow foolish face. Javanne had been lucky, being married outside direct Comyn lines. Her sons were all healthy and strong. Derik—looking at the young prince, Regis wondered if Derik would father anything but a string of halfwits like himself. And suddenly his blood iced; he looked at Derik and saw nothing, nothing but a grinning skull...*a skull, laughing*...he rubbed his hands over his eyes and Derik was simply sitting there with his good-natured dimwitted grin.

Hastur said quietly, "You have a good point, sir. But Prince Derik and *comynara* Linnell were childhood sweethearts, and it would be cruel to part them now. There are others who can bring fresh blood into Council."

Regis thought, cynically, *maybe that's a good name for what I am doing, fathering nedestro sons wherever I wish...the women don't seem to object, and neither do their fathers, since I am Hastur of Hastur*...and his thoughts slid aside, as he saw Lady Callina rise, looking tall and stately in her crimson ceremonial robes.

"This matter is not for Council meddling," she said, pale as death, "Linnell is *my* ward! I have given consent to her marriage and that is enough!"

"Meddling, lady?" asked Di Asturien, "That's a strange way to put it. Marriages in Comyn are supposed to be settled by the Council, aren't they?"

"I am Head of Aillard. Linnell's marriage is not for the Council to agree or disagree."

"But the prince's is," the old man insisted. "I protest it, and I'm sure there are others!"

Derik said amiably, "Can't you trust me to choose my own wife, sir? Or am I to imitate a Dry-Towner and have half a dozen wives and *barraganas*? Even a prince should have a few areas of private choice."

"What does the lady say about it?" asked old Di Asturien, and Linnell, sitting in Callina's shadow, colored and shrank away.

"This marriage was approved by the Council a long time

ago," she said, almost in a whisper. "If somebody was going
to protest against it, they should have done so years ago.
Derik and I were handfasted when I was fourteen and he was
twelve. There's been time enough to protest it before this,
and before we—before we had our hearts set on each other."

"That was a long time ago, and the Council was stronger
then," said the old man, grumpily. "There are plenty of
women in the Domains with good blood in 'em. He didn't have
to choose a sister of another Domain Head."

"With respect, sir," said Lord Hastur, "we have heard what
you have to say. Is there anyone within Comyn who wants
to speak on this?"

"I will not hear," said Callina, in pale rage. "I have given
consent to this marriage, and there is no other with the power
by law to change it."

"And if anyone tries," said Derik, "I will challenge him
anywhere." He laid his hand to sword-hilt.

And for a moment it seemed to Regis that he saw the
Council as Lerrys had seen it: children, squabbling over toys,
that contemptuous *You'll whip out your little sword and cut
me to pieces with it.* Derik had spoken as honor and Comyn
law demanded, yet he sounded like a blustering fool. Derik
was a fool, of course. But had he ever had a chance to be
anything else? Were they all, in Comyn, just such fools?

But Hastur was going, calmly, along with custom. He said
to Di Asturien, "Sir, are you ready to accept Prince Derik's
challenge?"

The old man shrank.

"All Gods forbid, sir! I, challenge Hastur of Elhalyn and
my lawful prince? I was just putting the question, Lord Hastur, no more than that." He bowed to Derik. *"Su serva, Dom."*
And Regis, watching the dignified old man retreat, almost
servile, heard again Lerrys's question...*playing at lords and
ladies*... why, because of his ancestry, should a fool like Derik
make an old and honorable man, of excellent lineage and
long service to his country, cringe like that?

*I get it too. From the time I was ten years old, Guards
following me around like so many governesses, for fear I would
break a toenail—why, in heaven's name?*

Preoccupied again, he missed the next words of Hastur,
and roused suddenly to shock when Hastur called out, "The
Seventh Domain! Aldaran!"

Then Regis heard a voice he had never thought to hear

again, speaking from behind the curtain; then the curtain
rings clashed with a small metallic clamor, and a tall man
came and stood at the edge of the railing.

He looked like Lew; older, and unscarred, but the resemblance was still there; he might have been Lew's elder
brother. He said, "I am here for Aldaran; Beltran-Kermiac,
Lord of Aldaran and Scathfell."

And the shocked silence in the Crystal Chamber was shattered by Lew's loud cry.

"I protest!"

Lew Alton's narrative

CHAPTER EIGHT

I didn't know I was going to protest until I heard myself doing it.

I heard them call Aldaran's name, and realized that this was actually happening; it was not a nightmare. I had heard the voice in nightmares, often enough. He was still so much like me that I have seen twins less alike; although now, no one could mistake us...bitterness overwhelmed me. It was he who had worked to summon Sharra; and there he stood, unscathed; while I, who had suffered to stem the fire-storm he had raised, and contain Sharra again, so that it should not ravage our world from the Bay of Storms to the Wall Around the World—I stood here, scarred and mutilated, more of an outcaste than he.

"I protest!" I shouted again, leaping down until I stood at the center of the open space, facing him.

Hastur said mildly, "We have not yet called for a formal challenge. You must state the reasons for your protest."

I fought to steady my voice. Whatever my own hate—and I felt that it would rise and swallow me—I must speak now calmly. Hysteria would only harm my cause; no matter what protests, incoherent accusations, were tumbling over one another in my mind, I must plead my cause with quiet rationality. I grasped at the presence in my mind, the alien memories I carried; how would my father have spoken? He had usually been able to make them do his will.

"I declare—" I began, trying to steady my voice against the flood, "I declare—the existence—of an unsettled blood feud." Blood feud was held, everywhere in the Domains, to be an obligation surmounting every other consideration. "His life is—is mine; I have claimed it."

To this moment our eyes had not met; now he raised his head, and looked at me, skeptical, concerned. I turned my own away. I did not want to remember that once I had called this man cousin and friend. Gods above, how could the man stand there and look me calmly in the eye and say, as he was saying now, "I did not know you felt that way, Lew. Do you blame me for everything then? How can I make amends? Certainly I was not aware of any such quarrel as that."

Amends! I clenched the stump of my arm with my good hand, wanting to shout, *can you make amends for this? Can you give me back six years of my life, can you bring back—Marjorie?* For once in my life I was grateful for the presence of the telepathic dampers without which all this would have blasted through the room with the full force of the hyper-developed Alton rapport—but I said doggedly, "Your life is mine; when, where and as I can."

Beltran spread his hands slightly, as if to say, "What is this all about?" Before the puzzled look in his eyes, I swear that for a moment I doubted my own sanity. Had I dreamed it all? My fingernails clenched in my wrist, and I reminded myself; *this* was no nightmare.

Hastur said sternly, "Your words are nothing here, Lord Armida." I remembered, after a shocked second; this was *my* name, not my father's; I was Lord Armida now.

"You have forgotten," Hastur went on, "blood feud is forbidden here in Comyn as among equals." The word was a counterplay on words; the word *comyn* meant, simply, *equals in rank or status.*

"And I state," said Beltran calmly, "that I have no grudge against my cousin of Alton; if he believes there is a blood-feud between us, it must arise from a time in his life when he was—" and I could see everyone in Council saying what he seemed, so kindly, to forbear saying: *from a time when he was mad....*

The very existence of Comyn, the Seven Domains of the Hastur's kin, was predicated on an alliance prohibiting blood-feud, Comyn immunity. Which Beltran, damn him, now enjoyed. Zandru send him scorpion whips! Was there no way to stop this farce?

Where I was standing I could not see her; but Callina rose and came forward, her crimson Keeper's veils fluttering as if in an invisible breeze. I turned as she spoke; she stood there, strange, distant, remote, not at all like the woman I had held in my arms and pledged to support. Her voice, too, sounded faraway and overly distinct, as if it came, not *from* her, but somehow *through* her.

"My lord Aldaran, as Keeper of Comyn I have the right to ask this of you. Have you sworn allegiance to Compact?"

"When I am pledged Comyn," Beltran said, "I am ready to swear."

She gestured and said, "Your army stands out there, bearing Terran weapons, in defiance of Compact. Are we to allow you in Comyn when you have not yet sworn to observe the first law of Comyn, in return for welcoming you among us?"

"When I swear to Comyn," said Beltran with silken suaveness, "my Honor Guard shall give up those weapons into the hands of my promised wife."

I saw Callina flinch at the words. There were telepathic dampers all over the room, but still it seemed that I could read her thoughts.

If I do not agree to this marriage, it means war. The last war in the Domains decimated the Comyn. Beltran could wipe us out altogether.

She raised her eyes and looked at him. She said, her words dropping into deathly silence, "Why, then, my lord of Aldaran, if you are content with an unwilling bride—" she hesitated; I knew she did not turn or look at me, but I sensed the trapped despair behind her words—"then I agree. Let the handfasting be held on Festival Night."

"Be it so," said Beltran, with that smile that was like a mask over his true feelings, and bowed. I stood, without moving, as if my feet were rooted to the floor of the Crystal Chamber. Were they really going to do this? Were they going to sell Callina to Beltran, to prevent war? Was there no one who could lift a hand against this monstrous injustice?

In a final appeal I cried out, "Will you have him in Council, then? He is sealed to Sharra!"

He turned directly to me, then, and said, "So are you, cousin."

To that, there was nothing I could say. I felt at that moment like doing what Lerrys had done, and storming out of the Council, cursing them all.

I have never been quite sure what happened next. I know that I made a move to resume my seat, had taken a few steps toward the Alton enclosure, when I heard a cry, in a woman's voice. For a moment it sounded so like Dio's that I stood frozen; then Derik cried out, too, and I turned to see Beltran take a step back and thrust out his hands, as if to guard himself.

Then there were cries everywhere, shouts of dread and terror; backing a little away into the enclosure, I saw it, hanging in the air above us, growing, menacing....

The form of a chained woman, hair of flame, tossing, ravening, growing higher, higher, with the crackling sound of forest-fire...Sharra! The fire-form, Sharra....Now I knew it was a nightmare from hell, I backed away, too, from the rising flames licking at us, the smell of burning, the flood of terror, of hate, the corner of hell which had opened up for me six years ago....

I clutched at vanishing self-control before I could cry out again and disgrace myself by screaming like a woman. The Form of Fire was there, yes; it hovered and flickered and trembled above us, the shape of a woman, her head thrown back, three times the height of a tall man, the flames licking at her hair. *Marjorie! Marjorie, burning, overshadowed by Sharra...*then I caught at vanishing rationality.

No, this was not Sharra as I had known it. My heart was beating fast from fright, but there was no true smell of burning in the room, the curtains of the enclosures did not smolder or catch into flame where the fire touched them...this was illusion, no more, and I stood, clenching the fist of my good hand, feeling the nails cut into the flesh, feeling the old burning pain in the hand that was not there...*phantom pain, as this was no more than a phantom, an image of Sharra....I would have known the real thing, I would feel my whole body and soul tied into that monstrous overshadowing....*

The Form of Fire thrust out an arm...a woman's arm lapped in fire...and Beltran broke, backed away...bolted from the Crystal Chamber. Now that I knew what it was, I stood my ground, watching him go, wondering who had done it. Kadarin, wherever he was, drawing the Sword, evoking the Form of Fire? No. I was sealed to Sharra, body and soul; if Kadarin, who had also been sealed to that unholy thing, had summoned, I too would have been consumed in the flame....I gripped my hand hard on the railing, wondering. The Comyn were milling around, crying out in confusion. Two or three others bolted, too, through their private entrances at the back of the enclosures.

Callina? No Keeper would profane her office that way, using it to terrify. I could have done it—even now I could feel the heat of flame in my useless matrix—but I knew I had not. Beltran, who also was Sharra-sealed? He had been the most frightened of all, for he had seen Caer Donn burning.

The Form of Fire flamed and died and was gone, like a candle blown out by the wind.

Danvan of Hastur, Regent of the Comyn, had stood his ground, but he was white as death, and he was holding the rail before him as he spoke, ritual words almost without significance.

"I declare...Council Session...closed for this year and all matters before it, adjourned until another year shall bring us together..."

One by one, those members who had not already run away went silently out of the Chamber, already shocked and ashamed of their terror. I, who had faced the reality of Sharra, found myself wondering how they would react to the real thing. Yet my own heart was still pounding a little; a fear bred in the bone, a gateway just dimly ajar between worlds to let in that monstrous shadow....I had seen those gates open halfway, and knew that they opened into fire and hell, like the living heart of a volcano.

Then, behind Danvan Hastur, I saw Regis standing very still, his hand just touching his matrix. He did not look at me, he was not looking at anything, but I knew, as clearly as if I had spoken:

Regis! Regis had summoned that image! But why? Why and how!

He lowered his hand. I could see fine beads of sweat around his hairline, but his voice sounded normal. "Will you have my arm, Grandfather?"

The old man snarled, "When I need help I will be dressed in my shroud!" and, throwing his head erect, marched out of the Chamber. Now only Regis and I remained.

I found my voice, bitterly.

"You did that. I don't know how or why, but *you* did that! Cousin—can you play with such things as a joke?"

His hand fell away from his matrix, hanging limp at his side as if it hurt him. Maybe it did; I was too agitated to care. At last he said in a strained voice, only a whisper, "It gave us—time. Another year. They cannot—cannot challenge your right to the Alton Domain, or pledge Beltran to Council, for another year. Council has been—closed." Then he swayed, and caught weakly at the railing where he stood. I pushed him down in a chair.

"Put your head between your knees," I said roughly, and watched him as he sat there, his head bent, while a little color began to come back into his cheeks. At last he sat upright again.

"I am sorry if the—the image—frightened you," he said. "It was the only thing I could think of to stop this Council. This farce. I wanted them to see what it was that they had to fear. So many of them don't know."

I remembered Lerrys saying, *You see Sharra as the bogeyman under every bed*...no. He had not said that to me, but to Regis. I looked at him, dazed. I said, "There are supposed to be telepathic dampers in here. I should not be able to read your mind, nor you mine. Zandru's hells, Regis, what is going on?"

"Maybe the dampers aren't working," he said, in a stronger voice, and now he sounded completely rational; only afraid, as he had every right to be. I was afraid myself.

"The image didn't frighten me," I said, "except for a moment at first. I have seen the reality of Sharra. What frightens me, now, is the fact that you could do that, with dampers all over the room. I didn't know you had that much *laran*, though I knew, of course, that you had some. What sort of *laran* can do that?" I went to the nearest of the telepathic dampers and twisted dials until it was gone, the unrhythmic waves vanished. Now I could feel Regis's agitation and fear, full scale, and wished I could not. He said, in a strained voice, "I don't know how I did it. Truly I don't. I was standing here behind Grandfather, listening to Beltran talk so calmly, and wishing there was some way to show them what it had been....and then—" he wet his lips with his tongue, and said shakily, "then it was there. The—the Form of Fire."

"And it scared Beltran right out of the room," I said. "Do you think he knows that Kadarin has the Sharra matrix?"

"I couldn't read him. I wasn't trying, of course. I—" his voice broke again. "I wasn't *trying* to do anything. It just— just happened!"

"Something in your *laran* you don't know about? We know so little of the Hastur Gift, whatever it was," I said, trying to calm him. "Hang on to the good part; it scared Beltran out of here. I wish it had scared him all the way back into the Hellers! I'm afraid there's no such luck!"

I was willing to leave it at that. But as I turned to the doorway, Regis caught at my shoulder.

"But how could I do that? I don't understand! You—you accused me of playing with it, like a joke! But I didn't, Lew, I didn't!"

I had no answer for him. I moved aimlessly around the room, turning out the rest of the dampers. I could feel his fear, mounting almost to panic, rising as the dampers were no longer there to interfere with telepathic contact. I even wondered, angrily, why *he* should be so afraid. It was I who was bound to Sharra, I who must live night and day with the terror that one day Kadarin would draw the Sword of Sharra and with that gesture summon me back into that terrible gateway between worlds, that corner of hell that I once had opened, which had swept away my hand, my love—my life...

Firmly I clamped down on the growing panic. If I did not stop this now, my own fear and Regis's could reinforce each other and we would both go into screaming hysterics. I caught at what I could remember of the Arilinn training, managed to steady my breathing, felt the panic subside.

Not so Regis; he was still sitting there, in the chair where I had shoved him, white with dread. I turned around and was surprised to hear my own voice, the steady, detached voice of a matrix mechanic, dispassionate, professionally soothing, as I had not heard it in more years than I liked to think about.

"I'm not a Keeper, Regis, and my own matrix, at the moment, is useless, as you know. I could try to deep-probe you and find out—"

He flinched. I didn't blame him. The Alton gift is nothing to play games with, and I have known experienced technicians, Tower-trained for many years, refuse to face that fully focused gift of rapport. I can manage it, if I must, but I was not eager. It is not, I suppose, unlike rape, the deliberate overpowering of a mind, the forced submission of another personality, the ultimate invasion. Only the probably non-existent Gods of Darkover know why such a Gift had been bred into the Alton line, to force rapport on an unwilling other, paralyze resistance. I knew Regis feared it too, and I didn't blame him. My father had opened my own Gift in that way, when I was a boy—it had been the only way to force the Council to accept me, to show them that I, alien and half Terran, had the Alton Gift—and I had been ill for weeks afterward. I didn't relish the thought of doing the same thing to Regis.

I said, "It might be that they could tell you in a Tower; some Keeper, perhaps—" and then I remembered that here in Comyn Castle was a Keeper. I tended to forget; Ashara of the Comyn Tower must be incredibly old now, I had never seen her, nor my father before me... but now Callina was there as her surrogate, and Callina was my kinswoman, and Regis's too.

"Callina could tell you," I said, "if she would."

He nodded, and I felt the panic recede. Talking about it, calmly and detached, as if it were a simple problem in the mechanics of *laran*, had defused some of the fear.

Yet I too was uneasy. By the time I left the Crystal Chamber, even the halls and corridors were empty; the Comyn Council had scattered and gone their separate ways. Council was over. Nothing remained except the Festival Night ball, tomorrow. On the threshold of the Chamber, we encountered the Syrtis youngster; he almost ignored me, hurrying to Regis.

"I came back to see what had happened to you!" he demanded, and, as Regis smiled at him, I quietly took my leave, feeling I made an unwelcome third. As I went off alone, I identified one of my emotions; was I jealous of what Regis shared with Danilo? No, certainly not.

But I am alone, brotherless, friendless, alone against the Comyn who hate me, and there is none to stand by my side. All my life I had dwelt in my father's shadow; and now I could not bear the solitude when that was withdrawn. And Marius, who should have stood at my side—Marius too was dead by an assassin's bullet, and no one in the Comyn except Lerrys had even questioned the assassination. And—I felt myself tensing as I identified another element of my deep grief for Marius. It was relief; relief that I would not have to test him as my father had tested me, that I need not invade him ruthlessly and feel him die beneath that terrible assault on identity. He had died, but not at my hands, nor beneath my *laran*.

I had known my laran could kill, but I had never killed with it.

I went back to the Alton rooms, thoughtfully. They were home, they had been home much of my life, yet they seemed empty, echoing, desolate. It seemed to me that I could see my father in every empty corner, as his voice still echoed in my mind. Andres, puttering around, supervising the other servants in placing the belongings which had been brought here from the town house, broke off what he was doing as I came in, and hurried to me, demanding to know what had happened to me. I did not know that it showed on my face, whatever it was, but I let him bring me a drink, and sat sipping it, wondering again about what Regis had done in the Crystal Chamber. He had scared Beltran. But, probably, not enough.

I did not think Beltran was eager to plunge the Domains into war. Yet I knew his recklessness, and I did not think we could gamble on that; not when his outraged pride was at stake, the pride of the Aldarans.

I said to Andres, "You hear servants' gossip; tell me, has Beltran moved into the Aldaran apartments here in Comyn Castle?"

Andres nodded glumly, and I hoped that he would find them filled with vermin and lice; they had stood empty since the Ages of Chaos. It said something about the Comyn that they had never been converted to other uses.

Andres stood over me, grumbling, "You're not intending to go and pay a call on him there, I hope!"

I wasn't. There was only one way in the world I would ever come again within striking range of my cousin, and that was if he had me bound and gagged. He had betrayed me before; he would have no further chance. Sunk in the misery of that moment, I confess, to my shame, that for a moment I played with the escape that Dan Lawton, in the Terran Zone, had offered me, to hide there out of reach of Sharra.... but that was no answer, and it left Regis and Callina at the mercy of whatever unknown thing was working in the Comyn.

I was not altogether alone. The thought of Callina warmed me; I had pledged to stand beside her. And I had not yet spoken alone with my kinswoman Linnell, except over the grave of my brother. It was the eve of Festival Night, when traditionally, gifts of fruit and flowers are sent to the women of every family, throughout the Domains. Not the meanest household in Thendara would let tomorrow morning pass without at least a few garden flowers or a handful of dried fruits for the women of the household; and I had done nothing about a gift for Linnell. Truly, I had been too long away from Darkover.

There would be flower sellers and fruit vendors doing business in the markets of the Old Town, but as I stepped toward the door, I hesitated, unwilling again to show myself. Damn it, during the time I had lived with Dio, I had almost forgotten my scarred face, my missing hand, and now I was behaving as if I were freshly maimed—Dio! Where was Dio, had I truly heard her voice in the Crystal Chamber? I told myself sternly that it did not matter; whether Dio was here or elsewhere, if she chose not to come to me, she was lost to me. But still I could not make myself go down to ground level of the enormous castle, go out into the Old Town through Beltran's damnably misnamed *Honor Guard.*

Some of them would have known me, remembered me....

At last, hating myself for the failure, I told Andres to see about some flowers for Linnell tomorrow. Should I send some to Dio too? I truly did not know the courtesies of the situation. Out there in the Empire, I knew, a separated husband and wife can meet with common courtesy; here on Darkover, it was unthinkable. Well, I was on Darkover now, and if Dio wanted nothing from me, she would probably not want a Festival gift either. With surging bitterness I thought, *she has Lerrys to send her fruits and flowers.* If Lerrys had been before me, at that moment, I think I would have hit him. But what would that settle? Nothing. After a moment I picked up a cloak, flung it about my shoulders; but when Andres asked where I was going, I had no answer for him.

My feet took me down, and down into courtyards and enclosed gardens, through unfamiliar parts of the castle. At one point I found myself in a court beneath the deserted Aldaran apartments—deserted all my life, till now. Half of me wanted to go in there and face Beltran, demand—demand what? I did not know. Another part of me wanted, cravenly, to walk through the city, take refuge in the Terran Zone, and then— then what? I could not leave Darkover, not while the Sharra matrix was here; I had tried. And tried again. It would mean death, a death neither quick nor easy.

Maybe I would be better dead, even that death, so that I was free in death of Sharra... and again it seemed to me that the Form of Fire raged before my eyes, a thrilling in my blood, cold terror and raging, ravening flame like ichor in my veins....

No; this was real. I tensed, looking up at the hills behind the city.

Somewhere there, strange flames burned, an incredible ninth-level matrix twisted space around itself, a gateway opened, and the fire ran in my veins.... There was fire before my eyes, fire all through my brain....

No! I am not sure that I did not scream that furious denial aloud; if I did no one heard me, but I heard the echoes in the courtyard around me, and slowly, slowly, came back to reality. Somewhere out there, Kadarin ran loose, and with him the Sharra matrix, and Thyra whom I had hated, loved, desired and feared...but I would die before they dragged me back into *that* again. Deliberately, fighting the call in my mind, I raised the stump of my arm and slammed it down, hard, on stone. The pain was incredible; it made me gasp, and tears came to my eyes, but that pain was *real;* outraged nerves and muscles and bones, not a phantom fire raging in my brain. I set my teeth and turned my back on the hills, and that call, that siren call which throbbed seductively in my mind, and went into the Castle.

Callina. Callina could drive these devils from my mind.

I had not been inside the Aillard wing of Comyn Castle for many years, not since I was a child. A silent servant met me, managed not to blink more than once at the ruin of my face. He showed me into a reception room where, he said, I would find *Domna* Callina and Linnell with her.

The room was spacious and brilliant, filled with sunshine and silken curtains, green plants and flowers growing in every niche, like an indoor garden. Soft notes of a harp echoed through the room; Linnell was playing the *rryl*. But as I came in she pushed it aside and ran to me, taking an embrace and kiss with the privilege of a foster-sister, drawing back, hesitant, as she touched the stump of an arm.

"It's all right," I said. "You can't hurt me. Don't worry about it, little sister." I looked down at her, smiling. She was the only person on this world who had truly welcomed me, I thought; the only one who had had no thought of what my coming would mean. Even Marius had had to think of what it would mean in terms of Domain-right. Even Jeff; he might have had to leave Arilinn and take his place in Council.

"Your poor hand," she said. "Couldn't the Terrans do anything for it?"

Even to Linnell I didn't want to talk about it. "Not much," I said, "but I have a mechanical hand I wear when I don't want to be noticed. I'll wear it when I dance with you on Festival Night, shall I?"

"Only if you want to," she said seriously. "I don't care what you look like, Lew. You're always the same to me."

I hugged her close, warmed as much by her accepting smile as by the words. I suppose Linnell was a beautiful woman; I have never been able to see her as anything but the little foster-sister with whom I'd raced breakneck over the hills; I'd spanked her for breaking my toys or borrowing them without leave, comforted her when she was crying with toothache. I said, "You were playing the rryl...play for me, won't you?"

She took up the instrument again and began to play the ballad of Hastur and Cassilda:

> The stars were mirrored on the shore,
> Dark was the lone immortal moor,
> Silent were rocks and trees and stone—
> Robardin's daughter walked alone,
> A web of gold between her hands
> On shining spindle burning bright...

I had heard Dio singing it, though Dio had no singing voice to speak of—I wondered, where was Callina? I should speak with her—

Linnell gestured, and I saw, in a niche beyond the fireplace, Callina and Regis Hastur, seated on a soft divan and so absorbed in what they were saying that neither had heard me come into the room. I felt a momentary flare of jealousy— they looked so comfortable, so much at peace with each other—then Callina looked up at me and smiled, and I knew I had nothing to fear.

She came forward; I wanted to take her in my arms, into that embrace which was so much more than the embrace I would have given a kinswoman; instead she reached out and touched my wrist, the feather touch with which a working Keeper would have greeted me, and with that automatic gesture, frustration slipped between us like an unsheathed sword.

A Keeper. Never to be touched, never to be desired, even by a defiling thought...angry frustration, and at the same time, reassurance; this is how she would have greeted me if we were both back in Arilinn, where I had been happy...even had we been acknowledged lovers for years, she would no more have touched me than this.

But our eyes met, and she said gravely, "Ashara will see you, Lew. It is the first time, I think, in more than a generation, that she has agreed to speak with anyone from outside. When I spoke to her of the Sharra matrix, she said I might bring you."

Regis said, "I would like to speak with her, too. It may be that she would know something of the Hastur Gift..." but he broke off at Callina's cold frown.

"She has not asked for you. Even I cannot bring anyone into her presence unless she wishes it."

Regis subsided as if she had struck him. I blinked, staring aghast at this new Callina, the impassive mask of her face, the eyes and voice of a cold, stony stranger. Only a moment, and she was again the Callina I knew, but I had seen, and I was puzzled and dismayed. I would have said something more, even to reassure Regis that we would ask the ancient *leronis* to grant him an audience, but Linnell claimed me again.

"Are you going to take him away at once? When we have not seen each other for so many years? Lew, you must tell me about Terra, about the worlds in the Empire!"

"There will be time enough for that, certainly," I said, smiling, looking at the fading light. "It is not yet nightfall... but there's nothing good to tell of Terra, *chiya;* I have no good memories. Mostly I was in hospitals..." and as I said the word I remembered another hospital in which not I, but Dio had been the patient, and a certain dark-haired, sweet-faced young nurse. "Did you know, Linnie—no, of course, you couldn't know; you have a perfect double on Vainwal; so like you that at first I called her by your name, thought it was you yourself!"

"Really? What was she like?"

"Oh, efficient, competent—even her voice was like yours," I said. And then I stopped, remembering the horror of that night, the shockingly deformed, monstrous form that should have been my son...I was strongly barriered, but Linnell saw the twitching of my face and put up her hand to stroke my scarred cheek.

"Foster-brother," she said, giving the word the intimate inflection that made it a term of endearment, "don't talk about hospitals and sickness and pain. It's all over now, you're here at home with us. Don't think about it."

"And there are enough troubles here on Darkover to make you forget whatever troubles you may have had in the Empire," said Regis, with a troubled smile, joining us at the window, where the sun had faded, blurred by the evening clouds. "Council was not properly adjourned; I doubt we've heard the last of that. Certainly not the last of Beltran..." and Callina, hearing the name, shuddered. She said, looking impatiently at the clouds, "Come, we must not keep Ashara waiting."

A servant folded her into a wrap that was like a gray shadow. We went out and down the stairs, but at the first turning, something prompted me to turn back; Linnell stood there, framed in the light of the doorway, copper highlights caught in her brown hair, her face serious and smiling; and for a moment, that out-of-phase time sense that haunts the Alton gift, a touch perhaps of the precognition I had inherited from the Aldaran part of my blood, made me stare, unfocused, as past, present, future all collapsed upon themselves, and I saw a shadow falling on Linnell, and a dreadful conviction....

Linnell was doomed....the same shadow that had darkened my life would fall on Linnell and cover her and swallow her....

"Lew, what's the matter?"

I blinked, turning to Callina at my side. Already the certainty, that sick moment when my mind had slid off the time track, was fading like a dream in daylight. The confusion, the sense of tragedy, remained; I wanted to rush up the stairs, snatch Linnell into my arms as if I could guard her from tragedy...but when I looked up again the door was closed and Linnell was gone.

We went out through the archway and into a courtyard. The light rain of early summer was falling, and though at this season it would not turn to snow, there were little slashes of sleet in it. Already the lights were fading in the Old City, or could not come through the fog; but beyond that, across the valley, the brilliant neon of the Trade City cast garish red and orange shadows on the low clouds. I went to the railed balcony that looked down on the valley, and stood there, disregarding the rain in my face. Two worlds lying before me; yet I belonged to neither. Was there any world in all the star-spanning Empire where I would feel at home?

"I would like to be down there tonight," I said wearily, "or anywhere away from this Hell's castle—"

"Even in the Terran Zone?"

"Even in the Terran Zone."

"Why aren't you, then? There is nothing keeping you

here," Callina said, and at the words I turned to her. Her cobweb cloak spun out on the wind like a fine mist as I pulled her into my arms. For a moment, frightened, she was taut and resisting in my arms; then she softened and clung to me. But her lips were closed and unresponsive as a child's under my demanding kiss, and it brought me to my senses, with the shock of *déjà vu...somewhere, sometime, in a dream or reality, this had happened before, even the slashes of rain across our faces....* She sensed it too, and put up her hands between us, gently withdrawing. But then she let her head drop on my shoulder.

"What now, Lew? Merciful Avarra—what now?"

I didn't know. Finally I gestured toward the crimson smear of garish neon that was the Trade City.

"Forget Beltran. Marry me—now—tonight, in the Terran Zone. Confront the Council with an accomplished fact and let them chew on it and swallow it—let them solve their own problems, not hide behind a woman's skirts and think they can solve them with marriages!"

"If I dared—" she whispered, and through the impassive voice of a trained Keeper, I felt the tears she had learned not to shed. But she sighed, putting me reluctantly away again. She said, "You may forget Beltran, but he will not go away because we are not there. He has an army at the gates of Thendara, armed with Terran weapons. And beyond that—" she hesitated, reluctant, and said, "Can we so easily forget—*Sharra?*"

The word jolted me out of my daydream of peace. For the first time in years, Sharra had not even been a whisper of evil in my mind; in her arms I had actually forgotten. Callina might be bound to the Tower by her vows as Keeper, but I was not free either. Silent, I turned away from the balconied view of the twin cities below me, and let her lead me down another flight of stairs and across another series of isolated courtyards, until I was all but lost in the labyrinth that was Comyn Castle.

Both of us, lost in the maze our forefathers had woven for us....

But Callina moved unerringly through the puzzling maze, and at last led me into a door where stairways led up and up, then through a hidden door, where we stood close together as, slowly, the shaft began to rise.

This Tower—so the story goes—was built for the first of

the Comyn Keepers when Thendara was no more than a
village of wicker-woven huts crouching in the lee of the first
of the Towers. It went far, far into our past, to the days when
the fathers of the Comyn mated with *chieri* and bred strange
nonhuman powers into our line, and Gods moved on the face
of the world among humankind, Hastur who was the son of
Aldones who was the son of light... I told myself not to be
superstitious. This Tower was ancient indeed, and some of
the old machinery from the Ages of Chaos survived here, no
more than that. Lifts that moved of themselves, by no power
I could identify, were commonplace enough in the Terran
Zone, why should it terrify me here? The smell of centuries
hung between the walls, in the shadows that slipped past, as
if with every successive rising we moved further back into
the very Ages of Chaos and before.... at last the shaft stopped,
and we were before a small panel of glass that was a door,
with blue lights behind it.

I saw no handle or doorknob, but Callina reached forward
and it opened. And we stepped into...blueness.

Blue, like the living heart of a jewel, like the depths of a
translucent lake, like the farther deeps of the sky of Terra
at midday. Blue, around us, behind us, beneath us. Uncanny
lights so mirrored and prismed the room that it seemed to
have no dimensions, to be at once immeasurably large and
terribly confined, to be everywhere at once. I shrank, feeling
immense spaces beneath me and above me, the primitive fear
of falling; but Callina moved unerringly through the blueness.

"Is it you, daughter and my son?" said a low clear voice,
like winter water running under ice. "Come here. I am waiting for you."

Then and only then, in the frosty dayshine, could I focus
my eyes enough in the blueness to make out the great carven
throne of glass, and the pallid figure of a woman seated upon
it.

Somehow I would have thought that in this formal audience Ashara would wear the crimson robes of ceremonial for
a Keeper. Instead she wore robes that so absorbed and mirrored the light that she was almost invisible; a straight tiny
figure, no larger than a child of twelve. Her features were
almost fleshlessly pure, as unwrinkled as Callina's own, as
if the very hand of time itself had smoothed its own marks
away. The eyes, long and large, were colorless too, though in

a more normal light they might have been blue. There was a faint, indefinable resemblance between the young Keeper and the old one, as if Ashara were a Callina incredibly more ancient, or Callina an embryo Ashara, not yet ancient but bearing the seeds of her own translucent invisibility. I began to believe that the stories were true; that she was all but immortal, had dwelt here unchanged while the worlds and the centuries passed over her and beyond her....

She said, "So you have been beyond the stars, Lew Alton?"

It would not be fair to say the voice was unkind. It was not human enough for that. Detached, unbelievably remote; it was all of that. It sounded as if the effort of conversing with real, living persons was too much for her, as if our coming had disturbed the crystalline peace in which she dwelt.

Callina, accustomed to this—or so I suppose—murmured, "You see all things, Mother Ashara. You know what we have to face."

A flicker of emotion passed over the peaceful face, and she seemed to *solidify,* to become less translucent and more real. "Not even I can see all things. I have no power, now, outside this place."

Callina murmured, "Yet aid us with your wisdom, Mother."

"I will do what I must," she said, remotely. She gestured. There was a transparent bench at her feet—glass or crystal; I had not seen it before, and I wondered why. Maybe it had not been there or maybe she had conjured it there; nothing would have surprised me now. "Sit there and tell me."

She gestured at my matrix. "Give it to me, and let me see—"

Now, remembering, telling, I wonder whether any of this happened or whether it was some bizarre dream concealing reality. A telepath, even an Arilinn-trained telepath, simply does not do what I did then; without even thinking of protest, I slipped the leather thong on which my matrix was tied over my head with my good hand, fumbled a little with the silken wrappings, and handed it to her, without the slightest thought of resisting. I simply put it into her hand.

And this is the first law of a telepath; nobody touches a keyed matrix, except your own Keeper, and then only after a long period of attunement, of matching resonances. But I sat there at the feet of the ancient sorceress, and laid the matrix in her hand without stopping to think, and although something in me was tensed against incredible agony...I

remembered when Kadarin had stripped me of my matrix,
and how I had gone into convulsions.... nothing happened;
the matrix might have been safely around my neck.

And I sat there peacefully and watched it.

Deep within the almost-invisible blue of the matrix were
fires, strange lights...I saw the glow of fire, and the great
raging shimmer...*Sharra!* Not the Form of Fire which had
terrified us in Council, but the Goddess herself, raging in
flame—Ashara waved her hand and it disappeared. She said,
"Yes, that matrix I know of old...and yours has been in
contact with it, am I right?"

I bowed my head and said, "You have seen."

"What can we do? Is there any way to defend against—"

She waved Callina to silence. "Even I cannot alter the
laws of energy and mechanics," she said. Looking around the
room, I was not so sure. As if she had heard my thoughts,
she said, "I wish you knew less science of the Terrans, Lew."

"Why?"

"Because now you look for causes, explanations, the fallacy
that every event must have a preceding cause...matrix mechanics is the first of the non-causal sciences," she said, seeming to pick up that Terran technical phrase out of the air or
from my mind. "Your very search for structure, cause and
reality produces the cause you seek, but it is not the real
cause...does any of this make sense to you?"

"Not very much," I confessed. I had been trained to think
of a matrix as a machine, a simple but effective machine to
amplify psi impulses and the electrical energy of the brain
and mind.

"But that leaves no place for such things as Sharra," Ashara said. "Sharra is a very real Goddess.... No, don't shake
your head. Perhaps you could call Sharra a demon, though
She is no more a demon than Aldones is a God.... They are
entities, and not of this ordinary three-dimensional world you
inhabit. Your mind would find it easier to think of them as
Gods and Demons, and of your matrix, and the Sharra matrix,
as talismans for summoning those demons, or banishing
them.... They are entities from another world, and the matrix is the gateway that brings them here," she said. "You
know that, or you knew it once, when you managed to close
the gateway for a time. And for such a summoning Sharra
will always have Her sacrifice; so she had your hand, and
Marjorie gave up her life...."

"Don't!" I shuddered.

"But there is a better weapon of banishing," Ashara said. "What says the legend..."

Callina whispered, "Sharra was bound in chains by the son of Hastur, who was the Son of Aldones who was the Son of Light...."

"Rubbish," I said boldly. "Superstition!"

"You think so?" Ashara seemed to realize she was still holding my matrix; she handed it carelessly back to me and I fumbled it into the silken wrappings and into its leather bag, put it back around my neck. "What of the shadow-sword?"

That too was legend; Linnell had sung it tonight, of the time when Hastur walked on the shores of the lake, and loved the Blessed Cassilda. The legend told of the jealousy of Alar, who had forged in his magical forge a shadow-sword, meant to banish, not to slay. Pierced with this sword, Hastur must return to his realms of light... but the legend recounted how Camilla, the damned, had taken the place of Cassilda in Hastur's arms, and so received the shadow-blade in her heart, and passed away forever into those realms....

I said, hesitating, "The Sharra matrix is concealed in the hilt of a sword...tradition, because it is a weapon, no more...."

Ashara asked, "What do you think would happen to anyone who was slain with such a sword as that?"

I did not know. It had never occurred to me that the Sword of Sharra could be used as a sword, though I had hauled the damnable thing around half the Galaxy with me. It was simply the case the forge-folk had made to conceal the matrix of Sharra. But I found I did not like thinking of what would happen to anyone run through by a sword possessed and dominated by Sharra's matrix.

"So," she said, "you are beginning to understand. Your forefathers knew much of those swords. Have you heard of the Sword of Aldones?"

Some old legend...yes. "It lies hidden among the holy things at Hali," I said, "spelled so that none of Comyn blood may come near, to be drawn only when the end of Comyn is near; and the drawing of that sword shall be the end of our world...."

"The legend has changed, yes," said Ashara, with something which, in a face more solid, more human, might have been a smile. "I suppose you know more of sciences than of legend....Tell me, what is Cherilly's Law?"

It was the first law of matrix mechanics; it stated that nothing was unique in space and time except a matrix; that every item in the universe existed with one and only one *exact* duplicate, except for a matrix; a matrix was the only thing which was wholly unique, and therefore any attempt to duplicate a matrix would destroy it, and the attempted duplicate.

"The Sword of Aldones is the weapon against Sharra," said Ashara. But I knew enough of the holy things at Hali to know that if the Sword of Aldones was concealed there, it might as well be in another Galaxy; and I said so.

There are things like that on Darkover; they can't be destroyed, but they are so dangerous that even the Comyn, or a Keeper, can't be trusted with them; and all the ingenuity of the great minds of the Ages of Chaos had been bent to concealing them so that they cannot endanger others.

The *rhu fead*, the holy Chapel at Hali...all that remained of Hali Tower, which had burned to the ground during the Ages of Chaos...was such a concealment. The Chapel itself was guarded like the Veil at Arilinn; no one not of Comyn blood may penetrate the Veil. It is so spelled and guarded with matrixes and other traps that if any outsider, not of the true Comyn blood, should step inside, his mind would be stripped bare; by the time he or she got inside, he would be an idiot without enough directive force to know or remember why he had come there.

But inside the Chapel, the Comyn of a thousand years ago had put them out of our reach forever. They are guarded in the opposite fashion. An outsider could have picked them up freely; but the outsider couldn't get into the Chapel at all. No one of Comyn blood could so much as lay a hand on them without instant death.

I said, "Every unscrupulous tyrant in a thousand years of Comyn has been trying to figure that one out."

"But none of them has had a Keeper on their side," said Ashara. Callina asked, "A Terran?"

"Not one reared on Darkover," Ashara said. "An alien, perhaps who knew nothing of the forces here. His mind would be locked and sealed against any forces here, so that he wouldn't even know they were there. He would pass them, guarded by ignorance."

"Wonderful," I said with sarcastic emphasis. "All I have to do is go thirty or forty light-years to a planet out there, force or persuade someone there to come back with me to this planet, without telling him anything about it so he won't know what he ought to be afraid of, then figure a way to get him inside the Chapel without being fried to idiocy, and hope he'll hand over the Sword of Aldones when he gets it into his enthusiastic little hand!"

Ashara's colorless eyes held a flicker of scorn, and suddenly I felt ashamed of my sarcasm.

"Have you been in the matrix laboratory here? Have you seen the screen?"

I remembered, and suddenly knew what it was; one of the almost-legendary psychokinetic transmitters... *instantaneously, through space, perhaps through time...*

"That hasn't been done for hundreds of years!"

"I know what Callina can do," said Ashara with her strange smile. "And I shall be with you..."

She stood up, extended her hands to us both. She touched mine; she felt cold as a corpse, as the surface of a jewel.... Her voice was low, and for a moment it seemed almost menacing.

"Callina..."

Callina shrank away from the touch and somehow, though her face was molded in the impassive stillness of a Keeper, it seemed to me that she was weeping. "No!"

"Callina—" the low voice was soft, inexorable. Slowly, Callina held out her hands, let herself touch, join hands with us....

The room vanished. We drifted, fathomless, in blueness, measureless space; blank emptiness like starless space, great bare chasms of nothingness. In Arilinn I had been taught to leave my body behind, go into the overworld of reality where the body is not, where we exist only as thoughts making form of the nothingness of the universe, but this was no region of the overworld I had ever known. I drifted, bodiless, in tingling mist. Then the emptiness between stars was charged with a spark, a flare of force, a stream of life, charging me; I could feel myself as a network of live nerves, lacework of living force. I clenched again the hand that had been cut from me, felt every nerve and sinew in it.

Then, suddenly in the emptiness, a face sketched itself on my mind.

I cannot describe that face, though I know, now, what it

was. I saw it three times in all. There are no human words to describe it; it was beautiful beyond imagining, but it was terrible past all conception. It was not even evil, not as men in this life know evil; it was not human enough for that. It was—damnable. Only a fraction of a second it burned behind my eyes, but I knew I had looked straight in at the gates of hell.

I struggled back to reality. I was again in Ashara's blue-ice room; had I ever left it? Callina's hands were still clasped in mine, but Ashara was gone. The glass throne was empty, and as I looked on it the throne, too, was gone, vanished into the mirrored shimmer of the room. Had she ever been there at all? I felt giddy and disoriented, but Callina sagged against me, and I caught her, and the feel of her fainting body in my arms brought me back sternly to reality. The touch of her soft robes, of the end of her hair against my hand, seemed to touch some living nerve in me. I clasped her against me, burying my face against her shoulder. She smelled warm and sweet, with a subtle fragrance, not perfume or scent or cosmetic, just the soft scent of her skin, and it dizzied me; I wanted to go on holding her, but she opened her eyes and swiftly was aware again, holding herself upright and away from me. I bent my head. I dared not touch her, and would not against her will, but for that dizzying moment I wanted her more than I had ever wanted any woman living. Was it only that she was Keeper and so forbidden to me? I stood upright again, cold and aching, my face icy where it had lain against her heart; but I had control of myself again. She seemed unaware, immune to the torrent of feeling that raged in me. Of course, she was a Keeper, she had been taught to move beyond all this, immune to passion....

"Callina," I said, "cousin, forgive me."

The faintest flicker of a smile moved on her face. "Never mind, Lew. I wish—" she left the rest unspoken, but I realized she was not quite so insulated from my own torment as I had believed.

"I am no more than human," she said, and again the faint feather-touch to my wrist, the touch of a Keeper, reassured me. It was like a promise, but we drew apart, knowing that there must remain a barrier between us.

"Where is Ashara?" I asked.

Once again the flicker of a troubled smile on her face. "You

had better not ask me," she murmured. "You would never
believe the answer."

I frowned, and again the uncanny resemblance troubled
me, the stillness of Ashara in Callina's quiet face—I could
only guess at the bond between the Keepers. Abruptly, Callina moved toward some invisible door and we were outside,
on the stone landing, solid, and I wondered if the blue-ice
room had ever existed, or if the whole thing had been some
kind of bizarre dream.

A dream, for there I was whole and I had two hands....
Something had happened. But I did not know what it could
have been.

We returned another way to the Tower, and Callina led
me through the relay chamber, into the room filled with the
strange and mysterious artifacts of the Ages of Chaos. It was
warm, and I pulled off my cloak and let the heat soak into
my chilled body and aching arm, while Callina moved softly
around the laboratory, adjusting specially modulated dampers, and finally gestured to the wide, shimmering glass
panel, whose depths made me think of the blue-ice room of
Ashara. I stared, frowning, into the cloudy depths. Sorcery?
Unknown laws, non-casual sciences? They mingled and were
one. The Gift I had borne in my blood, the freak thing in my
heredity that made me Comyn, telepath, *laranzu*, matrix
technician....for such things as this I had been bred and
trained; why should I fear them? Yet I was afraid, and Callina
knew it.

I was trained at Arilinn, oldest and most powerful of the
Towers, and had heard something—not much—about screens
like this. It was a duplicator—it transmitted a desired pattern; it captured images and the realities behind them—no;
it's impossible to explain, I didn't—and don't—know enough
about the screens. Including how they were operated; but I
supposed Callina knew and I was just there to strengthen
her with the strength of the Alton Gift, to lend her power
as—the thought sent ice through my veins—I had lent power
for the raising of Sharra. Well, that was fair enough; power
for power, reparation for betrayal. Still I was uneasy; I had
allowed Kadarin to use me for the raising of Sharra without
knowing enough about the dangers, and here I was repeating
the same mistake. The difference was that I trusted to Callina. But even that frightened me; there had been a time

when I had trusted Kadarin, too, called him friend, sworn
brother, *bredu.*

Again I stopped myself. I had to trust Callina; there was
no other way. I went and stood before the screen.

Augmented by the screen, I could search, with telepathic
forces augmented hundredfold, thousandfold, for such a one
as we wanted. Of all the millions and billions of worlds in
space and time, somewhere there was a mind such as we
wanted, with a certain awareness—and a certain *lack* of
awareness. With the screen we could attune that mind's vibrations to *this* particular place in time and space; here, now,
between the two poles of the screen. The space annihilated
by the matrix, we could shift the—well, we call them *energons,* which is as good a name as any—shift the energons of
that particular mind and the body behind it, and bring them
here. My mind played with words like matter-transmitter,
hyperspace, dimension-travel; but those were only words. The
screen was the reality.

I dropped into one of the chairs before the screen, fiddling
with a calibration which would allow me to match resonances
between myself and Callina—more accurately, between her
matrix and mine. I said, not looking up, "You'll have to cut
out the monitor screen, Callina," and she nodded.

"There's a bypass relay through Arilinn." She touched controls and the monitor surface, a glassy screen—large, but
half the size of the giant screen before me—blinked fitfully
and went dark, shunting every monitored matrix on Darkover out of this relay. A grill crackled, sent out a tiny stac-
cato signal; Callina listened attentively to no sound that I
could hear—the message was not audible, and I was too
preoccupied to merge into the relays. Callina listened for a
moment, then spoke—aloud, perhaps as a courtesy to me,
perhaps to focus her own thoughts for the relay.

"Yes, I know, Maruca, but we have cut out the main cir-
cuits here in Thendara; you'll have to monitor from there."
Again the listening silence, then she rapped out, "Put up a
third-level barrier around Thendara! That is a direct order
from Comyn; observe and comply!" She turned away, sighing.

"That girl is the *noisiest* telepath on the planet! Now everyone with a scrap of telepathy on the whole planet will know
something is going on in Thendara tonight!"

We had had no choice; I said so. She took her own place
before the screen, and I blanked my mind against it, ready

for whatever she should demand of me. What sort of alien would suit us? But without volition, at least on my part, a pattern shaped itself on the screen. I saw the dim symbols in the moment before my optic nerve overloaded and I went out; then I was blind and deaf in that instant of overload which is always terrifying, however familiar it may become.

Gradually, without external senses, I found orientation within the screen. My mind, extended through astronomical distances, traversed in fractional seconds whole galaxies and parsecs of subjective spacetime. Vague touches of consciousness, fragments of thought, emotions that floated like shadows—the flotsam of the mental universe.

Then before I felt contact, I saw the white-hot flare in the screen. Somewhere another mind had fitted into the pattern which we had cast out like a net, and when we found the fitting intelligence it had been captured.

I swung out, bodiless, divided into a billion subjective fragments, extended over a vast gulf of spacetime. If anything happened, I would never get back to my body now, but would drift on the spacetime curve forever.

With infinite caution I poured myself into the alien mind. There was a short, terrible struggle. It was embedded-enlaced in mine. The world was a holocaust of molten-glass fire and color. The air writhed. The glow on the screen was a shadow, then solid, then a clearing darkness....

"Now!" I did not speak, simply flung the command at Callina, then light tore at my eyes, there was a ripping shock tearing at my brain, the floor seemed to rock and Callina was flung, reeling, into my arms as the energons seared the air and my brain.

Half stunned, but conscious, I saw that the screen was blank, the alien mind torn free of mine.

And in a crumpled heap on the floor, where she had fallen at the base of the screen, lay a slight, dark-haired woman.

I realized after a moment that I was still holding Callina in my arms; I let her go at the very instant that she moved to free herself of me. She knelt beside the strange woman, and I followed her.

"She's not dead?"

"Of course not." With the instincts of the Arilinn-trained, Callina was already feeling for a pulse, though her own was still thready and irregular. "But that—transition—nearly killed us, and we knew what to expect. What do you think it must have been like for her?"

Soft brown hair, falling across her face, hid her features. I brushed it gently back, and stopped, my hand still touching her cheek, in bewilderment.

"Linnell—" I whispered.

"No," said Callina, "She sleeps in her own room..." but her voice faltered as she looked down at the girl. Then I knew who it must be; the young nurse I had seen on that dreadful night in the Terran hospital in Vainwal. Even knowing, as I did, what had happened, I thought my mind would give way. That transition had taken its toll of me too and I had to take a moment to quiet my own pulses and breathing.

"Avarra be merciful," Callina whispered. "What have we done?"

Of course, I thought. *Of course.* Linnell was near to us both; sister, foster-sister. We had spoken with her just tonight. The pattern was at hand. Yet I still wondered, why Linnell, why not duplicate myself, or Callina?...

I tried to put it into simple words, more for myself than Callina.

"Cherilly's Law. Everything in the universe—you, me, that chair, the drinking fountain in Port Chicago spaceport—everything exists in one, and only one, exact duplicate. Nothing is unique except for a matrix; even atoms have minute differences in the orbit of their electrons...there are equations to calculate the number of possible variations, but I'm not enough of a mathematician to calculate them. Jeff could probably reel them all off to you."

"So this is...Linnell's identical twin...?"

"More alike than that; only once in a million times or so would a twin be the duplicate under Cherilly's Law. This is her *real* twin; same fingerprints, same retinal patterns and brainwave patterns, same betagraphs and blood type. She won't be much like Linnell in personality, probably, because the duplicates of Linnell's *environment* are duplicated all over the Galaxy." I pointed to the small scar beside her chin; turned over the limp wrist where the mark of Comyn was embedded in the flesh. "Probably a birthmark," I said, "but it's identical with Linnell's Seal, see? Flesh and blood are identical; same blood type, and even her chromosomes, if you could monitor that deeply, would be identical with Linnell's."

Callina stared and stared. "She can live in this—this alien environment, then?"

"If she's identical," I said. "Her lungs breathe the same ratio of oxygen in the air as ours do, and her internal organs are adjusted to the same gravity."

"Can you carry her?" Callina asked, "She'll get a dreadful shock if she wakes up in this place."

I grinned humorlessly. "She'll get one anyhow." But I managed to scoop her up one-handed; she was frail and light, like Linnell. Callina went ahead of me, pulled back curtains, showed me where to lay her down on a couch in a small bare room—I supposed the young men and women who worked in the relays sometimes took a nap here instead of returning to their own rooms. I covered her, for it was cold.

"I wonder where she comes from?" Callina murmured.

"From a world with about the same gravity as Darkover, which narrows it a little," I evaded. I could not remember the nurse's name, some barbaric Terran syllables. I wondered if she would recognize me. I should explain it all to Callina. But her face was lined with exhaustion, making her look gaunt, twice her age. "Let's leave her to sleep off the shock—and get some sleep ourselves."

We went down to the foot of the Tower. Callina stood in the doorway with me, her hands lightly resting in mine. She looked haggard, worn, but lovely to me after the shared danger, the intimacy created by matrix work, a closeness greater than family, greater than that of lovers. . . . I bent and kissed her, but she turned her head so that my kiss fell only on a mouthful of soft, fine, sweet-scented hair. I bowed my own head and did not press her. She was right. It would have been insanity; we were both exhausted.

She murmured, as if finished a sentence I had started ". . . and I must go and see if Linnell is really all right. . ."

So she, too, had shared that sense of portent, of doom? I put her gently away, and went out of the Tower, but I did not go to my rooms to sleep as I meant to do. Instead I paced in the courtyard, like a trapped animal, battling unendurable thoughts, until the red sun came up and Festival dawned in Thendara.

CHAPTER NINE

The morning of Festival dawned red and misty; Regis Hastur, restless, watched the sun come up, and asked his body-servant to arrange for flowers to be sent to his sister Javanne.

I should send gifts, too, to the mothers of my children....

It was simple enough to arrange that baskets of fruits and flowers should be sent, but he felt profoundly depressed and, paradoxically, lonely.

There is no reason I should be lonely. Grandfather would be only too happy to arrange a marriage for me, and I could choose any woman in Thendara for wife, and have as many concubines as a Dry-Towner, and no one could criticize me, not even if I chose to keep a male favorite or two on the side.

I suppose, when it comes to that, I am alone because I would rather be alone, and responsible to no one...

...except the whole damned population of the Domains! I cannot call my life my own...and I will not marry so that they will approve of me!

There was only one person in Thendara, he reflected, whom he really wished to send a gift; and because of custom, he could not do that. He would not degrade what was between Danilo and himself by the pretense that it was the more conventional tie. He sat at his high window, looking out over the city, pondering yesterday's end to the Council, frightened because he had done what he had done, manifested the Form of Fire before them all. Somehow, without training more than the barest minimum, so that he could use his *laran* without becoming ill, he had acquired a new Gift he did not know he had, nor did he know what to do with it. He knew so little of the Hastur Gift and he suspected that his grandfather knew little more.

If only Kennard had still been alive, he would have gone to the kindly kinsman he had learned to call "Uncle" and set his puzzlement before him. Kennard had spent years in Arilinn and knew everything that was known about the Comyn powers. But Kennard was dead, under a faraway alien sun, and Lew seemed to know little more than himself. Moreover, Lew had his own troubles.

At this point he was summoned to breakfast with his grandfather. For a moment he considered sending a message that he was not hungry—he had made a point with his grandfather and was not inclined to give way on it—but then he remembered that it was, after all, Festival, and kinsmen should put aside their quarrels for the day. In any case he would have to confront his grandfather at the great ball tonight; he might as well meet him in private first.

Danvan Hastur bowed to his grandson, then embraced him and as Regis took a seat before the laden table, he noticed that his grandfather had ordered all his favorite delicacies. He supposed this was as near to an apology as he would ever have from the old man. There was coffee from the Terran Zone, in itself a great luxury, and various honey cakes and fruits, as well as the more traditional fare of porridge and nut breads. As he helped himself, Danvan Hastur said, "I ordered a basket of fruits and candies sent to Javanne in your name."

"You might have trusted me to remember, sir," said Regis, smiling, "but with that brood of children, the sweets won't go to waste."

But thinking of Javanne set him to remembering again the eerie power he had somehow acquired over Javanne's matrix when it had been possessed by Sharra....He did not understand and there was no one to ask. Should he go and demand the audience with Ashara which Callina had denied him? *Lew's matrix was overshadowed by Sharra; perhaps I would have power over that too....*

But he feared to try and fail. And then he remembered that there was another matrix, and one within his own reach, which had been overshadowed by Sharra; though at a greater distance than Lew's; Lew had been in the very heart of Sharra's flames...Rafe Scott was concealed in the Terran Zone, and Regis didn't blame him. But did Rafe even know that Beltran was here, threatening all of them? Yes, he would pay a call upon Rafe this morning.

He declined another cup of coffee...although he was grateful for the gesture his grandfather had made, he did not really like it...and pushed his chair back, just as the servant announced:

"Lord Danilo, Warden of Ardais."

Hastur greeted Danilo with affable courtesy, and invited him to join them at the table; Regis knew that his grandfather was underlining a conceded point. But Danilo, bowing to them both, said, "I am here with a message from Lord Ardais, sir. Beltran of Aldaran has brought his honor guard within the city walls and has invited you to witness his formal giving up of Terran weapons into the hands of his promised wife, Lady Aillard."

"Send a messenger to tell him I will be there within a few moments," said Hastur, rising. "Regis, will you join me?"

"Please excuse me, Grandfather, I have an errand elsewhere," Regis said, and though his grandfather did not look pleased, he did not question Regis.

"I'll leave you two alone, then," he said, and withdrew. Regis discovered his appetite had returned; he poured himself the coffee he had refused and some for Danilo too, and passed the platter of honey cakes. Danilo took one, and said, sipping curiously at the coffee, "This is a Terran luxury, no? If Lord Dyan has his way, there will be no more of this..."

"I can well do without it," Regis said. He took a handful of candied blackfruit and offered it silently to Danilo; Danilo, accepting the sweetmeats, smiled at him and said, "No, and I have no Festival gift for you, either....I am not Dyan, to send presents to his favorites as I would do to my sister if I had one."

We do not need to gift one another....

Still, it is a sign I wish I might show...

Regis said aloud, breaking the moment of intimacy that was more intense than any physical caress, "I must go to the Terran Zone, Dani; I must see if Captain Scott knows what is going on..."

"I will go with you, if you wish," Danilo offered.

"Thank you, but there is no need to anger your foster-father," Regis said, "and if you go there against his will, he will take it as defiance. Keep the peace, Dani; there are enough quarrels within Comyn, we need no more." He put his honey-cake aside, suddenly losing his appetite again. "Grandfather will be angry enough that I am not there to witness the Aldaran men giving up their Terran weapons. But Beltran will never love me, no matter what I do, and I would as soon not be there to see this—" he searched for a word, considered and rejected "farce," then shrugged.

"Dyan may trust Beltran; I will not," he said, and left.

Some time after, he gave his name and business to the Spaceforce guard, black-leathered, at the gates of the Terran Zone. The Spaceforce man stared, as well he might—one of the powerful Hasturs here with no more escort than a single Guardsman? But he used his communicator, and after a moment said, "The Legate will see you in his office, Lord Hastur."

Regis was not *Lord Hastur*—that was his grandfather's title—but there was no use expecting Spaceforce men to know proper courtesy and protocol. Lawton, in the Legate's office, rising to greet him, used his proper address and got his title right, even saying it with the proper inflection, which was not all that easy for a Terran. But then, of course, Lawton was half Darkovan.

"You honor me, Lord Regis," Lawton said, "but I hadn't expected to see you here. I suspect I'll be at the ball in Comyn Castle tonight—the Regent sent me a formal invitation."

"It's Rafe Scott I came to see," Regis said, "but I didn't want to do it behind your back and be accused of spying, or worse."

Lawton waved that aside.

"Would you rather see him here? Or in his own quarters?"

"In his quarters, I think."

"I'll send someone to show you the way," Lawton said. "But first, a question. Do you know the man they call Kadarin by sight?"

"I think I'd know him if I saw him." Regis remembered the picture he had seen in Lew's mind, the day the Alton townhouse had burned.

"What kind of chance would we have of finding him, if we sent Spaceforce into the Old Town? Is there anyone there who would try and hide him from justice?"

"He's wanted by the Guardsmen there too," Regis said. "It's fairly certain that he was responsible for a fire and explosion with contraband explosives..." Briefly, he outlined to Lawton what he had seen.

"Spaceforce could find him faster than your guards," the Terran Legate suggested. Regis shook his head.

"I'm sure they could," he said, "but, believe me, I wouldn't advise sending them."

"There ought to be a treaty that we could at least look for a wanted criminal," Lawton said grimly. "As it is, once he sets foot in the Old Town he's safe from our men—and if he

somehow sneaks into the Trade City, safe from your Guardsmen. I'd like to know why we can't have that much cooperation at least."

*So would I, sir. If I were in charge, you'd have it. But I'm
not, and Grandfather doesn't feel that way.* Regis realized
suddenly that he was ashamed of his grandfather's views.
They had indeed sworn to a certain amount of cooperation
with the Terrans, many times over the past years; more especially after the epidemic in which the Terran Medic division
had sent an expert to assist them. But now Kennard, who
had started this kind of cooperation, was dead, and it seemed
the informal alliance was falling apart; Regis wished Lawton
had enough *laran* so that he need not explain all this, through
the slow and clumsy medium of words.

He said, fumbling, "It's—it's not a good time to ask for
that, Mr. Lawton. It would take a lot of arranging. We'll deal
with Kadarin if we find him, and I assume you will if you
catch him here. But this is not the time to ask for formal
cooperation between the Guard and Spaceforce. The important thing is to catch that man Kadarin and deal with him—
not argue about whose jurisdiction he should be under."

Lawton struck the desk before him with an angry fist.
"And while we argue about it, he's laughing at both of us,"
he said. "Listen here. A few days ago, the Orphanage in the
Trade City was broken into, and a child's room was entered.
No child was hurt, no one was kidnapped, but the children
in that dormitory had a dreadful fright, and they described
the man to Spaceforce—and it seems likely that Kadarin was
the one. We don't know what he was doing there, but he
managed to escape again, and he's probably hiding out in the
Old Town. And now I've heard that Beltran of Aldaran has
brought an army down to Thendara—"

This was Comyn business; Regis had no wish to argue it
with a Terran, however friendly. He said somewhat stiffly,
"Even as we stand here, sir, Lord Aldaran is making a solemn
oath to observe Compact, and giving up all his Terran weapons. I know that old Kermiac of Aldaran was a Terran ally,
but I believe Beltran feels otherwise."

"But it was Beltran, not Kermiac, who managed to burn
the spaceport at Caer Donn, and half of the town with it,"
Lawton said. "How do we know that Beltran hasn't brought
his men here to join Kadarin, and try some such trick on the
Thendara spaceport? I tell you, we have to find Kadarin be-

fore that gets out of hand again. You probably don't realize that the Empire has sovereign authority over all its colonies where there's a threat to a spaceport; they're not under local authority at all, but under the interplanetary authority of the Senate. You people have no Senate representation, but you *are* a Terran colony and I *do* have the authority to send Spaceforce in—"

This sounds like what Lerrys was saying. Regis said, "If you ever want good relations with Comyn Council, Lawton, I wouldn't advise it. Spaceforce quartered in the Old Town would be looked upon as...."

As an act of war. Darkover, with swords and the Guardsmen, to fight the interplanetary majesty of the Empire?

"Why do you think I am telling you this?" Lawton asked, with a touch of impatience, and Regis wondered if indeed the man had read his thoughts. "We *have* to find Kadarin! We could arrest Beltran and call him in for questioning. I have the authority to fill your whole damned city with Terran Intelligence and Spaceforce so that Kadarin would have as much chance as a lighted match on a glacier!" He sounded angry. "I need some cooperation or I'll have to do *exactly* that; one of my jobs is to see that Thendara doesn't go the way of Caer Donn!"

"The agreement whereby you respect the local government—"

"But if the local government is harboring a dangerous criminal, I'll have to override your precious Council! Don't you understand? *This is an Empire planet!* We've given you a lot of leeway; it's Empire policy to let local governments have their head, as long as they don't damage interplanetary matters. But among other things, I am responsible for the safety of the Spaceport!"

Regis said angrily, "Are you accusing us of harboring Kadarin? We have a price on his life too."

"You have been remarkably ineffective in finding him," Lawton said. "I'm under pressure too, Regis; I'm trying to hold out against my superiors, who can't imagine why I'm humoring your Council this way with Kadarin at large, and—" he hesitated, "Sharra."

So you too know what Sharra's flames can do....

Lawton sounded angry. "I'm doing my best, Lord Regis, but my back's to the wall. I'm under just as much pressure as you are. If you want us to stay on our side of the wall, find us Kadarin, and turn him over to us, and we'll hold off. Otherwise—I won't have a choice. If I refuse to handle it, they'll simply transfer me out, and someone else will do it—someone without half the stake I have in keeping this world peaceful." He drew a long breath. "Sorry; I didn't mean to imply that any of this was your fault, or even that you could do anything about it. But if you have any influence with anyone in the Council, you'd better tell them about it. I'll send someone to show you the way to Captain Scott's quarters."

Rafe's voice said a careless "Come in," as Regis knocked; as he entered, Rafe started up from his chair. "Regis!" Then he broke off. "Forgive me. Lord Hastur—"

"Regis will do, Rafe," Regis said. After all, they had been boys together. "And forget that formal little speech about why am I honoring your house." A grin flickered on Rafe's face, and he gestured Regis to a seat. Regis took it, looking about him curiously; in his many visits to the Terran Zone he had never before been inside a private dwelling, but only in public places. To him the furniture seemed coarse, ill-made and badly arranged, comfortless. Of course, these were the bachelor quarters of an unmarried man, without servants or much that was permanent.

"May I offer you refreshment, Regis? Wine? A fruit drink?"

"It's too early for wine," Regis said, but realized that he was thirsty from all the talking he had been doing with the Legate. Rafe went to a console, touched controls; a cup of some white smooth artificial material materialized and a stream of pale-gold liquid trickled into it. Rafe handed him the cup, materialized and filled another for himself. He came back and took a seat.

Regis said, sipping at the cool, tart liquid, "I have seen what happened to your matrix. I—" suddenly he did not have the faintest idea how he was going to say this.

"I have discovered—almost by accident—" he fumbled, "that I have some—some curious power over—not over Sharra, just over—matrixes which have been—contaminated—by Sharra. Will you let me try it with yours?"

Rafe made a wry face, "I came here so that I could forget about that," he said. "It seems strange to hear talk of matrixes *here*." He gestured to the bare plastic room.

"You may not be as safe as you think," Regis warned him soberly, "Kadarin has been seen in the Terran Zone."

"Where?" Rafe demanded. When Regis told him, he leaned back in his chair, white as death. "I know what he wanted. I must see Lew—" and stopped dead. He fumbled for the matrix round his neck; unwrapped it. He held it out quietly on the palm of his hand. Regis looked fixedly at it, and saw it begin to flame and glow with that frightening evocation, the Form of Fire in both their minds, the reek and terror of a city in flames...

He tried to summon memory of what he had done with Javanne's matrix; found himself, after a brief struggle, wresting the Form of Fire slowly into a shadow, to nothing, a shred....

The matrix stared, blue and innocent, back at them. Rafe drew a noisy breath, color coming slowly into his face again.

"How did you do that?" he demanded.

That was, Regis thought with detachment, an excellent question. It was a pity he did not have an equally excellent answer. "I don't know. It may have something to do with the Hastur Gift—whatever that is. I suggest you try to use it."

Rafe looked scared. "I haven't been able to—even to try—since—" but he did take the crystal between his hands. After a moment a cold globe of light appeared over his joined hands, floated slowly about the room, vanished. He sighed, again. "It seems to be—free—"

Now, perhaps, I can face Lew and do that...

Rafe's eyes widened as he looked at Regis. He whispered, "Son of Hastur—" and bowed, an archaic gesture, bending almost to the ground.

Regis said impatiently, "Never mind that! What is it that you know about Kadarin?"

"I can't tell you now." Rafe seemed to be struggling between that archaic reverence and a perfectly ordinary exasperation. "I swear I can't; it's something I have to tell Lew first. It—" he hesitated. "It wouldn't be honorable or right. Do you command me to tell you, Lord Hastur?"

"Of course not," said Regis, scowling, "but I wish you'd tell me what you're talking about."

"I can't. I have to go—" he stopped and sighed. Then he said, "Beltran is in the city. I do not want to encounter him. May I come to Comyn Castle? I promise, I will explain everything then. It is a—" again the hesitation. "A family matter. Will you ask Lew Alton to meet me in his quarters in the Castle? He—he may not want to see me. I was part of that—

part of the Sharra rebellion. But I was his brother's friend,
too. Ask him, for Marius's sake, if he will speak with me."

"I'll ask him," Regis said, but he felt more puzzled than
ever.

When he left the Terran Zone, the Guardsman at his heels
drew diffidently level with him and said, "May I ask you a
question, Lord Regis?"

"Ask," Regis said, again annoyed at the archaic deference.
*I was a cadet under this man; he was an experienced officer
when I was still putting the chin-strap on the cinch-ring! Why
should he have to ask permission to speak to me?*

"Sir, what's going on in the city? They called all the Guards
out for some kind of ceremony—"

Abruptly, Regis remembered; his errand in the Terran
Zone had kept him away, and yet this might be called one
of the most important days in the history of the Domains.
The Seventh Domain of Aldaran was about to be restored
with full ceremony to Comyn, and in token of that Beltran
was to swear to Compact... he should have been there. Not
that he trusted Beltran to observe any oath one moment
longer than it was to his advantage to do so!

He said, "We'll go to the city wall; at least you'll see part
of it from there."

"Thank you, my lord," the Guard said deferentially.

Inside the city wall there were stairs, so that they could
walk atop the broad wall, past posted guards, each of whom
saluted Regis as he passed. Spread out below them, he could
see the men in Aldaran's so-called Honor Guard. *There must
be hundreds of them,* he thought, *it is really an army, enough
army to storm the walls of Thendara... he left nothing to our
good will.*

In a little knot at the head of them, he could see Beltran,
and a number of brightly clad cloaked figures; Comyn lords,
come to witness this ceremony. Without realizing he was
doing it, Regis enhanced his sight with *laran,* and suddenly
it was as if he stood within a few feet of his grandfather,
spare and upright in the blue and silver ceremonial cloak of
the Hasturs. Edric of Serrais was there too, and Lord Dyan
of Ardais, and Prince Derik, and Merryl; and Danilo at Dyan's
side, the two dressed identically in the ceremonials of Ardais;
and Merryl in the gray and crimson of Aillards, attending
Callina, who stood slightly apart from them, enfolded in her

gray cloudy wrap, her face partially veiled as befitted a Comyn lady among strangers.

One by one Beltran's men were coming up, laying down their Terran blasters before Lady Callina, kneeling and pronouncing the brief formula dating back to the days of King Carolin of Hali, when the Compact had been devised; that no man should bear a weapon beyond the arm's reach of him who wielded it, so that any man who would kill must dare his own death.... Callina looked cold and cross.

"Can't we go a bit nearer, sir? I can't see or hear 'em," the Guardsman asked.

Regis replied, "Go, if you like; I can see well enough from here." His voice was absentminded; he himself was down there, a few steps from Callina. He could sense her inner raging; she was only a pawn in this, and like Regis, she was at the mercy of Comyn Council, without power to rebel even as effectively as Regis could do.

Regis had protested once, long ago, that the path was carved deep for a Comyn son, a path he must walk whether he wished or no...stronger yet were the forces binding Comyn daughters. He must have thought this more strongly than he realized, for he saw Callina turn her head a little and look, puzzled, at the spot where Regis felt himself to be and, not seeing him, frown a little, but he followed her thoughts: *Ashara would protect me, but her price is too high...I do not want to be her pawn...*

The ceremony seemed endless; no doubt Beltran had structured it that way, so that the Comyn witnesses might witness his strength. There was a high heap of Terran weapons, blasters and nerve guns, at Callina's feet. *What in Aldones's name, does Beltran think we are going to do with them? Hand them over to the Terrans? For all we know, he might have as many more in Aldaran itself!*

Beltran has made a demonstration of strength. He hopes to impress us. Now we need some counter-demonstration, so that he need not go away thinking that he has done what we had not the power to make him do...

His eyes met the eyes of Dyan Ardais. Dyan turned, looking up at the distant spot on the wall where Regis stood. Regis did, without thinking about it, something he had never done before and did not consciously know how to do; he dropped into rapport with Dyan, sensing the man's strength and his exasperation at the way this put Beltran into a position of power.

Strengthen me, Dyan, for what I must do! He felt Dyan's thoughts, surprise at the sudden contact, an emotion of which Dyan was not quite consciously aware... *su serva Dom, a veis ordenes emprézi*... in the inflection with which he would have put himself at Regis's orders, now and forever, in life and death at the disposal of a Hastur... once, on the fire-lines during his first year as an officer in the Guards, he had been sent with Dyan into the fire-lines when forest-fire raged in the Venza hills behind Thendara, and once he had looked up and found himself working at Dyan's side, strained to the uttermost, shared effort in every nerve and muscle. It was very like being back to back, swords out, each guarding the other's back like paxman and sworn lord... he felt Dyan's strength backing his as he *reached out* blindly with his telepathic force....

GET BACK! It was a cry of warning, telepathic and not vocal, but everyone in the crowd experienced it, edged backward. The great heap of weapons began to glow, reddened, turned white-hot....

They vanished, vaporized; there was a great sickening stench for a moment, then that too was gone. Callina was staring, pale as death, at the empty blackened hole in the ground where they had been. Regis felt Dyan's touch almost like a kinsman's embrace; then they fell apart again....

He was alone, staring from his isolated watch-post on the wall at the empty space where the great heap of weapons had been. He heard his grandfather's voice, seizing this opportunity as if he himself had been responsible:

"Kneel now, Beltran of Aldaran, and swear Compact to your assembled equals," he said, using the word *Comyn*. Still somewhat dazed at the destruction which had overshadowed his dramatic gesture of giving up his weapons, Beltran knelt and spoke the ritual words.

"And now," he said, coming up to Callina and bending to kiss her fingertips, "I claim my promised wife."

She was rigid, conceding only the cold tips of her fingers, but she said, in a voice only half audible, "I will handfast myself to you tonight. I so swear." Regis could not see her now, he was too far away, but he knew she was cold with rage, and he did not blame her at all.

And then he caught another stray thought he hardly recognized.

I do not need these weapons, for there is a better one at my command than anything the Terrans have made....

Was that Dyan? He did not recognize the touch. Nor would he recognize Beltran's; when he had been imprisoned in Castle Aldaran he had been a boy, without *laran*, unwakened, and he would not have recognized Beltran's mental "voice."

But a cold and icy shudder went over him, as he knew just what weapon was meant. Was Beltran really mad enough to think of using—*that?*

And if I have power over Sharra, is it I that must face it?

He had a certain amount of power over the Form of Fire, at least when it manifested itself within a matrix. *But neither Rafe nor Javanne had been fully inside Sharra.* He did not think he could free Lew's matrix as he had freed theirs. Lew had been closely sealed to Sharra...and Regis cringed away from that thought.

But he must risk it...but first he should give Rafe's message. A brief, swift searching told him Lew was nowhere in the crowd at his feet, and he realized that something was happening to his *laran* for which he had not in the least been prepared: he was using it almost carelessly, without effort.

Is this, then, the Hastur Gift?

Forcibly he put that thought, that fear, aside, and went in search of Lew Alton. By the time he found him, Rafe would be there, and he sensed that Lew would not want to confront Rafe Scott unprepared.

Nor was Regis prepared for seeing Lew as he saw him when first old Andres ushered him into the Alton apartments. It did not seem, for a moment, that it was Lew at all, it did not seem that it was a person at all, just a swirling mass of forces, a presence of anger, a touch of a familiar voice...*Kennard? But he is dead*...and a swift awareness of the terrifying Form of Fire. Regis blinked and somehow managed to bring Lew's physical presence into focus, to bring the new and terrifying dimensions of his own *laran* under control. What was happening to him? He never used *laran* like this, he rarely used it at all...but now, giving it even the slightest mental lease seemed to mean that it would fly like a hawk, free, unwilling to return to being hooded....He forced it down, forced himself to *see* Lew instead of simply touching him. But the touch came anyhow, and through the texture of it he recognized something he had felt when he linked with Dyan. Quite simply he found himself saying aloud, "But of course; he was your father's cousin, and close kin to the Altons. Lew, didn't you know that Dyan had the Alton Gift?"

Of course, this is how he could force rapport on Danilo, this is how he makes his will known and enforces it...

But this is misuse... he uses it thus, to force his will... and this is the gravest crime for one with laran....

He was never trained in its use.... He was sent from the Tower.... The Alton Gift can kill, and they turned him loose, untrained, not knowing his own power...

Perhaps like mine, wakening late and suddenly growing as mine has grown, like growing out of my clothes when I was a lad, I am not strong enough nor big enough to contain this monstrous thing which is the Hastur Gift...

With main force Regis shut off the flow and said shakily aloud, "Lew, can you put a damper on? I'm not—not used to this."

Lew nodded, went quickly to a control, and after a moment Regis felt the soothing vibration, blurring the patterns. He was again alone, in control of his own mind. Exhausted, he dropped in a chair.

Dyan is not to blame. The Council did not do their duty by him, but turned him loose, his Gift untrained, unchanneled...

As with mine! But again Regis stopped the flow of thought; thinking, in dismay and outrage, that the damper should have done that. Before they could speak, the door opened and Rafe came in, unannounced.

Lew's face darkened; but Rafe said "Cousin—" in such a pleading way that Lew gave him an uneasy smile. He said, "Come in, Rafe. None of this is your fault; you're a victim too."

"It's taken me all this time to get up courage enough to tell you this," said Rafe, "but you have to know. Something the Legate said this morning meant that I didn't dare wait any longer. I want you to come with me, Lew. There's something you must see."

"Can't you tell me what it is?" Lew asked.

Rafe hesitated and said, "I would rather say this to you alone—" with an uneasy glance at Regis.

Lew's voice was brusque. "Whatever you have to say; I've no secrets from Regis."

Regis thought, *I don't deserve such confidence.* But he slammed his mind shut, wanting no more of the telepathic leakage he suddenly seemed unable to shut out of his mind.

"There was no woman here to take charge," said Rafe. "I went to your foster-sister. She agreed to take charge of her."

"Of whom, in God's name?" Lew demanded, then his mind quickly leaped to conclusions.

"This alleged child who's been gossiped about in the Guards?"

Rafe nodded and led the way. It was not Linnell, however, who faced them, but Callina.

"I knew," she said in a low voice. "Ashara told me... there are not many female children in the Domains who might be trained as I have been trained, and I think—I think Ashara wants her..." and she stopped, her words choking off. She gestured to an inner room. "She is there... she was afraid in a strange place and I made her sleep..."

In a small cot, a little girl, five or six years old, lay sleeping. Her hair was copper-red, freshly minted; scattered across her face, which was triangular, scattered with pale gold freckles. She murmured drowsily, still fast asleep.

Regis felt it run through Lew, like a powerful electric shock.

I have seen her before... a dream, a vision, a precognitive dream... she is mine! Not my father's, not my dead brother's, mine... my blood knows...

Regis felt his amazement and recognition. He said in a low voice, "Yes; it is like that." When first he had looked upon the face of his newborn *nedestro* son there had been a moment of recognition, absolute knowledge, *this is my own son, born of my own seed...* there had never been any question in his mind; he had not needed the monitoring to tell him this was his own true child.

"But who was her mother?" Lew asked. "Oh, there were a few women in my life, but why did she never tell me?" He broke off as the little girl opened her eyes...

Golden eyes; amber; a strange color, a color he had never seen before, never but once.... Regis heard the hoarse gasping cry Lew could not keep back.

"No!" he cried. "It can't be! Marjorie died... she died... died, and our child with her.... Merciful Evanda, am I going mad?"

Rafe's eyes, so like the eyes Lew remembered, turned compassionately on them both. "Not Marjorie, Lew. This is Thyra's child. Thyra was her mother."

"But—but no, it can't be," Lew said, gasping, "I never—never once touched her—I would not have touched that hellcat's fingertips—"

"I'm not quite sure what happened," Rafe said. "I was very young, and Thyra—didn't tell me everything. But there was a time, at Aldaran, when you were drugged... and not aware of what you were doing..."

Lew buried his face in his hand, and Regis, unable to shut out anything, felt the full, terrifying flow of his thoughts.

Ah Gods, merciful Evanda, I thought that was all a dream... burning, burning with rage and lust.... Marjorie in my arms, but turning, in the mad way dreams do, to Thyra even as I kissed her.... Kadarin had done this to me... and I remember Thyra weeping in my dream, crying as she had not done even when her father died.... It was not her choice either, Thyra was Kadarin's pawn too....

"She was born a few seasons after Caer Donn burned," Rafe said. "Something happened to Thyra when this child was born; I think she went mad for a little while.... I do not remember; I was very young, and I had been ill for a long time after the—the burning. I thought, of course, that it was Kadarin's child, he and Thyra had been together so long..."

And Regis followed Rafe's thoughts too, a frightening picture of a woman maddened to raving, turning on the child she had not wanted to bear, conceived by a shameful trick... with a man drugged and unaware. A child who had had to be removed to safety from time to time....

The little girl was awake now, sitting up, looking at them all curiously with those wide, improbable amber eyes. She looked at Rafe and smiled, evidently recognizing him. Then she looked at Lew, and Regis could feel it, like a blow, her shock at the sight of the ragged, ugly scars. Lew was scowling. *Well, I don't blame him—to find out, that way, that he had been drugged, used...* Regis had seen Thyra only once or twice, and that briefly, but he had somehow, even then, sensed the tension of anger and desire between Thyra and Lew. *And they had been together, sealed to Sharra...*

The little girl sat up, tense as a small scared animal. Regis could feel again Lew's shock at the sudden, frightening resemblance to Marjorie.

Then Lew said, his rough voice muted, "Don't be scared, *chiya.* I'm not a pretty sight, but believe me, I don't eat little girls."

The little girl smiled. Her small face was charming, pointed in a small triangle. A tooth had come out of the middle of her smile.

"They said you were my father."

"Oh, God, I suppose so," Lew said. *Suppose so. I know I am, damn it.* He was wide open now, and Regis could not shut out his thoughts. Lew sat down uneasily on the edge of the cot. "What do they call you, *chiy'lla?*"

"Marja," she said shyly. "I mean—*Marguerida*. Marguerida Kadarin." She lisped the name in the soft mountain dialect. *Marjorie's name!* "But I just be Marja." She knelt upright, facing him. "What happen to your other hand?"

Regis had seen enough of Javanne's children—and his own—to know how direct they were; but Lew was disconcerted by her straightforwardness. He blinked and said, "It was hurt and they had to cut it off."

Her amber eyes were enormous. Regis could feel her thinking this over. "I'm sorry—" and then she said, trying the word out on her tongue, "Father." She reached up and patted his scarred cheek with her small hand. Lew swallowed hard and caught her against him, his head bent; but Regis could feel that he was shaken, close to tears, and again could not shut out Lew's thoughts.

I saw this child once, even before Marjorie and I were lovers, saw her in a vision, and thought it meant that Marjorie would bear my child, that all would be well with us....I foresaw; but I did not foresee that Marjorie would have been dead for years before ever this daughter of mine and I should meet....

"Where were you brought up, Marja?"

"In a big house with lots of other little boys and girls," she said, *"They're* orphans, but I'm something else. It's a bad word that Matron says I must never, *never* say, but I'll whisper it to you."

"Don't," Lew said. He could guess; Regis remembered that there were still those who had called him bastard, even after he was acknowledged Heir to Alton. He had her snuggled on his lap now, in the curve of his arm.

If I had known, I would have come back—come back sooner. Somehow, somehow I would have managed to make amends to Thyra for what I did not remember doing...

Before Regis's questioning look, Lew raised his head. He said doggedly, "I was drugged with aphrosone. It's vicious stuff; you live a normal life—but you forget from minute to minute what is happening, remember nothing but symbolic dreams....I've heard that if you tell a psychiatrist what you remember of the dreams under the drug, he will be able to help you remember what really happened. I didn't want to know—" and his voice stuck in his throat.

That must have been after they escaped from Aldaran, Regis thought; *Marjorie and Lew escaped together, and Kadarin dragged them back, and drugged him, forcing him to serve as the pole of power for Sharra....No wonder he did not want to remember.*

"It doesn't matter," Lew said, reading Regis's thoughts, and his arm went around the child, so fiercely that she whimpered in protest. "She's mine anyhow."

He looks ugly but he's nice, I'm glad he's my father....

They all stared at her in astonishment; she had reached out and touched their minds. Regis thought, *but children never have the Gift....*

"Thyra was half *chieri*, they said," Lew said quietly. "Obviously, Marja *does* have it. It's not common, though it's not unknown. Your Gift waked early, didn't it, Rafe—nine or ten?"

Rafe nodded. He said "I remember our—foster-father Lord Aldaran—telling us about our mother. She was daughter to one of the forest-folk. And Thyra—" he hesitated, not wanting to say it.

"Go ahead," said Lew, "whatever it is."

"You did not know... Thyra. She was... like the *chieri. Emmasca;* no one was sure whether she was boy or girl. I can remember her like that, when I was very small, but only a little. Then Kadarin came—and very soon after, she began to wear women's clothing and think of herself as a woman... that was when we began to call her Thyra; before that, she had another name... you did not know that she was as old as Beltran, that she was past her twentieth year when Marjorie was born."

Lew shook his head, shocked. Regis picked up the thought, *I believed she was three or four years older than Marjorie, no more...* and a welter of images, resentment and desire, Thyra playing her harp, looking up at Lew in passionate wrath, Thyra's face suddenly, dreamlike, melting into Marjorie's

...Marjorie, saying gently; "You were a little in love with Thyra, weren't you, Lew?"

Lew set the child down. "I'll have to find a nurse for her; there's no woman in my apartments to look after her." He stooped down and kissed the small rosy cheek. "Stay here with my kinswoman Linnell, little daughter."

She caught at his hand and asked shakily, "Am I going to live with you now?"

"You are," Lew said firmly, and gestured to Rafe and Regis to leave the room with him. Regis said, with a note of warning, "They are going to use her to depose you..."

"I'm damned sure they'll try," Lew said grimly, "A nice, peaceful puppet, pliant in Hastur hands—no, I don't mean *you*, Regis, but the old man, and Dyan, and that precious kinsman of mine, Gabriel—the Council never did trust the male adult Altons too much, did they? So they exile me to Armida, or to a Tower, and bring this youngster up in the way they think she should go." His face looked strained and he clenched his good hand so tightly that Regis was glad he was not the object of Lew's wrath.

"Let them try," he said, and his hand twitched as if he had it around the neck of some one, "Just let them try, damn them! She's mine—and if they think they can take her away from me again, they are welcome to try!"

Regis and Rafe exchanged glances of mingled relief and dismay. Regis had hoped that something, somehow, would awaken Lew out of his deadly apathy, make him care for some one and something again. Now it seemed as if something had done just that. Well, they had raised the wind—but there might be hell to pay before this was over!

Lew Alton's narrative

CHAPTER TEN

The day was darkening toward twilight. Looking out over the city, I could see the streets beginning to fill with the laughing, masked, flower-tossing crowds of Festival Night. I would be expected to appear for the Alton Domain at the great ball in the Comyn Castle; it was simply part of being what I was, and although they had not made any overt move to depose me from my place as Head of the Domain, I intended to give them no chance to say I was neglecting any part of my duty. Now, among other things, I must somehow arrange proper care for Marja. Andres would guard her with his life, if he knew she were mine, but a child that age needed a woman to look after her, to dress her and bathe her and make sure she had proper playthings and companionship. Regis offered to place her in Javanne's care; his sister had twin daughters who were about her age. I thanked him but refused; Javanne Hastur has never liked me, and Javanne's husband, Gabriel Lanart-Hastur, was one of the main contenders for the Domain. The last thing I wanted was to place this child in his keeping.

I thought regretfully of Dio. I had been too quick to dissolve our marriage. She had wanted my child, and even though our son had died, perhaps she would have allowed this one to fill the place left vacant... but no; that would be asking too much, that she should love another woman's child as her own. When I thought of her, the old suffering and resentment surfaced. In any case, if she were here, I could consult her about the proper way to raise a girl child....I wondered how Callina would feel about it. And then I remembered that Callina had sworn to marry Beltran.

Over my dead body, I vowed silently, left Marja in Andres's care (he said that he knew a decent woman, the wife of one of my father's paxmen, who would come to care for her, if I took her home to Armida) and went to seek out Callina.

275

She looked weary and harried.

"The girl's awake," she said. "She was hysterical when she wakened; I had to give her a sedative. She's calmed down a little, but of course she doesn't speak the language, and she's frightened in a strange place. Lew, what are we going to do now?"

"I won't know till I see her. Where is she?"

So much had happened in the intervening hours that I had all but forgotten Ashara's plan, the woman who had been brought through the Screen. She had been moved to a spacious room in the Aillard apartments; when we came in she was lying across the bed, her face buried in the covers, and she looked as if she had been crying; but it was a tearless and defiant face she raised to me. She was still Linnell's double; even more so, having been decently dressed in clothing I supposed—correctly—to be some of Linnell's own.

"Please tell me the truth," she said steadily, as I came in. "Am I mad and locked up somewhere?" She spoke one of the dialects I knew perfectly well...of course; I had talked with her at length, that night on Vainwal when my son had been born, and died. And even as this crossed my mind I saw the memory reflected in her face.

"But I remember you!" she cried out, "The man with one hand—the one who had that—that—that terribly deformed—" My face must have done something she didn't know about, because she stopped. "Where am I? Why have you kidnapped me and brought me here?"

I said quietly, "You needn't be afraid." I remembered saying the same thing to Marja; she had been afraid of me too. But I could not reassure her with the same words that had comforted a five-year-old child. "Allow me to introduce myself. Lewis-Kennard Montray-Lanart, *z'par servu....*"

"I know who you are," she said steadily. "What I don't know is how I got here. A red sun—"

"If you'll be calm, I'll explain everything," I said. "I am sorry, I cannot remember your name—"

"Kathie Marshall," she said.

"Terranan?"

"Yes. But I know we're not on Terra, nor on Vainwal," she said, and her voice trembled; but she made no display of fear. I said, "The *Terranan* call this Cottman's Star. We call it Darkover. We brought you here because we need your help—"

"You must be crazy," she said. "How could I help you? And if I could, what makes you think I would, after you've kidnapped me?"

That was, I supposed, a fair question. I reached out to try to touch her mind; if she could not understand our language, at least this might reassure her that we meant no harm.

Callina said, "You were brought here because you were twinned in mind with my sister Linnell—"

She backed away. "Twinned minds? That's ridiculous! Do you think I believe in that kind of thing?"

"If you do not," said Callina quietly, "how is it that suddenly you can understand what I am saying?"

"Why, you're speaking Terran...no!" she said, and I saw the terror rise in her mind again. "Why, what language am I speaking—?"

It was reasonable that if she was Linnell's Cherillys double, she would have *laran* potential; at least she could understand us now. Callina said, "We hoped we could persuade you to help us; but there will be no compulsion and certainly no force."

"Where am I, then?"

"In the Comyn Castle in Thendara."

"But that's halfway across the Galaxy..." she whispered, and turned frantically to stare out the window, at the red light of the declining sun. I saw her white hands clench on a fold of curtain. "A red sun—" she whispered, "Oh, I have nightmares like this when I can't wake up..." She was so deathly white I feared she would collapse; Callina put an arm around her, and this time Kathie did not pull away.

"Try to believe us, child," Callina said. "You are here, on Darkover. We brought you here."

"And who are you?"

"Callina Aillard. Keeper of Comyn Council."

"I've heard about the Keepers," Kathie said, then, shakily, "this whole thing is crazy! You *can't* take a Terran citizen and pull her halfway across the Galaxy like this! My—my father will tear the planet apart looking for me—" She covered her face with her hands. "I—I want to go home!"

I wished that we had never started this whole thing. I was remembering the aureole of doom, fate, death which I had seen around Linnell...merciful Evanda, was it only last night? I wondered if this had endangered Linnell in some way; what happened when Cherillys duplicates met one another? There was not even a legend to guide me. There was an old legend from the Kilghard Hills, about a mountain chief, or a bandit lord—in those days, I supposed, it would be hard to distinguish between them—who had located his duplicate so that he could command his army by being in two places at once; but I couldn't remember any more than that, and I had no idea what had happened to the duplicate once his day was done. Possibly the bandit chief let his duplicate be hanged for his own crimes. In any case, I was sure he came to a bad end.

Would this woman's presence endanger Linnell? There was one precaution I could take; I could put a protective barrier around her mind, so that she would keep her invulnerability, her complete unawareness of these Darkovan forces. I hoped that in touching her mind, to give her knowledge of the language, I had not already breached that unawareness; at least I would make sure no one else did so. In effect, I meant to put a barrier around her mind so that any attempt to make telepathic contact with Kathie, or dominate her mind, would be immediately shunted, through a sort of bypass circuit built into the barrier, to me.

There was no sense in trying to explain what I meant to do. I would have to start by explaining the very nature of the *laran* Gifts, and since, as Linnell's exact duplicate, she had *laran* potential, when I had done explaining, she might be adapted and vulnerable to Darkovan forces. I reached out as gently as I could, and made contact.

It was an instant of screaming pain in every nerve, then it blanked out, and Kathie was sobbing convulsively.

"*What did you do?* I felt you—it was horrible—but no, that's crazy—or *I'm* crazy—what happened?"

"Why couldn't you wait till she understood?" Callina demanded. But I had done what I had to do, and I had done it now, because I wanted Kathie safely barriered before anyone saw her and guessed. But it hurt to see her cry; I had never been able to stand Linnell's tears. Callina looked up helplessly, trying to soothe the weeping girl.

"Go away. I'll handle this." And as Kathie's sobs broke out afresh, "Lew, go *away!*"

Suddenly I was angry. Why didn't Callina trust me? I bowed elaborately and said, "*Su serva, domna,*" in my coldest, most ironic voice, turned my back and went out.

And in that moment, when I left Callina in anger, I snapped the trap shut on us all.

As darkness fell, every light in the Comyn Castle began to glow; once in every journey of Darkover around its sun, the Comyn, city folk from Thendara, mountain lords with business in the lowlands, offworld consuls and ambassadors and Terrans from the Trade City, mingled together on Festival Night with a great show of cordiality. Now it involved everyone of any importance on the planet; and Festival opened with a great display of dancing in the great ball-room.

Centuries of tradition made this a masked affair, so that Comyn and commoner might mingle on equal terms. In compliance with custom I wore a narrow half mask, but had made no other attempt at disguise; though I had worn my mechanical hand, simply so that I would not be a marked man. My father, I thought wryly, would have approved. I stood at one end of the hall, talking idly with a couple of Terrans in the space service, and as soon as I decently could, I got away and went to one of the windows, looking out at the four miniature moons that had nearly floated into conjunction.

Behind me the great hall blazed with colors and costumes reflecting every corner of Darkover and much of our history. Derik wore an elaborate and gaudy costume from the Ages of Chaos, but he was not masked—one part of a prince's duty is simply to be visible to his subjects. I recognized Rafe Scott, too, in the mask and whip of a *kifirgh* duelist, complete with clawed gloves.

In the corner reserved by tradition for young girls, Linnell's spangled mask was a travesty of disguise. Her eyes were glowing with happy consciousness of all the eyes on her; as *comynara* she was known to everyone on Darkover—at least in the Domains—but she rarely saw anyone outside the narrow circle of her cousins and the few selected companions permitted to a lady of the Aillard Domain. Now, masked, she could speak to, or even dance with, complete strangers; the excitement of it was almost too much for her.

Beside her, also masked, I saw Kathie, and wondered if that was another of Callina's brilliant ideas. Well, there was no harm in it; with the bypass circuit I had put into her brain, she was safely barricaded; and there was hardly a better way of proving to her that she was not a prisoner but an honored

guest. They would probably think her a minor noble woman
of the Aillard clan.

Linnell laughed up at me as I approached her.

"Lew, I am teaching your cousin from Terra some of our
dances. Imagine, she didn't know them."

My cousin from Terra. I supposed that was another idea
of Callina's. Well, it explained the faint unfamiliarity with
which she spoke Darkovan. Kathie said gently, "I wasn't
taught dancing, Linnell."

"You weren't? What did you study, then? Lew, don't they
dance on Terra?"

"Dancing," I said dryly, "is an integral part of all human
cultures. It is a group activity passed down from the group
movements of birds and anthropoids, and also a social chan-
neling of mating behavior among all higher primates, including man. Among such quasi-human cultures as those of
the *chieri* it becomes an ecstatic behavior pattern akin to
drunkenness. Yes, they dance on Terra, on Megaera, Samarra, Alpha Ten, Vainwal, and in fact from one end of the
Galaxy to the other. For further information, lectures on an-
thropology are given in the city; I'm not in the mood." I turned
to Kathie in what I hoped was proper cousinly fashion. "Suppose we do it instead."

I added to Kathie as we danced, "Certainly you wouldn't
know that dancing is a major study with children here; Linnell and I both learned as soon as we could walk. I had only
basic instruction—after that I went to training in the martial
arts—but Linnell has been studying ever since." I glanced
affectionately back at Linnell, who was dancing with Regis
Hastur. "I went to a dance or two on Vainwal. Are our dances
so different?"

But as I talked I was studying the Terran woman carefully.
Kathie had guts and brains, I realized. It took them to come
here after the shock she had had, and play the part tacitly
assigned to her. And Kathie had another rare quality; she
seemed unaware that the arm circling her waist was unlike
any other arm and hand. That's not common; even Linnell
had given it a quick, furtive stare. Well, Kathie worked in
hospitals, she had probably seen worse things.

With seeming irrelevance, Kathie said, "And Linnell is
your cousin, your kinswoman—?"

"My foster-sister; she was brought up in my father's home.

We're not blood kin, except insofar as all Comyn have common ancestry."

"She's very—well, it's as if she were *really* my twin sister; I feel as if I'd always known her, I loved her the moment I saw her. But I'm afraid of Callina. It's not that she's been unkind to me—no one could have been kinder—but she seems so remote, somehow, not quite human!"

"She's a Keeper," I said, "they are taught not to show emotions, that's all." But I wondered if that were all it was.

"Please—" Kathie touched my arm, "let's not dance; on Vainwal I'm a good enough dancer, but here I feel like a stumbling elephant!"

"You probably weren't taught as intensively." To me that was the strangest thing about Terra; the casualness with which they regarded this one talent which distinguishes man from the four-footed kind. There is a saying on Darkover; *only men laugh, only men dance, only men weep.* Women who could not dance—how could they have true beauty?

I started to return Kathie to the corner where the young women waited; and as I turned, I saw Callina enter the ballroom. And for me, the music stopped.

I have seen the black night of interstellar space flecked with a hundred million stars. Callina looked like that, in a filmy web like a scrap torn out of that sky, her dark hair netted with pale constellations. I heard drawn breaths, gasps of shock everywhere.

"How beautiful she is," breathed Kathie, "but what does the costume represent? I've never seen one like it...."

"I've no idea," I said, but I lied. The tale was told in the *Ballad of Hastur and Cassilda*, the most ancient legend of the Comyn; Camilla, slain by the shadow-sword in the place of her bright sister, so that she passed away into the realms of darkness under the shadow of Avarra, Dark Lady of birth and death...I had no idea why a woman on the eve of her bridal, even in the case of so unappealing a marriage as this, should choose to come in such a dress. I wondered what would happen when Beltran of Aldaran caught the significance of that? A more direct insult would be hard to devise, unless she had come in the dress of the public hangman!

I excused myself quickly from Kathie and went in the direction of Callina. I agreed that this marriage was a sickening farce, but she had no right to embarrass her family like this. But Merryl reached her first, and I caught the tail end of his lecture.

"A pretty piece of spite—embarrass us all before our guests, when Beltran has made so generous a gesture—"

"He may keep his generosity as far as I am concerned," Callina said. "Brother, I will not look or act a lie. This dress pleases me; it is perfectly suited to the way I have been treated all my life by Comyn!" Her laugh was musical and bitter. "Beltran would endure more insult than this, for *laran*-right in Comyn Council! Wait and see!"

"Do you think I am going to dance with you while you are wearing that—" his voice failed him; he was crimson with wrath. Callina said, "As for that, you may please yourself. I am willing to behave in a civilized manner. If you are not, it is your loss." She turned to me and said, almost a command, "Lord Alton will dance with me." She held out her arms, and I moved into them; but this boldness was unlike her, and put me ill at ease. Callina was a Keeper; always, in public, she had been timid, self-effacing, overwhelmingly shy and modest. This new Callina, drawing all eyes with a shocking costume, startled me. And what would Linnell think?

"I'm sorry about Linnell," said Callina, "but the dress pleases my mood. And—it is becoming, is it not?"

It was, but the coquetry with which she glanced up at me, shocked and startled me; it was as if a painted statue had come to life and begun flirting with me. Well, she had asked me. "You're too damned beautiful," I said, hoarsely, then drew her into a recess and crushed my mouth down on hers, hard and savagely. "Callina, Callina, you're not going through this crazy farce of a marriage, are you?"

For a moment she was passive, startled, then went rigid, bending back and pushing me frantically away. "No! Don't!"

I let my arms drop and stood looking at her, slow fury heating my face. "That's not the way you acted last night— nor just now! What is it that you want anyhow, Callina?"

She bent her head. She said bitterly, as if from a long way off, "Does it matter what I want? Who has ever asked me? I am only a pawn in the game, to be moved about as they choose!"

I took her hand in mine, and she did not pull it away. I said urgently, "Callina, you *don't* have to do this! Beltran is disarmed, no longer a threat—"

"Would you have me forsworn?"

"Forsworn or dead rather than married to him," I said, rage building in me. "You don't know what he is!"

She said, "I have given my word. I—" she looked up at me and suddenly her face crumpled into weeping. "Can't you spare me this?"

"Did you ever think that there are things you might have spared me?" I demanded. "So be it, Callina; I wish Beltran joy of his bride!" I turned my back on her, disregarding her stifled cry, and strode away.

I don't know where I thought I was going. Anywhere, out of there. A telepath is never at ease in crowds, and I have trouble coping with them. I know that a path cleared for me through the dancers; then, quite unexpectedly, a voice said, "Lew!" and I stopped cold, staring down at Dio.

She was wearing a soft green gown, trimmed with white; her hair waved softly around her face, and she had done nothing to disguise the golden-brown freckles that covered her cheeks. She looked rosy and healthy, not the white, wasted, hysterical woman I had last seen in the hospital on Vainwal. She waited a minute, then said, as she had said the first time we came face to face, "Aren't you going to ask me to dance, *Dom* Lewis?"

I blinked at her. I must have looked a great gawk, staring with my mouth open.

"I didn't know you were in Thendara!"

"Why shouldn't I be?" she retorted. "Do you think I am an invalid? Where else would I be, at Council season? Yet you have not even paid me a courtesy call, nor sent flowers on the morning of Festival! Are you so angry because I failed you?"

A dancing couple reeled within a half-step of us, and a strange woman said irritably, "Must you block the dancing floor? If you are not dancing, at least get out of the way of those who are!"

I took Dio's elbow, not too gently, and steered her out on the sidelines. "I am sorry—I did not know you wanted flowers from me. I did not know you were in Thendara." Suddenly all my bitterness overflowed. "I do not yet know the courtesies of dealing with a wife who abandoned me!"

"*I* abandoned—" she broke off and stared at me. She said, evidently trying to steady her voice. "I abandoned *you*? I thought you divorced me because I could not give you a healthy son—"

"Who told you that?" I demanded, grasping her shoulders until she winced; I loosened my grip, but went on urgently, "I went back to the hospital! They told me you had left, with your brothers—"

Gradually the color left her face, till the freckles stood out dark against her white skin. She said, "Lerrys bundled me onto the ship before I could walk.... He had to carry me. He told me that as the Head of a Domain, you could not marry a woman who could not give you an Heir—"

"Zandru send him scorpion whips!" I swore. "He came to me, just after I came here—he threatened to kill me—said you had been through enough—Dio, I swear I thought it was what you wanted—"

Her eyes were beginning to overflow and I saw her bite her lip; Dio could never bear to cry where anyone could see her. She put out a hand to me, then drew it back and said, "I come here to Festival—hoping to see you—and I find you in Callina's arms!" She turned her back on me, and started to move away; I held her back with a hand on her shoulder.

"Lerrys has made enough mischief," I said. "We'll have this out with him, and we'll do it now! Is he here, that damned mischief-maker?"

"How dare you speak that way of my brother?" Dio demanded inconsistently. "He was doing what he thought was best for me! At that point I was hysterical, I never wanted to see you again—"

"And I was complying with your wishes," I said, drawing a deep breath. "Dio, what's the use of all this? It's done. I did what I thought you wanted—"

"And I come here to find you and see if it was what *you* wanted," Dio flung at me, "and I find you already consoling yourself with that damned frozen stick of a Keeper! I hope she strikes you with lightning when you touch her—you deserve it!"

"Don't talk that way about Callina—" I said sharply.

"She is sworn Keeper; what does she want with my husband?"

"You made it very clear that I was *not* your husband—"

"Then why was it I who was served with notice of a divorce? What a fool I will look—" Again she looked as if she were going to cry. I put my arm around her, trying to comfort her, but she pulled herself angrily away. "If that's what you want, you are welcome to it! You and Callina—"

I said, "Don't be a fool, Dio! Callina will be handfasted to
Beltran within the hour! I couldn't stop her—"

"I've no doubt you tried," Dio retorted. "I saw you!"

I sighed. Dio was determined to make a scene. I still
thought we should settle this in private, but I was on guard,
too. She had made me feel like a fool, not the other way
around; and she had had every right to leave me after the
suffering I had put her through; but I did not want to be
reminded again of the tragedy, I was still too raw about it.

"Dio, this is neither the time nor the place—"

"Can you think of a better?" She was furious; I didn't blame
her. If Lerrys had been there, I think I would have killed
him. So she had not left me, after all, of her own free will.
Yet, as I looked at her angry face, I realized that there was
no way to go back where we had left off.

Others were looking at us curiously. I was not surprised;
I, at least, must have been broadcasting my emotions—which
were largely confusion—all through the ballroom. I said, "We
had better dance," and touched her arm. It was not a couple-
dance and I was grateful; I did not want quite that much
intimacy, not now, not here, not with all that lay between
us. I moved into the outer ring of men, and Dio let Linnell
move to her side and draw her into the circle. Strange, I
thought, that Linnell, my closest kinswoman, did not know
of our brief marriage nor the disastrous way in which it had
ended. It was not, after all, the sort of story to tell a young
woman on the verge of her own marriage. I saw how she
looked at Derik as she pulled him into the set. Then the music
began and I gave myself up to it, as the figure of the dance
swept Dio toward me, with a formal bow, and away again.
At last, as the dance ended, we faced one another again and
bowed. I saw Derik slide his arm through Linnell's, and was
left with Dio again.

I said formally, "May I bring you some refreshment?"

Her eyes glinted tears. "Must you be so formal? Is this
nothing but a game to you?"

I shook my head, tucked my hand under her arm and led
her toward the buffet. Her head hardly came up to my shoulder. I had forgotten what a little thing she was; I always
remembered her as being taller. Perhaps it was the way she
carried herself, proud and independent, perhaps it was only
that on Vainwal, like many women, she had worn high-heeled
shoes, and here she had reverted to the low soft sandals that

women wore in the Domains. The pale green of her gown made her hair shine reddish gold.

Our separation need not be final. Dio as Lady Alton, and we could live at Armida...and for a moment I was overcome with a flood of homesickness for the hills of my home, the long shadows at twilight, the way the sun lowered over the line of tall trees behind the Great House...I could have this still, I could have it with Dio....

The long refreshment tables were laden with every kind of delicacy one could imagine. I dipped her up a cup of some sweet red fruit drink; tasting it, discovered it had been heavily laced with some strong and colorless spirit, for a single glass made me dizzy. Dio, watching as I drank, set hers down untasted and said, "I don't want to get drunk here tonight. There's something—I don't know what it is. I'm frightened."

I took that seriously. Dio's instincts were good; and she was one of the hypersensitive Ridenows. Nevertheless, I said, "What's wrong? Is it only that there are Terrans and off-worlders here tonight?" Lawton was there, with several functionaries from the Terran HQ, and it suddenly occurred to me to wonder if Kathie would see the Terran uniforms, appeal to them for protection, accuse us of kidnapping or worse. Most Terrans knew nothing of matrix technology, and some of them were ready to believe anything about it. And I was quite sure that what Callina and I had done was now against some law or other.

Dio was lightly in rapport with me, and she turned to say with asperity, "Can't you get Callina out of your mind for a minute, even when you are talking with me?"

I could hardly believe this; Dio was jealous? "Do you care, *preciosa?*"

"I shouldn't, but I do," she said, raising her face to me, suddenly serious. "I think I wouldn't mind...if she wanted you...but I don't want to see you hurt. I don't think you know everything about Callina."

"And of course, you do?"

She said, "It was I who should have gone to the Comyn Tower, to be trained as—as Ashara's surrogate. I did not want to be nothing more than—than a pawn for Ashara. I had known one of the—one of her other under-Keepers. And so I made certain that I was—" she hesitated, colored a little—"disqualified."

I understood that. There is now no reason why a Keeper

must be a sworn virgin, set apart, consecrated, near-wor-
shipped. For good reasons, they remain celibate while they
are functioning as Keeper in a circle; but not in the old,
superstitious, ritualistic way. There had been a time when
a woman chosen as Keeper entered upon a lifelong sentence
of alienation, chastity, separation; not now. Yet, for some
reason or another, Ashara chose her under-Keepers from
those who were trained as virgins; and Dio's way was as good
as any to avoid that sentence.

I understood, suddenly, why Callina had rebuffed me. The
marriage with Beltran was to be empty ceremonial, politi-
cally arranged; Callina had no intention of giving up her role
as Keeper in Ashara's place. I should have been compli-
mented—she was well aware that I would not accept that
kind of separation. She was *not* indifferent to me; and she
had let me know it. And for that reason she dared not let me
come near.

Folly, folly twice over, then, to love the forbidden. Yet the
thought that she might fall into Beltran's keeping frightened
me. Would he really be content with a formal arrangement,
where he had the name of consort, and no other privileges?
Callina was a beautiful woman, and Beltran was not indifferent....

"Lew, you are as far away from me as if you were on
Vainwal again," Dio said irritably, and took the glass of fruit
juice I had dipped up for her. I watched her, wondering what
would come next. I was a fool for thinking, even for a moment,
of Callina, who was forbidden to me, who had put herself
beyond my reach...Keeper or no, Beltran's wife would be
forbidden; I was sworn Comyn and they had conferred Comyn
immunity upon him. That was a fact, one I could neither
climb over nor go round. And this business with Dio loomed
between me and any life I might make for myself. I recognized, with a surge of humiliation, it was not for me to say,
I will have this woman or that; it was, rather, which of them
would have me. I seemed to have no choice in the matter, and
in any case I was no prize for a woman. *Mutilated, damned,
haunted*...I forced down the sickening surge of self-pity, and
looked up at Dio.

"I must pay my respects to my foster-sister; will you join
me?"

She shrugged, saying, "Why not?" and followed me. A nag-
ging unease, half telepathic, beat at me. I saw Callina, danc-

ing with Beltran, and stubbornly looked away. If that was her choice, so be it. Viciously, I hoped he'd try to kiss her. Lerrys, Dyan? If they were here, they were in costume and unrecognizable. Half the Terran colony could be here tonight, and I would not know.

But Linnell was dancing with someone I did not recognize, and I turned to where Merryl Aillard and Derik were chatting idly in a corner. Derik looked flushed, and his voice was thick and unsteady. "Ev'n, Lew."

"Derik, have you seen Regis Hastur? What's his costume?"

"D'know," Derik said thickly, "I'm Derik, tha's all I know. Have 'nough trouble 'memberin' that. You try it sometime."

"A fine spectacle," I muttered, "Derik, I wish you would remember who you are! Merryl, can't you get him out of here and sober him up a little? Derik, do you realize what a show you are giving the Terrans and our kinfolk?"

"I think—forget y'self," he mumbled, "Not your affair wha' I do—ain't drunk anyhow..."

"Linnell should be very proud of you," I snapped. "Merryl, go and drag him under a cold shower or something, can't you?"

"L'nell's mad at me," Derik spoke in tones of intimate self-pity. "Won' even dansh..."

"Who would?" I muttered, standing on both feet so I would not kick him. It was bad enough to need a Regency in times like these, but when the heir-presumptive to the crown makes a drunken spectacle of himself before half of Thendara, that was worse. I resolved to hunt up Hastur, who had authority I didn't, and influence with Derik—at least I hoped so. Merryl did, but he was no help. I scanned the riot of costumes, looking for Danvan Hastur, or even Regis. Or perhaps I could find Linnell, who might be able to persuade or shame him into leaving the room and sobering up.

One costume suddenly caught my eye. I had seen such harlequins in old books on Terra; parti-colored, a lean beaked cap over a masked face, lean and somehow horrible. Not in itself, for the costume was no worse than grotesque, but a sort of atmosphere—I told myself not to imagine things.

"No, I don't like him either," said Regis quietly at my side. "And I don't like the atmosphere of this room—or this night."

I said, "I keep thinking I have seen him before." I did not know what I was going to say until I heard myself saying it. "I feel—I feel as if all hell was going to break loose!"

Regis nodded gravely. He said, "You have some of the Aldaran Gift, don't you? Foresight..." he saw Dio was still at my elbow and bowed to her. "Greetings, *vai domna*. You are Lerrys's sister, are you not?"

I looked again at the harlequin-masked man. I felt I should know him, that somehow his name was on the very tip of my tongue. At the same time I felt a curious twisting fear; why could I not remember, not recognize him?

But before I could force myself further, the dome lights were switched off. Immediately the room was flooded with streaming moonlight. There was a soft "A-ahh—" from the thronged guests as through the clearing transparency of the dome, the four moons floated high, in full conjunction, one above the other; the pale violet face of Liriel, sea-green Idriel, the peacock shimmer of Kyrrdis, and the pale pearl of Mormallor. I felt a faint touch on my arm and looked down at Dio.

This is not how I had imagined we would return home together...for a moment I was not sure whether it was her thought or mine. Couples were moving onto the floor for the moonlight dance which was traditionally a dance for pledged couples; I saw Linnell approaching Derik—drunk or no, she would consider herself bound and obligated for this. I was unable, suddenly, to resist the old tie, the old attraction; I drew Dio into my arms and we moved onto the floor. Over her shoulder I saw that Regis was standing alone at the edge of the dance floor, his face cold and detached, in spite of the women who made a point of standing conveniently near in case he should choose one of them. Dio felt warm and familiar in my arms. Was this what I had wanted all along? I found that I resented that smile which took so much for granted. Yet the rhythm of the music pounded in my blood. I had forgotten this—the sense of being altogether in key with one another, resonating to the same music, like a single body moving to the sound, and as she had done once before, she reached out, almost without volition, and the mind-touch came between us, a locking closer than any physical intimacy...closeness, home, fulfillment. As the final chord of music rang in the night, I caught her close and kissed her, hard.

The silence was anticlimax. Dio slid from my arms, and I felt cold and alone again. The lights, coming on again under the dome, caught her looking up at me with a strange smile.

"So I have had that much of you," she said softly. "Was it never any more than that, Lew—that I was a woman, and you were alone and—in need? Was it never more than that?"

"I don't know, Dio. I swear I don't know," I said wearily. "Can't we leave it for now, and settle it sometime when— when half of Thendara isn't watching us?"

She said, unexpected, her face very grave, "I don't think we will be given that much time. I'm frightened, Lew. Something is very wrong. On the surface, everything's as it's always been, but there's something—something that shouldn't be here, and I don't know what—"

Dio had the sensitive Ridenow gift; I trusted her instincts. But what could I do? Certainly nothing could be done here, no one would dare strike at any of us before the City and the assembled guests. Still, Regis had said very much the same thing, and I was myself uneasy.

As I threaded my way through the crowd, in search of Linnell or Callina, I saw again the stranger in the harlequin costume. Whom did I know who was tall and rangy, like that, why did he strike me as strange, over-familiar? He was too tall to be Lerrys, yet it seemed the hostility which beat out toward me from him was very much like what I had sensed in Lerrys when he warned me to stay away from Dio.

(And Dio was at my side. Would Lerrys make good his threats, here and now?)

Again I moved through the crowd. I had spoken to Regis and forgotten to speak to him about Derik—there was too much on my mind, it seemed I had been moving aimlessly back and forth through this wretched yammering crowd all night, and my barriers were beginning to loosen; I would not be able to endure the mental jangle of it much longer. A few cadets were crowding near the long banquet tables, greedily attacking the heaped delicacies there, delighted at the change from barracks food. Among them I recognized both of Javanne's sons, Rafael and the younger Gabriel. I supposed one of them would still consider himself my Heir....

I have no son, I shall never have a son; but I have a daughter and I shall fight for her right to hold Armida after me... and then I was seized with a sickening sense of futility. Would there be anything to hold, after Beltran took his place in Comyn Council and destroyed us all? Would it not be better to take Marja—and Dio if she would come—and go back to

Terra, or Vainwal, or out to one of the worlds at the far edge
of the Empire where we could build a new life for ourselves?
I'm not a fighter. I can fight if I must, and my father tried
his best, from the day I was big enough to clasp my hands
around the hilt of a sword, to make certain that I would be
good at it, and I had learned because I had had no choice. But
I have never enjoyed it, despite his efforts to make me excel
in arms-play, in unarmed combat, as a soldier.

*Damn him, even his last words had been of battle ... I could
hear them now, surging inside me as if they were being spoken
now, not in memory: Return to Darkover, fight for your
brother's rights and your own ...*

and he had thrust me into this seething hell ...

"How you are scowling, Lew," Linnell said in pretty reproof. "This is supposed to be a celebration!"

I tried to move my face into something like a sociable
smile. Sometimes I would rather be in the ninth and coldest
of Zandru's hells than in a crowd where I have to be sociable,
and this was one of those times, but I was not going to spoil
Linnell's enjoyment. I said, "Sorry, this ugly mug of mine is
bad enough, I suppose, without making it worse."

"You're not ugly to me, foster-brother," she said, in the
intimate mode that made it an endearment. "If I wish your
face were unmarred it is only a way of wishing you hadn't
suffered so much. The flowers you sent me were beautiful,"
she added. "See, I am wearing some of them on my gown."

I smiled a little ruefully and said, "You must thank
Andres; he selected them. They suit you, though." I thought
Linnell herself was rather like a flower, rosy and bright,
smiling up at me. "I saw you dancing with Derik; I hope you
told that wretch Merryl to take him away and sober him up!"

"Oh, but he isn't drunk, Lew," she said seriously, laying
a hand on my wrist. "It's only his bad luck that he should
have one of these spells on Festival Night.... He gets like
this sometimes, and when he was younger, they used to keep
him in bed and out of sight—he doesn't drink at all, because
it makes him so much worse, he never even touches wine
with dinner. I was angry with him because he took one
drink—some fruit drink which had been doctored with strong
firi, and he wouldn't offend Merryl by refusing it...."

"That was a mean trick; I had some of it myself," I said.
"Now I wonder just who did that, in such a way that Derik
would get some?" I had a few suspicions. Lerrys, for instance,

would be glad to see our presumptive king, poor thing that he was, making more of a fool of himself than usual.

"Oh, surely, it was an accident, Lew," Linnell said, shocked. "No one would do a thing like that on purpose, would they? It does taste very good, I hardly knew there was anything in it; I might easily have drunk more than one glass, and of course, poor Derik, he's not familiar enough with drink to know that something which tasted only of fruits would make him so much worse—"

So someone who had a vested interest in proving Derik thoroughly incompetent had made sure he had some harmless-tasting drink which would emphasize his various impediments and confuse him worse than ever. Merryl? Merryl was supposedly his friend. Lerrys? He might do anything which would throw us into the arms of the Terran Empire, and he had the kind of devious mind which would enjoy a dirty trick like that. I wondered how, in that family, Dio had turned out so forthright and straightforward.

I said, "Well, he certainly appeared drunk, and I'm afraid most people would think it of him!"

"When we are married," she said, smiling gently, "I will make certain no one can lead him into such things. Derik is not always a fool, Lew. No, he is not brilliant, certainly he will always need someone like Regis—or you, Lew—to guide him in matters of policy. But he knows he is not very bright, and he will let himself be guided. And I will make certain that it is not Merryl who guides him, either."

Linnell might sound and look like a delicate, flowerlike, fragile young girl, but behind all that there was strong common sense and practicality, too. I said, "It's a pity you are not Head of the Domain, sister; they would never have been able to marry you off to Beltran." I turned and saw Kathie, who had been dancing with Rafe Scott, and hoped she had had sense enough not to say anything to him. And beyond her was the harlequin who had so deeply disturbed me...damn it, *who was he?*

"Lew, who is Kathie really? When I'm near her I feel terribly strange. It's not so much that she *looks* like me—it's as if she were a part of myself, I know what she's going to do before she does it...I know, for instance, that she's going to turn—there, you see? And she's coming this way...and then I feel, it's a kind of pain, as if I had to touch her, embrace her. I can't keep away from her! But when I actually do touch

her, I have to pull away, I can't endure it...." Linnell was
twisting her hands nervously, ready to burst into hysterical
tears or laughter, and Linnell wasn't a girl to fret over trifles.
If it affected her like this, it was something serious. What
did happen, I wondered, when Cherillys doubles came face
to face?

Well, I was about to see, whatever it was. As Kathie ended
the dance she moved toward Linnell, and almost without
discernible volition, Linnell began to move in her direction.
Was Kathie working some malicious mental trick on my little
cousin? But no, Kathie had no awareness of Darkovan powers,
and even if she had potential for *laran,* nothing could get
through that block I'd put around her mind.

Linnell touched Kathie's hand, almost shyly; in immediate
response, Kathie put an arm around Linnell's waist, and they
walked enlaced for a minute or two; then with a sudden nervous movement, Linnell drew herself free and came to me.

"There is Callina," she said.

The Keeper, aloof in her starry draperies, threaded her
way through the maze of dancers seeking new partners, moving toward the refreshment tables.

"Where have you been, Callina?" Linnell demanded. She
looked at the dress with sorrowful puzzlement, but Callina
made no attempt to justify or explain herself. I reached out
to touch her mind; but I felt only the strange, cold, stony
presence which I had felt once or twice near Callina, a door
locked and slammed, cold and guarded.

"Oh, Derik drew me off to listen to some long drunken
tale—I thought you told me he never drinks, Linnie? He
never did get it all told...the wine conquered him at last.
May he never fall to a worse enemy. I ordered Merryl to find
his body-servant and have him carried to his rooms, so you'll
have to find someone else to dance with for the midnight
dance, darling." She looked indifferently around the room.
"I suppose I'll be dancing with Beltran; Hastur is signaling
to me. Probably he intends to begin the ceremony now."

"Am I to come with you then?"

Callina said, still with that icy indifference, "I will not
give this farce any of the trappings of a wedding, Linnie. Nor
will I drag any of my kinsmen into it...why do you think I
made sure Merryl was well out of the way?"

"Oh, Callina—" Linnell said, reaching for her, but she

moved away, leaving Linnell with her arms outstretched, hurt and bewildered.

"Don't pity me, Linnie," she said tensely, "I—won't have it." I was sure that what she meant was, *I can't bear it.*

I don't know what I would have said or done at that moment, if she had turned to me; but she drew herself apart from us; her eyes brooded, blue ice like Ashara's, past me into silence. Bitter and helpless, I watched her move away through the crowds in that dress that was a reminder of death, doom, shadows.

I should have guessed everything, then, when she left us without a word or a touch, silent and remote as Ashara's self, making a lonely island of her tragedy and shutting us all away from her. I watched Beltran, at Hastur's side, advance to greet her, and saw that she gave him only a formal bow and not an embrace; listened as the bracelets were locked on their wrists.

"Parted in flesh, may you never be so in spirit; may you be forever one," Hastur said, and all over the room, wives reached for husbands, and lover for lover, to exchange the ritual kiss. Callina was Beltran's consort, the marriage a legal fact, from the moment Hastur released her hand. I did not turn to see if Dio was near me. The truth of the matter is, I had, at that moment, forgotten her existence, I was so caught up into Callina's anguish.

The next dance after a handfasting was always, by tradition, a dance for married or pledged couples. Callina, with the privilege of the bride, led Beltran onto the dance floor; but they moved with nothing touching but their fingertips. I saw Javanne and Gabriel move, smiling, onto the floor; the Regent bowed to an elderly dowager, one of Callina's distant kinswomen, and they moved into the sedate measure.

"Regis," Linnell said gaily, "are you going to disappoint every unwedded woman in the Domains again tonight?"

"Better disappoint them now than later, kinswoman," said Regis, smiling. "And I notice you are not dancing—where is our royal cousin?"

"He is ill—someone gave him some punch which had more to it than he knew," Linnell said, "and Merryl has taken him away, so I have neither kinsman nor lover to dance with me tonight—unless you would like to dance, Lew? You're more my brother than Merryl ever was," she added with a touch of annoyance.

"Forgive me, Linnie, I would rather not," I said, and wondered if I was still a little drunk; I felt uneasy, almost nauseated. Was it only the general unease of a telepath when the crowds are surrounding him too closely?

"Look, even Dyan is dancing with the widow of the old arms-master," Linnell said, "and Dio with Lerrys—look, isn't he a marvelous dancer?" I followed her look, saw the brother and sister dancing, closely gathered in each other's arms like lovers rather than sister and brother, and for a moment I wanted to storm across the floor in outrage, remind Lerrys that Dio was *mine*...but I felt unable to move. If I tried to dance surely I would fall down, but I had drunk only a very little of that same heavily spiked fruit drink.

Regis said, bowing to Linnell, "I will dance with you as Derik's surrogate, if you wish for it, cousin. It seems I am Derik's heir—may his reign be long," he added, with a wry smile.

"No, I would rather not," she said, a hand on his arm, "but you may stay and talk with me for this dance...Lew, do you know the man there in the harlequin costume? Who is the woman with him?"

For a moment I could not see the harlequin I had noticed before; then I saw him, dancing with a tall woman with dark-copper hair, wonderful thick curls that cascaded halfway down her back. The whirling movement of the dance suddenly turned them toward me, and—although the woman was masked—suddenly I knew her, knew them both, even behind the hideous harlequin mask.

Thyra! No mask could have concealed her from me...for a moment it seemed that the matrix at my throat burned as with Sharra's very fire. I stood shocked, unable to move, watching my sworn enemy, and wondering with desperate unease what brought them here, into the very heart of Thendara, with a price on Kadarin's head and the death sentence from Terran and Comyn at once! I gripped the dagger at my waist with my good hand, wishing I had not encumbered myself with the artificial one. Kadarin and Thyra, boldly dancing together here at the Comyn masked ball....

But now at the conclusion of this dance, all masks were coming off; I tore mine away, using the mechanical hand; the other was firmly gripped on my dagger. Did he think that I would not attack him here because it was in the middle of a ball?

And now I saw that Regis had recognized him too. I took a single step; Regis caught urgently at my arm.

"Steady, Lew," he muttered. "It's what he wants you to do, come after him without thinking...."

The matrix at my throat was suddenly alive with flame, and a voice whispered, called in my mind.

...I am here! I am here...all your rage, all the fury of frustrated lust, let it turn on them to serve me, burning, burning...

Sharra! The voice of Sharra, whispering like a frantic ghost in my mind, the fury of all my frustration, leaping up to betray me... Thyra's eyes, burning into mine, the red flame of her hair seeming to blaze up around her! And suddenly it flared all around her, as Thyra seemed to grow taller, to rise and tower above us into the heights of the ballroom, as I saw Kadarin's long fine hand, the hand of a *chieri*, flash and draw the sword, *that* sword....

It called to me. I had dragged it unwilling through half a Galaxy because I could not leave it behind, and now it summoned me, summoned me... half-aware, I slid my dagger back into its sheath; my place was at Kadarin's side, lending strength to the Goddess, pouring all my own rage and terror and frustration through it... my hand went to the matrix at my throat. I saw some woman whose name I could not remember staring at me with widening blue eyes....I heard her whisper a name I no longer associated with myself, but she was nothing to me, and a young man with the face of a mortal enemy... Hastur, he was Hastur... the mortal enemy, the first to strike! I felt his hand gripping at my arm and thrust him away with uncanny strength, so that his knees buckled and he spread to the floor; and all this time that pattern of hate and fear, mingled love and loathing, beat in my mind....I took a step, then another, toward where the Goddess flamed above me.

I must return... return to Sharra, return to the immortal who rose in flame above me forever, burn myself in the purging fire... she was there, Marjorie, calling me from within the flames of Sharra, those compelling amber eyes, the cascade of red hair wildly tossing sparks and flame and the smell of burning, as I burned for her with lust and terror...

The one I knew to be my mortal enemy was gripping me now with both hands as I fought my way, step by step, through the cries of the yammering crowd, to where Sharra burned...

"No, damn it, Lew," he gasped, "You're not going, if I have to kill you first and give you a clean death..." and he struck at me with the dagger, tearing a line of blood across my good arm. The pain made me waver, come to myself a little, know what was happening.

"Regis—help me," I heard myself whisper.

"Your matrix! Let me—" Before I could stop him, he snatched out his own dagger, cut the string which held my matrix round my neck; I tensed, in anticipation of agony unendurable... *once Kadarin had ripped it away and I had gone into convulsions...* but even through the leather bag and the silks I felt the touch....

The form of Sharra wavered, sank... I did not know what Regis was doing, but strand by strand, it seemed that the gripping call of Sharra lessened in my mind. I heard it still, a soft insidious voice whispering in my mind...

Return to me, return, take vengeance on all these who have scorned and despised you... return, return...

...to Darkover and fight for your brother's rights and your own... but now it was my father's voice; I had never thought I would be glad to hear that haunting voice in my mind, but now it recalled me wholly to myself, like a plunge into an icy stream. Then that too quieted, and I stood looking at Kadarin and Thyra where they stood together, the Sharra sword in Kadarin's hand, Thyra's hair still tossing with the last sparks of the dying flame.

Gabriel broke away from Javanne; made a quick step toward Kadarin, his sword in hand. Perhaps all he saw was the invasion by a wanted man; I never knew whether the Form of Fire had been real or whether anyone but myself had seen it. Kadarin whirled, shoving Thyra before him, as Gabriel shouted for the Guard and the young cadets started flocking toward him from everywhere in the room. I drew my dagger again and started for him too, then stood paralyzed....

The air seemed full of cold shimmering light. Kadarin and Thyra stood frozen, too, and I saw Kathie caught between them.

They did not physically touch her, but something shook her like the grip of some invisible thing with claws; tossed her aside and caught at Linnell. She was in their grip as if she had been bound, hand and foot. I think she screamed, but the very idea of sound had died in the thickening darkness around Kadarin and Thyra. Linnell sagged, held up hideously on empty air; then fell, striking the floor with a crushing impact, as if something had shaken her and then dropped her. I fought toward her, shouting soundless curses, but I could not move, could not really see.

Kathie flung herself down by Linnell. I think she was the only person capable of free movement in that hall. As she caught up Linnell in her arms I saw that the tortured face had gone smooth and free of horror; a moment Linnell lay quiet, soothed, then she struggled with a bone-wrenching spasm, and slackened, a loose, limp small thing with her head lolling on her twin's breast.

And above her the monstrous Form of Fire grew again for a moment, Kadarin's face and Thyra's blazing out from the center... then it all swam away and for a moment that cold and damnable mask I had seen in Ashara's Tower blazed out and swam before my eyes...

...and then it was gone. Only a little stirring in the air, and Kadarin and Thyra were gone, too; the lights blazed back and I heard Kathie scream, and heard the cries of the crowd as I elbowed my way savagely to Linnell's side.

She was dead, of course. I knew that even before I laid my hand over Kathie's in a vain attempt to feel any pulse of life. She was lying, a tumbled, pathetic little heap across Kathie's lap. Behind her, blackened and charred panels showed where warp and distortion had faded and Kadarin and Thyra were gone. Callina thrust her way through the crowd, and bent over Linnell. Around me I heard the sound of the Festival throng subsiding. Gabriel sent out the Guard that had gathered, in an attempt that I knew would be vain—Kadarin had not gone out of the castle in any recognizable way and searching the grounds would do no good, even if the Terran Legate joined his forces to ours for the man they both wanted. The other people in the crowd were wedging in around us, and I heard that horrible sound of horror and curiosity which runs through a crowd when tragedy strikes. Hastur said something, and people began silently leaving the ballroom. I thought, *this is the first time in hundreds of years that this Festival has been interrupted.*

Regis was still standing like one of the pillars of the Castle, his face pale, his hand still gripping his matrix. *The Hastur Gift.* We did not know what it was; but we had seen its power now for the second time.

Callina had not shed a tear. She was leaning on my arm,

so numbed with shock that there was not even grief in her
eyes; she only looked dazed. My main worry was now to get
her away from the inquisitive remnant of the crowd. It was
strange that I did not once think of Beltran, even though the
marriage-bracelet was still locked on her wrist.

Her lips moved.

"So this was what Ashara intended..." she whispered.

She collapsed and went limp in my arms.

BOOK THREE

The Hastur Gift

CHAPTER ONE

After Lew carried Callina from the ballroom, Regis Hastur's first thought was of his grandfather. He hurried toward the place where he had last seen Lord Hastur watching the dancers; he found him there, pale and shaken, but uninjured.

"Linnell is dead—" Regis said, and Danvan Hastur put a hand to his heart. He said, gasping, "What of the prince, what of Derik?" He tried to rise, but fell back, and Regis said "Keep still, sir—I'll see to it." He beckoned to Danilo, who broke into a run across the floor.

"Stay here," he said, "See that no one harms the Lord Hastur—"

Danilo opened his mouth to protest; didn't. He said *"A veis ordenes..."* and Regis shoved through the crowd, noticing Gabriel moving in on Beltran, who stood motionless, his mouth hanging open.

"Lord Aldaran," said Gabriel Lanart-Hastur, "I will have your sword, if you please."

"I? I have done nothing—"

"None the less," Gabirel said, evenly, "you were once among those who sought to bring Sharra among us. Your sword, sir." Half a dozen guards, with swords at the ready, moved in on him, and Beltran drew a long breath, looking from guard to guard and evidently calculating his chances; then he shrugged and handed his sword, hilt first, to Gabriel.

"Take him to the Aldaran quarters," said Gabriel, "and make certain that he does not leave them for any reason whatever, nor on any pretext, until the Regent has spoken with him and satisfied himself of his innocence. Make sure that he has no—" he hesitated, "unauthorized visitors."

The Prince. I must see what has happened to Derik. Even though he was not in the ballroom, if his shields were down—where, in the name of all the Gods, did Merryl take him?

Regis hurried up the stairs, racing through the long corridors, hallways. In the Elhalyn suite lights were blazing, and he heard a high shrill wailing. He knew, then, that he had come too late. In the main room, Derik was lying half

303

on, half off a divan; Merryl, beside him, was flung across his
body as if he had tried, at the last moment, to shield his
friend and lord from some unseen menace. He was sobbing;
but Derik was motionless and when Regis touched him, already cold. The wailing came from an old woman who had
been Derik's nurse when he was little, and had cared for her
sickly charge ever since. Regis looked down sorrowfully at
the young man's body.

Merryl stood up, trying to check his tears. He said, "I don't
know—suddenly he cried out as if he were fighting something
away, and fell like this..."

"Was it you, Merryl, who thought it funny to make the
prince drunk tonight?"

"Drunk?" Merryl looked up at him in bewilderment. "He
was not drunk—he had nothing but some drink made of
mixed fruits, so sweet that I could not touch it! He was
not—" then comprehension rushed over his face and he
stared, only beginning to realize the truth. "Then that was
why—*Dom* Regis, did someone meddle with that drink out
of malice?"

"Their malice was worse than they knew," Regis said
grimly, wondering afresh who had played that cruel trick.
Lerrys, perhaps, hoping Derik would make a drunken spectacle of himself before Comyn and Terran guests—to re-em-
phasize that the Domain of Elhalyn was in incompetent
hands? If so, he had overreached himself and done murder.
Not that Lerrys would have dirtied his hands in doing it
himself, but a judicious bribe to one of the dozens of waiters
and serving-folk, and it would be done. "If Derik's shields had
been halfway normal, he would have fought, and perhaps
conquered, as I did, and Lew—"

Merryl was weeping now, unashamed. Regis had always
believed that Merryl had hung around and flattered the
prince for his own advantage; now he realized that the youngster had genuinely cared for the prince. And Regis must break
more evil news to him.

"I am sorry to have to tell you this—Linnell is dead, too."

"Little Linnie?" Merryl wiped his eyes, but he looked
stunned and grieved. "It doesn't seem possible. They were
both so happy tonight—what happened, Regis?"

Regis found he could hardly speak the name. "The Castle
was invaded. Someone tried to summon—" he forced his lips

to pronounce the name but it came out only a whisper of horror; the Form of Fire was too new in his mind. "Sharra."

Merryl said, his voice hard and venomous, "This is the doing of that Alton bastard! I swear I will kill him!"

"You'll do no such thing," Regis said. "The—invaders—Kadarin and his crew—were trying to lure Lew back to them, and he fought and was—was wounded." Again he remembered the blood streaming down Lew's arm from the wound he himself had given him; but he had no regrets. Something like that had been necessary to bring Lew to himself, to gather his forces so that he might resist Sharra.

I seem to have some power over the Form of Fire. But without Lew I could do nothing.

"Merryl, I must go and tell my grandfather about Prince Derik. You can do nothing more for him now, lad," he added compassionately, and it did not seem at all strange to call Merryl "lad," though Merryl was only a year or two younger than himself, "You should go to your sisters."

"I am not Head of the Domain," said Merryl, "They will have no use for me." ...abruptly awe swept over his face and he knelt.

"Prince Derik is dead. May your reign be long, Prince Regis of Hastur and Elhalyn!"

"Zandru's hells!" Regis whispered. So swiftly had everything happened that he had not even realized; what he had always feared had come upon him. Derik had died, young and childless, and he himself, Regis, was nearest the throne. All the implications struck him dumb; he was now superior in rank even to his grandfather, for there was now no reason for a Regency. *I am Lord of the Comyn. I, Regis Hastur.*

He covered his face with his hands. It was simply too much to take in, and suddenly he realized that the battle with Sharra had left him drained and exhausted, far more than he realized. He thought he would fall to the ground; his knees would not hold him upright. *And I am not yet accustomed to the laran I used this night. I used it to free Lew from Sharra, not knowing how or why. Lord of Light! Where will this end?*

He said, faltering, searching for words, "Go and—and seek for Lord Hastur, Merryl; I must tell him of Derik's death—" and some part of him wanted to hide, to run away like a child, for once his grandfather knew this, the process would be inexorable, would roll over him and crush him like one of the great earth-moving machines he had seen on the Terran spaceport. *I to rule the Comyn?*

"Let me cover him first," said Merryl. He looked down again at the dead body of the prince; bent and kissed him on the forehead, then took off his own cloak and laid it gently over Derik, covering his face; tucked it around him as if he were comforting a little child who slept. He said, his voice unsteady, "There was more to Derik than most people ever knew," and Regis thought Derik could have had a worse epitaph.

So many deaths! Lord of Light, where will this end? Marius Alton. Linnell. Derik. Will Sharra reach out and destroy all that is left of the Comyn?

Merryl said, "I am at your orders, my prince," and went.

By the time the red sun rose over Comyn Castle on that morning after Festival, Derik and Linnell lay side by side in the Chapel of Comyn Castle, together in death as in their lives; Danvan Hastur had locked on their arms the copper marriage bracelets, the *catenas* they would have worn in just a few days more. Regis felt a poignant sorrow; they were both so young, and they would have been King and Queen of the Comyn. It would have been more just to give Derik the crown he had been denied so long.

I do not want it. But I have never been asked what I want.

The death of Derik, and the accession of Regis to the crown, had been proclaimed in Thendara, but the coronation itself would not take place for some time, and Regis was glad for that. He needed some time to assimilate what had happened.

I am Lord of the Comyn—whatever that may mean in these days of destruction!

"You must name Councillors," his grandfather had told him; almost the first thing he said, and Regis's first thought had been: *I wish Kennard were alive.*

Danvan Hastur was not a powerful telepath, but he had picked *that* up, He said gently, "So do I, my boy, but somehow you must manage without him. The strongest man within the Comyn is Lord Ardais, and he has always been your friend; he was your cadet-master in the Guards. If you are wise, lad, you will make certain that he is named as one of your first advisers."

Yes, Regis thought. *I suppose Dyan is my friend. I would rather have him friend than enemy, at least.* He said something like this to Danilo when they were alone, adding "I hope you will not mind—being paxman to a prince, Dani?"

Ten days ago Danilo would have passed this off with a flippant joke. Now he only looked at Regis seriously and said, "You know that I will do all I can for you. Only I wish this hadn't happened. I know you don't want it."

"I asked grandfather to take charge of the state funeral for Derik and—and Linnell," Regis said somberly. "It's my business to see to the living. I don't suppose Gabriel and his men have been able to find Kadarin—or Spaceforce, either?"

"No; but there's rioting in the city, Regis, because Spaceforce has come over on the Darkovan side, searching," said Danilo. "If you don't order them out, there's going to be a civil war."

"The important thing is to find Kadarin," Regis protested, but Danilo shook his head. "The important thing, just now, is peace in Thendara, Regis, and you know it as well as I do. Tell Lawton to call off his dogs, or Gabriel isn't going to be able to hold the Guards back. If they've made Thendara too hot to hold Kadarin for a few tendays, so much the better— if he can't poke his nose out into the marketplace without a guardsman or Spaceforce man grabbing him, then we don't have to worry about him. But we have to get those Terrans out of the Old Town, or, I tell you, there's going to be war!"

Regis said with a sigh, "It seems to me that we ought to be able to work together, Terran and Darkovan, against a common enemy, as we did over the Trailmen's fever, last time there was an epidemic. A few Spaceforce men looking for a hunted criminal aren't hurting anyone in Thendara—"

"But they're *there*," Danilo argued, "and the people of Thendara don't want them there!"

It still seemed to Regis that the highest priority just now was to catch Kadarin and eliminate the threat that he would try and raise Sharra again. Just the same, he knew that what Danilo said was true.

"I suppose I ought to make it a personal request to the Legate," he said wearily, "but I have to stay here and settle things among the Comyn. Grandfather—" he broke off, but he knew Danilo followed the words he could not bring himself to say.

Grandfather has aged overnight; I have always known he was very old, but until that Festival Night he had never shown his age.

"Perhaps," Dani said quietly, "he has borne this burden all these years because he knew Derik could not rule in his place if he gave up the Regency—but now he trusts you to guard the Comyn in his place."

Regis bowed his head as if this new burden had been piled physically on him, like a heavy weight. *I have known all along that this day would come; I have wished that my grandfather did not treat me like a child; and now when he does not, I am afraid to be a grown man in command of myself and others.* It was now his decision to make. He said, "Send a message to the Legate, asking him as a personal favor to me—emphasize that, Dani, as a *personal favor to me*—to withdraw uniformed Spaceforce men from the Old Town, and restrict them to the Trade City. Or better; write it and I'll sign it, and have it sent by the most prestigious escort you can find."

Danilo said, with a wavering grin, "We never thought it would come to this when we were together in Nevarsin and I learned to write a better hand than you. Now you can keep me on hand as your private secretary."

Regis knew what Danilo was trying to say without putting it into words. As Heir to Hastur he had been visible enough, always in the public eye. But he had done his duty to ensure heirs to the Hastur Domain, and for the rest he had told himself, fiercely, *I am not the only lover of men in the Domains!* But now, as Prince of the Comyn, he would be even more the public representative of the Comyn. Centuries ago, the Hastur-kin had separated the Hastur Domains of Hastur and Elhalyn, allotting to the Elhalyn all the ceremonial and public duties with the crown.

"A crown on a stick, that's what they want," he said grimly. "Something they can hang up in the marketplace and bow down to!" He thought, but did not say, that the Domains had effectively been without a King all during the two-and-twenty years of the Regency, ever since the infant Prince Derik was left fatherless, and the Domains had been none the worse for that lack.

"We had better make sure that there are any Domains to rule over," he said, when the message had been written, "Derik may not have been the only one to die. And whom shall we send with this message?"

"Lerrys?" Danilo suggested. "He knows the Legate personally—"

Regis shook his head. "Lerrys is too much a Terran sympathizer—I'm not sure he'd deliver the message at all," he said. "Lerrys's view is that the Terrans have every right to be here since we are a Terran colony. Merryl?"

"Couldn't trust him to keep his temper," Danilo replied promptly.

Regis said hesitantly, "I would send Lew Alton; but he was wounded Festival Night—"

And he is personally concerned in this business of Sharra...."I wonder, Danilo; if I asked Lord Ardais to go—"

"I think he would be pleased to carry such a message to the Legate," Danilo said, "for he knows what it will do to the city, having uniformed Spaceforce about, and he is always eager to keep the people calm."

"I won't order him to do it," said Regis. "I know he does not like to go among Terrans, but he may be willing to go if I ask it personally as Lord Elhalyn...."

And again the tragedy struck him; Derik was older than he was himself, yet Derik had died without so much as a *nedestro* son to carry on his name. He had loved Linnell and had waited for their marriage, so that Linnell might bear his Heir; and now they were both dead.

And I have never cared so much for any woman. So I have two sons and a daughter, since I had no hesitation in using a woman for that purpose. Gods! What irony!

Yet I shall not share my throne with any woman, at least not for a time, nor until I find one with whom I am content also to share my life.

"I will go and ask Dyan myself," he said, glancing at the climbing sun, and suddenly aware that he had had no sleep and that he was weary. "He should still be sleeping, but for this he will not mind being wakened."

But in the Ardais quarters there were only servants, and one of them told Danilo that Lord Ardais had gone out early.

"Do you know where he is?"

"Zandru's hells, sir, no! Do you think the Lord Ardais tells his comings and goings to the likes of *me*?"

"Damn! Now I'll have to hunt all through the Castle for him," Regis said, wondering whether Dyan had gone to the Guard hall to see if he, an experienced officer, could be of some help to Gabriel, or whether he had left the ballroom earlier on some private errand and was still abed somewhere with a new favorite. If so, he might not know anything of the destruction that had raged in the Comyn!

Had it been only the day before that he had discussed this very possibility—sending Spaceforce into the Old Town of Thendara to find Kadarin? He had advised against it then; but Lawton had that authority, and now Kadarin had appeared actually within the Comyn Castle, to try and lure Lew Alton back to them...had he any right to keep Lawton from finding this man who was wanted for murder, and other crimes, by both Terran and Darkovan?

"Gabriel may know," he said, "and there are guardsmen at the doors of the Aldaran suite; they may be able to tell us where Gabriel is—in the Guard Hall, or out hunting for our wanted man!"

The suite of rooms allotted in Comyn Castle to the Aldarans had stood empty ever since Regis could remember; it was in a wing of the Castle which Regis had never knowingly entered before. Two big Guardsmen stood outside the door which was bolted shut on the outside. They saluted Regis, and he greeted them politely.

"Darren, Ruyven—I have to speak with my brother-in-law. Do you know if *Dom* Gabriel is in the Guard Hall, or if he's gone into the city? I have to locate Lord Ardais—"

"Oh, I can tell you where the Lord Ardais is, sir," the Guardsman Ruyven said. "He's in there, talking to Lord Aldaran."

Regis frowned and said, "I heard Captain Lanart-Hastur give orders that no one should be allowed to speak with Aldaran—"

"I didn't hear him say that, sir, I only came on at dawn," Ruyven said, "and anyhow—" he looked down at his boots, but Regis knew perfectly well what the man was thinking; was he supposed to give orders to a Lord of Comyn, and, moreover, one who had been his own superior officer for many years? Regis said, "Never mind, then, Ruyven, but you'll have to let us in to see him, too."

When Regis was small, he had been curious about the locked, empty Aldaran apartments. As the Guardsman let him in, he noticed that a dank and empty smell still clung about the walls and the embroidered hangings with the Aldaran double-headed eagle. They found Beltran in the main presence-chamber; someone had brought him some breakfast and he was eating porridge and nut-bread from a tray on his lap. Dyan sat at ease in a nearby chair, drinking something hot from a mug.

He looked up curiously at the younger men, but Beltran grinned widely. Regis had forgotten how much alike he and Lew really were, even through Lew's scars.

"Well, Regis," he said, "at last we are even; you came as kinsman to my castle and I imprisoned you—and now I come as kinsman to yours, and you imprison me. I suppose it's only fair you should have your day."

It was like Beltran, Regis supposed, to put him immediately on the defensive. He said stiffly, "A word with you, if you please, Lord Ardais." He was not going to discuss Comyn business with Beltran present.

"Lord Aldaran is party to Comyn business," Dyan reminded them.

"Not this," Regis said coldly. "Are you aware, Lord Dyan, that Prince Derik died during the night?"

"Good riddance," said Dyan.

"Kinsman!" Danilo protested, and Dyan turned fiercely on him.

"Zandru's hells, must you be such a hypocrite? We all know that Derik was a weakling, about as fit to rule as my three-year-old son! Now, perhaps, there will be some force in the Comyn, and we can talk to these Terrans as they deserve!"

Regis said stiffly, "It will be my business now to talk with the Terrans, Lord Dyan. It was for that I came here—I wish you to act as my embassy to them, with a message—"

Dyan interrupted, "There is only one message I will bear to the Terrans, Lord Regis, and you as a Hastur know what that message will be: *get out!* Off our world, off our planet, and take your Empire along with you!"

Lord of Light! It is worse than I thought! Dyan went on fiercely, "We made a good start, you and I, Regis, when we destroyed the Terran weapons! Now let us have the courage to follow up that message with a stronger one, aimed directly at Thendara!"

Does he truly believe that I destroyed Beltran's weapons as a message to the Terrans? Regis said, "Lord Dyan, this is not the place to discuss long-range Comyn policy. At the moment, the Legate has sent Spaceforce into the city; I have written a formal request that they be withdrawn, so that the Guards may do their own work in looking for a wanted criminal— and murderer, or are you not aware that Kadarin's attack

last night cost us Prince Derik and Linnell, and came close
to destroying Lord Alton?"

"That would be a smaller loss than any," said Dyan coldly.
"With Derik gone, we have a chance at a show of strength.
Your grandfather has played both sides too long, Regis, and
the Altons have tried to back him up. Now it is time to make
it very clear to the Terrans where we stand, and now we have
Beltran on our side, with a stronger message than any...."

Regis realized that he should have known this all along.
He said, in a whisper—he could not make his voice work—
"Kinsman, are you seriously advocating the use of *Sharra*
against the Terrans?"

"Not advocating; stating a fact," Dyan said. "Those who
do not join with us—" he looked up, gave Regis a hard, une-
quivocal stare, "are traitors to Comyn, and should, for the
sake of our whole world, for the survival of Darkover, be
silenced! Zandru's hells, Regis, don't you realize this is the
only chance for Darkover to survive without becoming what
they call us—just another Terran colony?"

"The existence of the Comyn," Regis said quietly, trying
not to show the horror he felt, "is based upon the Compact.
Sharra when used as a weapon is in defiance of Compact—"

"And while we go on observing the forever-be-damned
Compact," said Dyan fiercely, "they surround us, they will
bury us! We are like rabbithorns before a pack of wolves—
and you sit here peacefully saying 'B-a-a-a' while the wolves
open their jaws! Do you really think that we can fight the
Empire with our swords and a scant six dozen Guardsmen?"

"Why do you assume that we need to fight the Empire?"

"Regis, I cannot believe that you, a Hastur, are saying
this! Are you going to hand us meekly over to the Terrans?"

"Of course not," said Regis, "but there has not been a real
war on Darkover for generations. My father died in an illegal
war with Terran weapons—"

"Isn't that reason enough to get them right off our world?"

Regis drew a long breath, clenching his fists to keep quiet
and not shout out his defiance. He wondered if Dyan was
mad, or if he really believed all this. Dyan looked at him and
his face softened somewhat. He said, "You have had no sleep;
and a lot has happened in this one night. This is neither the
time nor the place to discuss what we must do about the
Terrans. Have you had anything to eat since last night?"

Regis shook his head, and Beltran said, "Sit down and join us at breakfast, won't you? We can discuss politics later. Rogan—" he beckoned his servant, "plates for Lord Hastur and Lord Danilo." And before they knew what had happened, they were seated around the breakfast table, being served porridge and broiled rabbithorn. Regis did not feel hungry, but he knew enough of matrix mechanics to know that last night's battle with Sharra had left him drained and exhausted. He ate hungrily, while Beltran, putting hostility aside, became the gracious host.

When the Terrans are gone, then we can enforce Compact again without their vicious example....

But if we seriously use Sharra against them, then we must stand, not against the Terrans who are here, but against the whole Terran Empire and all their multitudes of worlds...

And Sharra is not to be tamed thus, it will turn on those who use it, and destroy...

Beltran said aloud, "I don't wish my cousin of Alton any harm. I would like to make peace with him. His Gift is necessary to the use of Sharra, and he is Tower-trained; he is the safety factor for the use of Sharra, his control and strength. Can you arrange for me to put this to him, Regis?"

"I think it would be no use," said Regis quietly. "I think he would rather die."

"That," said Dyan harshly, "would be *his* choice, not ours! But if he chooses to stand with the Terrans, then he must take the consequences—"

"No," said Beltran. "I think he is the only living man who holds the Alton Gift."

"No," Dyan said, "there is an Alton child. Lew's daughter." Beltran waved that away. "A girl child. It's a man we need, with Alton strength."

So I must keep that secret. Dyan, untrained, does not know the nature of his own Gift. He knows he does not have the Ardais Gift... he adopted Danilo because he found the Ardais Gift had passed to Dani through one of Dyan's father's nedestro daughters. But he does not know, and he must never know, his own Alton Gift.... Regis looked helplessly at Dyan, only now fully aware of what Dyan had always meant to him. He knew Dyan's cruelty, and yet he had never been able to blame him altogether, knowing what powerful forces drove Dyan; knowing Dyan a haunted man, and a desperately unhappy one.

Dyan is myself, myself as I might all too easily have been. How can I condemn him? But I cannot let him destroy the Domains in loosing this mad business of a Holy War on the Terrans, even if I must kill him—

Last night, forced by bitter necessity, I struck at Lew, who is more than friend, more than brother to me. Now it seems that I must condemn Dyan, who is no more than what I might have been, to a madman's death. What right have I to do all this?

He set down his fork, feeling that Beltran's hospitality would choke him. He held himself tightly barriered lest either of the older men pick up even a hint of his thoughts. "Forgive me, *vai dom'yn,* I have business elsewhere. Danilo, attend me," he said, rising, and turned away. "We will speak of this at the proper time, Lord Dyan."

I must see what is left of the Comyn after last night. Perhaps there is nothing left for me to rule!

Lew Alton's narrative

CHAPTER TWO

The sullen red of another day was dying when I woke; my head throbbed with the half-healed wound Kadarin had given me, and my arm was afire with the long slash from Regis's dagger. I lay and wondered for a moment if the whole thing had been a delirious nightmare born of concussion. Then Andres came in, and the deep lines of grief in his face told me it was real. He had loved Linnell, too. He came and scowled at me, taking off the bandage on my head and inspecting the stitches, then looked at the wound in the arm.

"I suppose you are the only man on Darkover who can go to a Festival Night ball and come home with something like this," he grumbled. "What sort of fight was it?"

So he had heard only that Linnell was dead—not of the monstrous visitation of Sharra. The cut hurt, but it was no more than a flesh wound. I'd have trouble using the arm for a while, but I held no resentment; Regis had done the only thing he could, releasing me from the call of Sharra. I said, "It was an accident, he didn't mean to hurt me," and let him think what he liked. "Get me something to eat and some clothes. I have to find out what's happening—"

"You look as if you needed a tenday in bed," Andres said crossly. Then his very real concern for me surfaced in a harsh, "Lad, I've lost two of you! Don't send yourself after Marius and Linnell! What's going on that you can't wait until tomorrow for it?"

I yielded and lay quiet. Somewhere out there Sharra raged, I supposed... but I would know if they came into the Comyn Castle (was I altogether freed? I did not dare look at my matrix to see) and there was nothing to be gained by going out and looking for trouble. I watched Andres grumbling around the room, a soothing sound I remembered from boyhood. When Marius or I had raced our horses at too breakneck

a pace and tumbled off, breaking a finger or a collarbone on
the way down, he had grumbled in exactly the same way.

Marius and I had never had the boyhood squabbles and
fistfights of most brothers I knew; there had been too many
years between us. By the time he was out of pinafores and
able to assert himself, I was already grown and into the cadet
corps. I had only begun to know what kind of man my brother
was, and then he was gone from me, the furthest distance of
all. I had dragged him, too, into the inexorable fates pursuing
me. But at least he had had a clean death, a bullet through
the brain, not the death in fire that waited for me.

For now that Kadarin was loose with the Sharra sword,
I knew how I would die, and made up my mind to it. Ashara's
plan, and the help of Regis Hastur's new and astonishing
Gift, which seemed somehow to hold power over Sharra,
might destroy the Sharra matrix; but I knew perfectly well
that I would go with it into destruction.

Well, that was what had awaited me for all these years,
bringing me back to Darkover at the appointed time, to the
death appointed, which I should have shared with Marjorie.

We had planned our death.... I remembered that morning
in Castle Aldaran when, hostages to the destruction Sharra
was sowing in the country round, showering on the Terran
spaceport in Caer Donn, I had been allowed to waken from
the drugs that had kept me, passive prisoner, chained to the
destruction and feeding power into Sharra. I never knew why
I had been allowed to come free of the drugs; certainly it had
not been any lingering tenderness on Kadarin's part for either
of us. But Marjorie and I had been prepared to die... knew
we must die in closing the gateway into this world that was
Sharra. And so she and I, together, had smashed the gateway...

But then I, using all the power of that matrix, had taken
her, and the Sword, and flung us through space bodily—the
Terrans called it teleportation, and I had never done it before
or since—to Arilinn; where Marjorie had died from her terrible burns, and I...

...I had survived, or some part of me had survived, and
all these years had despised myself because I had not followed
her to death. Now I knew why I had been spared: Kadarin
and Thyra still lived, and somehow they would have recovered the matrix and ravaged Darkover again with its fire.
This time there would be no respite; and when Sharra was

destroyed, none of us would be left alive. And so I must set
my affairs in order.

I called Andres back to me, and said, "Where is the little
girl?"

"Rella—that's the cook's helper—looked after her today,
and put her to bed in the room Marius had when he was a
little tyke," Andres said.

"If I live, I may be able to take her to Armida," I said, "but
if anything should happen to me—no, foster-father, listen;
nothing's certain in this life. Now that my father and brother
are gone—you have served us all faithfully for a quarter of
a century. If something should happen to me, would you leave
Darkover?"

"I don't know. I never thought about it," the old man said.
"I came here with *Dom* Kennard when we were young men,
and it's been a good life; but I think I might go back to Terra
in the end." He added, with a mirthless grin, "I've wondered
what it would be like, to be under my own blue sky again,
and have a moon like a moon ought to be, not those little
things." He pointed out the window at the paling face of Idriel,
greenish like a gem through water.

"Bring me something to write on." When he complied, I
scribbled with my good hand, folded the paper and sealed it.

"I can't leave Armida to you," I said. "I suppose Gabriel
will have it after me; it's in the Alton Domain. I would if I
could, believe me. But if you take this to the Terran Legate
in the Trade City, this will take you to Terra, and I'd rather
you would foster Marja yourself than turn her over to Gabriel's wife." *Domna* Javanne Hastur has never liked me; no
doubt she would do her best by Gabriel's kinsman, but it
would be a cold and dutiful best; and Andres, at least, would
care for my daughter for my father's sake and Linnell's if not
for mine. "My mother—and my father after her—owned
some land there; it had better go to you, then."

He blinked and I saw tears filling his eyes, but all he said
was, "God forbid I should ever have to use it, *vai dom*. But
I'll do my best for the little girl if anything happens. You
know I'd guard her with my life."

I said soberly, "You might have to." I did not know why,
but I was filled suddenly with icy shivers; my blood ran cold
in my veins, and for a moment, even in the dying light which
turned the whole room crimson, it seemed that blood lay over
the stones around me. *Is this then the place of my death?* Only

a moment, and it was gone. Andres went to the window, drew the curtains with a bang.

"The bloody sun!" he said, and it sounded like a curse. Then he tucked the paper I had given him, without looking at it, into a pocket, and went away.

That was settled. Now there was only Sharra to face. Well, it must come when it would. Tomorrow Katie and I would ride to Hali, and the plan I had made, for finding the Sword of Aldones and using this last weapon against Sharra, would either succeed or it would fail. Either way, I would probably not see another sunset. My head was afire with the stitches in my forehead. Scars to match those Kadarin had made on my face... well, there's an old saying that the dead in heaven is too happy to care what happens to his corpse, be it beautiful or ugly, and the dead in hell has too much else to worry about! As for me, I had never believed in either heaven or hell; death was no more than endless nothingness and darkness.

Yet it seemed I could hear again my father's last cry, directly to my mind.... *Return to Darkover and fight for your rights and your brother's! This is my last command...* and then, past that, as the life was leaving him, that last cry of joy and tenderness:

Yllana! Beloved—!

Had he, at the last moment, seen something beyond this life, had my half-remembered mother been waiting for him at that last gateway? The *cristoforos* believe something like that, I know; Marjorie had believed. Would Marjorie be waiting for me beyond Sharra's fire? I could not, dared not, let myself think so. And if it were so—I let myself smile, a sour little smile—what would we do when Dio turned up there? But she had already loosed her claim on me... if love were the criterion, perhaps she would seek Lerrys beyond the gates of death. And what of those husbands or wives given in marriage who hated their spouses, married out of duty or family ties or political expediency, so that married life was a kind of hell and death a merciful release, would any sane or just God demand that they be tied together in some endless afterlife as well? I dismissed all this as mad rubbish and tried, through the fierce pain in my head and the fiery throbbing of my wounded arm, to compose myself for sleep.

The last red light dimmed, faded and was gone. A chink of the curtains showed me pallid greenish moonlight, lying

like ice across my bed; it looked cool, it would cool my fever...there was a step and a rustle and soft whisper.

"Lew, are you asleep?"

"Who's there?"

The dim light picked out a gleam of fair hair, and Dio, her
face as pale as the pallid moon, looked down at me. She turned
and pulled the curtains open where Andres had closed them,
letting the moonlight flood the room and the waning moons
peep over her shoulder.

The chill of the moonlight seemed to cool my feverish face.
I even wondered, incuriously, if I had fallen asleep and was
dreaming she was there, she seemed so quiet, so muted. Her
eyes were swollen and flushed with tears.

"Lew, your face is so hot..." she murmured, and after a
minute she came and laid something cold and refreshing on
my brow. "Do you mean they left you alone here like this?"

"I'm all right," I said. "Dio, what's happened?"

"Lerrys is gone," she whispered, "gone to the Terrans, he
has taken ship and swears he will never return...he tried
to get me to come with him, he...he tried to force me, but
this time I would not go...he said it was death to stay here,
with the things that were coming for the Comyn..."

"You should have gone with him," I said dully. I could not
protect Dio now, nor care for her, with Sharra raging and
Kadarin prowling like a wild beast, Thyra at his side, ready
to drag me back into that same corner of hell....

"I will not go when others must stay and fight," she said.
"I am not such a coward as that..." but she was weeping.
"If he truly feels we are a part of the Empire, he should have
stayed and fought for *that*..."

"Lerrys was never a fighter," I said. Well, neither was I,
but I had been given no choice; my life was already forfeit.
But I had no comfort for Dio now. I said softly, "It is not your
fight, either, Dio. You have not been dragged into this thing.
You could make a life for yourself elsewhere. It's not too late."

Lerrys was one of the hypersensitive Ridenow; the Ridenow Gift had been bred into the Comyn, to sense these
other-dimension horrors in the Ages of Chaos; a Gift obsolete
now, when the Comyn no longer ranged through space and
time as legend said they had done in the heyday of the Towers.
As those who fight forest-fire keep cagebirds to tell when the
poison gases and smoke are growing too dangerous for living
things—because the cagebird will die of the poisons before

men are aware of them—so the Ridenow served to warn
Comyn less sensitive than they of the presence of forces no
man could tolerate. I was not surprised that he had fled from
Darkover now...

I only wished I could do the same!

"Dio, you shouldn't be here, at this hour—"

"Do you think I care about that?" she said, and her voice
was thick with tears. "Don't send me away, Lew. I don't—I
don't—I won't ask anything of you, but let me stay here with
you for tonight—"

She lay beside me, her curly head against my shoulder,
and I tasted salt when I kissed her. And suddenly I realized
that if I had changed, Dio had changed no less. The tragedy
of that thing in the hospital, which should have been our son,
was her tragedy too; more hers than mine, for she had borne
it in her body for months; yet I had been distraught with my
own selfish grief, and left no room for her. She had come into
my life when I had thought it was over forever, and given
me a year of happiness, and I owed it to her to remember the
happiness, not the horror and tragedy at the end.

I whispered, holding her close, "I wish it had been different. I wish I had had—more for you."

She kissed my scarred cheek, with a tenderness which
somehow drew us closer than the wildest passion. "Never
mind, Lew," she said softly into the darkness, "I know. Sleep,
my love, you're weary and wounded."

And after a moment I felt that she was fast asleep in my
arms; but I lay there, wakeful, my eyes burning with regret.
I had loved Marjorie with the first fire of an untried boy, all
flame and desire; we had never known what we would have
grown into, for Marjorie had had no time at all. But Dio had
come to me when I was a man, grown through suffering into
the capacity for real love, and I had never understood, I had
let her walk away from me in the first upheaval. The shared
tragedy should have drawn us closer, and I had let it drive
us apart.

*If only I could live, I could somehow make it up to Dio, if
I only had time to let her know how much I loved her....*

*But it is too late; I must let her go, so that she will not
grieve too much for me....*

*But for tonight I will pretend that there is something beyond
morning, that she and I and Marja can find a world somewhere, and that Sharra's fire will burn out harmlessly before*

the mingling of the Sword of Aldones and the Hastur Gift.... I
half-knew that I was already dreaming, but I lay holding Dio
sleeping in my arms until at last, near dawn, I fell asleep too.

Red sunlight woke me, and the closing of a door somewhere
in the Alton suite. Dio—had she really been there? I was not
sure; but the curtains she had opened to the moonlight were
open to the sun, and there was a fine red-gold hair lying on
my pillow. The pain in head and wounded arm had subsided
to the dullest of aches; I sat up, knowing that it was time to
act.

While I dressed for riding, I considered. Surely, this day
or the next, what was left of the Comyn would ride to Hali
for the state funeral for Linnell—and for Derik. Perhaps it
would be better to ride with them, not to attract attention,
and then to slip away toward the *rhu fead*...

No. There was no time for that. I had loved Linnell and
she had been my foster-sister, but I could not wait to speak
words of tenderness and regret over her grave. I could not
help her now, and either way, she had gone too far to care
whether or not I was there to speak at her burying. For
Linnell I could only try to ensure that the land she had loved
was not ravaged by Sharra's fires. It might be that we could
do something for Callina too; surely Beltran, who had been
part of the original circle who had tried to raise Sharra, would
die with us when we closed that gateway for the last time.
And then Callina too would be freed.

I went in search of Callina, and found her in the room
where I had seen Linnell playing her *rryl*, that night before
we had gone to Ashara's Tower. Callina was sitting before
the harp, her hands lax in her lap, so white and still that I
had to speak to her twice before she heard me; and then she
turned a dead face to me, a face so cold and distant, so like
Ashara's, that I was shocked and horrified. I shook her, hard,
and finally slapped her face; at that she came back, life and
anger in her pale cheeks.

"How dare you!"

"Callina, I'm sorry—you were so far away, I couldn't make
you hear me—you were in a trance—"

"Oh, no—" she gasped, her hands flying to cover her mouth
in consternation, "Oh, no, it can't be...." she swallowed and
swallowed again, fighting tears. She said, "I felt I could not
bear my grief, and it seemed to me that Ashara could give

me peace, take away grief... grief and guilt, because if I had not—not used the screen with you, not found that—that Kathie girl, Linnell would have been alive...."

"You don't know that," I said harshly. "There's no way of telling what might have happened when Kadarin drew—that sword. Kathie might have died instead of Linnell; or they might both have died. Either way, don't blame yourself. Where is Kathie?"

"I don't want to see her," Callina said shakily. "She is like—it's like seeing Linnell's ghost, and I cannot bear it—" and for a moment I thought she would go far away into the trance state again.

"There's no time for that, Callina! We don't know what Beltran, or Kadarin, may be planning," I said. "We don't have much time; things could start up again at any moment." How had I been able to sleep last night, with this hanging over us? But at least now I was strong enough for what I must do. "Where is Kathie?"

At last Callina sighed and showed me the way to where Kathie slept. She was lying on a couch, awake, half naked, scanning a set of tiles, but she started as I came in, and caught a blanket around her. "Get out! Oh—it's you again! What do you want?"

"Not what you seem to be expecting," I said dryly. "I want you to dress and ride with us. Can you ride?"

"Yes, certainly. But why—"

I rummaged behind a panel, finding some clothes I had seen Linnell wear. It suddenly outraged me that these lengths of cloth, these embroideries, should still be intact, with Linnell's perfume still in their folds, when my foster-sister lay cold in the chapel at the side of her dead lover. I flung them, almost angrily, across the couch.

"These will do for riding. Put them on." I sank down to wait for her, was recalled, by her angry stare, to memory of Terran taboos. I rose, actually reddening; how could Terran women be so immodest out of doors and so prudish within? "I forgot. Call me when you're ready."

A peculiar choked sound made me turn back. She was staring helplessly at the armful of clothing, turning the pieces this way and that. "I haven't the faintest notion how to get into these things."

"After what you were just *thinking* at me," I said stiffly, "I'm certainly not going to offer to help you."

She blushed too. "And anyway, how could I ride in a long skirt?"

"Zandru's hells, girl, what else would you wear? They are Linnell's riding-clothes; if she rode in them, you certainly can." Linnell had worn them to ride to Marius's funeral.

"I've never worn anything like this for riding, and I'm certainly not going to start now," she blazed. "If you want me to ride somewhere on a horse, you're going to have to get me some decent clothes!"

"These clothes belonged to my foster-sister; they are perfectly decent."

"Damn it, get me some *indecent* ones, then!"

I laughed. I had to. "I'll see what I can do, Kathie."

The Ridenow apartments were almost deserted this early, except for a servant mopping the stone floor, and I was glad; I had no desire to walk in upon Lord Edric. It occurred to me that Dio and I had married without the permission of her Domain Lord.

Freemate marriage cannot be dissolved after the woman has borne a child, except by mutual consent.

But that was Darkovan law. Dio and I had married by the law of the Empire... why was I thinking this, as if there were still time to go back and mend what had gone astray between us? At least I would see her once more. I asked the servant if *Domna* Diotima would see me, and after a moment, Dio, in a long woolly dressing-gown, came sleepily out into the main room. Her face lighted when she saw me; but there was no time for that. I explained my predicament, and she must have read the rest in my face and manner.

"Kathie? Yes, I remember her from—from the hospital," she said, "I still have my Terran riding things, the ones I wore on Vainwal; she should be able to wear them." She giggled, then broke off. "I know it's not really funny. I just can't help it, thinking—never mind; I'll go and help her with them."

"And I'll go down and see if I can find horses for us," I said, and went down, swiftly, by an old and little-known stairway, to the Guard hall. Fortunately there was a Guardsman there who had known me when I was a cadet.

"Hjalmar, can you find horses? I must ride to Hali."

"Certainly, sir. How many horses?"

"Three," I said after a moment, "one with a lady's saddle."

Kathie might ride like Dio, astride and in breeches like some

Free Amazon, but Callina certainly would not. I told him where to bring them, and went back to find Kathie neatly dressed in the tunic and breeches I had seen Dio wear.

I was happy then. But I did not know it, and now it is too late—now and forever.

Some Terran poet said that—that the saddest words in any language are always too late.

The door thrust suddenly open and Regis came in. He said, "Where are you going? I'd better come with you."

I shook my head. "No. If anything happens—if we don't make it—you're the only one with any strength against Sharra."

"That is exactly why I must come with you," Regis said. "No, leave the women here—"

"Kathie at least must come," I said. "We are going to Hali, to the *rhu fead*," and added, when he still looked confused, "It's possible that Kathie may be the only person on this world who can reach the Sword of Aldones."

His eyes widened. He said, "There's something I should know...Grandfather told me once—no, I can't remember." His brow ridged in angry concentration. "It could be important, Lew!"

It could, indeed. The Sword of Aldones was the ultimate weapon against Sharra. And Regis seemed, of late, to have some curious power over Sharra. But whatever it was, we had no time to waste while he tried to remember.

Regis warned, "If Dyan sees you, you'll be stopped. And Beltran has a legal right—if no other—to stop Callina. How are you going to get out of the Castle?"

I led them to the Alton rooms. The Altons, generations and generations ago, had designed this part of the castle, and they had left themselves a couple of escape routes. It occurred to me to wonder why they had guarded themselves against their fellow Comyn, in those days; then I grinned with mirth. This was certainly not the first time, in the long history of the Comyn, that powerful clan had warred against clan.

It might be the last, though.

I forced my mind away from that, searching out certain elegant designs in the parquetry flooring. My father had once shown me this escape route, but he had not troubled to teach me the pattern. I frowned, tried to sound, delicately, the matrix lock that led to the secret stairway.

Fourth level, at least! I began to wonder if I would need

to hunt up my old matrix mechanic's kit and perform the mental equivalent of picking the lock. I shifted my concentration, just a little...

...*Return to Darkover...fight for your brother's rights and your own...*.

My father's voice; yet for the first time I did not resent it. In that final, unknowing rapport he had forced on me, I was sure there had been some of his memories—how else could I account for the sudden, emotional way I had reacted to Dyan? Now I stood with my toes in the proper pattern, and, not stopping to think how to do it, *pushed* against something invisible.

...*to the second star, sidewise and through the labyrinth...*

My mind sought out the pattern; halfway through the flickering memory that was not mine faded into nonsense, evaporated with the sting of lemon-scent in the air, but I was deeply into the pattern now and I could unravel the final twist of the lock. Beneath me the floor tilted; I jumped, scrabbled for safety as a section of the flooring moved downward on invisible machinery, revealing a hidden stair, dark and dusty, that led away downward.

"Stay close to me," I warned, "I've never been down here before, though I saw it opened once." I gestured them downward on the dusty stair; Kathie wrinkled her nose at the musty smell, and Callina held her skirts fastidiously close to her body, but they went. Regis and Dio followed us. Behind us the square of light folded itself, disappeared.

"I wish my old great-great-whatever-great grandfather had provided a light," I fretted, "it's as dark in here as Zandru's—" I cut off the guard-room obscenity, substituted weakly "pockets." I heard Dio snicker softly and knew she had been in rapport with me.

Callina said softly, "I can make light, if you need it."

Kathie cried out in sudden fright as a green ball of pallid fire grew in Callina's palm, spread like phosphorscence over her slender six-fingered hands. I was familiar with the overlight, but it was an uncanny sight to see, as the Keeper spread out her hands, the pallid glow leading us downward. The extended fingers broke through sticky webs, and once I fancied that gleaming little eyes followed us in the darkness, but I closed my eyes and mind to them, watching for every step under my feet. We crowded so hard on Callina's heels that she had to warn us, in a soft, preoccupied voice, "Be careful not to touch me." Once Kathie slipped on the strangely sticky surfaces, fell a step or two, jarringly, before I could catch and steady her. I felt with my good hand along the wall, ignoring what might be clinging there, and once the stair jogged sharply to the right, a sharp turn; without Callina's pale light we would have stepped off into nothingness and fallen—who knows into what depths? As it was, one of us jarred a pebble loose and we heard it strike below, after a long time, very far away. We went on, and I felt my blood pounding hard in my temples. Damn it, I hoped I would never have to come down here again, I would rather face Sharra and half of Zandru's demons!

Down, and down, and endlessly down, so that I felt half the day must be passing as we threaded the staircase and the maze into which it led; but Callina led the way, with dainty fastidious steps, as if she were treading a ballroom floor.

At last the passageway ended in a solid, heavy door. The light faded from Callina's hands as she touched it, and I had to wrestle with the wooden bar which closed it. I could not draw it back one-handed, and Dio threw her weight against the bar; it creaked open, and light assaulted eyes dilated by the darkness of that godforgotten tunnel. I squinted through it and discovered that we were standing in the Street of Coppersmiths, exactly where I had told Hjalmar to bring the horses. At the corner of the street, through the small sound of many tiny hammers tapping on metal, there was a place where horses were shod and iron tools mended, and I saw Hjalmar standing there with the horses.

He recognized Callina, though she was folded in an ordinary thick dark cloak—I wondered if she had borrowed the coarse garment from one of her servants, or simply gone into the servants' quarters and taken the first one she found?

"*Vai domna,* let me assist you to mount..."

She ignored him, turning to me, and awkwardly, one-handed, I extended my arm to help her into the saddle. Kathie scrambled up without help, and I turned to Dio.

"Do you know where you are? How are you going to get back?"

"Not *that* way," she said fervently. "Never mind, I can find my way." She gestured at the castle, which seemed to be very high above us on the slopes of the city; we had indeed come a long way. "I still feel I ought to come with you—"

I shook my head. I would not drag Dio into this, too. She

held out her arms but I pretended not to see. I could not bear farewells, not now. I said to Regis, "See that Dio gets back safely!" and turned my back on them both. I hoisted myself awkwardly into the saddle, and rode away without looking back, forcing myself to concentrate on guiding the horse's hoofs over the cobbled street.

Out of the Street of Coppersmiths; out through the city gates, unnoticed and unrecognized; and upward, on the road leading toward the pass. I looked down once, saw them both lying beneath me, Terran HQ and Comyn Castle, facing one another with the Old Town and the Trade City between them, like troops massed around two warring giants. I turned my back resolutely on them both, but I could not shut them away.

They were my heritage; both of them, not one alone, and try as I might, I could not see the coming battle as between Terran and Comyn, but Darkover against Darkover, strife between those who would loose ancient evil in our world in the service of Comyn, and those who would protect it from that evil.

I had allied myself with the ancient evil of Sharra. It mattered nothing that I had tried to close the gateway; it was I who had first summoned Sharra, misusing the *laran* which was my heritage, betraying Arilinn which had trained me in the use of that *laran*. Now I would destroy that evil, even if I destroyed myself with it.

Yet for the moment, breathing the icy wind of the high pass, the snow-laden wind that blew off the eternal glacier up there, I could forget that this might be my last ride. Kathie was shivering, and I took off my cloak and laid it over her shoulders as we rode side by side. She protested, "You'll freeze!" but I laughed and shook my head.

"No, no—you're not used to this climate; this is shirt-sleeve weather to me!" I insisted, wrapping her in the folds. She clutched it round her, still shivering. I said, "We'll be through the pass soon, and it's warmer on the shores of Hali."

The red sun stood high, near the zenith; the sky was clear and cloudless, a pale and beautiful mauve-color, a perfect day for riding. I wished that there were a hawk on my saddle, that I was riding out from Arilinn, hunting birds for my supper. I looked at Callina and she smiled back at me, sharing the thought, for she made a tiny gesture as if tossing a *verrin* hawk into the air. Even Kathie, with her glossy brown curls, made me think of riding with Linnell in the Kilghard Hills

when we were children. Once we had ridden all the way to
Edelweiss, and been soundly beaten, when we came home
after dark, by my father; only now I realized that what had
seemed a fearful whipping to children twelve and nine years
old, had in reality been a few half-playful cuffs around the
shoulders, and that father had been laughing at us, less angry
than grateful that we had escaped bandits or banshee-birds.
I remembered now that he had never beaten any of us seriously. Though once he threatened, when I failed to rub down
and care for a horse I had ridden, leaving the animal to a
half-trained stableboy, that if I neglected to see to my mounts,
next time I too should have no supper and sleep on the floor
in my wet riding-clothes instead of having a hot bath and a
good bed waiting.

Harsh as he had been—and there had been times when
I hated him—it seemed that only now, facing my own death,
was I wholly aware of how he had loved us, of how all his
own plans for us had fallen into ruin. I started to say, "Linnie,
do you remember," and remembered that Linnell was dead
and that the girl who rode before me, clutching a cloak around
her with Linnell's very gesture, was a stranger, a *Terran*
stranger.

But I looked past her at Callina, and our eyes met. Callina
was real, Callina was all the old days at Arilinn, Callina was
the time when I had been happy and doing work I loved in
the Towers. The copper bracelet on her left wrist, sign of a
tie with Beltran, was a joke, an obscenity, entirely irrelevant.
I let myself dream of a day when I would tear it from her
wrist, fling it in Beltran's face...

Callina was a Keeper, never to be touched, even with a
lustful thought...but now she was riding at my side, and she
raised her face to mine, pale and smiling. And I thought;
Keeper no more; the Comyn married her off to Beltran as
they would dispose of a brood mare, but if she can be given
to Beltran, they cannot complain if—after she is properly
widowed, for while I lived Beltran would not take her as his
wife—if afterward she gives herself to me.

*And then...Armida, and the Kilghard Hills...and our
own world waiting for us.* She smiled at me, and for a moment
my heart turned over inside me at that smile; then I forced
myself to remember. The way out led through Sharra; and
it was very doubtful that I would be alive to see the sun set.
But at least Beltran, who had, like myself, been sealed to

Sharra, would go with me into the darkness. But still her eyes sought mine, and against all conceivable sanity, I was happy.

Below us, now, lay the pale shores of Hali, with the long line of trees fading in the mist. Here, so the legend said, the Son of Aldones had fallen to Earth, and lay on the shores of the Lake, so that the sands were evermore mirrored and shimmering.... I looked on the pale glimmer of the sands of the shores, and knew that the sands were of some gleaming stone, mica or garnet, beaten into sand by the waves of a great inland sea which had washed here long before this planet spawned life. Yet the wonder remained; along these shimmering shores Hastur had lain, and here came Camilla the Damned, and the Blessed Cassilda, foremother of the Comyn, and ministered to him...

The shadows were lengthening; the day was far advanced, and one of the moons, great violet-shining Liriel, was just rising over the lake, waning a little from the full. We had perhaps two hours before sunset, and I discovered I did not like to think about riding back to Thendara in the darkness. Well, we would ride that colt when he was grown to bear a saddle; our task now was within the *rhu fead*, the old chapel which was the holy place of the Comyn.

It rose before us, a white, pale-gleaming pile of stone. Once there had been a Tower here; it had fallen in the Ages of Chaos, burned to the ground in those evil old days by a *laran* weapon next to which the Sharra matrix was a child's toy. We reined in the horses, near the brink of the Lake, where mist curled up whitely along the shore. The sparse pinkish grass thinned out in the sands. I kicked loose a pebble; it sank, slowly turning over and over, through the cloud-surface.

"That's not water, is it?" Kathie said, shaken. "What is it?"

I did not know. Hali was the nearest of the half-dozen cloud-lakes whose depths are not water, but some inert gas... it will even sustain life; once I walked for a little while in the depths of that Lake, looking at the strange creatures, neither fish nor bird, which swam, or flew, in that cloud-water. Legend said that once these Lakes had been water like any other, and that in the Ages of Chaos, some sorcerer, working with the *laran* of that day, had created them, with their peculiar gaseous structure, and the curious mutated fishbirds which flew or swam there...I thought that just about as likely as the ballad which tells how the tears of Camilla had fallen into the water and turned them into cloud when Hastur chose Cassilda for his consort.

This was no time for children's tales and ballads!

Kathie said in confusion, "But—but surely I have been here before—"

I shook my head. "No. You have some of my memories, that's all."

"All!" Her voice held a note of hysteria. I said, "Don't worry about it," and patted her wrist, clumsily. "Here, come this way."

Twin pillars rose before us, a twinkling rainbow glimmering like frost between them; the Veil, like the Veil at Arilinn, to keep out anyone not allied to Comyn. If Kathie's genes were identical to Linnell's, she should be able to pass this Veil—but it was not a physical test alone, but a mental one; no one without *laran* of the Comyn kind...and Kathie had been brought here because of her own immunity to that Comyn mental set.

"Even blocked," I said to Kathie, "it would strip your mind bare. I'll have to hold your mind completely *under* mine." I seemed to speak out of some strange inner surety, knowing precisely what I should do, and in a small corner of my mind, I wondered at myself. She shrank away from the first touch of my mind, and I warned tonelessly, "I must. The Veil is a kind of forcefield, attuned to the Comyn brain; you wouldn't survive two seconds of it."

I bent and picked her up bodily. "It won't hurt me; but don't fight me."

I made contact with her mind; swamped it, forced resistance down—somewhere at the back of my mind, I remembered how I had feared to do this to Marius. It was a form of rape, and I shrank from it; but I told myself that without this overshadowing she could not survive....

The first law of a telepath is that you do not enter any unwilling mind....

But she had consented; I told myself that, and without further waiting, I covered the last resistance and her mind disappeared, completely held down within my own and concealed. Then I stepped through the trembling rainbow...

A million little needles prickled at me, nameless force spitting me through and through like a strangely penetrating

rain.... I was inside, through the Veil. I set Kathie down on
her feet and withdrew, as gently as I could, but she slumped,
nerveless, to the floor. Callina knelt, chafing her hands, and
after a moment she opened her eyes.

There were doors and long passages before us, hazy as if
the *rhu fead* were filled with the same gaseous cloud as was
the Lake; I almost expected to see the strange fishbirds swim-
ming there. Here and there were niches filled with things so
strange I could not imagine them; behind a rainbow of colors,
I saw a bier where lay a woman's body—or a wax effigy—or
a corpse, I could not tell; only the long pale reddish hair; and
it seemed to me that the woman's body was too realistic for
any unreality, that her breast seemed to rise and fall softly
as she slept; yet the rainbow shimmer was undisturbed, she
had slept there or lain there in unchanging, incorruptible
death for thousands of years. Behind another of the rainbows
was a sword lying on a great ancient shield—but the hilt
and shield glimmered with colors and I knew it was no simple
weapon and that it was not what we sought. *Regis should
have come with us, I thought, how will I know the Sword of
Aldones when I find it?*

"I will know," said Callina quietly. "It is here."

Abruptly the passage angled, turned, and opened up into
a white-vaulted chapel, with something like an altar at the
far end, and above it, done in the style of the most ancient
mosaics, a portrayal of the Blessed Cassilda, with a starflower
in her hand. In a niche in one of the walls was another of the
trembling rainbows, but as I drew near, I felt the sting of
pain, and knew this was one of those protected entirely from
Comyn.... Now was the time to see if Kathie could actually
reach these guarded things. Callina put out curious hands;
they jerked back of themselves. As if she had heard my
thoughts—and perhaps she did—Kathie asked, "Are you still
touching my mind?"

"A little."

"Get out. All the way..."

That made sense; if this forcefield was adjusted to repel
the Comyn, then the slightest touch of my mind would endanger her. I withdrew entirely, and she began to walk
swiftly toward the rainbow; passed through it.

She disappeared into a blur of darkening mist. Then a
blaze of fire seared up toward the ceiling—I wanted to cry
out to her not to be afraid; it was only a trick...an illusion.

But even my voice would not carry through the forcefield against Comyn. A dim silhouette, she passed on and through the fire; perhaps she did not know it was there.

Then there was a crash of thunder that rolled through the chapel and jarred the floor as if with earthquake. Kathie darted back through the rainbow. In her hand, she held a sword.

So the Sword of Aldones was a real sword, after all, long and gleaming and deadly, and of so fine a temper that it made my own look like a child's leaden toy. In the hilt, through a thin layer of insulating silk, blue jewels gleamed and sparkled.

It was so much like the Sharra sword that I could not keep back a shudder as I looked at it. But the Sharra sword now seemed like an inferior forgery, a dull copy of the glorious thing I looked on. It was shrouded in a scabbard of fine dyed leather; words, graved in fine embroidery with copper thread, writhed across the scabbard.

"What does it say?" Kathie asked, and I bent to read the words, but they were in so ancient a dialect of casta that I could not make them out, either. Callina glanced at them, and after a moment translated.

This sword shall be drawn only when all else is ended for the children of Hastur, and then the unchained shall be bound.

Well, one way or the other, the world we had known was at an end; and Sharra unchained. But I would not venture to draw forth the sword from the scabbard. I remembered what had happened to Linnell when she was confronted with her duplicate, and I—I had been sealed to the Sharra matrix; even now I did not think I was free, not entirely.

So we had the Sword of Aldones; but I still did not know how it could be used. *The unchained shall be bound.* But how?

A tingle of power flowed, not unpleasantly, up my arm; as if the sword wished to be drawn, to leap from its scabbard...

"No," Callina warned, and I relaxed, letting my breath go, shoving the sword back into the leather; I had drawn it only a few inches.

"I'll take it," she said, and I sighed with relief. Callina was a Keeper; she knew how to handle strange matrixes. And while the Sharra sword was a concealment for a great and powerful matrix, the Sword of Aldones was—I sensed this

without knowing how I knew—itself a matrix, and dangerous
to handle. If Callina felt capable of that risk, I was not going
to dispute with her about it.

"That's that," I said. "Let's get out of here."

The last light of the sun was setting as we came out of the
rhu fead. The women went ahead of me; there was no need,
now, for me to safeguard Kathie. The Veil was only to screen
against those not of Comyn blood getting *into* the chapel; it
had never occurred to my forefathers in the Ages of Chaos
to guard against anyone getting out. I lingered, half wanting
to explore the strange things here.

Then Kathie cried out; and I saw the dying sunlight glint
on steel. Two figures, dark shapes against the light, blurred
before my eyes; then, I recognized Kadarin, sword in hand,
and at his side a woman, slender and vital as a dark flame.

She did not, now, look much like Marjorie; but even so, I
knew Thyra. Kathie started back against me; I put her gently
aside to face my sworn enemy.

"What do you want?"

I was playing for time. There was only one thing Kadarin
could want from me now, and my blood turned to ice with
the horror of that memory, and around my neck my matrix
began to blaze and to pulse with fire...

*Come to me, return to me in fire...and I will sweep away
all your hatred and lust, all your fears and anguish in my
own flame, raging unchained, burning, burning forever....*

"Hiding behind women again?" Kadarin taunted. "Well,
give me what the Keeper carries, and perhaps I shall let you
go...*if you can!*" He flung back his head and laughed, that
strange laugh that carried echoes of a falcon's cry. He did not
look like a man now, or anything human; his eyes were cold
and colorless, almost metallic, and his colorless hair had
grown long, flying about his head; his hands on his sword
were long and thin, almost more like talons than fingers. And
yet there was a strange beauty to him as he stood with his
head flung back, laughing that crazy laughter. "Why don't
you make it easy for yourself, Lew? You know you'll do what
we want in the end. Give me that—" he pointed to the Sword
of Aldones, "and I'll let the women go free, and you won't
have *that* to torment yourself with..."

"I'll see you frozen solid in Zandru's coldest hell before
that, you—" I cried out, and whipped out my dagger; I stood
confronting him. There had been a time when I could probably

have beaten him in swordplay; now, with one hand, and a head wound and a slash in my good arm, I didn't think I had a chance. But I might, at least, force him to kill me cleanly first.

"No, wait, Lew," said Callina quietly. "This is—Kadarin?" There was nothing in her voice but fastidious distaste, not a trace of fear. I saw a shadow of dismay on Kadarin's face, but he was not human enough, now, to react to the words. He said, in a ghastly parody on his old, urbane manner, "Robert Raymon Kadarin, *para servirti, vai domna.*"

She raised the Sword of Aldones slightly in her hand.

"Come and take it—if you can," she said, and held it out invitingly to him. I cried out, "Callina, no—" and even Thyra cried out something wordless, but Kadarin snarled, "Bluffing won't help," and lunged at her, wresting the sword from her hand....

Her hand exploded in blue fire, and Kadarin went reeling back, in the blue glow; the Sword of Aldones flared with brilliance, the brightness of copper filings in flame, and flared there, lying on the ground between us, while Kadarin, stunned and half senseless, slowly dragged himself to his feet, snarling a gutter obscenity of which I understood only its foulness.

Callina said quietly, "I cannot take it now that it has touched Sharra, either. Kathie—?"

Slowly, hesitating, her hand reluctant, she knelt and stretched out her hand; slowly, frightened, as if she feared that the same blue blaze of power would knock her senseless. But her hand closed over the hilt without incident. Perhaps, to her, it was only a sword. She drew a long breath.

Thyra cried out, "Let me—"

"No, wild-bird." For an instant, I saw through the monstrous thing he had become, a hint of the man I had, once, loved as a sworn brother; the old tenderness as he drew Thyra back, holding her quiet. "You cannot touch it either—but neither can the Alton whelp, so it's a draw. Let them go; there will be a time and place—" he glared out at me again, the moment of gentleness and humanity gone. "And nothing will protect you then; who has been touched by the flamehair, she will claim again for her own. And then the hells themselves will burn in Sharra's flame...."

Gods above! Once this had been a man, and my friend! I

could not even hate him now; he was not human enough for that.

He was Sharra, clothed in the body of a man who had once been human...and he willed it so, he had surrendered of his own will to the monstrous thing he had become! I could hardly see Thyra at his side, through the illusion of tossing flames which raged between us...

"No," Thyra cried out, "not now! Not now!" and the flames receded. I could see her clearly now; there had never been any fire. She came toward me, hands outstretched; only a woman, small and frail with little bones like a bird's. She was dressed like a man for riding, and her hair was the same rich copper as Marjorie's, and her eyes, clear golden-amber like Marjorie's, looked up to me in the old sweet half-mocking way; and I remembered that I had loved her, desired her...

She said, reaching out for a half-forgotten rapport between us, "What have you done with my daughter? Our daughter?"

Marja! For a moment it seemed I could feel the touch of sweet memory, Marjorie merging into Thyra in my arms, a living flame, th touch of the child-mind....

Thyra was i r pport and her face changed.

"You have hei, ien?"

I said quietly, "You did not want her, Thyra. It was a cruel trick played on a drugged man, and you deserve all the misery you have had from it...."

But for a moment I had forgotten to watch her, forgotten that she was nothing, now, but Kadarin's pawn...and in that moment a stab of agony went through my shoulder and my heart felt the agony of death and I knew that Thyra's dagger had wounded me....

I reeled back with the shock of it. Callina caught me in her arms; even through pain and sudden despair...*this was the end, and Sharra still raged, I had died too quickly, I had died*...I was startled at the strength with which she held me upright. Kadarin made a lunge forward, hauled Thyra bodily off me.

"No! That's not the way—we still need him—ah, what have you done, Thyra—you've killed him—"

I felt myself fainting, darkness sinking down and covering my eyes, a horrid noise battering at my eardrums—was death like this, pain and noise and blinding light? No, it was a Terran helicopter, hovering, sinking, and loud shouts, and one voice suddenly coming clear.

"Robert Raymon Kadarin, I arrest you in the name of the Empire, on charges of . . . lady, drop that knife; this is a nerve-blaster and I can drop you in your tracks. You too—put that sword down."

Through the wavering darkness before my eyes I made out the dark-uniformed forms of Spaceforce men. I should have known they would find Kadarin, one way or the other, and with Terran weapons prohibited here in the Domains. I could bring charges against them, I thought weakly, they have no right to be here. Not like this. Not with blasters outside the Trade City. I should arrest them instead of them arresting us.

Then I sank into a darkness that was like death indeed, and all I could feel was an immense regret for all I had left undone. Then even that was gone.

CHAPTER THREE

Dio watched the horses out of sight, and as they turned out of the Street of Coppersmiths, it seemed to Regis that the woman was weeping; but she shook her head, and one or two bright drops went flying. She looked at him, almost defiantly, and said, "Well, Lord Hastur?"

"I promised I would see you safely back to the Castle, *Domna*," he said, offering his arm.

She laughed; it was like a rainbow coming out through the cloud. "I thank you, my lord. Not necessary. I've walked unguarded in worse places than this!"

"That's right, you've been offworld," Regis said, feeling again the old longing, the old envy; for all his suffering, Lew was freer than he was himself, with all the worlds of an interstellar Empire at his command. Oh, to go beyond the narrow skies of his own world, to see the stars...he knew now that he would never go. For better or for worse, his fate lay here, whatever it might be; an unwanted crown, the new *laran* which so weighed on him that he felt he would split asunder like a butterfly from its constricting cocoon. He was Hastur; the rest he should put aside, all his old dreams, like the brightly colored tops and balls of his childhood. He walked at Dio's side, along the Street of Coppersmiths, turning at the corner to take the road to the Comyn Castle, and heard the whispers, saw the crowd draw before him in awe and astonishment.

"Comyn..."

"It's the Lord Hastur himself...the prince..."

"No, for sure not, what would the likes o' he be doing here on the street and unguarded..."

"It's the Hastur prince, yes, I saw him on Festival Night..."

He could not walk down a fairly narrow and unimportant street without collecting a crowd. Lew, a marked man and disfigured, one hand sacrificed to the fires of Sharra, was still more free than himself.... If any man stared at Lew it was only with pity or curiosity, not this entire trust, that sense

that whatever might come to Darkover, the Hastur-kin would
protect them and shield them.

*Like my own laran, it is too much for me ... too much for
any mortal man less than a God!*

He drew a fold of his cloak over the concealment of his red
hair, all unshielded to the mental leakage of the crowd, wonder, astonishment, curiosity.... *I cannot dance with a woman
or walk with one down the street but my name is linked to
hers ...*

"I'm sorry, Dio," he said, trying for lightness, "but I'm
afraid they have you marked out for my Queen already; it
is a pity that we must disappoint them. Now, I suppose, I will
have to explain to my grandfather that I do not intend to
marry you, either!"

She gave him a small wry smile. "I have no wish to be a
Queen," she said, "and I fear, even if you wished to marry
me, Lord Danvan would be scandalized...."

*I have cheapened myself with other men on Vainwal; and
now I am sister to the traitor who has fled from Darkover into
the Empire....*

He said, gently, "I did not know Lerrys was gone. But I
do not blame him for running away, Dio. I wish I could."
After a moment he added, "And if you are a traitor's sister,
that does not make you traitor; but the more credit to you
that you have remained when others have fled."

They were standing now before the gates of the Comyn
Castle; he saw one of the Guardsmen stare at him, alone and
unattended and with Lady Dio Ridenow, and although he
was trying not to read the man's mind, he could sense the
man's shock and amazement; *Lord Regis, here and without
even a bodyguard, and with a woman ...* and a secret pleasure
at this morsel of gossip he could spread among his fellows.
Well, everything Regis did created gossip, but he was heartily
sick of it.

He crossed the courtyard, wanting to say a polite word or
two to Dio and dismiss her. He had too many troubles to share
them with any woman, even if there was a woman alive with
whom he could share anything except a brief moment of passion or pleasure. And, abruptly, looking at Dio, he was torn
by her despair.

"What is it, Dio?" he asked gently, and felt it flood through
him.

He was so sure he was going to die! All he sees is his own

*death... I would have gone to death, even that, beside him,
but he can only see Callina...*

He was struck numb by the quality of her pain. No woman
had ever loved him like that, none ever shown him that kind
of loyalty and staunchness....

*He has gone to die, to hurl himself against death in finding
the weapon against Sharra....*

Regis realized that he should have gone with Lew himself;
or he should have taken his matrix, cleansed it as he had
done to Rafe's. What gave him this strange power, not over
Sharra, but over the Form of Fire? Kadarin was somewhere,
with the Sharra matrix, and Lew might fall into his hands....

He should have gone with Lew, or cleansed Lew's matrix.
Or at least demanded that Callina take him to Ashara, so
that the ancient Keeper of the Comyn could explain this new
and monstrous Hastur Gift. *Lew at least is Tower-trained, he
knows what strengths he has... and what weaknesses; he faces
death with full knowledge, not blinded as I am by ignorance!*
What was the good of being Hastur, and Lord of Comyn, if
he could not even know what this new *laran* might bring
him?

Dio was trying to conceal her tears. Part of him wanted
to reassure her, but he had no comfort for her and in any case
Dio did not want facile lies; she was one of the sensitive
Ridenow and she would see through them at once. He said
quietly, "It may be that we are all going to die, Dio. But if
I have a chance I would rather die to keep Sharra from destroying Darkover—Terran and Comyn alike. And so would
Lew, I think; and he has the right to choose his own
death... and to make amends..."

"I suppose so." Beneath the understanding, she turned to
him, no longer trying to conceal her tears, and somehow he
realized that this was a kind of acceptance. "It's strange; I
have seen so much of his—his weakness, his gentler side, I
forget how strong he is. He would never run away to the
Terrans because he was afraid; not even if they burned off
his other hand first..."

"No," said Regis, suddenly feeling closer to her than to his
own sister, "he wouldn't."

"You wouldn't either, would you?" she asked, smiling at
him through the tears in her eyes.

He is Hastur... and he will stand by Comyn... and then,
even in Dio, the curious and inevitable question: *I wonder*

*why he has never married? Surely he could have any woman
he wanted...surely it is not true that he is, like Lerrys, like
Dyan, only a lover of men, he has had women, he has* nedestro
children....

And then, Regis felt it, a return of her own despair and
pain, *our son, Lew's and mine, that frightful thing, and I
rebuffed him...it was only because I was so sick and weak,
I did not hate him or blame him, and then Lerrys took me
away, before I could tell him...Merciful Avarra, he has suffered so much, and I hurt him again, all that horror, when
I had promised that he would never have to hide himself from
me...*

*...and he will die still thinking I had rebuffed him because
of that horror....*

And suddenly Regis found himself envying Lew.

*How he has been loved! I have never known what it was
to love a woman like that or to be loved...and I shall die never
knowing if I am capable of that kind of love...*

Oh, yes, there had been women. He was capable of sudden
flaring passion, of taking them with pleasure, given and received; but once the flare of mutual lust had burned out,
sometimes even before the woman knew herself pregnant
with his child, he had been all too aware of what it was they
felt for him; pleasure at his physical beauty, pride that they
had attracted the attention of a Hastur, greed for the status
and privilege that would be theirs if they bore a Hastur child.
Any one of the five or six would gladly have married him for
that status; but he had never felt for any of them anything
more than that brief flaring of passion and lust; the vague
distaste and even revulsion, knowing that their feeling for
him was based on greed or pride.

*But never this kind of disinterested love...will I die without
ever knowing if I am capable of attracting that kind of love
from a woman? No one has ever loved me thus unselfishly but
Danilo, and that is different, the love of comrades, a shared
companionship...and even that, all men seem to despise...a
thing to be put aside with boyhood...is there no more than
this? Why can Lew attract this kind of love, and not I?*

But with what was hanging over them, there was no time
for this either. He turned to speak some word of recollection
to Dio, when suddenly a shriek of wild terror surged through
their minds, a wordless cry of despair and fright and utter
panic, pain and fear. *A child, a child is crying in terror...* Regis

was not sure whether it was his thought or Dio's, but all at once he knew what child it was who shrieked out in such agonized fright, and he pushed Dio before him and ran, ran like a possessed thing toward the Alton apartments.

Marja! But who would so terrify a child?

The great double doors to the Alton suite were standing ajar, swinging on one hinge. Old Andres was lying in a pool of his own blood, half over the threshold where he had been struck down.

He guarded her with his life, as he had sworn... Regis felt dismay; he too had been befriended and fathered by the old *coridom*. Then he realized that Andres was still moving feebly, though he was long past speech. He knelt, tears swelling up in his own eyes for the faithful old man, and Andres, with his last strength, whispered, "Dom Regis...lad..."

Regis knew that Andres did not see him; the dying eyes were already glazed, past sight. He saw only the boy of ten, Kennard's fosterling, Lew's sworn friend. And with his last strength Andres formed a picture in Regis's mind...

Then it was gone and there was nothing living in the room except himself. Regis stood up, stricken with pain. *"Beltran! But how, in all of Zandru's hells, did he manage to come here, when I left him safely imprisoned..."*

He did not even need to ask. He had left Beltran with Lord Dyan; and Dyan had agreed with Beltran that Sharra was the ultimate weapon against the Terrans...Lew was beyond their reach. But there remained an Alton child....

There remained an Alton child; and one Gifted, even at five years old, with the *laran* of her house...and of her *chieri* blood. Regis felt sick; would anything human stoop to use a small child in *Sharra?* He had had reason to know that Dyan could be cruel, could be unscrupulous, but *this?*

He realized that all through this, he had been hearing somewhere in his mind, ringing louder and wilder, the terrified shrieks of the child, the sudden flame and terror of the Form of Fire...and then it was gone, so suddenly that for a moment Regis was shocked, feeling that Marja must suddenly have died of terror, or been struck silent by a blow of terrifying cruelty...

What madness was this? Around him was the silence of death in the Alton rooms, the horrified gasps of Dio who stood on the threshold, but somewhere he was hearing a voice he knew, or was it a telepathic touch rather than a voice?

*Fool, this is nothing for a girl-child! I have the strength
and I am not squeamish...I am not one of your Tower-trained
eunuchs, let me take that place rather than one you can never
trust...* and then almost laughter, silent laughter in mockery.
*No, she's not dead, she is beyond your reach, that is all...pick
on someone your own size, Beltran!*

"Lord of Light!" Regis gasped in shock, knowing what had
happened. Dyan had *chosen* Sharra, despite every warning,
he had walked of his own free will into that horror which had
cost Lew his hand and his sanity, which even now overpowered Regis with dread and terror...

*Does this mean Lew is free? No, never, never, he is still
bound to Sharra...*

"Lord Hastur! Lord Regis—" a gasping servant, come in
search of him, stopped in shock, staring at the dead body of
the old *coridom* on the floor. "Good Gods, sir, what's happened?"

Regis said, clutching at calm and ordinary things, "This
man died defending his master's—his foster-son's property
and his child. He should have a funeral fit for a hero. Find
someone who can see to it, can you?" He rose slowly, staring
at the dead man and at the servants clustering in the doorway
of the Alton suite. Then he saw the man who had come to
look for him.

"Sir, the Lord Hastur—your grandsire, sir—he has ordered—" again the man, confused, shifted ground, "he has
asked if you will come and attend on him..."

Regis sighed. He had been expecting that; what conflicting
demands was his grandfather to make on him now? He saw
Dio and knew she could not bear to be left out of what was
happening now. Well, she had a right to know.

"Come along," he said, "Lew and I were *bredin,* once, and
you have a claim on me, too."

He found his grandfather in the small presence-chamber
of the Hastur apartments; Danvan Hastur said, "Aldones be
thanked, I have found you! The Terran Legate has sent a
message to you personally, Regis; something about a Captain
Scott and permission to authorize Terran weapons—" he
looked at his grandson, and tried to speak with the old authority, but only managed a shocking parody of his old
strength. "I don't know how you came to put yourself in a
position where Terrans could bid you come and go, but I
suppose you'll have to deal with it—"

He is old. I am the real power of Hastur now and we both
know it; though he will never say so, Regis thought, and
spoke to the unspoken part of his grandfather's words, whatever the actual words had been.

"Don't trouble yourself, sir; I'll go and deal with it." He
suddenly felt deep compassion for the old man, who had spent
so many years holding the power of the Comyn, without even
laran to sustain him.

*He has had all the troubles of a Hastur and none of the
rewards,* he thought, and then was startled and shocked at
himself. Rewards? This monstrous *laran* which threatened,
unwanted, to split him asunder, so that he walked with the
terrible knowledge of a power whose forces he could not even
imagine?

Gift? The Hastur curse, rather! He felt as if his very arms
and legs were too big for him, as if he walked halfway between
earth and sky, his feet hardly touching the ground, and all
without knowing why. Desperately, he wanted Danilo at his
side. But there was not even time to send a message to his
paxman, and in any case, if Dyan had flung himself recklessly
into the danger and terror of Sharra, Danilo was Lord Ardais,
for Dyan was as good as dead, and so were they all; let Danilo
stay free of this if he could. He said brusquely to the Spaceforce man who had brought the message, "I'll come at once."
Dio turned to follow him and he said, "No. Stay here." He
could not encumber himself with any woman now, certainly
not when Danilo had been denied the privilege of attending
him.

"I *will* go," she said wildly, "I am a Terran citizen; you
cannot prevent me!"

It wasn't worth arguing. He signaled to the Spaceforce
man to let her come, and together they clambered into the
surface car. Regis had never ridden in a Terran vehicle before;
he hung on breathless, as it tore through the streets, men
and women and horses scattering as it roared and jolted over
the cobbles; he thought irrelevantly, *we must forbid this, it
is too dangerous on such old and crowded streets.* Once
through the gates into the Trade City the streets were a little
smoother and he hung on desperately, not wanting to show
his fright before Dio who was apparently accustomed to this
kind of breath-taking transport.

Through the HQ gates, the Spaceforce driver barely stopping to flash a pass of some sort at the guard, then tearing

across the abnormally smooth terrain to the very gates of the skyscraper; and up in the lift, Dio doggedly keeping at his heels all the way, then into Lawton's office.

Rafe Scott, white as death, was there, and Lawton didn't waste words. He gestured, and Rafe poured it out.

"Kadarin has gone to Hali! I suddenly discovered that I was reading Thyra—I don't know why—"

Regis did. He could *feel* Sharra, through and around Rafe, a monstrous and obscene flame, unbodied, inchoate...and Rafe was part of that ancient bonding.

Kadarin, bearing the Sword. Thyra. Beltran....

Dyan, who had recklessly flung himself into the volcano.

And Lew, somewhere, somewhere...bound, sealed, doomed...

"Well?" Lawton said crisply, "Will you authorize me to send a helicopter, and men properly armed with blasters, to arrest Kadarin out there? Or are you going to stick to the letter of your Compact, while they work with something which is farther outside of your Compact than a super-planetbusting bomb, let alone a blaster or two?"

Am I going to authorize...who does he think I am? Then, in the sudden humility of power recognized and feared, Regis knew that he could no longer avoid the responsibility. He said, "Yes. I'll authorize it." He managed to write his name, though his hand shook, on the form Lawton held out to him. Lawton spoke into some kind of communicator.

"All right; Hastur authorized it. Let the copter go."

"I want to—" *I should go with the copter. Maybe I can still do something for Lew...or his matrix if it's sealed to Sharra...*

Lawton shook his head. "Too late. They've taken off. All you can do now is *wait.*"

They waited, while the sun sank slowly behind the mountain pass. Waited, while time wore away and dragged, and finally Regis saw the helicopter, a tiny black speck hovering over the mountain pass, coming nearer, nearer.

Dio rose and cried out, "He's hurt! I—I have to go to him—" and dashed for the lift. Lawton simultaneously answered some kind of blinking light, listened, and his face changed.

"Well," he said grimly to Regis, "I waited too long, or you did, or somebody. They've got Kadarin, yes, but it looks as if he's managed to commit another murder while everybody stood by and watched. They're going to take him down to Medic. You'd better come along."

Regis followed, through the sterile white walls of the Medical division. An elevator whined softly to a stop and Spaceforce men hauled out prisoners. Dio had eyes only for Lew, carried between two of the uniformed men. Regis could not tell whether he was alive or dead; his face was ghastly, his head lolled lifeless, and the whole front of his shirt was covered in blood.

Bredu! Regis felt shock and grief surging over him. Dio was clinging to Lew's lax hand, crying now without trying to hide it. Behind, Kadarin moved manacled between two guards. Regis barely recognized him, he was so much older, so much more haggard, as if something were consuming him from within. Thyra, too, was handcuffed. Kathie looked pale and frightened, and one of the guards was carrying Callina, who appeared to have fainted; they set her in a chair and gestured to someone to bring smelling-salts, and after a minute Callina opened her eyes; but she swayed, holding to the chair. Kathie went swiftly to her and held her up. One of the Medic personnel said something and she frowned and said, "I'm a nurse; I'll look after her. You'd better look after Mr. Montray-Alton; the woman stabbed him, and it looks as if it may have finished him—he was still alive when the helicopter landed, but that's not saying much."

But Regis looked at the long sword Kathie had let slide to the floor; and something inside him, something in his blood, suddenly awoke and shouted inside his veins.

THIS IS MINE!

He went and picked it up; it felt warm and *right* in his hands. Callina opened her eyes, staring, a strange, cold, blue gaze.

The moment Regis had the sword in his hands, looking at the curling letters written on the scabbard, all at once he seemed to be everywhere, not just where his body was, but as if the edges of his body had spread out to encompass everything in the room. He *touched* Callina and saw her with a strange double sight, the woman he knew, the plain quiet Keeper, still and prim and gentle, and at the same time she was overlaid with something else, cold and blue and watchful, like ice, strange and cold as stone. He *touched* Dio and felt the flood of her love and concern and dread; he *touched* Kadarin and drew back, THIS IS THE ENEMY, THIS IS THE BATTLE... NOT YET, NOT YET! He *touched* Lew.

Pain. Cold. Silence. Fear and the consuming flame...

Pain. Pain at the heart, stabbing pain...Regis spread out into the pain, that was the only way to explain it, felt the broken torn cells, the bleeding out of the life....NO! I WILL NOT HAVE IT SO! The trickling silence that was Lew was suddenly flooded with terrible pain, and then with heat and life and then Lew opened his eyes, and sat up, staring at Regis. His lips barely moved and he whispered, "What—what are you?"

And Regis heard himself say, from a great distance, "Hastur."

And the word meant nothing to him. But the gaping wound had closed, and all around him the Terran medics were standing and staring; and in his hand was this sword which seemed, now, to be more than half of himself.

And suddenly Regis was terrified and he slid the sword back into its sheath, and suddenly the world was all in one piece again and he was back in his body. He was shaking so hard that he could hardly stand.

"Lew! *Bredu*—you're alive!"

Lew Alton's narrative, concluded

CHAPTER FOUR

I have never remembered anything about that helicopter ride to the Terran HQ, or how I got to the Legate's office; the first awareness was of hellish pain and its sudden cessation.

"Lew! Lew, can you hear me?"

How could I help it? She was shouting right in my ear! I opened my eyes and saw Dio, her face wet with tears.

"Don't cry, love," I said, "I'm all right. That hell-cat Thyra must have stabbed me, but she seems not to have hurt me much."

But Kathie motioned Dio back when she would have bent to me, saying with professional crispness, "Just a moment; his pulse was nearly gone." She took some kind of instrument and cut away my shirt; then I heard her gasp.

Where Thyra's knife had gone in—perilously near the heart—was only a small, long-healed scar, paler and more perfectly cicatrized than the discolored scars on my face.

"I don't believe this," she protested. "I saw it, and *still* I don't believe it." She took something cold and wet and washed off the still-sticky smears of half-dried blood which still clung to the skin. I looked ruefully at the ruined shirt.

"Get him a uniform shirt, or something," said Lawton, and they brought me one, made out of paper or some similar unwoven fiber. It had a cold and rather slippery texture which I found unpleasant, but I wasn't in a position to be picky; besides, the medical smells were driving me out of my mind. I said, "Do we have to stay down here? I'm not hurt—" and only then did I see Regis, the Sword of Aldones belted around his waist, an unbelieving look of awe on his face. Later I learned what he had done; but at the moment—everything was so mad already—I simply took it for granted and was grateful that the Sword had come to the hands of the one person on this world who could handle it. I think, originally, I had supposed that Callina, or perhaps Ashara, would have

347

to take it, as Keeper. Now I saw it in Regis's custody, and all
I could think was, *oh, yes, of course; he is Hastur.*

"Where is Thyra? Did she get away?"

"Not likely," said Lawton, grimly, "She's in a cell down-
stairs, and there she'll stay."

"Why?" Kadarin asked. His voice was calm, and I stared,
unable to believe my eyes; on the shores of Hali he had appeared to me as something very far from human; now, curiously, he looked like the man I had first known, civilized
and urbane, even likable. "On what charges?"

"Attempted murder of Lew Alton here!"

"It would be hard to make a charge like that stick," Kadarin said. "Where is the alleged wound?"

Lawton stared irritably at the blood-soaked shirt which
had been cut from me. He said, "We've got eyewitnesses to
the attempt. Meanwhile we'll hold her for—oh, hell!—breaking and entering, trespass, carrying concealed weapons, indecent language in a public place—indecent exposure if we
have to! The main thing is that we're holding her, and you
too; we need to ask you some questions about a certain murder
and the burning of a townhouse in Thendara..."

Kadarin looked directly at me. He said, "Believe what you
like, Lew; I did not murder your brother. I did not know your
brother by sight; I did not know who he was until afterward,
when I heard in the street who it was that had been killed.
To me he was simply a young Terran I did not know; and for
what it is worth, it was not I who killed him but one of my
men. And I am sorry; I gave no orders that anyone should be
killed. You know what it was that I came for, and why I had
to come."

I looked at this man and knew that I could not hate him.
I too had been compelled to do things I would never have
dreamed of doing, not in my right mind; and I knew what
had compelled him. It was belted, now, around his waist; but
through that I could see the man who had been my friend.
I turned my face away. There was too much between us. I
had no right to condemn him, not now, not when through my
own matrix I could feel the pull, irresistible, of that unholy
thing.

Return to me and live forever in undying reviving fire... and
behind my eyelids the Form of Fire, between me and what
I could see with my physical eyes. Sharra, and I was still a
part of it, still damned. I took one step toward him; I do not

know even now whether I meant to strike him or to join hands with him on the hilt of the Sharra matrix concealed in its sword.

Hate and love mingled, as they had mingled for my father, whose voice even now pulsed in my mind, *Return . . . return . . .*

Then Kadarin shrugged a little and the spell broke. He said, "If you want to throw me in a cell, that's all right with me, but it's only fair to warn you I probably won't stay there long. I have—" he touched the hilt of the Sharra sword and said lightly, "a pressing engagement elsewhere."

"Take him away," Lawton said. "Put him in maximum security, and let him see if he can talk himself out of there."

Kadarin saved them the trouble of taking him; he rose and went amiably with the guards. One of them said, "I'll have that sword first, if you please."

Kadarin said, still with that impeccable grin, "Take it, if you want it."

Watching, I wanted to cry out a warning to the Spaceforce men; I knew it was not a sword. One of them thrust out his hand . . . and went flying across the room; he struck his head against the wall and sank down, stunned. The other stood staring at Lawton and turning back to Kadarin; afraid and I didn't blame him.

"It's not a sword, Lawton," I said. "It's a matrix weapon."

"Is *that*—?" Lawton stared, and I nodded. There was no way, short of killing Kadarin first, that they could get it away from him; and I was not even sure that he could be killed while he wore it, not by any ordinary weapon anyhow. I did warn them, "Don't put him and Thyra in the same cell."

Not that distance would make any difference, when that sword was drawn. And would I go with them? Just the same, I was glad to have Kadarin, and the Sharra matrix, out of my sight. I started to rise, only to have the young doctor push me down again on a seat.

"You're not going anywhere, not yet!"

"Am I a prisoner, then?"

The doctor looked at Lawton, who said, scowling, "Hell no! But if you try to walk out of here, you'll fall flat on your face! Stay put and let Doctor Allison go over you, why don't you? What's the hurry?"

I tried to stand up, but for no discernible reason I found myself as weak as a newborn rabbithorn. I could not get my legs under me.

I let the young doctor go over me with his instruments.
I hated hospitals, and the smell was getting to me, reviving
memories of other hospitals on other worlds, memories I
would rather not have to face just now; but there seemed no
alternative. I noticed Kathie talking to one of the doctors
and, as on Festival Night, I wondered if she would accuse us
of kidnapping or worse. Well, if she did, the story was so
unlikely on the face of it that probably no one would believe
her; Vainwal was half a Galaxy away!

There were times when I didn't believe it myself....

Before the doctor had finished listening to my heart and
checking every function of my body—he even had me unstrap
the mechanical hand, looked at it and asked if it was working
properly—Regis had come back into the room. He looked
grave and remote. At his side was Rafe Scott.

"I've seen Thyra," he said abruptly.

So had I, I thought, *and I wish I had not.* Even though
her attempt to kill me had been thwarted, I found I could not
bear to think of her. It was not all her fault; she was Kadarin's
victim as much as I, a more willing victim, perhaps, eager
for the power of Sharra. But thinking of the woman made me
remember the child, and I saw Regis's face change. I was not
used to this, Regis had never been so sensitive a telepath as
that...but I was beginning to realize that this new Regis,
with the sudden opening of the Hastur Gift, was a different
Regis from the youngster I had known most of my life.

Regis said, "I have bad news for you, Lew; the very worst.
Andres—" his voice caught, almost choking, and I knew.
During those carefree years at Armida, Andres had been like
a father to him, too.

My father, Marius, Linnell...now Andres. Now, more
than ever, I was wholly alone. I was afraid to ask, but I asked
anyhow.

"Marja?"

"He—defended her with his life," Regis said. "Beltran—
would have taken her into Sharra; she has the Alton Gift.
But Dyan..."

I was braced to hear that Dyan had been party to this; I
was not prepared for what Regis told me next.

"Somehow—he thrust her out—*elsewhere.* I could find no
trace of her, even telepathically. I do not know where he has
her hidden; but somewhere, she is safe from Sharra. And
Dyan—did you know he has the Alton Gift, Lew?"

In the confusion I had forgotten. But I should have known, of course. Power to force his will on another mind, even unwilling...and Dyan had Alton blood; he and my father had been first cousins. My father's mother was own sister to Dyan's father, and there were other kin-ties, further generations back.

Once, under terrible pressure—I had used a little-known power of the Altons, I had teleported from Aldaran to the Arilinn Tower. Dyan might, for some reason, have done this to Marja—but he could have sent her anywhere on Darkover, from Armida itself to Castle Ardais in the Hellers—or to the Spaceman's Orphanage in Thendara where she had been brought up.

When there was time, I would have to make a search for her, physical and telepathic; I did not think Dyan could hide her from me permanently, or even that he would want to. But before that, Kadarin held the Sharra matrix, and if he chose to draw it, I knew I could never trust myself again. I tried to warn Regis of this. He touched the Sword of Aldones, and he looked grim. "This is the weapon against Sharra. Since I belted it on...there are many things I know," he said, strangely, "things I had not learned. I have known for days that I have a strange power over Sharra, and now, with *this*—" it was as if something spoke *behind* and *through* the Regis I knew; he looked haggard and worn, years older than he was. But now and then, as I looked into his eyes, the other Regis, the youngster I knew, would peep through; and he looked frightened. I didn't blame him.

"Show me your matrix," he said.

I balked at that. Not without the presence of a Keeper. I said, "If Callina is there," and he turned to one of the doctors and asked what had happened to her.

"She was faint," said Kathie, "I took her into one of the cubicles to lie down. It must have been all the blood."

That alerted me to danger. Darkovan women don't faint at trifles, or at the sight of blood. I had to shout and create a scene, though, before they would take me to her; and I found her in one of the small cubicles, seated stone-still, her eyes withdrawn and pallid, as if she were Ashara's self, gazing at nothing in the world we could see...

Regis shouted at her, and so did I, but she was motionless, her eyes gazing into nowhere unfathomable distances. At last I reached out, tried to touch her mind—I felt her, very far

away, some cold icy *otherness*...then she gasped, stared at
me, and came back to herself.

"You were in trance, Callina," I told her, and she looked
at us in consternation. I believe that even then, if she had
taken us into her confidence, it might have been different...but
she made light of the curious trance, saying lightly, "I was
resting, no more...half asleep. What is it, what do you want?"

Regis said quietly, "I want to see if we can clear his matrix
and free him from the...the Sharra one. I did it for Rafe. I
think I could have done it for Beltran if he had asked me."
I picked up the unspoken part of that: Beltran was still eager
to use Sharra, he had regarded it as the ultimate weapon
against subjection to the Terrans...blackmail to get them
off our world forever.

*And Dyan, wrong-headed and desperately anxious for
power the weakening Comyn Council would not yield to him,
had followed him into subjection to Sharra....* I could feel
Regis's grief and sorrow at that, and suddenly for a moment
I saw Dyan through Regis's eyes; *the older kinsman, handsome, worldly, whom the younger Regis had liked and ad-
mired...then feared, with still the extreme fascination that
was closely akin to love...the only kinsman who had wholly
accepted him.* I had seen Dyan only cruel, threatening, harsh;
a martinet, a man eager for power and using it in brutally
unsubtle ways; a man sadistically misusing his power over
cadets and younger kinsmen. This other side of Dyan was
one I had never seen, and it gave me pause. Had I, after all,
misjudged the man?

No; or else even his love of power would never have misled
him into the attempt to that ultimate perversion of the Comyn powers: *Sharra's fire*...I had been burned by that fire,
and Dyan had seen the scars. But in his supreme arrogance,
he thought he could succeed where I had failed, make Sharra
serve him; be master, rather than slave to Sharra's fire...and
Dyan was not even Tower-trained?

"All the more reason, Lew, that you must be freed," Regis
argued. After a moment I slipped the leather thong off over
my head and fumbled one-handed to unwrap the silks. Finally
I let it roll out into my palm, seeing the crimson blaze
overlaying the blue interior shimmer of the matrix....

Callina focused her attention on me, matching resonances,
until she could take it into her hand; the trained touch of a
Keeper, and not overwhelmingly painful. Then I felt some-

thing like a tug-o-war in my mind, the call, restimulated, of Sharra, *Return, return and live in the life of my fires*...and through it I felt Marjorie...or was it Thyra? *In my embrace you shall burn forever in passion undiminished*...

I felt Regis, through this, as if he were somehow reaching into my very brain, though I knew it was only my matrix he was touching, disentangling it thread by thread...but the more he worked on it, the stronger grew the redoubled call, the pulse of Sharra beating in my brain, till I stood burning in agony....

The door was flung open and Dio was in the room, rushing to me, physically flinging Callina aside. "What do you think you are doing to him?" she raged.

The flames diminished and died; Regis caught at some piece of furniture, staggering, hardly able to stand erect.

"How much do you think he can stand? Hasn't he been through enough?"

I collapsed gratefully into a chair. I said, "They were only—"

"Only stirring up what's better left alone," Dio stormed. "I could feel it all the way up to the eighth floor above here...I could feel them *cutting* at you..." and she ran her hands over me as if she had expected to see me physically covered in blood.

"It's all right, Dio," I said, knowing my voice was hardly more than an exhausted mumble. "I was trained to—to endure it—"

"What makes you think you're able to endure it now?" she demanded angrily, and Regis said, in despair, "If Kadarin draws the Sharra sword..."

"If he does," Dio said, "he will have to fight; but can't you let him get together enough strength to fight it?"

I did not know. Rafe had never been farther than the outer layer of the circle we had formed around Sharra; I had been at its very heart, controlling the force and flow of the power of Sharra. I was doomed, and I knew it. I knew what Callina and Regis had been trying to do, and I was grateful, but for me it was too late.

My eyes rested on Callina, and I saw everything around me with a new clarity. She was everything of the past to me; Arilinn, and my own past; Marjorie had died in her arms, and then I had found in her the first forgetfulness I had known. Kinswoman, Keeper, all the past...and I ached with regret that I would not live to take her with me to Armida, to reclaim my own past and my own world. But it was not to be. A darker love would claim me, the wildfire of Sharra surging in my veins, the dark bond to Thyra who had made herself Keeper of that monstrous circle of Sharra, fire and lust and endless burning torture and flame...Callina might call me to her, but it was too late, now and forever too late. Dio spoke to me, but I had gone back to a time before she had come into my life, and I hardly remembered her name.

What were we doing here within these white walls?

Someone came into the room. I did not recognize the man although from the way he spoke to me I knew that he was someone I was supposed to know. One of the accursed Terrans, those who would die in the flames of Sharra when the time was ripe. His words were mere sounds without sense and I did not understand them.

"That woman Thyra! We had her in one of our strongest cells, and she's gone—just like that, she's gone out of a max-mimum security cell! Did you witch her out of there some-how?"

Fool, to think any cell could hold the priestess and Keeper of Sharra the Fire-born....

Space reeled around me; there was a slamming thunder-clap and I stood braced on the cobblestone of the forecourt of the Comyn Castle, my feet spanning the enlaced symbols there...and I knew Kadarin had unsheathed the Sword. Kadarin stood there, his pale hair moving in an invisible wind, his hands on Thyra's shoulders, his metallic eyes cold with menace, and Thyra...

Thyra! Flames rose upward from her copper hair, sparks trembled at the tips of her fingers. In her hands she held naked the Sharra Sword, cold flames racing from hilt to tip. Thyra! My mistress, my love—what was I doing here, far from her? She raised one hand and beckoned, and I began nervelessly to move forward, without being conscious of the motion. She was smiling as I knelt at her feet on the stone, feeling all my strength going out to her, and to that fire that flowed and flamed in her hands...

Then the flame flared blue and wild to the heights of the castle, and I knew Regis had unsheathed the Sword of Al-dones. They were there, there physically, standing across from me, Regis and Callina, and she *reached* for me, enfolding me in the cold blue of Ashara's icy limbo, and then we were not in the Castle courtyard at all, but in the gray spaces of the overworld...far below I could see our bodies like tiny toys from a great height, but the only reality in the world was those two swords, crimson with flame and cold ice-blue, crossed and straining at one another, and I....

I was a puppet, a mote of power in the astral world, something stretched to breaking between them...Callina's voice, reminding me of Arilinn and all of my past, Thyra's crooning call, enticing, seductive, with memories of lust and fire and power...I was torn, torn between them as I felt myself a link between the two circles, Regis and Callina with the Sword of Aldones, Thyra and Kadarin, each pulling at me fiercely to make a third, to lend my power....

And then there was another strength in the linked circles...something cold and arrogant and brutal, the harsh touch as of my father's own strength, the Alton Gift which had opened my own to power, but this was not my father's touch....*Dyan! And he had always disliked me...and I was at his mercy...*

I did not mind dying, but not like this.... Again in my mind was the final cry of my father's voice, and we were so deeply enlaced that I could see Dyan look past me at Regis with infinite warmth and regret that in the end they should have been on opposite sides. *I wanted to stand at your side when you were King over all of Darkover, my gallant Hastur cousin...* and then, through me, I could feel Dyan's touch on the memory of my father's destroying call, the last thought in his dying mind...

And Dyan, in a moment of anguish and grief:

Kennard! My first, my only friend...my cousin, my kinsman, bredu...and there is no other, now, living, who bears your blood, and if I strike now I shall have killed you past death or any immortality... and then a final, careless thought, almost laughter, *this son of yours was never fit for this kind of power...*

And abruptly I was free, free of Sharra, thrust entirely away, and in that moment of freedom I was locked into the closing rapport of Regis and Callina, the sealed circle of power...

The fire-form reared high, higher, the size of the castle, the size of the mountain, with a scorching darkness at its heart...but from Regis, risen now to giant-size, blazing cold lightning struck at the heart of Sharra as he held the Sword of Aldones, poised to strike...

Sharra was bound in chains by the Son of Hastur who was the Son of Light...

And clothed in his cloak of living light Aldones came!

Now there was nothing to see, no human form, only fire lapping higher and higher, the spark of the Sharra matrix blazing out from the center of that darkness, and the core of brilliance through the veils clothing the figure of the God, like Regis in form, but Regis looming high, higher, not one of the Hastur-kin but the God himself...

Two identical matrixes cannot exist in one time and space; and once before, so the legend said, Sharra had been chained by the Son of Aldones, who was the Son of Light....

I cannot explain the legend, even now, although I saw it. I had felt the daemon-touch of Sharra. Infinite good is as terrifying, in its own way, as infinite evil. It was not Regis and Kadarin fighting with identically forged swords, one a copy of the other. It was not even matrix battling against space-twisting matrix, though that was nearer the truth. Something tangible and very real fought behind each sword, something that was not on this plane of reality at all, and could manifest itself and maintain a foothold in this dimension only through the swords. Lightnings streamed between them, wrapped in the rainbow aura that was Regis and Hastur, coiling into the licking flames at the heart of which Thyra glowed like a burning coal.

And then for an instant I felt that last bright arrogance reach out, Dyan shining across the space, his hawk-face keen and curious. For an instant then I think the linkage broke and the swords were only swords, and for a split second we stood in the courtyard of the Castle again and the cobbles were unsteady under my feet. And in that moment I know that he could have reached out and killed either of us....

And for a moment Thyra stood before me, only a woman again, although the Form of Fire still licked around her, and the smell of burning beat on the air, and her throat was naked to my knife...

I had sworn their death in vengeance for my hand. But in that moment I could remember only that there had been a time when she stood before me, only a frightened girl, terrified by her own growing powers. If the Gods themselves had put a dagger into my hand at that moment I could not have struck her down, and for a moment it seemed as if a great question vibrated in the overworld, and in this world and through all the universes of my mind;

Will you have the love of Power or the Power of Love?

And everything in me surged toward Kadarin, whom I had once loved as a brother, and to the young and beautiful Thyra whom I, as much as Kadarin, had destroyed. I have never been able to explain this, but I knew in that one searing moment of testing that I would die in Sharra's fire myself rather than hurt either of them any further than they had already been hurt. Everything in me cried out an enormous and final *No!*

And then we were battling again in the gray limbo of the overworld, and the two swords crossed and blazed like interlaced lightnings...

Then the flames sank and died, and a great darkness blazed at the heart of the Sharra matrix. I saw a blaze of endless fire, and the searing flame strike inward, and then a great vortex seemed to open inwards, into a great whirling nothingness. Into that nothingness were swept away Kadarin and Thyra, two tiny, disappearing figures, whirled away and apart...and a great wordless cry of pain and despair and at the last instant, so faint that I never knew whether I heard it or not, a split-second cry of joy and rediscovery which made me hear again in my mind my father's last cry...

"Beloved—!"

Silence and nothingness, and darkness...and the great and damnable Face that I had seen in Ashara's overworld of blue ice....

And then I was standing in the gray light of dawn on the cobblestones in Comyn Castle, facing Regis, only a shrinking, hesitant young man again, with the Sword of Aldones halfraised in his hand, and Callina pale as death beside him. There was no sign anywhere of Kadarin or Thyra, but sprawled on the cobbles before us, broken and dying, Dyan Ardais lay, his body blackened as if with fire. The Sword of Sharra lay broken in his hand. There were no jewels in the hilt of the sword now; they lay charred and ugly, burnt pebbles which, even as the first rays of the sun touched them, evaporated into pale gouts of rising smoke, and were gone forever...as Sharra's power was gone forever from this world.

Regis sheathed the Sword of Aldones and knelt beside Dyan, weeping without shame. Dyan opened pain-filled eyes,

and I saw recognition in them for a moment, and pain beyond
the point where it ceases to have meaning. But if Regis had
hoped for a word, he was disappointed; Dyan's eyes glinted
up at him in a moment, then fell back and stared at something
which was not in this world. But for the first time since I had
known him, he looked content and at peace.

*If he had been willing to kill us all, Sharra would have
triumphed*... I knelt, too, beside his body, conceding his hero's
death, as Regis laid his own cloak over Dyan's body. He still
held the Sword of Aldones, but from that, too, all glow and
power had faded; the blade was blackened all along its length
as if with the strange fire in which it had been quenched.
After a moment Regis laid the Sword of Aldones on Dyan's
breast, as a fallen hero's sword is laid to be buried with him.
None of us protested. Then Regis rose, and the rays of the
rising sun touched his hair... snow white.

It was over; and beyond hope I was free, and alive... beyond
countless, measureless havoc, I had come free. I turned to
Callina, and at last, knowing we were free, caught her for
the first time in my arms and pressed her lips hungrily to
mine.

And all desire died in my heart and mind as I looked down
into the chill eyes of Ashara.

I should have known, all along.

Only a moment and she was Callina again, clinging to me
and crying, but I had seen. I let her go, in horror... and as
my arms released her, Callina crumpled very slowly to the
pavement and lay there unmoving, beside Dyan.

I knelt again, turning her over, catching her up in my
arms, uncaring; but she was still, unmoving, already cold.
And now I knew....

Generations ago, a powerful Keeper, of the Hastur line,
had held all the power of the Comyn... and as she grew older,
had been reluctant to set aside her power; and so she had
concentrated power in the Aillard line, and many of those
women had been her under-Keepers, giving their own powers
to Ashara, so that Ashara, whose flesh had failed and who
lived now within the matrix, went abroad in the body and
personality, like a garment, of her newest Keeper... and of
these, my young kinswoman had been the last. I had wondered why I could never touch her mind, nor come near, except
now and again for a moment....

And again the terrifying question from the overworld

seemed to beat in my heart; *the Love of Power or the Power of Love?*

I will swear to my dying day that Callina had loved me....

Otherwise, would that ancient Hastur sorceress have risked the end of her undying mind and all her power, to risk all for my freedom from Sharra's bondage? Regis and I, alone, could never have faced that last undying blaze of Sharra's fire. But with Callina recklessly throwing all of Ashara's powers into the fray, through the body of the young Hastur who was her far kinsman, so that the strength of the first Hastur, whoever and whatever He was, manifested itself through the Sword of Aldones... so that Regis took on the majesty and power of the Son of Light, even as the one who held Sharra took on the Form of Fire...

Dyan, too, in the end, had not been able to strike with Sharra to wipe out his kin. All his life he had fought for the honor of the Comyn, though in strange ways, and in the end he had acted first to protect my daughter, then to protect me, and finally he could not strike down Regis...

The Love of Power or the Power of Love? I wonder if that question had beat in his mind, too, during the final moments of that battle?

Somewhere above me in the castle, I heard a sound, not with my physical ears, but in the recesses of my mind; cleared now from the searing presence of Sharra, I was conscious of it all through me; the sound of a child crying, a telepath child, alone, hungry, frightened, wailing for her mother who was dead and the father she half feared, half loved. And I knew where she was. I saw Regis, his shoulders bowed beneath his new and terrible burden, his hair incredibly turned white in that all-consuming battle, and saw him turn wearily toward the Castle. Had his grandfather survived that battle which must have rung in the minds of all the Comyn?

Yes; Danilo went to him and cared for him, lent him strength...

Regis heard the crying too, and turned to me, with a weary smile.

"Go and look after your daughter, Lew; she needs you, and—" unbelievably he smiled again, "she's old enough to have the Gift but not old enough to hold it within reasonable bounds. Unless you go and comfort her, she'll drive everyone in the Castle—everyone in the City—mad with her wailing!"

And I went in and ran unerringly up the stairs to the one

place where Dyan had known I would not search for Marja and where she would be safely concealed; the Ridenow apartments which Lerrys and Dio had shared. And as I burst in through the great outer doors, hurrying to the empty room, I saw Dio holding Marja on her lap, but she could not silence her wailing and struggling until I bent over them and clasped them both in my arms.

Marja stopped crying and turned to me, the telepathic shrieking suddenly quieted, only soft hiccuping sobs remaining as she clung to me, sobbing. "Father! Father! I was so scared, and you didn't come and you didn't come and I was all alone, all alone and there was a fire, and I cried and cried and nobody heard me except this strange lady came and tried to pick me up..."

I quieted the hysterical outburst, pulling her to me.

"It's all right, *chiya*," I crooned, holding her in one arm and Dio in the other. "It's all right, Father's here—" I could not give Dio a child of her own. But this child of my own blood had somehow survived out of all the holocaust that had raged in the Comyn...and never again would I mock at the power of love which had saved us both. I had wanted to die; but I was alive, and miraculously, beyond all, I was glad to be alive and life was good to me.

Laughing, I set Marja down, drawing Dio into my arms again. Never once did she ask a question about Callina. Perhaps she knew, perhaps she had been a part of all that great battle which, even now, I was beginning to doubt—had it ever happened except in my own mind? I never knew.

"We have just time," I said, "to file a stop on that Terran divorce action. I think it hasn't been ten days yet—or have I lost track of the time?"

She laughed, a wavering smile. "Ten days? No, not quite."

Marja interrupted us, setting up her telepathic demand again. *I'm hungry! And scared! Stop kissing her and hold me!*

Dio drew her close between us. "We'll get you a big breakfast right away, *chiya*," she said softly, "and then someone will have to try teaching you the elementary manners of living in a telepathic family. If you are going to do that every time I kiss your father—or anything else, little daughter—I am afraid that I will start making noises like a wicked stepmother from the old fairy tales! So you will have to learn some manners, first thing!"

Incredibly, that made all three of us laugh. And then we went back to the Terran Zone to withdraw an unnecessary divorce decree. Somewhere along the way—I forget just where—we stopped and ate fresh hot bread and porridge at a cookstall, and everyone who looked at us took it for granted that I was out for an early breakfast with my wife and daughter. And I found I liked the feeling. I no longer felt them staring only at my scars.

If Dio had not accepted Marja... but she was not that kind of person. She had wanted my child, and now I had put my child in her care. The hurt would never leave her, for that pitiful monstrosity which should have been our son; but Dio never lived in the past. And now we had all the future before us.

Marja held on to my hand and Dio's as we went into the Terran Zone. I looked back, just once, at the Comyn Castle which lay behind us.

I knew we would never go back.

But I did go back, just once more. It was only a few days later, but Marja had already begun to call Dio "Mother."

Epilogue

"Crowned King? King of *what?*" Regis said, shaking his head gently at his grandfather. "Sir, with all respect, the Comyn effectively do not exist. Lew Alton survives, but he does not wish to remain at Armida—and I cannot see any reason why he should. The Ridenow have already bowed to the inevitable, and applied for their status as Terran citizens. Dyan is dead—and his son is a child three years old. The Lady of Aillard is dead, and so is her sister; no one remains among the Aillard but Merryl...and his twin sister, who is the mother of Dyan's son. The Elhalyn are gone...do you still think we must treat the Terrans as enemies, sir? I think it is time to accept that we are what they say—one of their lost colonies—and apply for protected status, to keep our world as it should be...immune to being overrun by Empire technology, but still part of the Empire."

Danvan Hastur bowed his head. He said, "I knew it would come to this in the end. What is it that you want to do, Regis?"

With that new and terrible sensitivity, Regis knew what his grandfather was feeling, and so his voice was very gentle as he spoke to the old man.

"I have asked Lawton to come and see you, sir. Remember he is blood kin to the Ardais and to the Syrtis, sir; he might have been among the Comyn."

Dan Lawton came into the room, and to Regis's surprise he bowed deeply and knelt before Danvan Hastur.

"*Z'par servu, vai dom,*" he said quietly.

"What mockery is this?" demanded Hastur.

"Sir, no mockery," said Lawton without rising. "I am here to serve you in any way I can, Lord Hastur, to be certain that your ancient ways will not suffer."

"I thought we were now no more than a Terran colony..."

"I do not think you understand what it is to be an Empire world, *vai dom,*" said Lawton quietly. "It means that you have the right to define what Darkover will become; you who inhabit Darkover alone. You may share or not share your own fields of learning—though I hope we will be allowed to

362

know something of matrix technology, so that nothing like this Sharra episode may ever arise again without our knowledge. You and you alone—you people of Darkover, I mean, not you personally, with all respect, sir—may determine how many Terrans and on what terms may be employed here or may settle here. And because your interests must be protected in the Federation of worlds that is the Empire, you have the right to appoint, or to elect, a representative in the Empire's Senate."

"A fine thought," said Danvan Hastur wearily, "but who is left that we could trust, after all the deaths in the Comyn? Do you think I am going to appoint that scamp Lerrys Ridenow, just because he knows Empire ways?"

"I would gladly serve you myself," said Lawton, "because I love my home world—it is my home world as well as yours, Lord Hastur, even though I have chosen to live as a Terran; I too was born beneath the Bloody Sun, and there is Comyn blood in my veins. But I think my task is here, so that there may be a Darkovan voice in the Terran Trade City. Regis has found a candidate, however."

He gestured to the door, and Lew Alton came in.

His scarred face looked calm now, without the tension and torment which had inhabited it for so long; Regis, looking at him, thought: *here is a man who has laid his ghosts. Would that I could lay mine!* Within him the memory blurred, *a time when he had been more than human, reaching from the center of the world to the sky, wielding monstrous power* . . . and now he was no more than human again and he felt small, powerless, shut up inside a single mind and skull . . .

"A man who knows Darkover and Terra alike," said Regis quietly, "Lewis-Kennard Montray-Alton of Armida, first Representative to the Imperial Senate from Cottman Four, known as Darkover." And Lew came and bowed before Lord Hastur.

"By your leave, sir, I am going out on the ship which takes to the stars at sunset, with my wife and daughter. I will gladly serve for a term, after which you will be able to educate the people of Darkover to choose their own representatives . . ."

Danvan Hastur held out his hand. He said, "I would gladly have seen your father in this post, *Dom* Lewis. The people of Darkover—and I myself—have cause to be grateful to the Altons."

Lew bowed and said, "I hope I may serve you well," and

Hastur said, "All the Gods bless you and speed you on your way."

Regis left his grandfather talking with Lawton—he was sure a time would come when they would like and respect one another, if not yet—and went out into the anteroom with Lew. He took him into a kinsman's embrace. "Will you come back when your term is over, Lew? We need you on Darkover—"

A momentary look of pain crossed Lew's face, but he said, "I don't think so. Out there—on the edge of the Empire—there are new worlds. I—I can't look back."

There have been too many deaths here....

Regis wanted to cry out, "Why should you go into exile again?" But he swallowed hard and bent his head, then raised it, after a moment, and said, "So be it, *bredu*. And wherever you go, the Gods go with you. *Adelandeyo.*"

He knew he would never see Lew again, and his whole heart went after him as he went out of the room. *The Empire is his, and a thousand million worlds beyond worlds.*

But my duty lies here. I am—Hastur.

And that was enough. Almost.

As the red sun was setting behind the high pass, Regis stood with Danilo on a balcony overlooking the Terran Zone, watching as the great Terran ship skylifted, bound outward to the stars. *Where I can never go. And he takes with him the last of my dreams of freedom, and of power....*

Do I want the love of Power or the Power of Love?

And suddenly he knew that he did not really envy Lew. No woman had ever loved him as Lew had been loved, no. But Dyan had left, in his death, a shining legacy of another kind of love; something he had heard, and only half remembered from his years in St. Valentine-of-the-Snows, returned suddenly to his mind,

"Dani, what is that thing the *cristoforos* say...greater love hath none...."

Danilo returned, in the most ancient dialect of *casta*, the one they had spoken at the monastery:

"Greater love no man knoweth than he who will lay down his life for his fellow."

Dyan had laid his life down for them all, and in his death, Regis had come to a new understanding; love was love, no matter whence it came or in what form. Some day he might love a woman in this way; but if that day never came, he would accept the love that was his without shame or regret.

"I will not be King," he said, "I am Hastur; that is enough." An echo stirred in his mind, a memory that would never wholly surface.

Who are you?

Hastur... it was gone, like a stilled ripple in the Lake. He said, "I'm going to need a lot of—a lot of help, Dani."

And Danilo said, still in the most ancient dialect of Nevarsin, "Regis Hastur, I am your paxman, even to life or death."

Regis wiped his face... the evening fog was condensing into the first drops of rain, but it felt hot on his eyes. "Come," he said, "my grandfather must not be left too long alone, and we must take counsel how to educate our sons—Mikhail, and Dyan's little son. We can't stand here all night."

They turned and went side by side into the Castle. The last light faded from the sky, and the great ship, outward bound into the Empire, was only a star among a hundred thousand other stars.